LAMB TO THE SLAUGHTER

JAMES HARPER

This is a work of fiction. Names, characters, organisations, places, events and incidents are either products of the author's imagination or are used fictitiously. Any resemblance to actual persons, living or dead, or actual events is purely coincidental.

Copyright © 2025 James Harper

All rights reserved

No part of this publication may be reproduced, or stored in a retrieval system, or transmitted, in any form or by any means, electronic, mechanical, photocopying, recording, or otherwise, without express written permission of the publisher.

www.jamesharperbooks.com

ISBN: 9798296970350

PROLOGUE

One week ago

Perfect, he thought, as he pulled into the lay-by on the B3035 Botley Road and saw a blue, ten-year-old BMW estate parked at the far end nearest the stile leading into the field. He navigated his way around the worst of the puddles left by the recent rain, tyres crunching on gravel as early evening shaded into night. He pulled cautiously forward until there was only six inches to spare between the two vehicles, despite there being room for at least two or three cars behind the BMW. He killed the engine and sat for a while with the window rolled down, enjoying the quiet of the evening as the natural world wound down at the end of another day. Admiring its deceptive beauty that hid so much savagery—some of which wouldn't remain hidden for much longer.

He would've happily sat there all night, but time wasn't on his side. Leaning between the front seats, he pulled a heavy herringbone-tweed field coat and a wide-brimmed waxed-cotton hat off the rear seat, then climbed out.

The jacket was too big, but rather that than too small, the hat a good fit. He turned up the collar against the unseasonably chill wind blowing from the east, pulled the brim of the hat low over his face. Collected a backpack from the boot, its weight an unwelcome reminder of what it contained, the unholy use those contents would soon be put to.

He checked in front of the BMW, a foot to spare between its front bumper and a solid wooden fence post.

Rather you than me, he thought, smiling to himself as he imagined the BMW driver's irritation as they manoeuvred back and forth to get out of the impossibly tight space. Satisfied, he went to lean against the stile, gazing out across the fields, the lightly-trampled grass of the footpath on the left proof that it wasn't a popular route.

Despite that, a dog walker was visible in the distance when he threw his leg over the stile, jumped down and set off, pulling his scarf up over his chin and mouth until only a thin strip of his face was visible—his nose and not a lot else. And he had a very ordinary-looking sort of nose.

The dog came rushing and bounding to meet him as he strode out towards the far side of the field and the derelict barn beyond it. An over-excited young spaniel, God knows what they put in dog food these days. It was obvious it had found a muddy puddle, and now it bounced on its hind legs and barked at him, then rested its muddy paws on his jacket, a string of viscous drool hanging from its jowls, bright eyes staring up at him, waiting for its head to be scratched. Any other time and he'd have obliged.

The old biddy owner came hurrying up, her voice apologetic but lacking the authority to make a blind bit of difference to the dog.

'*Down Lola, down!*' Then followed it with that dog-walker's perennial favourite. 'She's only playing. She won't bite.'

He felt like hitting it around the head with the backpack, that'd teach it. Instead he pushed it roughly away, hissed a warning at it, the dog cowering as if in the presence of evil.

Dipping his head, he walked on. Gave the old woman a wide berth, his face averted.

Her apologies died on her lips as he ignored her, the unnecessary rudeness stealing her voice. But he heard her plainly enough when she found it again, felt the intensity of her glare on his back.

'What a rude man.'

Wait until you see where I've parked, he thought with silent malice, continuing towards the barn standing in front of a small stand of field maples a couple of hundred yards away.

Over a five-bar gate and off the public footpath now, he was at the barn a couple of minutes later, his heart going *thump, thump, thump* in his chest, and not because of the exertion. Turning to look back the way he'd come, he saw the BMW's lights come on, then an inordinate amount of toing and froing as the dog walker manoeuvred in the tight space before she was gone on her indignant way.

He turned back to the barn, took a wrecking bar from the backpack. Old and derelict the barn might be, but the farmer had still put a padlock on it. Not that a padlock is any use when the wood the hasp is bolted to is rotten. He worked the wrecking bar in, prised and levered it back and forth until the wood split, too rotten to even screech in protest. The whole thing came away in a rush, sent him stumbling backwards. He staggered, managed to keep his footing, righted himself. A few muddy paw marks on the front of the jacket he could live with. He didn't want to go arse over tit and risk ripping the jacket or staining it too badly.

Inside the barn, he took a battery-powered camping lantern from the backpack, held it high to illuminate the still, dusty interior. Unseen rodents scurried into the darkest corners, the smell of decay, of unloved neglect, in his nose after time and the elements had taken their relentless toll.

The roof had collapsed completely in one corner, the darkening evening sky visible through it. On a sunny day, gaps in the wooden siding would turn the interior into an ever-shifting magical place, sunlight slanting across the uneven floor, dust motes dancing in the air. Now, it was the east wind that made its presence felt, nothing magical about its touch.

On the back wall a section of newer siding marked the place where repairs had been made before the farmer gave up the fight against the inevitable altogether. The old siding lay in an untidy heap on the floor, its removal more effort than it was worth to a busy man with fields to plough.

A pipistrelle bat silently darted and flitted above his head and then out through the broken roof as he crossed the barn to the pile of discarded siding. He prodded the planks with his toe, sorted through them. They were of varying lengths from splintered pieces a couple of feet long to full lengths of eight feet or more, but they were too rotten to be of any use, as well as being too wide and not thick enough for what he had in mind.

He was starting to worry he'd never find anything suitable when he came across a couple of broken joists from the collapsed roof—one length of seven feet and another of six. At two inches thick and six inches wide, they were more appropriate than the siding. When he was satisfied there was nothing better, he took a heavy claw hammer from the backpack along with a bag of nails, then hammered the two lengths into a makeshift cross. Stood it on its end and leaned it against the wall, the camping lantern on the ground behind it.

His phone pinged in his pocket as he stood admiring his handiwork, its cruel purpose now all the more evident.

Everything okay?

Looking at the cross backlit by the lantern's glow, he smiled to himself as he tapped out a reply.

Perfect. Any problems your end?

Don't worry. You've got plenty of time.

Easy for you to say, he thought, pocketing the phone.

Time to go.

He jammed the barn door shut, fixed the padlock back in place as best he could. It wouldn't bear close scrutiny, but the farmer had probably forgotten the old barn even existed.

It was almost dark as he made his way along the footpath to where the car was parked. Back in the lay-by, he used his phone's flashlight to inspect the front bumper, the lack of dings or scratches proof of how careful the old biddy had been when manoeuvring to get out.

He took a final look across the fields towards the derelict barn before driving away, pulse quickening and a tight knot of trepidation in his gut at the thought of the unspeakable horrors awaiting him the next time he entered it.

1

One week later

Detective Inspector Max Angel was halfway through a mouthful of steak when his phone rang.

'Where are you?' DS Catalina Kincade said.

'In the Jolly Sailor in Bursledon. Why?'

'On your own?'

'Who is it, Max?' Siobhan Angel demanded before he could answer, looking as if she was about to snatch the phone out of his hand.

'You're with your mother?' Kincade said, recognising the harsh Belfast accent even above the background noises of the busy pub.

'We're just having a bite to eat.'

'Bit late for Mother's Day, isn't it, sir?'

'I get fed up to the back teeth cooking meals for him he gets home too late to eat,' Siobhan said, as if the roles were reversed and Kincade was responsible for her son's long and irregular hours.

'Better chew quickly, sir,' Kincade said.

'What is it?'

'We've got a body in a barn about a mile west of Bishop's Waltham.'

'Evidence of foul play?'

'It doesn't come much fouler or more evident than this.'

'I can hear something in your voice, Sergeant . . .'

She laughed at being caught out, her words riding out on the back of it.

'This one's made for you, sir. I'll be with you in ten minutes.'

The phone went dead in his ear before he could ask what she meant, what it was about sudden violent death that amused her. Siobhan wagged her finger at him as he took a quick swallow of beer, then went back to his steak and chips as if he hadn't eaten for a week.

'Don't bolt your food, Max. You'll give yourself indigestion.'

He shook his head at her, didn't risk a further reprimand for talking with his mouth full. Then tuned her out as she resumed the litany of petty irritations that filled her day, a single thought in his mind.

I get the feeling indigestion's going to be the least of my problems.

KINCADE REFUSED TO SAY WHAT HAD AMUSED HER FOR THE WHOLE of the five-mile drive to the lay-by on the B3035, despite Angel's reminders about their respective ranks, the repeated mantra—*you'll see*—the only thing he could get out of her. It made him feel like one of her girls in the days leading up to Christmas.

The road had been closed between Bishop's Waltham and the junction with Calcot Lane, halfway to Curdridge. Kincade parked at the end of a long line of vehicles, immediately behind one of the crime scene technicians' vans. Fifty yards ahead, a lay-by on the right was empty apart from a silver Ford Focus parked at the far end next to a stile that led into the adjoining field.

Craig Gulliver and Lisa Jardine arrived within minutes and parked immediately behind Kincade's car, then everybody made their way to where the first responder was waiting beside the Ford Focus.

'Michael Browning and Simone Grainger,' PC Andy McNab said, indicating the couple inside the car. 'They discovered the body.'

Angel performed a piece of very elementary mental police work. Given the approaching nightfall and the remoteness of the barn visible across the fields, it was obvious what their intentions had been before their evening took a turn for the worse.

'I'll talk to them after I've had a look in the barn,' he said, then climbed over the stile, the other three following behind.

'Wouldn't it be a coincidence if this is the barn Doctor Death roosts in,' Kincade said to nobody in particular.

Angel kept his eyes front, didn't let her see the smile on his lips. Her creativity when insulting the pathologist, likening her to one of the undead or a blood-sucking vampire, never ceased to amaze him.

He increased the pace, Gulliver easily keeping up, the two women dropping slightly behind. Kincade fell silent as he'd hoped.

Ahead of them the barn was lit up like something off a poster for a horror movie. A brilliant white light from the arc lamps spilled out of the open barn doors, the vertical slits between the wooden siding similarly illuminated, and behind it all the low rumble of the mobile generators like a slumbering beast awakened.

Kincade put on a spurt as they got to within twenty yards of it, her voice now serious as she drew alongside him.

'I know I said it's made for you, sir, but there's nothing remotely funny about what's inside.'

'I didn't think there would be for one second.'

Despite that, he couldn't deny the biblical nature of the scene as he stepped into the open doorway, the intensity of the light dazzling him. Immediately ahead of them a shirtless man was nailed to a wooden cross leaning against the barn wall, his chin on his sunken chest and his upper body streaked with blood.

Angel was aware of the suppressed smiles on Gulliver and Jardine's faces, everybody enjoying the connection to his previous life as a Catholic priest. He surprised them with an irreverent remark of his own.

'I don't suppose he'll be rising from the dead in three days' time.'

With that, he pulled on a pair of protective booties and stepped into the too-bright interior of the barn, crossing to where the pathologist waited for him.

'Don't say it, Isabel.'

Durand gave him a look like butter wouldn't melt, her characteristic emotionless facade slipping.

'Say what, Padre?'

He shook his head at her.

'You're as bad as Kincade.'

'I heard that,' Kincade said, joining them in front of the gruesome tableau.

'What do you think?' Angel said, knowing how much she liked to demonstrate her powers of observation and deduction to the pathologist.

'Arms nailed to the cross through the wrists, not the palms. I expect you'll find evidence of restraints around the wrists which were removed after nailing. Unless there were four of them, you'd never hold him still.' She indicated the victim's feet. 'The feet are tied. I'm guessing it's harder to nail through two feet one on top of the other—'

'It would be,' Durand confirmed.

'—even if you could hold them still in the first place. Looks like the killer was prepared to forego some of his enjoyment in the interests of practicality.'

'I think he more than made up for it,' Angel said, his eyes on the victim's blistered and blackened feet, the smell of charred flesh mercifully no longer present. 'Somebody used a blow torch on him.'

'That's what it looks like to me,' Durand agreed, her nose wrinkling in disgust as if a waft had just reached her.

'For sadistic pleasure or to get information?' Kincade said, voicing the question on all their minds.

Angel supplied the equally-obvious answer.

'Probably both.'

It was clear from the wound it wasn't a case of a quick flick of the flame over the victim's feet. Even after obtaining the information they were interested in, the killer continued for the fun of it. Because nobody fails to give up information instantly when the flame of a blow torch is lifting the skin from their flesh like old paint from woodwork.

'This is one sick puppy,' Kincade said, to solemn nods all round.

They spent a moment contemplating what might motivate such cruelty before Angel moved them away from the *why* and back into the safer realms of the *how*.

'Cause of death, Isabel? Crucifixion or the stab wound?'

'Given what else he did, I have no doubt the killer would have loved to pull up a chair and watch this poor man's slow and painful death by crucifixion—a combination of myocardial rupture, asphyxiation and shock. However, that can take up to a couple of days, depending on the health and strength of the victim, making it impractical.' She pointed towards the two-inch-wide horizontal wound between the fourth and fifth ribs Angel had referred to, a mass of congealed blood extending from it down the victim's stomach and soaking into his trousers, and from there down over his feet, pooling on the floor at the foot of the cross. 'He didn't have the time to wait around, obviously. From the amount of blood and the position of the wound, I'd say it was made with a blade long enough to pierce the heart.'

'Time of death?'

'Rigor mortis is completely gone. Livor mortis is well-established.' She indicated a greenish-blue discolouration of the skin spreading across the victim's abdomen. 'The marbling here indicates that putrefaction is well underway, and the presence of the maggots here'—pointing at the crusty blood surrounding the fatal wound—'all suggest he's been dead at least forty-eight hours.'

'Some time Friday night.'

'I'm sure that's what the post-mortem will confirm, yes.'

'Any ID or personal effects?'

'Nothing. No wallet, car keys or phone.'

Angel stepped back to get a better overall look, Kincade coming with him as he let his thoughts flow.

'The cross must have been lying on the ground. They, and it has to be at least two of them, knocked him unconscious, laid him on the cross. Tied his wrists to the cross-member with cable ties like you said, then bound his feet to the upright. It looks like ordinary clothes line to me. Once he was secured, they hammered the nails through his wrists.' Pointing to a couple of evidence markers spaced six feet apart next to corresponding blood stains on the floor. 'They then cut away the cable ties. Took hold of an end of the cross-member each, lifted him up and leaned the whole lot against the wall. You can see the indentations in the dirt where something heavy was dragged.'

That wasn't all Kincade could see. It looked as if there'd been a hoedown or some arcane sacrificial dance to celebrate the crucifixion, the dirt floor of the barn churned up where the killers had shuffled and struggled under the weight and awkwardness of the cross as the man on it writhed in agony. From a casual glance, it could've been two people or ten responsible.

Good luck, SOCOs, she thought, relieved she wasn't the one responsible for giving a definitive answer about how many people had been present. Instead, she stuck to the obvious as they took a last look at the man on the cross.

'Then the sick bastards went to work on him with a knife and the blow torch.'

They left Durand to it, drifted slowly back towards the door, looking up and around as they went. A cursory glance to get a feel for the scene in advance of more details resulting from the forensic technicians' search. He noticed a large hole in the roof where part of it had collapsed, called over one of the SOCOs.

'You need to get that hole covered.'

The officer looked where Angel was pointing, his face mask covering any embarrassment that might have been there for not already having done so.

'Will do, although there's no rain forecast.'

'I wasn't thinking about that. The media are going to be all over this. I don't want them flying a bloody drone through it.'

'At least we know where to start,' Kincade said, as they made their way back to where the couple who'd found the body waited in their car.

He didn't need to look at her to know she was about to be facetious.

'Really?'

'Uh-huh. We need to identify the twelve people he had supper with last night. I bet one of them betrayed him.'

He bit his tongue, refused to laugh. Knowing similar irreverent jokes would be rife in the days ahead. For now, he changed the subject, keeping it light-hearted with a nod towards the witnesses' car.

'What's the betting they're both married and having an affair?'

'If they are, tonight is going to have a very beneficial effect on their marriages going forward.'

'Always look on the bright side, eh?'

From their faces when they climbed out of their car, Michael Browning and Simone Grainger didn't look as if there was much bright side in evidence. In their late twenties, they were both pale and haggard-looking, and Angel was relieved they chose to talk outside the car. Its interior smelled like a stale ashtray—as did their breath.

They'd been offered the opportunity to go home and be interviewed there in comfort later, but had declined. The way Browning cleared his throat made it clear they'd discussed what they saw as their biggest problem while they waited in the car.

'We're both married . . .'

'To other people,' Simone added, a challenge to criticise them in her voice.

'That's why we didn't want to be interviewed at home,' Browning explained unnecessarily, his guilt and shame behind it.

'It's all going to come out, isn't it?' Simone said, resignation replacing the aggression of a moment ago.

Angel nodded apologetically.

'I'm afraid so.'

The couple shared a look, then Simone brightened suddenly.

'What if you never catch the killer?'

Angel took a deep breath. Counted to ten. He felt he'd been more than fair to indulge them. Allow them to air their selfish concerns first, before getting down to the important details that might see justice served rather than saving two marriages that looked to be on the rocks anyway.

'Then I'd say it's a very sad day for that man's family.' Pointing across the fields in the direction of the derelict barn as he said it.

'But even if we never catch the killer,' Kincade said, not bothering to hide the distaste on her face, 'I'm sure we'll need to interview both of you again a number of times.'

She let a tight smile finish the sentence for her.

Until your spouses wonder what the hell's going on.

'If you could now tell us exactly what happened,' Angel said, 'then you can be on your way.'

Browning took on the role of lead spokesman, explaining how he'd seen the old barn when driving past a week earlier. That evening, they'd parked in the lay-by which had been empty, not having seen any other vehicles in the vicinity as they approached. They'd arrived at seven p.m., climbed the stile and crossed the fields. They didn't see another soul. An unspoken subtext—*that's why I chose this place*—underscored everything he said.

Angel had noticed the padlock still attached to the hasp on the open barn door and the splintered wood it had been ripped from.

'Was the barn door locked?'

'No. We wouldn't have broken in. The padlock was already hanging off. Looked like somebody used a wrecking bar on it.'

What would you have done if it had been locked? Kincade thought. *Had a quickie up against the wall?*

Angel's thoughts were more constructive. If the killer had planned ahead, it meant they'd carried out a reconnaissance. Only an idiot would fail to check whether he could get into his chosen execution chamber until the night of the murder itself.

'What happened next?'

'The broken lock made me wary,' Browning admitted.

What they heard: *I thought somebody might have had the same idea as us.*

'I poked my head around the edge of the door. That's when I saw him . . .'

'He screamed like a baby,' Simone said, made Kincade want to slap her.

'I tried to stop Simone from going in,' Browning went on, 'but she wasn't having any of it.'

Simone nodded, *you got that right.*

'I thought he was arsing around. Trying to scare me. I pushed him out of the way and went in.' She swallowed thickly, the horror of what she'd seen reflected in her eyes. 'I wish I hadn't now.' She threw an evil glance Browning's way, an irritating whine entering her voice. 'We should've gone to a motel like I wanted to, but, oh no, Mr Romantic here wanted to do it in a shitty old barn. He's not the one who gets straw in the crack of his arse.'

'Did you go all the way into the barn?' Angel asked, before a full-scale argument broke out.

Simone looked at him as if he'd asked her if she wiped her finger in the victim's blood and tasted it to see if it was real.

'You're kidding, aren't you? Michael was already puking in the bushes. I just about held it in until I got there myself.'

Kincade didn't need to put words to the look she gave Browning.

Was that the sort of romance you had in mind? Throwing up together in the bushes.

'That's when I phoned you lot,' Browning said with a quick sideways glance at Simone.

'Mr Goody Two-Shoes always has to do the right thing,' Simone muttered under her breath, oblivious to the contradiction in a man involved in an extra-marital affair.

They had no trouble imagining the indecision and argument that had preceded the call.

Should they get the hell out of there and say nothing? Call it in anonymously?

The way Simone was glaring at her lover suggested she'd been in favour of option one. Browning had the vestiges of a conscience and was more realistic. An anonymous call would be traced back to him, resulting in a visit to his house where everything would definitely come out. Angel doubted the relationship would last, even if their spouses never discovered their infidelity.

'She's a piece of work,' Kincade said, watching them drive away, the argument that had already started clearly audible through the open window. 'I feel like calling her husband, giving him the heads up. Do the poor bastard a favour.'

2

'This is stupid,' he said through gritted teeth, glancing nervously up and down the quiet lane. 'Absolutely bloody stupid.'

'You say that one more time and I'm going to punch you.' Looking like she meant it, too. Then a contemptuous note entered her voice. 'You want to be a pussy, go and sit in the car. See if I care.'

He was tempted to call her bluff. Except she'd do it without him. And every minute she was out of his sight was a minute spent worrying.

'Well?' she said. 'What's it going to be?'

He looked at the massive stone gate posts, the rusted and padlocked wrought-iron gates between them. Overgrown, impenetrable thorny hedges on either side that would rip an undernourished fox to shreds, let alone a person.

He felt like taking a step back, watching her try to get over on her own. Again, she'd find a way. Blind determination bordering on insanity always finds a way.

'You're pathetic,' she mocked, when he still didn't move.

Up yours, he thought, the anger surging inside him. *Pathetic?* After what he'd already helped her do?

She changed tack before he found the words he wanted to say, manipulating him like she always did. Dropped the mocking tone, the contempt. Laid her hand on his arm, as if to say, *don't forget what I did for you.* Her voice was a mix of reasonableness and wistful longing when she put it into words.

'It's all for nothing if we don't do this part.'

'Hardly nothing. The bastard's dead.'

'You know what I mean.'

Sometimes he thought that was the problem. He *did* know what she meant. That's what scared him.

As always, there was no point in arguing. He didn't know why he'd wasted the last five minutes, risked a car driving past. Nobody could say they weren't acting suspiciously as hell.

He leaned his shoulder against the weathered stone of the right-hand gate post, anchored his feet. Bent his knees and made a stirrup of his hands. She stepped into it with a smug smile at getting her way. He straightened his legs, boosted her up, high enough for her to clamber precariously onto the top of the gate post.

'How are you going to get over?' she said through the gate after she'd dropped to the ground on the other side.

'I'm not. I'm going to be a pussy and wait in the car.'

He took a step away, the predictable response stopping him before he took a second.

'Don't be a dickhead.'

This time, there was no malice behind it. Just more of the smug satisfaction that it was only ever a question of time before he gave in to her.

He was taller than her, stronger and more agile. He backed away from the gates, then took a run at them, leaping, his momentum bouncing him off a horizontal strut and upwards, grabbing one of the ornamental spikes along the top of the gate, using the strength in his arms to push himself up until his waist was level with the row of spikes. Then one leg up, his body following, a smooth fluid movement, over and dropping to the cracked concrete drive on the other side.

He stifled an involuntary hiss of pain as he landed, but there was no damage done. He'd jumped from higher roofs more times than he cared to remember. A few paces up and down and he was right as rain.

'I'm impressed,' she said. 'You're like Spider-Man.'

Yes, and you're a black widow, he thought, setting off.

'C'mon, let's get this over with.'

They followed the drive through the middle of an untamed jungle on either side, feral rhododendrons and rampant brambles and stunted saplings colonising what had once been manicured gardens. A larger, older tree lying across the drive forced them to clamber over what remained of its rotting trunk, then onwards, the house coming into sight ahead of them as they rounded the curve.

He almost put his hand on her arm, stopped himself in time. It would only be rejected.

'Are you okay?'

'Of course I'm okay.' The sharpness of her tone telling him she was anything but.

She stopped at the end of the drive, a dried-up circular fountain ahead of her, the house itself beyond that. Its lower windows were boarded over with ply, those above empty save for the occasional broken shard of glass, a thick coating of pigeon droppings covering every ledge. Broken roof tiles littered the ground beside crumbling render that had come away from the wall in a single sheet, exposing the old red brick beneath. Weeds sprouted from every crack and cranny, a monstrous buddleia taking up residence in the shelter of the once-impressive porte cochère.

She took half a dozen photographs on her phone—he guessed so that she had a permanent reminder that the past dozen years had not been kind to it, either—but knew better than to ask.

When she was done, they made their way around to the right of the house, past the detached garage block and onto the wide rear terrace that ran the length of the building, an ancient oak pergola overgrown with vines at the far end.

'We'll never get through that,' he said, as they stood contemplating the wilderness stretching away to the trees in the distance. 'It'd be easier approaching from the fields on the other side of the trees.'

She spun around to face him, the earlier sharpness still in her voice, irritation on her face.

'I didn't risk breaking my neck climbing over that stupid gate just to climb back out again, and then do what we should've done in the first place if you'd had your bright idea before it was too late.'

He recognised the time to keep his mouth firmly shut, wishing he'd had the foresight to bring a machete.

They went right, to the far edge of the terrace where the beginnings of a path that had once skirted the lawns disappeared into what nature had reclaimed for its own. Fighting their way through, they found their progress easier than anticipated. *Obsession crossing the line into insanity*, he thought to himself as he followed behind her resolute back, then took his turn forging the way after she tripped on ivy as thick as her wrist and he had to drag her out of the brambles that swallowed her. From the sour scowl on her face, he'd be hard-pressed to say which of them was the most prickly.

They stopped for a rest beside a massive oak at the edge of the trees, turning to look back at the house.

'We haven't come far,' she said, echoing the thoughts he hadn't dared voice.

'It'll be easier from here. The leaf canopy keeps it dark. The undergrowth won't be as bad.'

With his back against the oak, he took out his phone, opened the compass app.

'That way.' Pointing in a south-westerly direction.

As he'd predicted, their progress was faster, the undergrowth thinning progressively as they moved deeper into the trees. A quarter mile later, the path they were following ended on the bank of a large ornamental pond choked with water lilies and bulrushes. A startled moorhen went skittering across the top of the lily pads, its explosive panicked cries startling them every bit as much.

'There,' she said, pointing to what remained of a wooden boathouse on the far side.

He took a deep breath. Held it. Let it out slowly as the memories his subconscious had protected him from for the past twelve years threatened to overwhelm him. Forced them back into the dark recesses of his mind, ignoring the sharp sting of remembered pain in his hands, and set off towards it.

Progress slowed again, the break in the leaf canopy above the pond allowing the light in, thirsty roots from the bankside vegetation benefitting from the ready supply of water.

Despite that, they made it without either of them falling in, cursing and swearing at nothing and everything as they went. He stepped up onto the sagging boathouse porch, the railing coming away in his hand.

'Stop wasting time,' she hissed, as he jumped down again before the rotting floor gave way under his weight.

Her agitation was palpable as she led the way to the rear of the building, then dropped to her knees in the middle of a small clearing somehow spared from encroachment by the towering trees all around, as if even they had some respect.

He stood immediately behind her, rested his hand on her shoulder. Saying nothing. Waiting for her, as was appropriate. Her voice caught momentarily when finally, she spoke.

'You'd never know.'

'That was the whole idea.' For a split second, he thought she was about to snap at him, but he was wrong. The memories had sucked the venom out of her, left a hollow void behind. 'It wasn't your fault.'

She acted as if he hadn't spoken.

'I wish I'd brought flowers.'

You'd have dropped them in the brambles wasn't what she needed to hear.

'Better that you didn't.'

She placed her hand over his still resting on her shoulder, squeezed.

'I know. Maybe one day.'

The moment of melancholy was over as quickly as it came. Jumping to her feet, she pulled out her phone, opened Google maps. Zoomed in as far as possible, the pond behind them clearly visible. She dropped a pin, dragged up the details, the exact latitude and longitude displayed in five-decimal-point detail. She highlighted it, copied it, then pasted it into the notes app. The location would be a lot easier to find the next time she wanted it, that was for sure.

'Let's try the fields,' he said, studying their location on Google maps on his own phone. 'It's only about a quarter of a mile.'

She paused for a poignant farewell glance, then followed him in the same south-westerly direction, the edge of the woods as close by as he'd promised it would be, open fields ahead of them beyond a barbed-wire fence. He stood on the bottom strand pushing it down, pulled up the one above to allow her to duck and step through the gap, then she did the same for him, the back of his jacket snagging and ripping on the wire when he failed to stoop low enough.

'Told you it'd be easier,' she said, claiming the credit for his good idea, as they skirted the field boundary back to where their car awaited.

3

'It brings it home when you actually see a man nailed to a cross,' Lisa Jardine said, staring out of the window at the countryside flashing by.

'Brings what home?' Gulliver replied, the depth of feeling behind his partner's remark surprising him.

'You know, Christ on the cross and all that. You get the story stuffed down your throat growing up, but it's all about the spiritual side of things. You never actually think about the physical aspect. You've got nails through your wrists with all your weight hanging on them, so you try to take some of the weight with your legs, but you've got a nail through your feet, and that's even worse . . . and it might go on for days. Up down, up down, up down. It's exhausting just thinking about it.'

'You're not coming over all religious, are you? Thinking it'll get you in the boss' good books?'

She gave him a very non-religious look.

'Don't be a twat, Craig. I'm just saying, it makes you think.'

Nice that something does, he thought and kept to himself.

As conversations in the car between them went, it broke new ground. A pleasant change for him from Jardine's usual acerbic observations as they drove to Warren Wood Farm to speak to the owner of the barn-cum-execution chamber, Clive Ratliff.

Ratliff was everybody's idea of a good ol' boy farmer, his face weathered and prematurely aged by the elements, the sleeves of his thick check shirt rolled up over muscular forearms, a flat cap that he no doubt wore in bed wedged on his head.

He took them through into a large farmhouse kitchen where a pot of coffee sat keeping warm on the AGA, a pile of paperwork on the table beside a half-empty mug.

'Might as well do something useful while I'm waiting,' he said, as polite a way of saying *I'm a busy man, be quick about it* as Gulliver had ever heard.

Ratliff maintained the role of caricature country bumpkin, pulling off his cap and scratching his head when they confirmed a man had been murdered in his barn, which is why he hadn't been allowed access when he turned up the previous night to see what all the fuss was about.

'Is it true he was crucified?'

They weren't surprised details had leaked out. A killer wanting to catch people's attention would've struggled to find a better way to dispatch his victim. Nobody wanted to think about what the media was going to make of it.

'When was the last time you went to the barn?' Gulliver said, the way he ignored the question effectively confirming it for Ratliff and anyone he talked to in the days ahead.

Off came the cap again. Another thoughtful scratch, his eyes on the floor.

'I haven't been inside it for months. But I was over that way the Friday before last.'

Exactly a week before he was killed, Gulliver thought.

'Would you have noticed that the lock had been broken?'

'Definitely. It might not be much use to me, but I don't want kids sneaking in for a smoke and burning it down with a careless cigarette butt. The insurance company would think I'd done it deliberately to get a nice new barn for free.'

'You actually got up close, not just a quick glance from ten yards away?' Jardine said.

'That's right.' Shaking his hand back and forth as if rattling the padlock to make sure it was secure. 'It was exactly as I'd left it. You think the killer broke the lock in advance?'

'There's a good chance. Do you remember seeing anyone in the vicinity between the day you checked the padlock and Friday evening? Parked in the lay-by? Hikers or dog walkers on the public footpath?'

Ratliff's mouth turned down at the mention of people on the footpath, although, as far as they knew, he didn't keep livestock that uncontrolled dogs might worry.

'I don't have time to pay attention to every car that parks in the lay-by. And there are always dog walkers.'

'Any regulars? People you know who stop for a chat?'

He looked as if he was about to say how busy he was again, thought better of it. It was a murder investigation, after all.

'There's a woman with a young cocker spaniel I see quite often. But I've never talked to her.'

'Do you know who she is, even if you're too busy to stop and talk? Someone who lives nearby?'

'No. I recognise the dog more than her. She used to have a much older dog. Another spaniel. It must have died. I remember because we used to have one like it.'

'Is there anyone who breeds them nearby?'

'Don't think so. We got ours from a dog rescue home.'

They wrapped it up after that. Ratliff had provided vital confirmation of the week-long window during which the killers made their advance preparations, as well as identifying a potential dog-walking witness. He was now itching to get outside and get ploughing or whatever else fills a farmer's day.

'I suppose there'll be hordes of rubberneckers tramping over my fields to take a look,' he said with a scowl as he showed them out.

'Perhaps, until public interest dies down,' Jardine admitted.

'It's not a crime to sell tickets, is it?'

Only against human decency, Jardine thought, leaving him to his new business plan.

THE VICTIM'S IDENTITY PROVED STRAIGHTFORWARD TO ESTABLISH. Working on the assumption that anybody wanting to approach Clive Ratliff's barn would keep to public footpaths, all such footpaths in the vicinity of the barn were identified, the access points to those routes searched.

An abandoned Volvo V90 was found in a similar lay-by to the one used by Michael Browning and Simone Grainger, the footpath leading from it passing within spitting distance of the stand of trees adjacent to the barn. Entering the registration details into the PNC produced a photograph held by the DVLA for Dominic Thomas Orford, aged forty-two, of Morestead Road, Morestead. It matched the crucified man to a T.

Whoever killed him and removed his ID and personal effects had bought themselves less than twelve hours, if that had been the purpose of taking them in the first place.

IF ANGEL THOUGHT NOTIFYING DOMINIC ORFORD'S NEW WIDOW of her husband's violent death was the worst thing he would have to deal with that morning, he was mistaken.

He was at his desk, trying to get the image of Orford nailed to a DIY cross out of his mind as he prepared himself mentally for one of the worst aspects of the job, when Sergeant Jack Bevan rang him from the front desk.

Bevan was an escapee from a remote village with an unpronounceable name in darkest Wales. Their business dealings were always prefaced by a good-natured exchange of banter—Bevan would make irreverent remarks about Angel's previous life as a Catholic priest, and Angel would refer to people eating their own young in Bevan's home town.

Not so today.

Bevan sounded as if he'd rather deliver the death message to Mrs Orford himself than say what he did next.

'Better get down here asap, Padre. There's someone to see you. I thought I was going to have to sit on her to stop her from coming up.'

'Who is it?'

Bevan hesitated, dropped his voice to a whisper.

'Catherine Beckford.'

Angel closed his eyes, wishing he'd already left the office.

'I'll be down in a sec.'

'What's up?' Kincade said, catching sight of his face.

He had no good choices. A straight lie was out. The truth was worse. Telling her it was nothing wouldn't wash—not after she'd seen his expression.

'Catherine Beckford is in reception.'

She stiffened. It might not be DS Stuart Beckford, her sorely-missed predecessor currently on long-term sick leave, but the surname was sufficient to raise her hackles.

'What does she want?'

It would've been a stupid question if they didn't both already know.

'It's got to be about Balan's offer. Stu must have told her.'

'And she came here? Don't they have a telephone?'

He gave her a disappointed look. She was a woman herself. She should understand why Catherine Beckford wanted to rip into him face-to-face, enjoy his pain first-hand.

'Want me to do the Orford notification while you deal with her?' she offered.

He let out a heavy sigh, shook his head.

'Thanks for offering, but no. It'll feel like light relief after ...' Pointing at the floor, rather than trying to describe what awaited him downstairs.

The reception area was empty when he got there, apart from Bevan behind the counter. Irrational hope surged in Angel's breast. Had Catherine got fed up waiting and left? Taken the lift up as he came down the stairs?

Bevan killed his hopes dead.

'I put her in interview room one.'

It was further proof of how seriously Bevan was taking the matter. Angel couldn't think of another occasion on which Bevan hadn't referred to it as *confessional* number one when Angel was presiding. Bevan pointed at the ceiling, his tone conspiratorial.

'I didn't want to risk anyone from the top floor passing and recognising her. I wouldn't know what to tell them.'

Nice try, Angel thought, in response to Bevan's thinly-disguised fishing trip for details. He nodded his thanks, left Bevan to his imagination. It couldn't be worse than the reality.

Catherine started yelling before Angel had even closed the interview-room door.

'What the hell do you think you're playing at, Max?'

Now was not the time to point out that *playing at* was not an appropriate way of describing things. In fact, now was not the time for Angel to say anything at all. Catherine was in full-flow, pacing the room as her frustration and anger fought for dominance.

'We've been trying to move past it. God knows, it hasn't been easy. Now you go and resurrect it.'

It was the death of Angel's wife, Claire, killed in a head-on collision when a Romanian lorry driver fell asleep at the wheel and ploughed into Stuart Beckford's car while the four of them were out for the evening.

Angel forced himself to keep his voice level, not respond to the unfair accusation with his tone of voice as well as the words themselves.

'*I* haven't resurrected it.' Jabbing his chest with an angry finger. 'Virgil Balan has—'

'*Balan, Balan, Balan.* I'm sick of hearing that bloody name. Who the hell is he? Stu was very evasive about him.'

I bet he was, Angel thought, a chill settling in his stomach. He was getting the feeling Stuart Beckford had fed his wife an extremely edited version of events.

'He's a Romanian detective with a connection to another case. He took a personal interest in me—'

'Stu told me you aren't sure if he's legit or not.'

Seemed to Angel that Stuart Beckford wasn't the only one who liked to filter what he divulged. Catherine's memory about what she had and hadn't been told was something of a moveable feast.

In this instance she was right. Virgil Balan had offered to find Bogdan Florescu, the Romanian lorry driver responsible for the fatal accident, who'd immediately absconded back to Romania. Angel couldn't decide whether Balan was offering official assistance to extradite Florescu back to the UK to stand trial, or a personal offer to find and capture Florescu, then leave him at Angel and Beckford's mercy in a filthy basement, bring your own brass knuckles.

There was no point in Angel answering. Balan was already dirty in Catherine's mind.

'*I knew it!*' she exclaimed, when he didn't respond. 'You should have told him to piss off.' Her voice took on the moral conviction of a person who doesn't have to make the difficult decisions. 'It's wrong on so many levels. You can't justify revenge, ever. Being police officers makes it even worse.'

He waited, mentally rolling his hand—*keep it coming*—fully expecting her to drag up his past life as a priest on top of being a serving police officer.

She must be saving it for later, he thought when she failed to do so, her next words demonstrating that in her mind Balan was not only dirty, he'd already found Florescu and was holding him in secret and against his will while her husband and Angel booked their flights to Bucharest.

'What do you plan to do to him, Max? Take out all your anger and grief and guilt on him while he's tied to a chair? Will you use your fists? Or a baseball bat?'

He almost accused her of becoming hysterical, of letting her imagination get out of control. He caught himself in time, avoided answering the unanswerable.

'One step at a time, Catherine.'

'That's not a bloody answer.'

'It happens to be how I'm taking things.'

It was as if he hadn't spoken, Florescu's face already a bloodied pulp in front of her eyes.

'How can you possibly think it will help? You, an ex-priest, of all people.'

Got there at last, he thought sourly, then played on the advantage she'd given him.

'Maybe I want to forgive him in person.'

She snorted derisively.

'*Bollocks!* You never believed in any of that claptrap.' She shook her head, confusion and frustration in the gesture. 'I don't understand why you were so bloody determined to go ahead. Maybe if you hadn't been so obsessed, Stu would've written it off as what it is—a stupid idea.'

A wave of dismay swept through him. He hadn't known what

to do when Balan made the offer. He'd left the decision to Beckford, who'd given it the thumbs-up. It saddened him that his friend had turned that situation on its head, blamed him.

He shrugged apologetically. Feigned embarrassment that he couldn't justify his unreasonable decision. One day, Catherine might learn the truth, but it wouldn't be from him.

Except it wasn't as easy as that.

They'd known each other a long time.

Now, she narrowed her eyes at him, uncertainty colouring her voice.

'Stu wasn't lying to me, was he? Was he the one who wanted to go ahead, and you're the one going along with it?'

He shook his head at her, big long strokes from side to side —*what a ridiculous idea.*

'It was my idea, Catherine. I'm sorry if it's causing problems between you.'

She studied him a long time without saying anything. Until she did.

'For a copper, you're a shit liar, Max. Once a priest, always a priest, eh?'

There wasn't anything to say that wouldn't make the situation worse. It felt to him as if she'd exhausted her supply of venom, rolled out all the accusations she'd come armed with. She looked drained. The weariness in her voice spoke of acceptance, of dealing with a situation she couldn't prevent.

'Who have you told?'

'My mother.'

'Really?'

'Yes, *really*. She's living in my house, for Christ's sake. There's no way I could hide it. My sister thinks we're all Nazis torturing false confessions out of innocent suspects in the cells. She should see her own mother when she gets into her stride. The IRA missed a trick when they didn't employ her services.'

Catherine smiled with him, then it was gone. And he found out the hard way he'd been wrong about her stock of venom running dry.

'You haven't told your new DS, have you? What's her name? Kinsale?'

'Kin*cade*.'

'You have, haven't you? I can see it written all over your face. *Jesus Christ, Max!* I bet she's loving it. Egging you on. There's no chance of Stu getting his job back if he gets caught going along with your crazy plan.'

Angel almost laughed out loud. They were back to it being his fault—until Catherine got home to her hapless husband, that is.

'She's doing the exact opposite,' he said, in Kincade's defence. 'She thinks it's a stupid idea, too. Even though she's the one who'll end up in my job if we got caught doing what you're so convinced we're about to do.'

She gave him a pitying look that he should be so naive.

'You shouldn't be so trusting, Max. It's the priest in you coming through again. I know what women like her are like. Two-faced cow.' She jabbed her index finger at him a couple of times. 'Mark my words, she's after your job.'

He gave up.

It wasn't even worth pointing out that if Kincade was promoted into his job, Beckford would get his back from her.

Sometimes, facts have no place in an argument.

4

'I wasn't going to,' Kincade said, when Angel came back into their shared, broom-cupboard-sized office, and slumped in his chair as if he'd been shot in the chest.

'Wasn't going to what?'

'Ask.'

'Good.'

'About the only thing that is?'

'You got that right. And you are asking, in a very underhand, female way.'

'Got something of a temporary downer on women after the last fifteen minutes, by any chance?'

'Nothing temporary about it.'

'So? How about ruining somebody else's day to make you feel you're not alone?'

He laughed, a wheezy strangled sound he couldn't stop from leaking out. Sat up straight, pulled himself together.

'I know you're not asking, but we were right. Stu told his wife about Balan's offer.'

She winced as if she'd trapped her finger in the door.

'How was it left?'

With her hating me, he almost said before stopping himself. He didn't want to poison her mind by letting her know Beckford had put all the blame on him—even though she would've felt better knowing the man she was scared was about to reclaim his job from her wasn't such a saint after all.

'No change. She was letting off steam, that's all. She knows talking to me won't make any difference. If Stu's decided he wants to do this, he's going to do it, whatever anybody says.'

'Pig-headed, eh?'

He grinned at her, the truth hidden behind his joking words as he pointed at her chair.

'I think it's part of the job description for sitting in that chair.'

She tried to look offended, didn't quite pull it off.

'At least it made you smile. Can't have you breaking down in tears before his wife does.'

'It's almost as if the method of killing him matches the victim's name,' Kincade said, when they were in the car and on the way to where the unsuspecting Mrs Orford waited in Morestead, ten miles away.

Angel smiled to himself at the way they were growing together—in their thought processes, if nothing else.

'A religious undertone, you mean? Dominic sounds like the sort of name a monk would have. Brother Dominic.'

'Yeah. Or a priest. Wouldn't it be funny if he turned out to be one?'

Fucking hilarious, he thought, and replied in a similar vein.

'Or a police officer who made too many irreverent remarks?'

'I've got no idea who you might be thinking of, sir.'

The light-hearted banter continued all the way to Morestead, a welcome respite for him sandwiched between the argument with Catherine Beckford and the upcoming emotional disaster zone.

'Nice house,' Kincade said, as he pulled onto the drive of a large house directly opposite Morestead Church. 'Must've been doing okay.'

'Or maybe Mrs Orford is a successful banker?' he said, the reference to her own estranged banker husband living in a big house in Highgate in London reminding her not to jump to conclusions.

'True.' She paused, on the face of it thoughtful—if he didn't know better. 'Even so, somebody paid a lot of money for the house. Maybe we're looking at Harold Shipman reincarnated.'

'Let's go find out, shall we?'

As was often the case, Mrs Orford knew who they were and why they were on her doorstep as soon as she opened the door. The speed with which she opened it suggested she'd been waiting close behind it, sick with worry after her husband failed to return home the previous two evenings. Personally, Angel thought it was more of a primeval sixth sense at work.

Whatever it was, her knees buckled as her hand went to her mouth. Angel stepped smartly in, caught her by the elbow and steered her into a large, comfortable sitting room on the left while Kincade closed the front door on a world that would never be the same again for Louise Orford.

As always, Kincade marvelled at the way he delivered the life-changing news, unable to identify whether it was the words he chose or the way in which he said them—most likely a combination of both—that made her determined to practice in front of the mirror. At times, she thought it was his background as a priest, all those hours spent in the confessional, his empathy deepened by the horrors he'd witnessed as an Army chaplain in Iraq and Afghanistan. At other times, she thought it was simply him. He'd have been the same if he'd sold second-hand cars before joining the police.

None of it counted for anything when the difficult questions came, of course. And come they always did, once the initial shock subsided sufficiently for the newly-bereaved to ask about the things they didn't want to hear.

The shortest question was always the hardest, and Louise, like everybody else, started with it, addressing Angel as if Kincade was part of the furniture.

'How?'

'He was murdered.'

'How?'

If only that was an echo, he thought, sticking to clinical facts in an attempt to steer away from the awful details.

'A fatal stab wound to the heart.'

He hadn't volunteered that it happened in a derelict barn, so why should he say her husband had been nailed to a cross at the time?

It wouldn't help in the long run, but it was a detail to save for another day. In a perfect world, it might never be necessary to divulge every grisly detail, but the farmer's question to Gulliver and Jardine about crucifixion proved there was already a leak— one the media would soon exploit to squeeze every last penny from a public that gorged itself on human tragedy.

An excruciating silence descended as Louise tried to process the alien words being spoken to her. Kincade slipped away, headed down the hall to the kitchen overlooking a substantial back garden and got busy with making tea.

Louise produced a tissue from nowhere as women do, dabbed her eyes and blew her nose, a pointless exercise that did nothing to stem the flow of silent tears. She swallowed thickly, forged on with her questions, all of which sounded like *why?* to Angel.

'When did it happen?'

'On Friday night. He was found Sunday evening without any identification on him. We located his car this morning which allowed us to identify him.'

'He told me he was attending a conference,' Louise said, confusion in her voice at why her husband should lie about being murdered.

Kincade returned with a tray containing three mugs of tea before Angel followed up on the conference that may or may not have been an excuse. Louise took a mug before the tray was down, cradling it in both hands, then sipped gratefully from it, the sugar Kincade had added fuelling a hope-filled question.

'Do you know who did it?'

'I'm afraid not,' Angel replied, taking a mug of tea for himself. 'He was found in a derelict barn about a mile from Bishop's Waltham—'

'That's not far from where he works,' Louise said, as if deriving comfort from the reference to life as it used to be. 'I thought there was something not right about the conference. We ended up having a big argument about it. That's why I didn't report him as missing when he didn't come home.' She looked directly at Kincade as if she would understand the childish things men do when they're annoyed. 'I thought he'd gone to stay at his parents' house. They're away at the moment.'

'What sort of a conference?' Angel said, his interest fuelled by Louise's suspicions.

'A doctor's conference, what do you think?'

Saves having to ask what he did for a living, Angel thought, then confirmed it anyway.

'Dominic was a doctor?'

'That's right. A GP in a practice in Waltham Chase.' She smiled briefly, more like a nervous tic. 'That's where we met. I used to work in the pharmacy there. I was made redundant and didn't bother looking for another job. Dominic was doing well and ... it doesn't matter.'

'Everything matters in a case like this, Mrs Orford,' Kincade said gently.

Louise looked at her as if the seat cushion had spoken.

'I was going to say Dominic's parents helped out. Doctors make a good living, but we could never have afforded this house on our own, not after I gave up work. We were trying for children, but it never happened.' She gave Kincade a sad smile. 'Do you have children?'

'Two girls.'

'I hope you realise how lucky you are.'

Luckier still if they lived with me and not Elliot and his gold-digging bunny-boiler, Hannah, she thought and chose not to share in the circumstances.

'I do, Mrs Orford. How long have you been married?'

'Eight years. We got married in two thousand and sixteen. Dominic finished his training as a GP up in London the year before, then moved back down to take up a position in the local practice.' She glanced around as if she'd heard somebody eavesdropping at the door. 'To tell you the truth, I think his father had a quiet word with the senior partner. I never said that to Dominic, of course. Men are so concerned about their pride.' Looking directly at Angel as if he personified the sin. 'Anyway, that's how we met, and things progressed from there.'

The fresh tears rolling down her cheeks spoke the final sentence for her.

I thought we'd have a lot longer than eight short years together.

She produced an asthma inhaler that, like the tissue, had been secreted around her person, sucked hard on it.

Angel decided to call it a day. There would be follow-ups, and they would search the study-cum-office Dominic Orford no doubt maintained in the big old house. They would take away his computer and pick apart his online life in as much detail as his physical one, but for now Angel finished with a catch-all question.

'Has anything unusual occurred in the recent past that you think we should know about?'

Louise studied the inhaler still in her hands as she tried to coax memories from her reeling mind, her response not one they anticipated.

'How recent?'

They'd normally expect *yes, no* or *my mind's a blank*. Angel couldn't remember being asked to be more specific before.

'That doesn't really matter. It's more a case of what might have happened, not when.'

'But you said recent.'

Angel curbed his frustration, kept his voice level.

'Generally, we're more interested in recent events, but that doesn't preclude us looking further back.'

Louise promptly shook her head.

'Nothing comes to mind.'

Then why did you bloody ask about the time frame? Angel thought, as they saw themselves out.

'I WONDER WHAT HAPPENED THAT SHE DIDN'T WANT TO TELL US about?' Kincade said, echoing Angel's thoughts once they were back in the car and still parked outside Louise Orford's big empty house.

'He's a doctor. Maybe somebody complained about inappropriate behaviour while he was examining them.'

Kincade shook her head, the memory of the last time she'd undergone an intimate examination in her mind, the coldness of the implements.

'There's always a chaperone in the room these days.'

'Maybe the chaperone's body will turn up soon.'

She twisted towards him, even though she didn't need to see his face to know he wasn't being serious.

'Nobody crucifies a man for touching them inappropriately.'

'Full-on rape?'

'In a doctor's surgery?'

'Doesn't have to be.'

'Then the fact that he's a doctor is irrelevant.'

He had to give her that one.

It still didn't explain a curious phenomenon he'd encountered before. That even in the face of a brutal murder, those left behind can be more concerned about protecting their loved one's posthumous reputation at the expense of helping find who killed them. They were the ones who had to go on living. In the absence of evidence painting the deceased in a poor light, their loved one remained the innocent victim of a mindless crime, rather than a person whose own crimes had brought their death upon them.

All he knew for sure was that it didn't make their job any easier.

5

DS Dave Garfield leaned back in his chair, hands clasped behind his head. Staring at the email that had arrived five minutes earlier, the same old question in his mind.

A crank? Or not a crank?

Except there was something different about this one. A lot of nutters were highly intelligent, but the sender of this email was in a different league.

He grabbed his empty coffee cup, thinking he might as well kill two birds with one stone.

Sergeant Nick Ensign on Bridgwater Police Centre's front desk eyed him suspiciously when Garfield put a steaming cup of coffee down on the counter five minutes later.

'You're after something.'

Garfield shook his head sadly.

'So cynical.'

'You try spending a day on this desk, see how much of your faith in human nature is left by the end of it. So? What do you want?'

'Have you taken any calls asking for me?'

'Not specifically. The call handlers put a young woman

through. She wanted to know who was in charge of mispers. I gave her your name.'

'And my email address?'

Ensign gave him the sort of look Garfield hadn't been on the receiving end of since his first day.

'She asked for it, so I asked her what it was about. She immediately hung up.'

They both knew it made no difference whether Ensign had supplied Garfield's email address or not. All anybody needed was an officer's name and the force location. There were plenty of subversive websites out there happy to instruct the crazies in the standard police email format including the force's server address.

The email Garfield received had come through on *david.garfield@avonandsomerset.pnn.police.uk*. The fact that *Garfield* wasn't a common name meant the sender didn't even need his collar number.

'I'm assuming she emailed you,' Ensign said.

'Somebody did. Too much of a coincidence if it wasn't her. Anything distinctive about her voice?'

'Nothing that would help to identify her.'

Back at his desk, Garfield thought the situation through. Asking the name of the officer in charge of missing persons was a clever ruse. If she'd asked who was in charge of murder investigations, alarm bells would have rung.

He was still staring at—or through—the email, his mind churning away, when DC Vicky Cook walked past.

'Bit young to be having a senior moment, Dave.'

Garfield startled, grinned at her.

'It's called thinking, Vicky. That's why you didn't recognise it.' Then, before she came back with a snappy response, 'Take a look at this.'

She leaned in, resting her hand on his shoulder, the smell of her perfume in his nose. He was okay with the familiarity, apart from the fact that Human Resources would be getting their knickers in a twist if it was the other way around.

'It's a crank,' Cook said, no room for doubt in her mind.

'Very specific for a crank.'

Cook read the short message a second time.

A body is buried at 51.18943, -3.18056

'I suppose, giving the map coordinates like that. It's still just a crank who knows how to use Google maps. Probably thinks giving the coordinates will make you take it seriously.'

It's worked, Garfield thought.

'Have you checked the location?' Vicky said, when he didn't respond. 'Probably in the middle of the Bristol Channel.'

'Not yet.'

'Who's it from?' She peered at the screen, read it aloud. '*Never_forgotten2012@gmail.com.* Good luck with tracing it, if that's how you choose to waste your time.' With that, she pushed herself off his shoulder, left him to it, her perfume lingering on.

Garfield wasted no time entering the coordinates into Google maps, nodding thoughtfully to himself when he saw the location. He'd heard of it. Kilstock Court. About ten miles away, out in the sticks between the villages of Kilton and Knighton, although Kilton wasn't even a village, just a church and a few farms and cottages on a bend in the road. It had been before his time, but he'd heard the stories. Maybe he'd have a word with one of the old-timers.

It was obvious now why the sender had emailed—they weren't about to give detailed coordinates over the phone, check that the officer had taken them down correctly.

The question was, had Vicky been right? Were the precise details simply a clever ploy by the sender to give added authenticity? Or was the sender actually not a crank at all?

Five minutes later and he'd forgotten all about it, a genuine missing thirteen-year-old schoolgirl claiming all his attention.

Angel didn't like to admit it to himself, but delivering the death message to Louise Orford achieved what Kincade predicted—not exactly making him feel better, but putting his own problems into perspective.

What he didn't need as he prepared for the initial team briefing was for Stuart Beckford to call him and complicate matters all over again.

He knew who it was when his phone rang—not because of a distinctive ringtone like the sound of seagulls fighting over fish heads he'd assigned to his sister—but because he just knew. It was the way life worked.

He glanced at the phone screen briefly to confirm his suspicions, let it go to voicemail.

Sure enough, it pinged a minute later as Beckford texted instead.

He opened it, if for no other reason than a text message can't get out of hand unless you reply. It was short and to the point.

Sorry about Catherine ambushing you this morning. I'll call you later.

Six weeks later sounds good, he thought, pocketing the phone, the damage to his focus already done.

'Ready?' Kincade said brightly, coming back into the room after visiting the ladies' loo.

'As I'll ever be.'

'You sound as if you're about to sit down to your own last supper.'

He shook his head, *don't ask*.

She didn't need to, humming Chopin's *Marche Funèbre* to herself as she followed him into the incident room.

. . .

Given the easy opportunities the manner of Dominic Orford's death offered for irreverent gallows humour, Angel was surprised to find the incident board devoid of it. He'd been expecting a heading *SUSPECTS* with the numbers from one to twelve arranged in a column beneath it, or the question *last meal?* next to an image of fish and loaves beside a glass of red wine.

He couldn't even blame the absence on Detective Superintendent Marcus Horwood's missing presence in the room. The Super was elsewhere, busy climbing the greasy pole while he left the real police work to others. DCI Olivia Finch was sitting on the sidelines, but she was still one of them, her presence not deterring Gulliver or Jardine—the usual suspects —from lightening the atmosphere.

Nobody could deny it needed lightening in any way possible.

A graphic full-length image of Dominic Orford nailed to a home-made cross took pride of place, smaller images of the nails driven through his wrists and the blackened and blistered gas-torch burns on his feet supporting it. Angel felt a more visceral reaction to the image of Orford's feet than he did the others. It was impossible to imagine having six-inch nails hammered through your wrists, but anyone who'd burned their hand on an oven door had an uneasy understanding of the agonies Orford endured.

'Dominic Thomas Orford . . .' Angel began, and quickly took the room through the basics of Orford's life and profession, before moving onto an aerial view of the murder scene and surrounding area on the board, the two public footpaths that might have been used by the killers.

'We're definitely talking killers plural are we, Padre?' Olivia Finch asked from the side.

'Theoretically, it's possible for one strong man to have shouldered the cross with Orford on it and dragged it up against the barn wall. The marks on the ground suggest otherwise. That it was dragged by a person holding each end of the cross member.' He rocked his hand. 'Slight variations might imply one person took more of the weight than the other.'

'A man and a woman?'

'Very possibly. It's also looking like at least one of them carried out a recce and broke the lock at the same time.'

'Meaning it's well planned.'

'I'm sure we'll find more evidence of that, yes.'

'A random attack or targeted?'

Had they been in Finch's office, Angel might have said he doubted some nutter woke up one morning and thought to himself, *I feel like crucifying somebody today*. Given that they weren't, he played it straight.

'I'm leaning towards targeted, ma'am. Unless we're looking at a genuine psychopath, I'd say there's a degree of viciousness that implies it's personal.'

'Revenge?'

'One of the best motives out there.'

Finch's mouth turned down, although not at Angel's words, but at an added problem that crossed her mind.

'Given the way he was killed, we can expect the media to be all over it.'

'There's already a leak, I'm afraid.' He caught the horror on Finch's face, did his best to reassure her. 'No crime scene photographs or anything like that, but a rumour he was crucified.'

Finch relaxed marginally, but not so that anyone would notice. She gestured towards everyone assembled in the room.

'Sorry, Padre, I'm monopolising you.'

'Plenty of him to go around since his mother's been fattening him up,' Kincade said under her breath, a remark nobody except Angel caught.

'Going back to the way he was killed,' Gulliver called out as Angel sucked his stomach in. 'I don't think it's only about revenge. He was tortured, wasn't he? I'm not an expert, but it strikes me that the killer started on his feet with the blowtorch, got the information he wanted, then killed him quickly with a knife. If it had been all about revenge, he'd have carried on working up his body with the blowtorch until he died.'

'That sounds like an expert talking if you ask me,' Jardine said, to much laughter.

Angel waited for it to die down before going back to Gulliver.

'You've got a point, Craig.'

'We also need to look at it from the victim's side,' Jardine said, as if keen to prove she was more than the joker her sharp tongue suggested. 'Orford lived in Morestead, six miles away from where he was killed. They must have lured him there somehow. Something they had over him, or something he wanted from them.'

'Very true, Lisa,' Angel agreed, 'which brings us onto what we learned from his wife. He lied to her. Told her he was attending a conference. That suggests to me the killers contacted him, demanded a meeting. It was something he didn't want to tell his wife about, so he invented the conference.'

Kincade raised a finger to interrupt.

'He's not the only one who lied. We both got the impression she was lying when we asked her if anything unusual had happened recently. As if she was protecting his reputation. I did a search and he's not on the PNC. I couldn't find any news articles on the web about scandal, either. That doesn't mean there isn't any, of course. Being a doctor means there's plenty of scope, from inappropriate behaviour all the way up to killing off old ladies for their money.'

'Harold Shipman rides again,' Gulliver called out, to general murmurs of agreement.

'One other thing,' Angel said, before he left Kincade to start allocating responsibilities. 'His parents obviously played a major part in his life—'

'What's his mother's name?' Jardine asked. 'Something beginning with *M*?'

Better late than never, Angel thought as the room laughed at Jardine's biblical reference.

'No, Lisa, not Mary. It's Helen. His father is Nigel. Anyway, they helped them buy their house and his wife also told us she thought his father fixed him up with his job. They're in France at the moment, due back in the next couple of days. We'll be talking to them as soon as they return. I get the feeling they might know more about their son's life than his wife ever did.'

6

'First things first,' George Leather said to the young woman who'd been put through to him. 'Can I take your name?'

'Jane.'

Why don't I believe you? he thought, dropping his chewed Bic ballpoint on his desk and not bothering to make a note of it. Despite having already written the call off, he played along for a little longer.

'How can I help you, *Jane*?'

'You got that the wrong way around. It's how I can help you.'

What is this? National cliché day?

'Okay. I'm all ears.'

'Give me your email address. I want to send you something.'

He hesitated, took a moment to phrase his next question.

'I'm assuming this is the first step towards us paying you for a story?'

'You assume wrong. I don't want money. Are you going to give me your email address or should I call one of your competitors?'

When you put it like that, he thought, and recited it to her.

The phone went dead in his ear the moment he'd finished,

not a thank you or a goodbye or *I'll be in touch*. He waited for a minute to see if anything came through immediately, wondering if he was about to get a picture of a naked young woman off her meds displaying her wares. When nothing arrived, he pushed back in his chair, went to grab a cup of coffee, the young woman already half forgotten.

She was one hundred per cent fully remembered when he got back ten minutes later after stopping off for a chat at a number of colleagues' desks and dropped into his chair.

The subject line hit him first, as if the young woman was trying to write his headline for him.

Man crucified in barn.

The email body was empty. George got the feeling the attached image file was going to make words redundant. He opened it, horror and excitement and confusion all jostling in his mind as he stared at the image, then immediately closed it again before anybody walked past and saw it.

In the good ol' days, he'd have been reaching for his cigarettes about now, lighting up right here at his desk.

In the current tofu-eating, health-Nazi environment, he glanced around at his editor's closed door, a bitter taste in his mouth as past resentments surged inside him. Of disappointing, aka non-existent, pay rises. Of being passed over for promotion in favour of less-well-qualified colleagues who ticked other boxes senior management decided were more important in order to display the paper's woke credentials, and bollocks to who can string more than two words together without resorting to text-message-style abbreviations and emojis.

But, try as he might, he couldn't see any way to turn this opportunity to his personal advantage. Worse, he had a sneaking suspicion Ms Jane Not-My-Real-Name was at this very moment duplicating the call she'd made to him to every other crime desk she could identify on the internet.

He crossed the busy newsroom at a brisk march, knocked briefly on Cherie Frost's door and barrelled into the room without waiting for a response. Cherie and another woman he didn't know but who he thought worked in the legal department—what he thought of as the *you can't publish that* department—looked up, irritation on their faces.

'I'm in the middle of something, George,' Cherie said, the annoyance in her disapproving tone making him feel like a puppy who'd crapped on the carpet.

'Sorry, Cherie, but you need to see this.'

'We're almost done here—'

'*Now!*'

The two women jumped at the sharpness of his bark, but Cherie didn't argue any more.

You don't need to bother coming, he thought with a sour glance at the legal department spoilsport, but she came along to piss on his parade all the same.

Mercedes Cortés walked the half mile from Southampton Central railway station to the Pig in the Wall hotel located at the bottom of Western Esplanade, hoping to ease the stiffness still in her legs after twenty-odd hours in goat class on a plane, followed by the train journey down from London.

She looked up at the relentless grey of the sky above as she strode out, her backpack slung over her shoulder, wondering why anybody in their right mind would choose to live in the UK. At least that was something she could thank her mother for, taking her away from it all.

It was about the only thing that came to mind.

She stopped outside the hotel for a moment to admire the elegant facade built into the old city walls, then went inside, the old-world charm of the interior making up in a small way for the depressing weather outside.

'Is that a faint Australian accent I detect?' the reception clerk said, after the formalities were completed and he'd handed over the key card.

Stupid question, she thought, *seeing as you've just seen my Australian passport.*

She smiled anyway. He was only making conversation, although the way he'd run his eyes up and down her when she walked in suggested he'd like to do a lot more.

Dream on.

'Yeah. I was born over here, but my mum took me to Oz when I was young. I never really picked up much of an accent, despite being at an impressionable age.'

Why am I talking so much? she thought, making a conscious effort to shut up before she showed him a picture of the house back home and the swimming pool and their dog. *It's the nerves*, she told herself. *Jesus!* All she'd done was check into a bloody hotel.

'Are you over for business or pleasure?' he said, continuing with his script.

You think I've got a business suit in this backpack?

She immediately felt guilty for the thought. It wasn't such a stupid question, after all. Things were so much more relaxed than in the old days her mother was always banging on about.

'Definitely not business.'

He gave her a curious look at the unusual way she answered, but soon got his plastic smile back in place.

'That must make it pleasure.'

She shrugged, the doubts coming through in her voice.

'We'll see.'

She didn't mean to be unnecessarily rude or unfriendly, but she was dog-tired, even if she guessed it was more the nervousness and uncertainty about what lay ahead. At least it stopped him from asking more questions. Or worse—offering to show her around after his shift ended.

She waved away the offer of assistance, carried her backpack up to her room, then lay for a while on the bed staring up at the ceiling, her doubts intensifying.

She needed a drink, that's all there was to it.

She showered first, changed into some fresh, if crumpled, clothes, her hair in a loose ponytail at the nape of her neck. Then headed back downstairs, ordered a beer and went outside to sit at one of the tables on the small terrace at the front of the building.

Her phone rang when she was halfway through her first beer.

She knew who it was, checked anyway, proved herself right a moment later—her mother. She let it go to voicemail, hoping the call wasn't indicative of how the whole trip would be, expecting regular updates on the ins and outs of a duck's arse every two minutes. For somebody who didn't want her to come, her mother seemed pretty bloody interested.

Seeing as her phone was already in her hand, she opened the image gallery, scrolled slowly through.

Except all that did was make the uneasy sense of foreboding surge inside her again.

MERCEDES CORTÉS WASN'T THE ONLY ONE NOT ANSWERING THEIR phone to people they didn't want to speak to. Angel was giving Stuart Beckford the same treatment. He was still disappointed in Beckford for blaming him for the decision to give Virgil Balan the green light, a decision that might have life-changing consequences for all of them.

With the memory of Catherine Beckford's accusations still

fresh in his mind, he wasn't sure he'd be able to keep his feelings under wraps. The situation was difficult enough and fraught with competing emotions as it was. It didn't need them falling out over it after only recently having re-established contact. The easiest option was to continue to ignore Beckford's calls for the time being.

Again, like Mercedes, the answer felt as if it was waiting to be found in the bottom of a pint glass. Temporary cerebral reset courtesy of alcohol. Kincade had already left, roadworks on the A36 making the thirty-mile journey to Upper Woodford, a few miles north of Salisbury, where she lived with his father, longer than usual.

Gulliver and Jardine were both busy working their way through the list of local dog breeders and pet shops hoping to identify the potential dog-walker witness that the farmer, Clive Ratliff, had mentioned.

Angel bumped into Olivia Finch in the corridor as he headed out, thought about asking her if she was interested in a quickie—not that he'd have phrased it that way—then decided against it. She'd only want to talk about the investigation, or, worse, the complete shambles that passed for his private life.

Which is how he ended up at The Jolly Sailor in Bursledon, *tout seul*. A couple of sanity-preserving beers before going home to do battle with his cantankerous mother.

Or so he thought.

He'd only taken a couple of paces into the pub's interior when he saw her sitting at a table, her back to him. She was wearing a floral dress he hadn't seen before and had made more of an effort with her hair than he could remember. He got the impression he'd only need to take a step further into the room to be punched on the nose by her perfume.

She'd often joked that now she knew the location of his favourite watering hole where he stopped off for a quick one on the way home, she would join him there, making it pointless for him to go there in the first place.

That was not the situation he was now faced with.

She was sharing the table with a man—and it wasn't his father. Angel recognised him. A part-time barman in the pub called Roger, a man of the same sort of age as his mother. On a previous occasion when Angel had taken his mother there, they'd shown a passing interest in one another.

That interest appeared to have progressed.

Suddenly, Angel wasn't thirsty.

He turned on his heel and headed out again, sat for a while thinking in his car with the window down, the breeze off the River Hamble doing nothing to clear his mind. He didn't have anything against his mother starting a new relationship—beyond the natural distaste of any child not wanting to think about their parents at it, preferring to explain their own existence by either immaculate conception or courtesy of a passing stork.

Siobhan had been split from Carl for fifteen years, living back in Belfast until her recent visit to the mainland on account of her estranged husband's suspected late-onset Huntington's disease. As Carl unkindly said, she'd come to watch him die—apart from the fact that to do so they would have to meet. So far, they hadn't.

Thinking didn't get him anywhere beyond an acceptance of *que sera, sera.*

Back home, he chilled a couple of cans of Brewdog Hazy Jane IPA in the freezer, then sat drinking them in the small gazebo he'd built at the bottom of the garden with his cat, Leonard, curled up asleep on his lap, snoring softly.

He felt like the roles had been reversed, him waiting up for his own mother to get home, a single thought in his mind.

What next?

7

'I'M GLAD I'M NOT YOU, PADRE,' JACK BEVAN SAID THE NEXT morning when Angel walked past the front desk.

'The feeling's mutual, Jack.' He waved the newspaper in his hand—what he guessed was behind the Welshman's remark—in Bevan's face. 'The difference is, I'll still feel the same way when this dies down.'

'*If* it dies down, Padre, not when. *If.*' He flicked his fingers at Angel, *gimme here*. 'Let's have another look.'

Angel handed it over, happy to be rid of it.

'Keep it.'

He left Bevan smiling to himself, a final *I'm glad I'm not you* cut off by the lift doors as they closed.

'Finch wants to see you,' Gulliver said, leaning backwards as Angel passed his desk.

'I bet she does.'

'Have you seen the paper?' Patting a copy on his desk.

'Yep. Any joy working through the dog breeders?'

Gulliver rolled with the disappointment of Angel's refusal to join in with the anti-journalist sentiment in the room.

'Actually, yes. One of the breeders gave us a name.

Dorothy Bancroft. She recently bought a cocker spaniel puppy from him after her old dog had to be put down. She lives on the outskirts of Bishop's Waltham. It means a short drive to get to the footpath leading to the barn. She would've parked in the lay-by the killers might have used.' He tapped the newspaper again. 'Don't forget Finch was looking for you, sir.'

'Thank you, Craig. It hadn't slipped my mind.'

He knocked on Finch's open door a minute later, went in and made a beeline for her private coffee machine, the lack of aroma not registering.

'It's broken,' she said, the scowl on her face intensifying.

He gave her an apologetic smile.

'I think you might have over-estimated my technical skills, ma'am. I can try changing the fuse, but if that doesn't work . . .'

'Don't be an arse your whole life, Padre. That's not why I wanted to see you. Have you seen the paper?' Thrusting a copy at him as she said it.

'Why? You think there might be a coffee machine repair man who advertises in it?'

'If there is, he's going to have a hard time fixing it, given where it's going to be very shortly.'

'Where the sun don't shine, ma'am?'

'Precisely, Padre.' She thrust the paper at him a second time. 'Look at that.'

He took it from her, read the headline he knew by heart.

Man crucified in barn near Bishop's Waltham.

Told you we had a leak wasn't the way to go.

Bet the Super isn't happy wasn't going to cut the mustard, either.

He sucked the air in through his teeth instead, made a vaguely positive observation, the memory of asking one of the SOCOs to cover up the hole in the barn roof in his mind.

'At least it's only a photograph of the exterior of the barn. We're not looking at something from our own files.'

'*Yet.*'

He skimmed the article again, as he had earlier, smiling when he got to the same line that made him smile the first time.

'I fail to see what's so amusing, Padre,' Finch snapped.

'The line where he says, *let's hope we don't have to wait as long for an answer to this mystery.* He's obviously got a sense of humour.'

'Great. So long as you're not the one tasked with solving it. Did you notify his widow?'

'Yesterday. But I didn't say anything about crucifixion.'

She shook her head in defeat, staring at the headline jumping off the page mocking them.

'We can't win, can we? Try to spare the next-of-kin's feelings and it ends up backfiring. You need to speak to this George Leather character. The tone of the article makes it sound as if they're very sure about their facts. They wouldn't lead with such a sensationalist headline based on a rumour doing the rounds of the local community.'

'Already on the list, ma'am.'

'Anything else I need to know?'

Not unless you're interested in my mother dating a local barman, he thought, and saved for another time.

'You'll be the first to know when there is.'

'I very much doubt that, Padre.'

She let him get as far as the door before calling him back, a rare smile on her face.

'Have a quick look at the fuse in the coffee machine for me, will you . . .'

. . .

'You'll never guess what Jack Bevan told me,' Jardine said, her voice hushed as if there was somebody else in the car earwigging.

I don't want to, Gulliver thought, the potential for gossip appalling him. Should there ever be a contest to identify the numero uno gossipmonger, it would be a hard-fought battle between Bevan and Jardine. The thought of the two of them hunched together over the front desk, whispering like a pair of schoolchildren, made Gulliver shudder.

'You're right. I'll never guess. Because I'm not even going to try.'

'Don't you want to know?'

'I didn't realise what I wanted came into it.'

She nodded to herself, *good point.*

'Catherine Beckford came into the station yesterday. The boss had a long discussion with her. Although Jack said it was more of an argument from the sound of the shouting.'

Gulliver applied the usual filters. He downgraded *long discussion* to *short chat* and dialled *shouting* down to *raised voices*. Still, it got his attention, even if he'd never let Jardine see the interest on his face.

'Did Jack hear what it was about?'

She grinned at him, a teasing note entering her voice.

'*Oh!* So you *are* interested now?'

'Not really.'

'Liar. Anyway, somebody walked in off the street, so Jack had to—'

'Do his job instead of eavesdropping?'

'—deal with them, but he thinks—'

'Decided to make up.'

'—that the boss is putting the block on Beckford coming back. Beckford's missus got wind of it and came in to give the boss a bollocking.'

'Bollocks.'

'That's what I just said.'

'*No*. You're talking bollocks.'

She shook her head at him in despair.

'Sometimes I think you're happy to walk around with your head up your arse.'

'*No*. Head in my work. Talking of which, we're here.'

Here was the dog walker, Dorothy Bancroft's, house. Jardine rolled her eyes as she climbed out of the car.

'We're always *here*.' Pointing at the ground. 'We can't be over there, can we?' Now pointing across the street. 'I'm over there.'

Gulliver wasn't sure what he might have done or said, had they not got the interview with Ms Bancroft to occupy them.

She was exactly as Gulliver imagined her to be, given her name. Dorothy Bancroft sounded like an old maid's name to him. She was anything between sixty and eighty, her steel-grey hair uncoloured and cut short in an unflattering style, her dress something that had gone out of style in the early Victorian era, her shoes sensible and laced. Gulliver sniffed the air as she invited them in, expecting to smell cakes baking or perhaps boiled cabbage. He guessed she helped out at the local church, cleaning the aisle she'd never walked down on her father's arm when she wasn't walking her dog.

She directed them into the front sitting room, continuing down the hall towards the kitchen where everything for tea and refreshments was already prepared, waiting for the boiling water to be added to the teapot. She carried it all back in on a tray, her dog coming with her when she didn't get the kitchen door closed with her foot in time.

It came rushing into the front room, bounded up onto the sofa where Jardine was perched, onto her legs, off again and onto the floor, then the same with Gulliver, on, off, and down, ready for another lap until Gulliver grabbed its collar to allow

Dorothy to put the tray down without everything ending up on the floor.

'She's very excitable,' Dorothy said, as if they'd somehow failed to notice when the dog used their legs as part of its exercise circuit. 'Her name's Lola.'

Everybody said *hello* to Lola, who immediately started barking.

Gulliver wasn't sure if he'd rather be back in the car listening to Jardine's verbal diarrhoea.

'It's the first time I've been interviewed by the police,' Dorothy said, which surprised nobody, Lola included.

'We'll try to make it as painless as possible,' Gulliver replied with a smile, eyeing up the slices of fruit cake piled up on the plate—as was Lola. 'We understand you regularly walk Lola over the fields near Warren Wood Farm.'

'That's right.' She leaned sideways and picked up a well-chewed copy of that morning's paper from the floor at the side of her chair. 'I assume it's about this dreadful murder.'

'It is, yes.'

'*Crucified!* It beggars belief. The murderer must be some kind of religious crackpot.'

Gulliver chided himself for his earlier churchy assumption, got to the point.

'We're interested to know if you've seen anything unusual while you've been walking Lola recently. Not necessarily on the evening in question, but also in the days leading up to it.'

Dorothy poured the tea before answering, handed out cups, ignoring the slices of fruit cake, an omission that did not go unnoticed. Gulliver's stomach growled.

Dorothy took a sip of tea, then scowled.

Mine tastes alright, Gulliver thought, *although I'd be better with a slice of cake.*

Except it was another incorrect assumption on his part as Dorothy's words made clear.

'I came across a very rude man a couple of evenings before the murder. I always park in the lay-by. We got there at about six o'clock, like we normally do. We have a number of routes we walk.' She glanced at her dog as if expecting a tail wag or bark of confirmation, except all of Lola's concentration was on the fruit cake—unlike Gulliver who was only giving it fifty per cent. 'It was near the end of our walk as we were approaching the lay-by. He'd climbed over the stile and was walking towards us. I didn't get the lead on Lola in time, and she went bounding towards him and jumped up at him. She put muddy pawprints on the front of his jacket, but it wasn't that bad. I was apologising, but he pushed Lola roughly away and carried on walking as if I wasn't even there.' She paused, taking a thoughtful sip of tea—and still forgetting to offer the slices of cake around. Then she nodded to herself with a quick glance at the newspaper. 'I know I'm probably imagining things after the event now that I know about the murder, but it seemed to me he was very keen for me to not see his face. His collar was turned up and he had a scarf over his mouth and chin. It was a bit windy, but it's only September. And he had a hat with a wide brim pulled down low over his face.' She smiled suddenly, gave them a flash of horsey teeth. 'If you want to show me pictures of men's noses, I might be able to recognise him.'

They smiled with her, then Jardine took over.

'It was definitely a man, was it?'

'I think so. From his build . . .'

'What is it?' Jardine said as Dorothy trailed off.

'I was going to say his coat was too big for him, so I suppose it could've been a woman in a man's coat, but I don't think so.' She looked at her hands, which were on the masculine side, the veins and sinews prominent on the backs of them. 'He definitely had a man's hands. I noticed them when he pushed Lola away.'

'Is there anything else about him you remember?'

Dorothy came alert as if Jardine had slapped her, a look of horror on her face.

'I forgot to offer you cake.'

Jardine's heart fell after the uptick caused by Dorothy's reaction. Gulliver's did the opposite.

'Don't mind if I do.' Taking the largest slice as he said it.

'How about you, dear?' Dorothy said to Jardine, eyeing her up and down as if she thought she needed a bit of fattening up —that, or a bit of sweetness.

'I'm fine, thank you. Going back to the man you saw . . .'

Dorothy dragged her eyes away from watching Gulliver devour his piece of cake, a satisfied smile—*my kind of young man* —on her face.

'Sorry.' Then to Gulliver. 'Do have another piece.'

'Thank you, I think I will.'

Tough luck, Lola, Jardine thought, *there ain't gonna be any left for you.*

'About the man, Ms Bancroft . . .'

'Yes, sorry. I remember his coat. A herringbone tweed field coat. The sort of thing people wear for shooting with big cartridge pockets. With a contrasting green, loden collar. I was standing glaring at his back as he walked away after ignoring me and noticed it. He'll wish he'd been friendlier when you arrest him for murder. I wouldn't have turned around and taken such notice if he hadn't been so rude.'

'That's very helpful,' Jardine said, not commenting on how, in Dorothy's mind, the murderer was as good as behind bars already. 'It's lucky Lola jumped up at him, too. You can never get all the mud out.' She raised an eyebrow at Gulliver who'd just shovelled a huge piece of cake into his mouth. 'Any more questions, Craig?'

Gulliver knew exactly what she'd done, waiting until his mouth was full. He needn't have worried. Dorothy suddenly sat up as if Lola had made her move for the remaining cake.

'There was something else. The lay-by was empty when I arrived. I parked at the end beside the stile. There was enough room behind me for four more cars, at least. Despite that, the man we're talking about parked this close to me.' Holding her hands six inches apart as she said it. 'There was a fence post in front of me, and I had to manoeuvre back and forth a dozen times before I could get out. I thought maybe he did it deliberately hoping I would damage his car and then he'd make a claim against me for damage he'd done himself. He probably took a picture of my car. I made very sure I didn't hit his.'

A silent exchange passed between Gulliver and Jardine—who would ask the question they knew would lead to the biggest disappointment of the day?

Jardine took it upon herself while Gulliver continued to chew contentedly.

'I don't suppose you took a picture of his car?'

Dorothy shook her head, looking as if she felt responsible for the whole investigation grinding to a halt.

'I'd forgotten to charge my phone. I'm always doing it. It was completely dead.'

'Can you remember the number plate?'

'I remember that it wasn't in the middle like most number plates. The car was a dark blue Alfa Romeo. It looked peculiar with the number plate at the side.'

'Can you remember any part of the registration itself? We don't need much if we know the make and colour.'

'Sorry.'

But I bet you remember the recipe for half a dozen different types of cake, in ounces or grams, Jardine thought, and asked something more pertinent.

'Did you notice if he was carrying anything with him?'

Dorothy brightened as the opportunity to answer positively presented itself.

'He had a small backpack. It looked heavy. I was worried he was going to hit Lola with it. I suppose the nails he used to crucify that poor man were in it.'

'More likely a crowbar he used to break into the barn,' Jardine replied, knowing she'd done nothing to curtail Dorothy's imagination.

They wrapped it up after that. Jardine could've bet everything she owned and ever would own on what happened next. Dorothy gathered up the tray and carried it through to the kitchen. She was back a minute later, a package wrapped in tin foil in her hands for Gulliver.

'You needn't have bothered with wrapping it, Ms Bancroft,' Jardine said. 'He'll have eaten it all before we get back to the car.'

Dorothy ignored her, her thoughts written all over her face.

My kind of young man.

'BE SICK BEFORE WE GET IN,' JARDINE WARNED, AS THEY approached the car.

'It's my car and I'll be sick wherever I want. Except I'm not going to be sick at all. Besides, there's nothing wrong with having a healthy appetite.'

'*Healthy?*' Poking her index finger into his midriff. 'You've just eaten half your body weight in sugar, as well as everything else.'

'We can't all live on our nerves.'

'I don't know what you're talking about.'

Except she did. The situation with her younger brother,

Frankie, in trouble with their colleagues in the North East, was ever present in her mind—however much she tried to not let it show.

It wasn't something he wanted to get into now, falling back on the safety of work.

'What do you think? Was it the killer on his way to breaking into the barn?'

'There's a good chance. Except something's not right.'

'The situation with the car, you mean?'

'That's one. And why go at prime dog-walking time when it's still daylight? Why not wait until it's dark?'

'It's as if he wanted to be seen and remembered.'

'Either that, or just plain stupid.'

They both knew the world was filled with stupid criminals. Despite that, it didn't feel as if they were dealing with one of them on this occasion.

8

DS DAVE GARFIELD WAS HAVING A PROBLEM SCRATCHING THE ITCH that started when he received the email sent from the *never_forgotten2012@gmail.com* email address, claiming a body was buried in the grounds of Kilstock Court.

The missing thirteen-year-old schoolgirl who temporarily distracted him turned out to be a false alarm. An over-reaction by her parents—understandable, but annoying and time wasting, nonetheless.

He was back to the itch. He'd had no luck finding an old-timer to grill about the rumours surrounding the place. Deep down, he'd known what he was going to have to do all along—go there himself.

He thought about taking DC Vicky Cook with him, quickly discounted it. She'd dismissed the email as the work of a crank, and he had a feeling everyone else would agree with her. Best to establish some facts himself before inviting ridicule.

Which is how he ended up sitting in his car outside the padlocked gates to Kilstock Court, Google maps open on his iPad. He'd been surprised when he did a search on Google and discovered that five-decimal-point coordinates—the standard given by Google maps—equates to one-point-one metres on the ground. The level of accuracy astounded him.

Now all he had to do was get into the grounds. He didn't fancy climbing over the gates. He wasn't as young or fit as he used to be, and the pointy spikes on top looked lethal. Zooming out on Google maps, he saw it was possible to access the woods at the bottom of the property's grounds via the adjacent fields.

He backed the car up until he saw somewhere to park that gave easy access to the fields. Then he parked on the opposite side of the lane, went to inspect the location he'd just identified, careful not to contaminate the surrounding ground.

A quick visual didn't tell him much. It was possible there were fresh tyre marks, but he wouldn't bet his pension on it. Still, better safe than sorry. With that in mind, he went twenty yards further down the lane, climbed over the barbed-wire fence and made his way across the field, keeping away from the easier going on the unploughed verge.

A similar barbed-wire fence marked the boundary between the farmer's fields and Kilstock Court's grounds. At a point that gave direct access through the woods to the location corresponding to the emailed coordinates, he saw a sag in the wires—they'd been pulled apart to let somebody through. He marked the spot, then moved on until he found a broken fence post that made it easier to clamber over the wires without risking castrating himself.

A quarter mile into the woods and he was standing in front of a small clearing behind a derelict boathouse on a small lake. He put the coordinates into Google again, got the same result.

It was the spot where the person behind the *never_forgotten2012@gmail.com* email address claimed a body was buried. The email address suggested it happened in 2012.

From looking at the undisturbed ground, it was difficult to see how she would know. She'd either buried it there herself, or somebody had told her about it. DC Vicky Cook's preferred option couldn't be ignored, either—there wasn't anything but worms down there.

He skirted around the boathouse, noticed a section of broken handrail from the front porch lying on the ground. The clean exposed break suggested it had been recently snapped off. Behind him, a path had been beaten through the rampant undergrowth surrounding the lake. He orientated himself to the map on his iPad, calculated that if he followed the path of trampled vegetation, then struck out through the woods directly opposite the boathouse, he'd come to the main gardens behind the house. They were likely to be equally as overgrown.

Whoever had trampled the path had come the hard way, climbing over the gates and fighting their way from there. It was a hell of a thing to do just to send a hoax email.

Maybe *never_forgotten2012@gmail.com* wasn't a basket case off her meds, after all.

'I'M GOING TO STOP ANSWERING THE PHONE TO YOU, JACK,' ANGEL said, when Bevan called him from the front desk. 'Who is it this time?'

'After this morning's newspaper headline, it's the last person in the world you want to talk to.'

Angel's heart sank as he made an easy guess.

'Mrs Louise Orford?'

'In person.'

'What's her mood like?'

'You mean, has she got a rolled-up copy of the paper in her clenched fist, ready to beat you around the head with? No. If you want my opinion, I don't think she's seen the paper yet.'

'Tell her I'll be right down.'

'Louise Orford's downstairs?' Kincade guessed, as soon as he got off the phone.

'Yep. We might have a second chance. Jack doesn't think she's seen the paper.'

'Who's she asking for?'

He pointed directly at her.

'You.'

'Really? Then why did Jack call you?' She pushed herself to her feet, shrugged herself into her jacket. 'Let's talk to her together.'

'Don't want to miss anything in case she's decided to come clean about what she wouldn't say yesterday, eh?'

'If only.'

Like he had with Catherine Beckford, Bevan had parked Louise Orford in interview room one. Angel got a better reception from her than he had from Catherine when he walked in, no yelling at him before the door was shut. Her composure slipped when she caught sight of Kincade a couple of paces behind, jumped to an obvious conclusion.

More bad news.

Then it was his job to confirm it.

'I told you yesterday Dominic died from a fatal stab wound. There are other details I withheld in an attempt to soften the blow, allow you some time before telling you everything. Unfortunately, my hand has now been forced. The newspaper has got hold of those details—'

'How?'

'At the moment, we don't know. Rest assured, investigating how it happened is a priority.'

'It must be one of you.' Looking from him to Kincade and back again, as if she meant them personally. He wasn't sure she didn't.

'I very much hope it isn't, Mrs Orford . . .'

She waved the pointless words away, not interested in hearing the rest of the guff about leaving no stone unturned.

'What details?'

He hesitated, searching for an easy way to put it. Except there were none. *Nailed to a cross* was worse than using the word that described it perfectly, even if that word was loaded with two thousand years' worth of conflicting emotions.

'Before being stabbed, Dominic was crucified.'

Louise stared at him open-mouthed, no sounds escaping as she struggled with the last thing she ever expected to hear.

'What? Like Christ? Nailed to a cross?'

The newspaper article made no mention of Orford's wrists being nailed, but Angel was beyond withholding details in the hope they never saw the light of day. Should they catch the killer, every gruesome detail would be put before the court.

'His wrists were nailed, but not his feet. They were tied.'

Despite his decision of a moment ago, he held off from telling her that her husband had been tortured with a blow torch.

She wouldn't have taken it in, anyway. Her head was in her hands, a stuttering, nervous cross between a laugh and a cry of anguish on her lips.

'Would you like to break for a while?' Kincade offered.

'No. Let's get it over with.'

She did her party trick making a tissue appear out of thin air, dabbed her eyes and blew her nose. Forced out a couple of long breaths as if trying to expel all the sadness from inside her.

'I phoned Dominic's parents and told them. They're cutting their trip short. They'll be back later today if they can get booked on a ferry or Eurotunnel. Tomorrow at the latest.'

'That makes our job a lot easier, thank you,' Angel said, and waited. She wouldn't have come in personally to tell them such a minor detail. He was hoping the sleepless night she'd endured had persuaded her to tell them what she decided against saying the previous day.

He was wrong.

'I couldn't stop thinking about Dominic lying to me about attending a conference. He's never lied to me before.' She gave them a brief smile. 'That I know of. But it's not as if he could suddenly say to me out of the blue, *I'm off to a conference now*. He told me a few days in advance. It made me think he knew something really bad was coming and he was preparing to deal with it.'

Something in the way she said *deal with it* registered with Angel. It had a very permanent ring to it, gave him an idea about what was coming.

'I checked his gun cabinet. One of his shotguns is missing. He was so worried about whatever it was, he was prepared to . . .'

She tailed off, unable to say the words that described an unrecognised aspect of her husband's life that horrified her almost as much as his death.

They got to him before he got to them, Angel thought more succinctly, and saw the same reflected in Kincade's eyes.

'We need to collect your husband's computer as a matter of urgency. Whatever scared him, started him down this path, will be on there, or on his phone. We should have those records very soon.'

Louise nodded as if it was all gobbledegook to her.

'Whatever you need, just ask.'

It was too good an opportunity to miss. Angel let Kincade take it.

'We asked you yesterday whether there was anything we should know about. We got the impression something crossed your mind, but you decided not to mention it.'

Louise took a deep breath, let it out.

When is this ever going to end?

'Some stupid woman made a complaint about him at work. You're better off asking them about it. He never lied to me, but that's not the same as volunteering every last little detail.'

And that has to be the understatement of the century, Angel thought, showing her out.

'Exactly what we don't need,' Kincade said, as they headed back upstairs. 'A lunatic who likes crucifying people on the loose with a stolen shotgun. Not a good combination.'

'Something to bear in mind if we get to the point of arresting him,' he agreed. 'What do you think about the complaint made against him?'

She stopped on the stairs, gave it some thought.

'You don't crucify a man as payback for touching you inappropriately. Besides, if that was the reason, you'd mutilate him as well.' Pointing at his crotch as she said it. 'It wouldn't have been his feet they used the blowtorch on.'

He shuddered and felt an unpleasant twinge below the belt at the thought of it, then resumed climbing the stairs.

'I agree. It's unlikely to be the reason he was killed, but it might be an indicator of the sort of man Orford was. I get the feeling the deeper we dig, the more we're going to find.'

'The more reasons to kill him,' she said more accurately, and didn't hear any disagreement from him.

9

DCI Finch was at the drinks machine beside the lifts when Angel and Kincade came through the doors from the stairwell.

How the mighty have fallen, he thought, and phrased it differently.

'Coffee machine still broken, ma'am?'

'I'm not drinking this muck out of solidarity with you and everybody else, Padre.' Holding the plastic cup of brown sludge towards him as if he didn't know exactly what it looked and tasted like. 'Anyway, I'm glad to see you getting some exercise taking the stairs. Can't have you getting too fat now your mother's feeding you.'

'Making personal remarks because your coffee machine is broken does not reflect well on you, ma'am.'

'Bollocks. Come and look at this. You too, Cat.'

She led them through the incident room, everybody trying hard not to smile at the sight of her carrying a cup of what they had to suffer on a daily basis.

'Want me to take a look at the machine, ma'am?' Kincade said, drifting across to inspect it while Finch got settled behind her desk.

'You can have it, Cat.'

'You didn't offer it to me,' Angel said.

Finch gave him a wide smile.

'Us girls have to stick together. You men get everything else your way.'

It wasn't a road Angel planned to go down. Behind him, Kincade was busy rooting behind the filing cabinet the coffee machine sat on, trying to unplug it.

'What did you want to show us, ma'am?'

'I took a call from that journalist's editor. Cherie Frost . . .'

'Did she live up to her name?'

'If she ever fancies a double-barrelled name, *Ice-Maiden* would fit the bill. I reckon their legal department leaned on them and she wasn't happy about it. She called me to tell me she wanted to send me a photograph that had been emailed to George Leather. She also gave me the email address it was sent from.'

'Gmail?'

'Of course.' She squinted at her screen. '*Never_forgotten2012@gmail.com*. Apparently, Leather took a call from a young woman asking for his email address. Leather told Frost there was nothing remarkable about the woman or the call to help identify her.'

'Basically saying, *leave me out of it*.'

'No surprises there. Frost agreed to supply their call logs, which is something.' She turned her computer screen to enable them to see it, Kincade having temporarily abandoned trying to unplug the coffee machine. 'This is what was sent to them.'

'That's why Leather was so confident about Orford being crucified,' Angel said, for the sake of something to say to mask his surprise.

Finch beamed at him like she couldn't have wished for a more perceptive SIO on the investigation.

'Exactly, Padre. If somebody sends you a photograph of a man nailed to a cross, you can feel confident saying he was crucified.'

Angel ignored the sarcasm, leaned in to get a closer look. Stated the obvious a second time.

'At least it's not one of ours. The definition isn't good enough. The killers took it on a phone.'

Finch sipped her coffee and grimaced, looking like she'd have spat it out again if they hadn't been in the room. Angel knew exactly what she was about to say.

'C'mon, Padre. Explain it to us. What are they up to?'

'Why is it you think the worse the behaviour, the better I understand it?'

'It's obvious.' Glancing at Kincade and getting a firm nod back. 'All those hours in the confessional listening to people's sins.'

'I don't recall anyone ever admitting to crucifying a man, ma'am.'

She waved the objection away.

'Don't be pedantic. It gave you a good understanding of the worst side of people.'

'And your twenty years as a police officer have shown you the positive aspects of human nature on a daily basis, have they?'

'But you've got both, Padre.'

'My life's been filled with nothing but the worst of people, you mean?'

'Exactly, Padre. No wonder you're the way you are. So?'

Not for the first time he was reminded that Finch had been a woman long before she became a police officer.

'It's inconsistent. On the one hand, it's as if they're taunting us, rubbing our noses in it. Tipping off the newspaper, as well as the situation with the dog walker. The man she saw went out of his way to ensure she would remember the encounter.

On the other hand, crucifying a man has a very personal feel to it.'

Finch sipped absentmindedly at her coffee, even forgetting to grimace, as she thought about it.

'People who kill for personal reasons usually do their utmost to conceal the crime, knowing we'll be looking at them as soon as it's discovered.'

'Exactly.'

'Maybe it's personal for one of them, and the other one is using that as an opportunity to play with us.'

'*Got it!*' Kincade said triumphantly.

They both looked expectantly at her, still busy beside the filing cabinets.

She smiled apologetically.

'The coffee machine plug, I mean. Stupid place to put a filing cabinet, right in front of the wall socket.'

'Thank you for that contribution, Cat,' Finch said drily, looking as if she was about to revoke her earlier offer as Kincade lifted the machine off the cabinet.

'Probably needs a new fuse,' Angel said, ushering Kincade out, her arms clamped protectively around her prize.

'IT'S LUCKY THE BOSS DIDN'T WANT TO INTERVIEW ORFORD'S WORK colleagues himself,' Jardine said, as Gulliver pulled into the last available space in the Oaks Medical Centre's small car park.

Gulliver was busy concentrating on manoeuvring into the too-tight space, and foolishly responded without thinking first.

'Why's that?'

'You can ask them about getting a gastric band fitted. You'll need one after all the cake you scoffed.'

'Is that so? You think they also do tongue clamps? Although anything powerful enough to hold yours still wouldn't fit in a normal person's mouth.' He made a point of studying hers. 'It's not going to be a problem in your case.'

With that, he opened his door and got out. She tried to do the same, immediately discovered why he was looking so pleased with himself.

'You haven't left me enough room to get out.'

She could see as well as he could that if he'd parked in the middle of the tight space, neither of them would have been able to open their door wide enough.

'Who's the one who needs a gastric band now?' he said, after she gave up trying to squeeze through and shifted across into the driver's seat to get out.

'I didn't want to dink the other car.'

'Of course you didn't.'

'You need to learn how to park properly.'

'You need to lose a bit of weight off your arse.'

The light-hearted banter stopped the minute they got inside the surgery. A harassed-looking receptionist led them to a meeting room down a dog-legged corridor off the main waiting room filled with sickly old people and crying babies, then went to find the practice senior partner, Felix Corbyn.

Neither of them was surprised when Corbyn kept them waiting for ten minutes. It was written into a doctor's contract, after all.

He was exactly as Jardine expected when he finally joined them, no excuse offered. Tall and slim in a well-cut suit, his wire-rimmed glasses balanced on an aquiline nose above a neatly-trimmed white beard. The way he looked disapprovingly over his glasses at them made her instantly regret all her unhealthy habits.

He took the chair at the top of the table as was his right, rested his hands on it, fingers interlaced. The picture of a man comfortable in his own skin and proud of the practice he'd built up, whatever grubby little policemen might try to imply with their impertinent questions.

'What can I do for you today?'

The question made Jardine's blood boil. As if she was a patient with a minor ailment bothering a busy man, not a detective investigating the brutal murder of one of his colleagues.

'You're aware that Dominic Orford was murdered four nights ago?'

'I am. A terrible shock to all of us here. I've already telephoned his wife and expressed my personal and his colleagues' condolences. He will be sorely missed.'

'I'd like to get a bit of background, if that's okay. How long has he worked here?'

Corbyn smiled like an oncologist delivering the all-clear.

'Ten years, almost to the day. We all went out for a meal to celebrate his ten-year anniversary only a couple of weeks ago.'

'We understand he qualified as a GP up in London, then moved down to take up a position at this practice.'

Jardine saw what passed behind Corbyn's eyes—*I've got the measure of you*. He responded accordingly, anticipating where the line of questioning was headed.

'Dominic's father, Nigel, is a good friend of mine. Why wouldn't I offer his son a position here? You might have a problem with nepotism, but I don't.'

'Makes it more difficult if things don't work out.'

Corbyn dipped his silver-haired head in acknowledgement.

'Then it's lucky it did.'

'How was his performance?'

'More than satisfactory. I'd be a happy man if all of his colleagues were equally as competent.'

'What about ethically?'

Jardine saw the change of attitude reflected in the hardness of Corbyn's eyes. *I've got the measure of you* had just ramped up to *you impertinent bitch.*

'It didn't take long to get around to that, did it? The man's not even in his grave yet.'

Jardine gave him a tight smile.

'And his murderer is still walking around a free man.'

Gulliver wasn't sure how the antagonism between Jardine and Corbyn had developed so rapidly. Perhaps because she'd taken the lead and the same would've happened with him, or perhaps Corbyn was an arrogant misogynist. Either way, he stepped in, re-phrased Jardine's last remark in a more tactful way.

'We wouldn't be doing our jobs if we ignored it, Doctor. I take it complaints are not everyday occurrences, part and parcel of being a doctor?'

'Thankfully not. Certainly not in this practice.'

'Could you tell us what the complaint involved, please?'

Corbyn gave Jardine a pointed look that was easy to interpret.

See? That's how you speak to an important person like me.

Corbyn cleared his throat, straightened his waistcoat, as if he was in front of the General Medical Council's disciplinary board.

'The allegation was completely unfounded and was ruled to be so.'

'What exactly was the allegation?' Gulliver pressed.

Corbyn pursed his lips.

'The daughter of an elderly female patient alleged he'd shouted at her mother and threatened her during a house call.'

'Threatened her how?'

Corbyn gave him a look—*this is so tiresome.*

'She alleged Dominic threatened to administer a lethal dose of diamorphine.' He unclasped his fingers long enough to hold up a hand. 'Yes, the same way in which Harold Shipman murdered his victims. At least she didn't accuse Dominic of trying to force her mother to alter her will in his favour.'

'How did the allegation come to be dismissed? Surely it was his word against the two of them?'

'The patient was suffering from advanced Alzheimer's, amongst other things. Her opinion didn't count for much. It was Dominic's word against that of the daughter.' He smiled thinly, and Gulliver saw the pleasure he'd got in the result. 'However, the daughter was proved to be a serial accuser who'd brought similar claims against doctors in other practices with the intention of claiming compensation. Her case was thrown out and Dominic was cleared of any wrongdoing. Nobody here doubted him for a minute.'

'Glad to hear it, Doctor,' Jardine said. 'Should we talk to the receptionist to get the patient and her daughter's details? You do realise we'll want to talk to them?'

Corbyn dipped his head again, although this time it was an attempt to hide his anger.

'Talk to Theresa, yes.'

'And who should we talk to regarding access to Doctor Orford's computer systems?'

'Why on earth would you want to look at those? Besides, they're confidential.'

'You were the one to mention Harold Shipman, Doctor. I'm sure you appreciate we don't want to risk a repeat of the accusations of incompetence made against the police in that case. We *will* be looking at his computer, even if we have to get a warrant to do so. If you're worried about patient confidentiality, we're more interested in his email. Presumably your staff and colleagues get personal email coming through to their work email addresses, like anywhere else.' She cocked her head at him.

'Of course. I don't know who you need to speak to about it.'

He gave a dismissive wave. 'I'll find out and ask them to get in touch. Is that all?'

'One last thing. Mrs Orford said her husband told her he was attending a conference at the time he was killed. Do you know anything about that?'

Corbyn shook his head emphatically.

'It's nothing we sent him on. He'd taken the day off work for personal reasons on the day he was killed, but I don't know anything about a conference.'

Everybody got up at once and headed for the door, Gulliver in the lead. He stopped in front of it, a final question for the impatient Corbyn who couldn't get past without being rude.

'Was there anything unusual in his behaviour in the days or weeks leading up to his death? I'm asking you as the friend of his father, not in your role as his employer.'

Corbyn relaxed visibly at the mention of his friend, considered the question.

'Nothing that I'm aware of. But you're welcome to speak to his colleagues. They're all very busy, but I'm sure they'll find time to speak to you in the circumstances. Dominic was well-liked and respected. I'm confident you won't find whatever led to his death here.'

And I'm confident Harold Shipman's colleagues said the same about him, Jardine thought, giving Corbyn a perfunctory handshake on the way out.

THE RECEPTIONIST, THERESA, HAD NO PROBLEM FINDING THE patient records for Maureen Fowler and for her daughter, Angela, also a patient at the surgery. She didn't have a problem giving them her opinion, either.

'She's a real trouble-maker. I've got a friend who works at a practice in Eastleigh who said she did the same thing with one of their doctors.'

They hadn't doubted what Corbyn told them, but it was useful to have it confirmed. It also told them something about Theresa. Despite giving the impression of being rushed off her feet, she was still happy to talk. As one of the three receptionists working on the front desk in the midst of the busy clinic, she was in the thick of it, well placed to observe the comings and goings of patients, staff and anybody else.

Gulliver and Jardine shared a look, then he collared the woman sitting next to Theresa as soon as she got off the phone, asked her to check if any of the other doctors were available for a quick chat.

Jardine concentrated on Theresa. She suggested they step outside for some privacy, an excuse for an unscheduled break Theresa jumped at. Jardine started probing as soon as they were sitting side-by-side on the low wall separating the wheelchair ramp from the car park.

'What did you think of Dominic Orford?'

'He was alright. You met Corbyn. You saw what he's like . . .'

Jardine grinned conspiratorially at her.

'I got a good idea, yeah.'

'Dom was nothing like that. There's no way he'd do what that cow Angela Fowler accused him of.'

'We heard his old man is friends with Corbyn and got him the job. It makes us wonder if he was incompetent or had something in his past that meant he couldn't get a job on his own.'

Theresa stuck her bottom lip out, shook her head.

'Not at all. A lot of patients asked for him. Turned down earlier appointments to wait for him. Nobody does that with Corbyn, that's for sure.'

Jardine was tempted to ask what Theresa's last pay rise had

been like, whether that was behind the obvious dislike. Except she wasn't here about Dr Felix Corbyn.

'Has anything unusual happened that you think might be relevant?'

'Not really.' It was an automatic response, a holding statement while she thought about it. 'Although there was a strange incident about a month ago. Dom had a female patient complaining of stomach pains. He was examining her. It's not like it was an intimate examination.' She touched her own stomach to reinforce the point. 'And there was a chaperone in the room. One of the nurses. Maeve Kelly. I wasn't on duty that day, but I heard the patient jumped off the examining couch as soon as Dom touched her, ran screaming from the room. Went out through the pharmacy and knocked a bloody great display stand over in her panic. It was really weird.'

Jardine filtered out the likely exaggerations, her interest piqued nonetheless

'What was her name?'

'I could probably find it for you, but you'd be better off talking to Maeve. She's not in today, but she'll be in tomorrow.'

Jardine saw the desperate plea in Theresa's eyes—*please don't ask me to trawl through all the appointments about a month ago or maybe more or maybe less and I wasn't even on duty ...*

'It's okay. I'll phone tomorrow. I assume the pharmacy has CCTV?'

'Definitely.' She checked her watch, glanced behind her. 'I ought to be getting back.'

They both stood up, dusted off their backsides as they drifted slowly back inside, the flow of information at an end. Gulliver was already back at the reception desk. He hooked his thumb at the door Jardine and Theresa had just come through.

'Good ol' Dom was a great guy, *rah, rah, rah,*' he said, once the door had closed behind them. 'I don't think we're going to get much more than that out of any of them. What about you?'

She rocked her hand.

'Might be nothing, but . . .'

Gulliver's interest increased as she took him through Theresa's story, his assessment more a reflection on Angel's character than anything else.

'The boss is going to love that.'

'You bet. The stranger it is, the more he likes it. We'll probably find out the woman was Orford's long-lost daughter, and she freaked out when she felt daddy's hands on her.'

'Then she killed him because he'd given her mother a lethal dose of diamorphine like Angela Fowler accused him of threatening her mother with.'

Jardine pulled her head back to get a better look at him, her voice filled with admiration.

'I'm impressed, Craig. You're getting the hang of this.'

God help me, he thought, *I hope I'm not turning into you.*

10

Mercedes Cortés spent the morning in bed recovering from twenty-four hours of travelling followed by too many beers on an empty stomach the previous evening, attempting to anaesthetise herself to the anxiety threatening to overwhelm her.

She rolled out of bed a few minutes before midday, showered and then did her best to iron the worst of the creases out of a clean, crumpled blouse. Not that her grandparents would care. They wouldn't notice if she turned up in a muddy potato sack.

She walked the same route as on the previous day, but in the opposite direction, back to the train station, where she caught the 13:30 departure for Winchester, only seventeen minutes away. From there, she took a cab to her grandparents' house.

It was obvious her grandmother had been standing at the window waiting. The front door flew open before the taxi had driven away, and Maria Cortés came rushing out to greet her, smothering her in a hug, a stream of excited Spanish in her ear.

'Slow down or speak English, Gran,' Mercedes laughed,

disentangling herself from Maria's suffocating embrace. 'You know my Spanish isn't great.'

Maria held her at arm's length, tried to work a disapproving note into her voice.

'I'll never forgive your mother for not bringing you up bilingual.'

That's not the only thing you've never forgiven her for, Mercedes thought, and said something different.

'I'll never forgive her for naming me after a car.'

Maria shook her head and tut-tutted at her granddaughter's ignorance and lack of respect for tradition and the old ways.

'The name came first, Mercedes. It's a beautiful name. Do you still use Mercy?'

'That's even worse.'

Maria clucked her disapproval some more, then led Mercedes into the house. As with the hotel she was staying in, Mercedes had to admit the quaint charm of the old cottage and the lush beauty of its early-autumn garden as the leaves started to turn compensated in a small way for the dreary weather.

'Where's Granddad?' she asked, once they were in the kitchen and Maria was busy making coffee.

'Playing golf. Where else?'

'Really?'

'Yes, really.'

'I remember when he used to describe it as a good walk ruined.'

Maria shrugged at the unpredictable ways of the world and the people who populate it.

'Me, too. At least it gets him out of the house. Keeps him busy.'

Mercedes stopped what she'd been doing, nosing through the photographs and keepsakes on the painted wooden dresser.

'If he wants something worthwhile to do instead of hitting

little balls with a stick, he should come to Sydney. Open a tapas restaurant. He'd make a fortune.'

Maria placed a cup of coffee on the kitchen table for Mercedes, kept hold of her own as she leaned her traditionally-sized rump against the counter.

'For one, we don't want or need a fortune. We made enough money when we sold the restaurant to see us out.' She ducked her head to look out at the grey skies outside. 'And if we get fed up living here and never seeing the sun, we wouldn't move to a godforsaken place like Australia—'

'It is not.'

'—we'd move back to Seville.'

Mercedes resumed prowling the big kitchen, coffee cup in hand, as her grandmother watched her with undisguised pleasure. She picked up a framed photograph sitting on the dresser, showed it to her.

'What about this? Doesn't look so godforsaken to me. Is that a smile wide enough to split your face in two I can see?'

'No, dear, that's fear.' She took the photograph from Mercedes, smiled at the memory. 'Maybe terror is a better word. Your grandfather, too.'

Mercedes went to lean against the counter beside her, studied the happy scene with her. The five of them—herself, her grandparents, her mother and her partner, Paul—all dressed in blue and grey jumpsuits attached by harnesses to the guard rail on the top of the Sydney Harbour Bridge, one hundred and thirty-four metres above the water.

'I've never been so scared in my life,' Maria said. 'I wouldn't do it again.' She went to give the photograph back to Mercedes to put back on the dresser, hesitated. 'How's Paul?'

'He's fine.'

'Are you getting along with him any better?'

'Yeah, we're good. I decided I needed to grow up—'

'You *did* grow up, dear.'

'—and get over myself.'

'And we missed most of it. Are you hungry?'

'Starving.'

Maria narrowed her eyes at her, although there was a smile trying to break through.

'Not eating for two, are you, Mercedes?'

Are you scared of history repeating itself? Mercedes thought, but would never say.

'That doesn't deserve an answer.'

Maria gave her a knowing look, headed towards the fridge.

'Got anything that isn't Spanish?' Mercedes asked, her grandmother hearing the mischief in her voice even if she didn't see it on her face as she inspected the fridge's contents.

'Cheeky monkey.'

'Actually, Gran . . .' Mercedes started, the anxiety surging inside her. 'Before you do that . . .'

Maria closed the fridge door, nodded *of course*, then left the kitchen and went into a small home office—in reality a glorified alcove under the stairs housing a small desk with a computer on it. She came back a minute later with a slim manila folder in her hand, saw the look on Mercedes' face and laughed.

'I know. It looks like a police file on a suspect. Your grandfather watches far too many cop dramas on the TV. Either that, or he's harboured a secret desire to be a policeman he never told me about. He'd never admit it, but he enjoyed doing it. Not only because he was doing something he knows is important to you.' She sighed, a sudden regret colouring her voice. 'But it made him angry at the same time. Stupid, I know, but that's your grandfather for you. Old fashioned. I think it's best if you put it in your bag and we try not to mention it over dinner.'

She handed Mercedes the file, but kept hold of her end

when Mercedes took the other, as if it were a Christmas cracker they were about to pull.

'Are you sure this is a good idea?'

'Not at all. I'm worried sick. But I can't stop myself.'

Maria shook her head, a sad weary gesture that the world was full of people hell-bent on complicating their lives rather than enjoying them.

'You're just like your mother.'

She released her end and Mercedes carried the file out into the hall where she'd left her backpack, a whispered mantra on her lips.

Wait until you get back. Wait until you get back. Wait until you get back.

But it was hard. So very hard.

'What do you fancy to eat?' Maria asked brightly when Mercedes came back into the kitchen, the fridge door wide open. 'I've got boquerones, puntillitas, chorizo, jamón . . .'

Despite her earlier tongue-in-cheek request for anything that wasn't Spanish, Mercedes' mouth watered as her grandmother ran through a list of tapas that would put many a restaurant to shame.

'And I've got a chilled Albariño in the fridge, or a Marqués de Riscal Reserva Rioja, if you prefer red.'

'I suppose we'll have to speak Spanish at the dinner table, too.'

'We will if your grandfather has anything to do with it. The practice will do you good.' She cocked her ear towards the front of the house at the sound of a key in the front-door lock. 'That sounds like him now . . .'

Mercedes' anxiety spiked, a sudden visceral surge in her stomach at the thought of all the questions she so desperately wanted to ask her grandfather but knew she wouldn't ever dare.

. . .

'Everything okay?' Kincade said, when Angel hadn't spoken for five minutes as they drove to Bishop's Waltham to interview Nigel and Helen Orford, who'd managed to catch a last-minute ferry back from France.

'Why shouldn't it be?'

'*Ha!* People never realise that when they answer like that, they might as well save some breath and just say *no*.'

'Really? Women never realise that a man not talking for more than a minute and a half doesn't imply something's wrong.'

'So, what is it?'

'Nothing.'

'Liar ... *sir*. You've definitely got something on your mind.'

He gave her a sideways look, saw the mischief in her eyes.

'You didn't proposition Doctor Death, did you?' she said, when he failed to volunteer anything. 'And she turned you down.'

'I thought according to you we've been at it for years. On the dissecting table after every autopsy...'

She nodded, *you've got a point*.

'Are you going to tell me or not?'

It was obvious she wasn't going to let it go. There wasn't actually any reason not to tell her. As he knew all too well, she was a past master at keeping secrets—admittedly, mainly about herself.

'I went to The Jolly Sailor the other night—'

'As you always do'

His mouth turned down, not because she'd interrupted, but at the implications.

'Maybe not for much longer. I saw my mother in there on a date with a man.'

She twisted to face him, check if he was being serious. The scowl still on his face suggested he was.

'A date?'

'Yep.'

'What were they doing?'

'Having a drink.'

'Not kissing and cuddling?'

He pulled a face as if he'd taken a mouthful of sour milk.

'No, but they're of an age where public displays of affection are taboo.'

'Holding hands?'

'Not that I saw.'

She shook her head, no room for doubt in her voice.

'You're overreacting. I'd understand your concern if you couldn't get to sleep because of the bed banging against the wall in the spare bedroom . . .'

If he hadn't been driving, he'd have put his hands over his ears. As it was, he held one of them up as if directing traffic.

'*Enough!* And you wonder why I didn't want to tell you.'

He kept his eyes on the road. Refused to look at her, see the grin he felt warming the side of his face. He knew she'd been deliberately provocative to make him squirm. That didn't mean he had to look at her enjoying his discomfort.

'It doesn't sound like a date to me,' she said, dialling it down. 'Anyway, so what if it was?'

'Don't say anything to my father, okay?'

'I think it's quite sweet.'

'Don't forget, she still wants to meet you.'

If he was hoping to shut her up by mentioning the meeting she was determined to put off for as long as possible, it backfired.

'I suppose I should. Maybe she'll ask me to be a bridesmaid . . .'

Next time, I'm putting her in the boot, he thought, and savoured the idea for the rest of the journey.

. . .

Nigel and Helen Orford lived in a substantial three-storey, weathered red brick Georgian property with a white-painted portico over the front door and massive, ornate chimney stacks on the ends of each of the twin gables. Angel drove over the ancient cobbled drive, through eight-foot-high gateposts flanked by curved lichen-stained brick walls, and parked next to a black Porsche Taycan Sport Turismo.

Nigel Orford was a stocky man in his late sixties with a full mane of silver-grey hair swept back off his face. Dressed in a button-down shirt and stone-coloured chinos with well-worn boat shoes and no socks completing the preppy ensemble, he was a far cry from the raspberry cords and mustard pullover Angel had been expecting. He'd happily bet his pension on Orford being a keen yachtsman with a mooring on the Beaulieu River.

His wife wasn't quite so pukka.

She wore a pale-peach leisure suit that showcased surgically-enhanced curves that laughed in the face of age and gravity, at the same time proving that all the money in the world can't buy you breeding or good taste, her blond-out-of-a-bottle shoulder-length hair still damp from a recent shower.

A stack of wooden wine cases stamped with the names and illustrations of up-market French chateaux was piled immediately inside the front door, awaiting transfer to the underground spiral wine cellar.

Kincade reckoned if she slipped on something underfoot, it would most likely be a loose fifty-pound note.

The Orfords led them through into a spacious timber conservatory overlooking the rear garden, two glasses of the spoils from their cut-short trip to France on a low coffee table.

Angel and Kincade both declined the offer of a glass for

themselves, then Angel got them started. He moved quickly through their condolences, then listening patiently and respectfully as the Orfords expressed their horror, disbelief, sadness and outrage.

He was expecting the Chief Constable's Christian name to be dropped into the conversation when he admitted they didn't already have a suspect in custody, but thankfully it didn't happen.

'We'd like to talk about Dominic's early life. We've spoken to his wife, but she told us she's only known him since two thousand and sixteen.'

The Orfords shared a look. Then Nigel took the lead, as everyone in the room knew he always did.

'What's to talk about? He was like any other normal young man, although he was harder-working than most. He chose to read medicine at Bristol University.'

'Are you a doctor yourself, Mr Orford?'

'Good God, no. I'm a businessman.'

'Nigel owns a very successful engineering company,' Helen chipped in, as if worried they might think he had a market stall selling junk imported from China.

Orford cleared his throat, uncomfortable at having his achievements shouted from the rooftops by his wife.

'Anyway, Dominic completed his undergraduate studies, then did his two-year stint working like a dog as a junior doctor at University College London Hospital. After that, he trained as a GP. I would've liked him to become a surgeon, but that takes longer. To tell you the truth, he'd had a bellyful of studying by then.'

'Then he moved back down here to take up a position in a local practice?' Angel prompted.

'That's right.' He glanced at his wife, as if seeking

permission, then continued. 'If you've talked to Louise, you'll already know I helped him get that position.'

'She mentioned it, yes. It sounds to me as if it caused a bit of friction.'

Orford knocked back the last of the wine before replying, placed the glass carefully back on the table.

'It did. Louise always thought we should butt out of Dominic's life.'

Helen let out a sharp bark of laughter.

'We didn't hear much talk of butting out when we helped them buy the house. And if Nigel hadn't got Dominic his job at the surgery, they wouldn't have met and she'd still be a pharmacy sales assistant.'

Angel was getting a flavour of the Orford family dynamic, petty grievances and jealousies rife. It was no different to other families, although exacerbated by money.

'This was a very brutal murder. It suggests very strong emotions. There was also evidence of torture, perhaps to get information. Do you know of anything in Dominic's early life that could be responsible for such a deep-seated grudge?'

Orford looked at his wife again, found no help there. He blew the air from his cheeks, tried to put his frustration into words.

'Like I said, he was a normal, hard-working young man. Like me, he chose a course at university that meant he had to work hard. I studied engineering. It was full-on, like medicine is. Not like media studies or fashion design where you have two lectures a week and one assignment per term. We were very proud of him.'

'Very proud,' Helen echoed.

'You never wanted him to take over the reins at your company?'

'Before he took an interest in medicine, definitely. But anyone can make money. Not everyone has got what it takes to be a doctor. We were very happy when he told us that's what he wanted to do with his life. If we helped him along the way, so bloody what? It's a cliché to think that a person has to suffer hardship in order to be a good person, do something worthwhile with their life.'

He certainly died like a martyr, Angel thought, and kept very much to himself.

'Give me one word to describe Nigel Orford,' Angel said, when they were back in the car and heading home.

'I'd rather give you one to describe his wife.'

'I'm sure you would. I don't suppose you'd be happy with only one, either. So?'

She didn't even have to think about it.

'*Defensive*. The way he kept stressing how hard Dominic worked. Anyone would think he was actually a lazy sod and the old man was trying to convince himself he wasn't. Except if he'd been lazy, he'd never have qualified as a doctor. Daddy can't sit the exams for him, or do his shifts as a junior doctor.'

Angel couldn't disagree. But something was scratching away at the back of his mind, trying to get in. He had a feeling he needed to pick Isabel Durand's brains—and that wasn't something he was about to arrange with Kincade sitting beside him.

'Fancy a quick beer in The Jolly Sailor?' she said, then clamped her hand over her mouth. '*Oops!* I forgot. We can't. Not unless we want to watch your mum snogging some bloke in the corner.'

Funny how the same thoughts about folding her into the boot and closing the lid on her head were back in his mind again.

11

Angel felt like a teenager on his first date with the prettiest girl in the class as he walked through the bowels of Southampton General Hospital towards the autopsy suite presided over by Isabel Durand.

Apart from encountering her at the scene of Dominic Orford's crucifixion, he hadn't seen or spoken to her since she asked him to have a quiet word with her son in the hope of dissuading him from becoming an Army surgeon.

The meeting with Oliver Durand had been an unmitigated disaster. Oliver had no interest in what his mother or Angel thought about his choice of career. He only agreed to meet with Angel to satisfy his curiosity. Two things—*accusations* was a better word—stuck in Angel's mind from that meeting.

You're part of the reason my parents got divorced.

She never shuts up about you. Padre this, Padre bloody that.

The revelations had rocked Angel to his core. Forced him to re-evaluate every interaction with the pathologist in the light of the insight provided by her son. When they first met, they'd both still been married. Now, he was a widower and she divorced. It never crossed his mind she might be hoping the relationship between them progressed beyond the professional as a result. That the merciless ribbing from Kincade might actually be based on truth. Was she able to see what he couldn't because she was a woman?

The fact was, nothing had changed as far as Durand was concerned. All the changes were in his head—and perhaps heart. Hence the nervousness. Would he treat her any differently? Should he stick rigidly to the professional, ask her what he wanted to discuss with her in her subterranean office, rather than doing it over a convivial drink?

The decision, of course, was not his to make.

'Thank God you're here, Padre,' Durand exclaimed, the minute he entered her office.

'What? You need a hand snipping through some particularly tough ribs to get inside a cadaver's chest cavity?'

'What I need is somebody to take me for a drink.'

'There's a worrying amount of desperation in your voice, Isabel.'

'You try spending all day up to your elbows in dead bodies, see what it does for your sobriety.'

She was already out from behind her desk and heading for the door. Once outside in the corridor, she linked her arm through his. He glanced down at her hand.

'I hope you washed your hands after the last autopsy.'

'You obviously don't pay much attention, Padre, or you'd have noticed I wear gloves. Otherwise I might well be using your jacket sleeve to clean my hands. Or maybe even your face.'

And all he heard was *She never shuts up about you. Padre this, Padre bloody that.*

'The Pig in the Wall?' he suggested.

'Where else? It's almost becoming our local.'

It was where she'd first asked him to speak to Oliver. It was also where he'd met with her son. He hoped by suggesting it, she wouldn't suspect what a disaster that meeting had been. Her enthusiastic agreement implied her son had said nothing about how the meeting had deteriorated.

They drove there separately, each of them planning to drive home after a quick drink—a useful constraint on potential over-indulgence and whatever that might lead to. The Pig in the Wall was a hotel, after all.

As on the last occasion, she chose a Campari and soda, he a margarita, heavy on the salt.

'I don't want to talk about your discussion with Oliver,' she said, once they were settled in the leathery ambience of the hotel bar.

That makes eleven of us, he thought, counting his own vote ten times.

'I need to let him make his own decisions,' she went on. 'What people describe as making his own mistakes.'

'And how's that working out?'

'It's hard. Anyway, you're starting to talk about it.'

'You'd think I was being rude if I said nothing and changed the subject.'

She took a sip of Campari, then changed the subject herself.

'So? What brought you to the hospital? I haven't even performed the post mortem, so you can't be hassling about that.'

'*Hassling?*'

'It means to annoy or harass repeatedly or chronically.'

He raised his glass to her.

'Thank you for today's vocabulary lesson.'

She raised her own glass, *you're welcome*.

'And you certainly didn't come specifically to take me for a drink. The look of horror on your face when I suggested it made that very clear.'

He narrowed his eyes at her.

'Are you sure you didn't have a couple of nips of formaldehyde before I arrived?'

'Do you mean because I'm so well-preserved?'

'Fishing for compliments is not a good trait, Isabel.'

She pulled a face.

'You don't leave me much choice. You certainly don't volunteer them.'

His head was starting to spin—and it wasn't from two sips of margarita.

What had gotten into her? Or had she always been the same, and he'd never noticed?

'I'd be up before a disciplinary before I knew it if I went around complimenting female colleagues on a daily basis.'

She put down her glass, rested her hand on his. It was nothing she hadn't done a thousand times before, but now it felt different.

'Once in a while wouldn't hurt, Padre.'

He nodded firmly, a decision made.

'I'll need to practice in the mirror first.'

'You're not bloody kidding, you will.' She let go of his hand, leaned back in her seat, looking as if she'd enjoyed the gentle teasing, even if he hadn't. 'Anyway, what brought you to my door?'

'I don't suppose you knew Dominic Orford was a doctor?'

'I didn't, no.'

'A GP. By the way, does that mean you'll be more respectful when you desecrate his body?'

'I do love it when you say things like that to me, Padre.' She wriggled in her chair. 'It sends a little shiver down my spine.'

Serves me right for starting it, he thought, and got to the point.

'I've got a niggling doubt about his training and his age. How long does it take to train as a doctor?'

She beamed at him as if he'd taken her earlier remarks to heart and paid her a compliment.

'You ought to know that. Claire was a doctor.'

'She trained before I met her.'

'And you could easily have looked it up on the internet. You *did* want to take me for a drink, after all. I *knew* it.' With that, she downed what was left of her Campari. 'Let's have another to celebrate the truth finally making it out into the open.'

The way she phrased it made him think. Had her son told his mother about the things he'd said to Angel, after all? Was she now more relaxed, teasing and flirting with him, as a result of her cards being on the table?

It was more than he was up to thinking about at the end of a busy day. Waving at a member of staff and ordering the second round of drinks he could just about manage.

'So? How long?'

'It depends.'

'I could've worked that out for myself.'

'It's a minimum of five years at medical school as a university undergraduate. An additional year if you haven't got enough of a science background. Then you do your foundation training in a hospital for two years. What used to be called a junior doctor, but is now called a resident doctor, like it is in America.'

'That's the period when you're working ridiculously long hours?'

'Being taken advantage of, yes.'

He sucked the air in through his teeth.

'So cynical in one so young.'

She grinned at him for the unintentional compliment.

'See? It's not so difficult, is it? Anyway, after that, it depends on what you decide to specialise in. The speciality training to become a GP takes three years. It's longer for a surgeon and other disciplines. Does that help?' A mischievous smile curled her lips before he could answer. 'Don't be embarrassed to use the calculator on your phone if you need to.'

This was not the Isabel Durand he knew of old. It was going to take some getting used to. He only hoped she didn't carry on in the same vein when Kincade was present.

'A minimum of ten years,' he said. 'Eleven if you haven't got enough science. Assuming Orford went to university at eighteen like most people do, that means he should've qualified as a GP at age twenty-nine at the latest.'

'Well done, Padre. No calculator. I'm impressed.'

'The senior partner in Orford's practice told us they'd recently celebrated Orford's ten-year anniversary. He's forty-two, meaning he qualified when he was thirty-two. There's a gap of four years. Three if he had to do an extra year in medical school.'

They held each other's gaze for a long moment. Once again, all he could hear was her son's voice.

She never shuts up about you. Padre this, Padre bloody that.

'Maybe not,' she said. 'Was the celebration to mark ten years with his current practice or ten years as a GP?'

It was a valid point. They would have to check.

'What?' she said. 'I can see that's got you thinking.'

'Orford's father got him the job. We assumed it was immediately after qualifying. Maybe Dominic tried for three years, couldn't get a job himself, and daddy stepped in and asked a favour of his friend at that point. Nigel Orford didn't want to admit that to us. He doesn't mind admitting to nepotism, but he doesn't want to paint his son as a man nobody wants to employ.'

'It's possible, but unlikely. The NHS is crying out for doctors.'

He knew she was right. It wasn't only that he was as aware as anyone else in the UK of the difficulty in getting a doctor's appointment. He knew it as a premonition he felt in the secret oozings of his gut, a suspicion that things are never as they appear. A three-year gap in anyone else's career wouldn't have caused him to bat an eyelid. But in a man nailed to a cross and tortured...

The remainder of their quick drink together passed in exactly that manner—quickly. Leaving, she linked her arm though his as she had earlier. Catching sight of themselves in a mirror on the way out, he had to admit they looked good together. Nobody would ever look at them in the street and think, *what a strange couple.*

They didn't even notice the young woman coming in as they went out, and nor did she them.

His mind was too full of Oliver Durand's words—*She never shuts up about you. Padre this, Padre bloody that*—and as for the young woman, she couldn't think about anything other than the contents of the backpack slung over her shoulder, a slim dossier she'd somehow managed not to read on the train journey back from her grandparents' house.

12

'It was the fuse in the plug, after all,' Kincade said happily the next morning, as what used to be DCI Olivia Finch's personal coffee machine whirred and gurgled into life. She made them both a cup and they sat enjoying it—as well as the greater sense of satisfaction that fate hated Finch more than it did them.

'I'll have to make sure I've got a cup of it in my hand next time I'm summoned to her office,' he said.

'What a nasty streak in a man who used to be a priest.' Looking like she wished she'd thought of it first.

He sucked the last drips out of his cup, smacked his lips and moved them on.

'Something was bugging me about Orford's training. I did a search on the internet on how long it takes to train as a GP . . .'

She finished her own coffee more leisurely as he explained, came to the same conclusion.

'There's a three-year gap.'

He was tempted to repeat what Durand had said to him the previous evening, congratulate her on performing the calculation without recourse to a calculator. He kept it simple, instead.

'Exactly.'

They shared a knowing look. An unexplained period of time always got their juices flowing. Especially one that proud parents had omitted to mention.

'I wonder when it was?' she said, thinking out loud. 'If it was early on in his career and his death is related to it, it suggests his killer has been holding a grudge for a very long time. That might explain the brutality of the murder if it's been festering all that time.'

They would follow up with both Orford's wife and his parents. The parents felt like a better bet, especially after the way they'd stressed what a normal, hard-working man their son had been.

Gulliver stuck his head around the door as they were contemplating the awkward interview ahead. He sniffed suspiciously.

'That doesn't smell like the crap out of the drinks machine.'

'That's because it's not,' Kincade said, neither she nor Angel explaining. 'So? What's up?'

'Some interesting things from the call logs...'

The newspaper had supplied their own call logs with public-spirited alacrity. The number used by the female killer who emailed the paper an image of Orford nailed to the cross was quickly identified. Its call logs and cell-site data were then requested from the service provider. It hadn't taken Gulliver long to go through it.

'It's a burner, as you'd expect. There are only two calls on it. The most recent one is the call made to the journalist, George Leather. Guess where it was made from?'

'Downstairs in reception,' Kincade said flippantly.

'Not as far off as you might think.' Gulliver pointed out of the window at the train station on the other side of Mountbatten Way.

'Really?' Angel said.

'Yep.'

'Piss-taking bastards.'

'Well-put, sir. The other call was received from Dominic Orford's number two days before he was killed.'

'Received from?' Kincade said, looking for confirmation.

'Uh-huh. It suggests they contacted him some other way and gave him the number, told him to call them.'

'We need to chase forensics for the contents of his email systems,' Angel said, stating the blindingly obvious. 'What was the location for that call?'

'West Quay shopping centre. Under a minute duration. Just long enough to give details of where and when to meet. Obviously, we'll review CCTV footage from both locations, try to identify a person common to both.'

It was needle-in-a-haystack time. They were both busy locations, chosen for that very reason. Not only that, a woman had called George Leather. If her male accomplice had been carrying the burner phone at the time Orford called, they would never make a match. It had to be attempted, nonetheless.

'Keep us posted, Craig,' Angel said, expecting Gulliver to head off. Then, when he didn't, 'Something else?'

Gulliver's demeanour made clear there was, and something a lot more promising than two phone calls.

'They're not stupid. They obviously keep the phone switched off when they're not using it—'

'I sense a *but*.' This from Kincade.

'—but it was switched on again the day after Orford was murdered.'

'Switched on but no call?' Angel said.

'That's right. Either they decided not to make a call, or they turned it on for another reason.'

'To take a photograph?' Kincade suggested.

'That's what I'm thinking, Sarge. The thing is, the location was close to a village called Knighton.'

Angel and Kincade both stared at him uncomprehendingly. Angel put it into words.

'Where the hell's that?'

'Somerset.'

'Carrot-cruncher territory,' Kincade said, adding nothing to the progress of the investigation.

'Exactly, Sarge. I know the cell-site data isn't accurate down to the last couple of feet, but I studied the map of the area, anyway. The only thing I saw was a big property called Kilstock Court. That must be what they took a picture of. It's that, or open fields.'

The significance wasn't lost on anyone. They were working on the basis that Orford had been lured to the derelict barn where he was killed. He'd been suspicious enough to take a shotgun with him, even if it hadn't done him any good.

Kincade stated the obvious.

'Maybe a picture of Kilstock Court is what lured him to the barn.'

'I looked at it on Street View,' Gulliver said. 'All I could see was some big old gates that didn't look as if they'd been opened for years. The driveway was overgrown and curved away, so it wasn't possible to see the house itself. I'll see what I can find out about the place, see if anybody is living there, despite what it looks like.'

'Maybe it was an asylum and Orford was a patient there during his missing years,' Kincade said, then wished she hadn't bothered when she had to run through the timeline for Gulliver's benefit.

'Good work, Craig,' Angel said, ignoring Kincade's facetious remark as Gulliver went off to start digging. He was aware of her staring at him. 'What?'

'Thinking about the timeline and Orford's training. You didn't have to spend time researching it on the internet. You should've asked Doctor Death. Gone for a drink while you were at it.'

'I'll remember that for next time.'

'When I say at it, I mean *about* it, not *at* it.'

'Thank you for that much-needed clarification, Sergeant. Don't think I'm not grateful you didn't actually wink at me.'

'My pleasure, sir.'

DS DAVE GARFIELD WASN'T SURPRISED WHEN HE RECEIVED A second email from the *never_forgotten2012@gmail.com* address. He expected it to display anger or petulance, some indication the sender was growing frustrated when he didn't play their game.

As it turned out, it was identical to the first one. Short, and to the point.

A body is buried at 51.18943, -3.18056

He smiled to himself. It was as if the sender recognised that all they had to do was keep their message in the forefront of his mind, and that same inquisitive organ would do their work for them, the nagging doubts intensifying until he got a shovel and went digging himself.

He was tempted to email back.

I can't take you seriously until you tell me who you are and how you know. If you're not prepared to do that, I have to ask you not to waste any more police time.

He couldn't stop himself from glancing at his boss' door. DI Jay Chopra would laugh in his face. Offer to show Dave where the *delete* key was located on his keyboard. Suggest Dave use that same key the next time he had any stupid ideas about applying for promotion.

Bollocks to you!

He typed out the reply, hit send before he changed his mind. He didn't expect to get a response. One bounced back almost immediately, nonetheless, mimicking his tone.

I can't do that. If you're not prepared to do your job, a killer will continue to walk free.

This time, Dave did laugh out loud. A sudden bark that made DC Vicky Cook give him a curious look.

'I've received another one.'

She got up from her desk, came over to take a look. Hand on his shoulder again, perfume in his nose. This time, she wasn't so adamant in her dismissal.

'I still think it's a crank. But I'm happy to take a drive out there with you if you want.'

The offer surprised him. He responded to it with a guilty admission.

'I already did. There's nothing there you can see. But there's evidence of somebody having been there recently.'

Now, they both glanced at their boss' door.

'How much of a dent can one cadaver dog for an hour make in your budget?' she said, already on the way across the room.

Attagirl, Garfield smiled to himself, well aware—as was everybody with eyes in their head—that Jay Chopra couldn't ever say *no* to flirtatious Vicky Cook.

13

'I knew it!' Angel exclaimed, putting the phone down. He gave Kincade—who'd just made herself yet another cup of strong coffee—a disapproving look. 'You'll end up as hyper as your girls if you keep drinking that stuff.'

'Knew what?' she said, ignoring the remark.

'Nigel Orford is hiding something. I called to arrange a follow-up interview. He told me he's with his wife at their son's house with Louise. I said, perfect, we'll speak to the three of you together, save the taxpayer some petrol.'

'You didn't actually say the bit about saving petrol, did you?'

He looked down his nose at her, wishing he wore glasses to reinforce the effect.

'I think all that caffeine is starting to kick in already. Anyway, you've never heard anyone go into such a panic. He was so desperate we didn't go to Louise's house, he offered to come here.'

'Meaning he's hiding something from her, not us.'

They were prevented from exploring it further by Finch's arrival in the doorway.

'I can smell that bloody coffee all the way from my office.'

They both smiled the smile of new coffee machine custodians at her.

Welcome to our world.

'Help yourself to a cup, ma'am,' Kincade said.

Finch came all the way into the room, but didn't take them up on the offer. Instead, she gave them the evil eye.

'You know, if I hadn't seen how awkward it was for you to unplug it in my office, Cat, I'd say one of you snuck in and removed the fuse from the plug.'

They both looked horrified.

Who? Us?

'Maybe Cat made a big fuss about unplugging it so that you didn't suspect us, ma'am,' Angel said.

'I think I'm going to lock up the coffee and ration it, if this is the result.'

'If you've got any left over, we'll take it off your hands,' Kincade said, as if Finch hadn't spoken. 'And those little Italian biscotti, if you've got any.'

Finch gave her a withering look.

'You're not in Highgate now, Cat, or some other lah-di-dah London neighbourhood.'

'Chocolate digestives?'

'You know, I've actually forgotten what I came in to say.'

'Try drinking more coffee, ma'am,' Angel said to her retreating back, as she left the room in despair. 'That keeps the old brain cells alert.'

Finch's reply drifted back over her shoulder.

'A double whisky is what I need after trying to talk sense to you two.'

They shared a satisfied smile, feeling like a pair of schoolchildren who'd got the better of the headmistress.

That worked a treat.

Sadly, the fun and games ended as soon as Jack Bevan called

up from the front desk to say that Nigel and Helen Orford had arrived.

NIGEL ORFORD LOOKED MUCH AS HE HAD THE PREVIOUS DAY. His wife looked as if she was going to a wedding, although without the hat or fascinator. Interview room one was also far too small for the amount of overpowering, cloying perfume she wore. No doubt her captain-of-industry husband smoked cigars to retaliate when at home.

'How old was Dominic when he went to university to study medicine?' Angel started.

It was an easy question, but it took Nigel Orford a while to answer. He'd seen the way the interview was about to go already.

'Eighteen.'

'And had he studied sufficient science subjects to spend five years as an undergraduate?'

Orford hesitated again, but they all knew he had no way out of the corner Angel was boxing him into.

'No. He spent six years at university before doing his foundation training.'

'Which lasts two years?'

'That's correct.'

'Then a further three years to train as a GP?'

This time, Orford nodded without confirming it verbally.

'He had a nervous breakdown,' Helen Orford blurted. 'Stop playing games. Yes, he should have qualified when he was twenty-nine, but he was thirty-two. Why couldn't you simply ask the question instead of showing us how bloody clever you are?'

'If you'd volunteered the information when we last spoke, I wouldn't have needed to,' Angel said, his voice level. 'We made it very clear we were interested in his early life before he met his wife.' He looked from Helen to her husband and back again.

'Your request to come here today suggests she knows nothing about the breakdown.'

'She knows about it,' Orford said, 'but it's a very delicate matter. We don't talk about it.'

'When did it occur?'

Angel had addressed the question to Orford, but his wife jumped in again, on the attack once more.

'I'm sure you work very hard yourselves, but I bet it's nothing like junior doctors have to work. And talk about stress! If you cock it up, a guilty man might get away with a crime. If a doctor gets it wrong, people can die. It all got too much for him. He had a breakdown at the end of his two-year foundation training.' She glared at them both, challenging them to criticise her son, or herself and her husband for covering up for him. The anger was gone from her voice when she carried on after neither of them did so. 'He took a three-year break and then started his training as a GP.'

'Where was he during this period?' Kincade asked, a mental image of a big old house called Kilstock Court down in Somerset in her mind.

'He spent a few weeks at a residential clinic in London,' Orford said, taking over from his wife. 'Then he went travelling with his girlfriend.'

'Not Louise?'

'No. He hadn't met her at that point.'

'What was her name?'

Orford looked to his wife for help.

'I think it was the Cross girl,' she said. 'Juliet. And no, we don't have contact details for her. It was fifteen years ago.'

'Was she from around here, or somebody he met during his training?' Kincade pressed.

'Around here, I think.'

'Presumably they didn't spend the whole time travelling? Three years, apart from a few weeks in the clinic?'

Orford cleared his throat. Not only to tell his wife that he would take over, but an indicator of his unease.

'I gave him a job at my company. As I told you yesterday, Louise has got a problem with us interfering, as she sees it, in Dominic's life. I helped him get the position at the practice where he worked—'

'And we helped them buy their house.' Helen, of course.

'I didn't want her to know that I also gave him—'

'A cushy number?' Kincade, this time.

'—somewhere to work that wasn't too stressful while he was recovering from his breakdown.'

'Weren't a few months spent lounging on a beach in Bali or Thailand sufficient to achieve that?' Kincade said.

Orford gave her a thin smile.

'Clearly, his doctor thought not. I'm very pleased I was in a position to provide him with something useful to do during that period, however much you or other cynics might mock him, call him a poor little rich boy who couldn't stand on his own two feet. There's not much point in me working my fingers to the bone for the last forty-odd years if I can't help my own son when he needs it, is there?'

Don't ask her if she's got children, Angel thought, and stepped in to smooth the waters.

'It's all very understandable, Mr Orford. Things would have been so much simpler if you'd mentioned it earlier.'

Orford shrugged, a dismissive gesture.

'I'd just been told about my son's horrific murder. Maybe I wasn't thinking straight. Maybe my priority wasn't making your job easier.' He gave Kincade a particularly vitriolic look as he said it, then back to Angel. 'Please accept my sincere apologies.'

Angel nodded his acknowledgement, echoed Orford's unctuous tone.

'Now that you've had a short while to adjust to the awful reality of the situation, are you satisfied there isn't anything else you need to tell us? Anything that might help us catch Dominic's murderer. Because that's our number one priority here.'

Orford glanced at Kincade again, as if unsure whether her priority wasn't to get in as many snide remarks as possible.

'Nothing comes to mind at the moment. Rest assured that if anything does, you'll be the first to know, Inspector. Is that all?'

Angel scrunched his face as if he'd love to say *yes*, but his hands were tied.

'Just one more thing. Was Dominic religious in any way? The manner of his death isn't something I've come across before. It makes me wonder if the cross is significant?' Congratulating himself on not using the word *crucifixion*.

Orford glanced at his wife before answering.

'Neither of us is religious. Dominic wasn't, either. We didn't bring him up that way, and as far as we know, he didn't take an interest in later life. Louise is the same.'

'A mystery then?'

'Some religious nutter,' Helen spat, the depth of feeling behind it surprising them. 'Doing the Lord's bidding, killing sinners because Jesus comes to him in the night dressed as the Easter Bunny. Religion has got a lot to answer for, if you ask me.' Looking accusingly at Angel as if she'd somehow identified his previous calling.

'It's one possibility,' he said, then wrapped it up.

Nigel Orford made a point of not shaking hands with Kincade. His wife swept from the room with her nose in the air, not bothering to say anything to either of them.

'God, I hope we find something else he hasn't told us,' Kincade said, once the Orfords were out of earshot.

'Do you think there's something to find?'

'Definitely. They're still too defensive. It's nothing to do with Orford being on the back foot about helping his son every step of the way. Every parent would do the same in his position. I certainly would. There's something else. It could be connected to her problem with religion. We need to find the girlfriend and look into his time in the clinic.'

'I saw how disappointed you were that it wasn't the big old house in Somerset that Craig identified.'

'Maybe they shipped him down there from London and he didn't go travelling at all.'

'Is there anything he said you do believe?'

Her brow furrowed as she thought about it.

'Not sure. But his wife was bang on the money when she said how hard we work.'

Too much caffeine, he thought, as she bounded up the stairs ahead of him, her voice echoing in the stairwell.

'Gotta make sure Finch hasn't nicked our coffee machine . . .'

14

'I wonder what it's like being a chaperone at a doctor's surgery,' Jardine said out of the blue, an occurrence Gulliver was used to.

'A bit like being a doctor, I suppose. Except you don't have to put your finger anywhere.'

'But it's not, is it? If you decide to be a doctor or a nurse, you know you're going to have to examine people. It's part of the job. It's different if you're a receptionist and the doctor says, *come and get an eyeful while this patient strips off.*'

'They probably phrase it differently.'

'Doesn't make any difference. You might meet them in the supermarket or the pub. You'd be thinking, *don't I know you?* You might even say it. Then you both suddenly remember. It'd be so embarrassing.'

'How about if patients wore a hood?'

She pulled her head back to get a better look at him. It was something she did on a regular basis. One day, she was going to get stuck in the position.

'I worry about you sometimes, Craig. Where does that even

come from? Is that what they teach you at Oxford Bloody University?'

You worry about me? he thought, and went back to concentrating on the road.

They were on their way to the Oaks Medical Centre to interview the nurse, Maeve Kelly, who'd acted as a chaperone when a young woman inexplicably rushed from the room when Dominic Orford started to examine her.

She was a few years older than Orford had been, with a lot more experience than his ten years. As Jardine later said to Gulliver, *I bet she's lanced a lot of boils.*

She took them into Orford's now-vacant consulting room, killing two birds with one stone—it was available, and it facilitated a demonstration of her story.

'What exactly happened?' Jardine started.

'Dom had a patient complaining of stomach pains.' She held up a finger that had spent a lot of time in places Gulliver didn't want to think about. 'I looked her up on the system when they told me you wanted to speak to me. Caitlin Fox. She's twenty-nine and a pretty girl. Dom came out and asked me to act as a chaperone while he examined her. I came in and she was sitting right there.' Pointing to the chair at the side of the desk that looked very empty after Orford's computer had been removed. 'She was fully clothed and looked perfectly at ease. There wasn't an atmosphere in the room or anything. Dom asked her to lie on the couch and pull her top up.' She put her hands at her waist as if taking hold of the hem of an imaginary sweater, pulled them up until they were immediately below her bust. 'You couldn't even see the bottom of her bra. Just her exposed stomach above her jeans which were buttoned up.'

'And she was still okay at this point?' Jardine checked.

Maeve smiled at the memory.

'She even made a joke about it. Said she hoped he didn't

have cold hands. They were both smiling at each other about it. Then he touched her.' She placed two fingers side-by-side immediately below her rib cage. 'That's when she froze and then said she had to go. Like she'd remembered another urgent appointment. She grabbed her coat off the chair and left the room. It was the strangest thing I ever saw. He didn't have his fingers on her skin for more than five seconds.'

Maeve lapsed into silence, shaking her head to herself.

'Theresa on reception told us she was screaming and knocked over a display stand in the pharmacy,' Jardine said.

Maeve threw her eyes heavenwards, her voice long-suffering.

'Why am I not surprised? Theresa loves to exaggerate. Caitlin mumbled an apology and walked out the same as any other patient.'

'How did Dr Orford react?'

'Like you'd expect. He was as surprised as I was.'

'Anything else?'

Maeve considered her, as if assessing a persistent malingerer requesting a sick note on a sunny day.

'He looked worried and relieved at the same time. Worried about the potential consequences, then relieved I was in the room.'

'And you had an uninterrupted view of him touching her, did you? His body wasn't blocking your view of his hands?'

Maeve shook her head vehemently.

'There's not much point me being there if I don't make sure I can see what's going on.'

'Is there a chance he examined her previously and something happened on that occasion?' Gulliver chipped in.

'No. I checked. She was a new patient. Even if she hadn't been, Dom's behaviour was always exemplary.' She glanced at the door as if she'd heard somebody with their ear to it. 'We've had a few here that I wouldn't be so confident saying that about. But not Dom.'

'We heard a complaint had been made against him.'

Maeve looked as if she wanted to spit.

'Anyone can make a complaint. Doesn't mean it's true. That woman's a serial trouble-maker. She's the one who ought to be reported.' Looking at them as if they could think up an offence on the spot.

'Is there anything about him we ought to know?' Jardine said. 'I realise nobody likes to speak ill of the dead, but it is a murder enquiry. We're not here to judge. We don't care if he goosed one of the female members of staff at the Christmas party, if it helps us find his killer.'

Maeve laughed at Jardine's colourful example.

'I wouldn't have minded if he'd goosed me. When you get to my age, you're glad of any attention you get.'

Her eyes lost some of their focus, but neither of them thought for a moment it was because she was imagining being squeezed into a broom cupboard with Dominic Orford after they'd both had a few too many.

'What is it?' Jardine said.

Maeve waved it away, but explained anyway.

'It's nothing to do with when he worked here . . .'

She was too lost in whatever had crossed her mind to notice the effect her words had on them. Whatever came next, she couldn't have started in a way that would've grabbed their attention more forcefully.

'My younger sister was at school with him. She always said he was a bit odd. He went by his middle name, Tom. He hated Dominic. I suppose he started using it again when he became a doctor. It's got a better ring to it. Doctor Dominic Orford. Back then, everybody used to take the piss, call him Brother Dominic. You know, because Dominic sounds like a monk's name? And he got into meditation and alternative religions. I think he was even a Buddhist for a while. I'll ask Erin, if you like.'

'That'd be great,' Jardine said. 'Anything she can remember.'

'It was twenty-five years ago. I'll ask her, but don't hold your breath.'

'Did he have girlfriends at school?'

'As far as I know. He was a good-looking young man. Wasn't a bad looking older man, either. Charismatic, too, when he wanted to be.'

'Can you ask your sister if she remembers any of his girlfriends? We're particularly interested in somebody called Juliet Cross he might have gone travelling with when he was in his mid-twenties.'

If it crossed Maeve's mind that Orford should have been in the middle of his training and not swanning around the globe, she didn't show it.

'I'll ask her, but—'

'We won't hold our breath,' Gulliver finished for her.

'I TOLD YOU THERE WAS A RELIGIOUS CONNECTION,' JARDINE SAID triumphantly.

'There's a potential connection based on Maeve Kelly's recollection of what her teenage younger sister might have said about the local oddball twenty-five years ago,' Gulliver agreed. 'Does that sum it up?'

'*Jesus Christ, Craig!* Just agree for once, will you?'

'Yes.'

'Is that you agreeing to the religious connection or me telling you to agree.'

'Yes.'

'Are you the biggest dickhead ever to walk the earth?'

He wagged his finger at her, *oh no you don't.*

'It's understandable why his parents told us he wasn't religious,' she went on. 'He's not going to tell them if he'd got into some really weird stuff.'

'Human sacrifices, you mean?'

'Take the piss all you like. It all works in my mind.'

Something has to, he thought, and tried not to think too deeply about that strange and foreign land that was his partner's mind.

15

'I don't know about you,' Kincade said, as they made their way down the corridor towards the autopsy suite where Isabel Durand was scheduled to begin Dominic Orford's post mortem in the next five minutes, 'but it feels like forever since I've been down here.'

She must have installed a tracking app on my phone, Angel thought, throwing her a sideways glance to see if she was grinning knowingly at him.

'You almost sound like you've missed it.'

'Yeah, right. About as much as I'd miss a malignant tumour cut out of my colon.'

He shuddered at the graphic example but didn't reply, too busy hoping Durand didn't refer to their discussion of the previous evening.

'Afternoon, Padre,' the pathologist said breezily when they entered the sterile environment of the autopsy room, sounding as if they'd met in the park on a sunny summer's day. 'And to you, too, Sergeant Kincade.'

Good God, what's got into her? Kincade thought. *All that children's blood she drinks must be invigorating her.*

'You're full of the joys of spring, Doctor.'

'And why not, Sergeant, why not?'

How many reasons do you need? We're in a cold antiseptic room reeking of death. You're about to carve up a man until he looks like a pile of discarded scraps in a butcher's shop. Should I go on?

She glanced surreptitiously at Angel, but he was too busy avoiding her eye.

Something was up.

He normally kicked off the proceedings by reciting the last rites or playing *The Last Post* on his mouth organ while Durand pretended to be irritated at his disrespectful antics. Today, he looked as if he was holding his breath.

'Anything useful come out of that timeline we discussed, Padre?' Durand said, pulling on her gloves.

'Making progress, Isabel,' he replied, sounding as if he'd got a train line, forget about a timeline, stuck in his throat.

Just wait until I get you outside, Kincade thought, staring pointedly at the side of his averted face.

For practical purposes, Orford's body had been removed from the cross at the scene. Apart from that, he was as he'd been found, shirtless and barefoot, but still wearing his blood-soaked trousers.

Durand started her external examination from the top, with the head, immediately identifying something that hadn't been obvious at the scene. She leaned in closer, inspected his mouth with a hand-held lens.

'There are lesions on the oral commissure...'

'The oral *what?*' Angel interrupted.

Business as usual, Kincade thought, when Durand pursed her lips at him—secret liaison or not.

'The oral commissure, Padre. The place where the upper and lower lips meet.' Demonstrating on her own mouth as she said it.

'You learn something new every day,' he said, having made a point of not meeting Kincade's eye at any time when the word *oral* was in the sentence. 'Presumably he was gagged. Not by stuffing a rag into his mouth, but stretched across it and tied at the back.'

'That would be my assessment, yes. To muffle his screams.'

It was clear to everybody present that there would have been plenty of those.

Durand then continued with the extremities, moving down to Orford's wrists.

'Ligature marks are clearly evident, as we suspected.'

As I suspected, Kincade corrected under her breath.

Durand studied the puncture wound where one of the six-inch nails that had been removed at the scene had been hammered through Orford's wrist, shaking her head as she did so.

'What is it, Isabel?' Angel said, misinterpreting the gesture.

She gave him a look as if he was responsible for what she now said.

'Anyone would think the human wrist had been designed specifically for the purpose of crucifying a man. The nail has pierced the interosseous membrane which spans the space between the radius and ulna bones. It's a dense fibrous sheet of connective tissue perfect for suspending the weight of a man's upper body from. It's not even necessary to go through any bone. Not only that, the ulnar and radial arteries are spaced sufficiently far apart that you're unlikely to pierce them, which would spoil the fun if the victim bled to death quickly instead of hanging suspended for hours or days on end.'

It was a very out-of-character remark for Durand, known for sticking to an emotionless description of the wounds she documented.

'Sounds like you don't even need to know what you're doing,' Angel said.

'No. Any idiot could do it. Go through the middle and you'll be okay.'

'But the feet are different?'

'Very different, Padre,' she said moving down to the bottom end of the autopsy table. 'You've got the three cuneiform bones, the cuboid, the navicular...'

'The thigh bone's connected to the hip bone...' Kincade sang quietly to herself, and earned an elbow in the ribs from Angel as Durand continued.

'Driving a nail long enough to go through all of that, and with one foot on top of the other, is a very different kettle of fish to the wrists. I'm not surprised they decided to bind them using clothesline.'

Like the nails that had been prised out of the makeshift cross at the scene, the clothesline had been cut away to facilitate removal of the body. It would be subjected to detailed forensic examination, but for now, Durand's observations were limited to the resulting ligature marks.

'As you can see, Padre, the lower trouser legs have been pushed up before securing the ligature. I can't suggest any reason why that would be done rather than going around the trousers as well...'

'Stop them from catching fire when they used the blowtorch on his feet?'

Durand nodded approvingly.

'Your practical approach and ability to think ahead clearly matches that of the killers' own.' She smiled briefly, then went back to the body. 'The pattern of ligature marks suggests violent movement while he was constrained—'

'Someone played a blowtorch flame over my feet, I'd jerk my legs,' Kincade said.

'Exactly, Sergeant. It wouldn't surprise me to find a fracture of the fibula if the contraction was violent enough.' She took a deep breath, let it out. 'And now, the feet . . .'

'Can we re-cap before moving on?' Angel said.

'As you wish, Padre.' Making it sound like, *if we must*.

I'd have got a straight no, Kincade thought.

'I'd like to get the sequence of events clear in my mind,' Angel started. 'It's likely he was knocked unconscious . . .'

'I expect to find confirmation of that when I turn him over,' Durand agreed.

'His wrists were then secured to the cross using cable ties. They then tied his ankles to the upright member of the cross . . .'

'I shall be looking for evidence that one of them sat astride his legs while they were being secured. Depending on how long he was out for, he may have started to struggle as he came round.'

'And finally, they hammered the nails through his wrists.'

'That would be my assessment, yes. There is no other practical way to achieve it, short of having half a dozen people to hold him still. I'm not quite sure why you are so interested in the sequence, Padre.'

'It proves that the nails were solely for the purpose of punishment.'

'Not necessarily,' Kincade said. 'It might be to send a message.'

'I'll leave the two of you to work out what that might be,' Durand said. 'May I move onto the feet now?'

'I can't wait, Isabel,' Angel said, with a quick glance at the charred and puckered skin that would put him off summer barbeques for a while.

'The high pressure of a blowtorch flame applied for any length of time means we're looking at third degree burns at a minimum. A cursory inspection of the wound indicates that the flame has destroyed the epidermis and dermis. There may also be damage to the underlying bones, muscles, and tendons—what is sometimes referred to as a fourth-degree burn.'

His skin would've been bubbling like pizza topping, Angel thought, and put it in a less visceral way.

'Third, fourth or tenth degree, it would have been excruciating.'

'I don't think anybody could disagree with that, Padre. If they were after information, and he had it, he would have given it to them. I hope for his sake he had something to satisfy them quickly.' She held up a cautionary finger. 'Don't even think about asking me whether the flame was applied for longer than was strictly necessary as added punishment.'

'The fatal knife wound suggests they were done with punishment, wanted to end the job quickly.'

Durand nodded her agreement, moving back up the body to inspect the chest wound.

'A clean, two-inch-wide incision between the fourth and fifth ribs to the left of the sternum,' she said, glancing at Kincade. 'As you'll be aware, Sergeant, the inferior tip of the heart, the apex, lies to the left of the sternum between the junction of the fourth and fifth ribs near their articulation with the costal cartilages.'

Kincade smiled back like a cruising great white shark.

'I was aware of that, Doctor, yes. It's also my understanding that the average distance from the heart to the rib cage is one-and-a-half to two inches. Since two thirds of the heart's mass is located to the left of the body's midline, it would be entirely possible to pierce it with an everyday kitchen knife with a four-inch blade given the location of the wound. Or, if you want to be on the safe side, a six-inch carving knife. The two-inch-wide incision would also suggest a carving knife.'

'You took the words out of my mouth, Sergeant,' Durand

said, sounding as if she wanted to take Kincade's eyes out of their sockets with her fingernails.

Angel stepped in before the two women started hissing at each other.

'It sounds as if whoever did it knew what they were doing.'

'Definitely,' Durand confirmed. Then, with a look Kincade's way, 'However, five minutes on the internet would provide you with all the information you'd require. Any idiot can use the internet.'

That didn't work out how I planned it, Angel thought, and tried again.

'So we're looking at a fatal haemorrhage as the cause of death?'

'Given the position of the wound and the absence of any others sufficiently serious, it's looking that way.'

'Could you flip him over and take a look at the back of his head before we go?'

Durand's look said she could, but she didn't appreciate having her routine dictated to her. She stepped back for the mortuary assistants to turn the body over, nonetheless. A quick inspection of the back of Orford's head while parting his hair with her fingers was all she needed.

'There is evidence of blunt force trauma consistent with his being knocked unconscious. Minimal bleeding suggests something flat, like a plank of wood. It doesn't look too severe, so the period of unconsciousness wouldn't have lasted long. Hopefully we'll find trace evidence on his trousers if one of them sat astride his legs while he was coming to.' She raised an eyebrow at him. 'I assume you'll be leaving now? Before I begin the internal examination?'

He worked a look of regret onto his face, into his voice.

'I'd love to stay, but—'

'Fresh air calls,' Kincade interjected. 'It's been a pleasure, Doctor. As always.'

'The pleasure's all mine, Sergeant.'

Which gland is responsible for producing insincerity? Angel thought, steering Kincade by the elbow out of the room.

He soon wished he'd left her to continue sparring with the pathologist.

'*I did a search on the internet on how long it takes to train as a GP,*' she said, working a sing-song note into her voice as she mimicked him. 'I'll have to stop calling Durand Doctor Death and start calling her Doctor Internet.'

'I checked the details with her afterwards,' he lied, hoping she didn't also remember that Claire had been a doctor.

'Really? Funny pillow talk, if you ask me.'

'You've used that line before.'

'People have said the world isn't flat lots of times. Doesn't mean it isn't true.'

'I'm thinking about ordering you back in there for the internal examination.'

'I'm thinking about being insubordinate.'

He stopped walking, gawped at her.

'*Thinking about?*'

She shrugged, resumed walking.

'Okay, you got me. *Sir.*'

'You know, that word sounds really strange coming out of your mouth. Maybe it'll sound better with practice.'

'I'm not sure we'll ever find out.'

At least we're agreed on something, he thought, as they came out into the much-needed fresh air.

16

'C'mon boy, walkies time,' Graeme Laing said, working an enthusiasm he didn't feel into his voice, the leash swinging from his hand.

The black Labrador that had been snoring contentedly in its basket in front of the radiator raised its head, looked disapprovingly at the swinging leash and settled back down again. Closed its eyes.

What you can't see can't hurt you.

Laing crouched down, gave the dog a brisk rub behind the ears, more of a command in his voice now.

'C'mon, Harvey. I need this, even if you don't.'

The dog knew there was no point arguing. It yawned second-hand dog food in Laing's face, got to its feet and stretched. Then went to wait by the front door while Laing got his Barbour jacket on and his waxed-cotton flat cap. It was threatening to rain, and it didn't hurt to play safe.

He patted his jacket pocket to make sure he had everything he needed, then let them out, the dog trotting ahead of him, looking for places to cock its leg.

From Brookvale Road they bore left at the mini-roundabout

onto Blenheim Avenue, then left again and straight down Oakmount Avenue. At the far end, they went through the two bollards between the old brick gateposts, crossed Lover's Walk and through the trees before crossing The Avenue—the main North-South route into the town centre—and from there onto Southampton Common proper.

Harvey led the way on the familiar route towards the Model Yachting Pond, the occasional jogger and fellow dog-walkers paying them no attention. They walked an anti-clockwise lap of the pond as they always did, then headed north-west towards Ornamental Lake. Once there, Laing sat on what he thought of as *his* bench overlooking the wind-ruffled water. Harvey got comfortable by his feet.

In the old days, Harvey wouldn't have sat still for a moment. He'd have been chasing squirrels and ducks, although he'd always been wary of the hissing Canada geese. Laing would even have thrown a tennis ball for him to fetch when he'd scared off all the wildlife.

These days, they were both content to sit and think—in Laing's case—or snooze, in Harvey's. Except Laing didn't only think. Thinking was thirsty work. And sometimes the things he thought about made him reach for the hip flask in his pocket for reasons other than to slake his thirst.

He took a nip of whisky now, the dog's nose twitching at the familiar smell. Felt its warmth sliding down his gullet as the equally-familiar thoughts plagued him.

Where had the last twelve years gone?
Would he ever find the peace that answers bring?
Did he even care anymore?

Except today was different, an additional thought drowning out the old favourites.

Should he have called the phone number on the note, after all?

Harvey raised his head at the sound of an angler at one of

the nearby fishing platforms landing a decent-sized fish. In those far-off old days, Harvey would've gone to investigate, made a nuisance of himself. Now, it was as if he, too, was tired of life. To be fair, he had a lot less of his left than Laing did.

The fisherman decided to go out on a high, not sit for another hour and perhaps catch nothing more. He packed up his tackle and headed for home, nodding amiably to Laing as he walked past, the two men vaguely recognising each other.

'How big was it?' Laing asked, thinking he shouldn't allow himself to withdraw completely from the human race.

'Six-and-a-half-pound common carp.'

'Nice way to end the day.'

'Yeah. Do you fish?'

Laing held his hand horizontally three feet off the ground.

'Not since I was this high. The amount of time I spend sitting here, I might as well bring a rod with me.'

The angler smiled and resumed walking. Laing took another sip once he was out of sight. He might be a saddo drinking his life away on a park bench, but that didn't mean he wanted people thinking it. Just a quick sip, mind, not taking the time to admire the beauty of the flask itself with its graceful curves, feel the smoothness of old silver in his hand. Except that had nothing to do with keeping his drink problem away from prying eyes.

It was the inscription engraved into the flask that caused him to close his eyes each time he tipped it to his lips, the loving words turned to bitter accusation in the bleak wasteland of his heart.

Daytime went and evening came over the course of the next hour and a half as he sat there, the temperature dropping steadily. He pushed himself to his feet when the inner warmth from the whisky lost the battle against the cooling wind, and headed home. The sky was clear and cloudless, a quarter moon providing more than enough illumination. Not that he nor Harvey needed it. They could both have found their way home blindfolded.

He touched his cap in a salute to the pond and his bench —*see you tomorrow*—oblivious to the fact that his depressing, soul-destroying routine would soon be brought to an abrupt and unwelcome end.

TEN MILES AWAY, ANGEL WAS SITTING OVERLOOKING A DIFFERENT stretch of water. After Dominic Orford's autopsy and the graphic way it brought home what had been done to him, he'd felt the need for fresh air. He'd called Vanessa Corrigan, suggested they meet for a drink and a bite to eat at The Titchfield Mill, a country pub restaurant situated halfway between his home and where she lived in Southsea in Portsmouth.

The pub was housed in the converted mill buildings and had a number of cosy, wood-panelled bars, but he opted to sit outside on the raised deck overlooking the River Meon while he waited for Vanessa to arrive.

She was ten minutes late and wore faded jeans and a plain white shirt under a floral duster coat, her long dark hair tied back in a ponytail at the nape of her neck. A deliberate attempt to dress as differently as possible to the tailored and sober business suits she favoured for work as Deputy Governor of HMP Isle of Wight.

'How was your day?' she said, after he got back from the bar with a glass of Sauvignon Blanc for her and a half of Proper Job to top up the pint he'd bought when he first arrived.

'As good as can be expected when you've spent the afternoon attending an autopsy.' He swept his hand in an expansive arc, took in the beer garden and the river beyond it, the trees on the other side moving gently in the breeze. 'Hence the need for fresh air and good company.'

She smiled, raised her glass towards him.

'That's a different sort of compliment. I've never thought of myself as an antidote for watching dead bodies being cut up. How was he killed?'

'Crucified.'

Maybe it was her job, the need to stay calm and collected whatever the men in her charge got up to, but she didn't bat an eyelid.

'That's different, too.'

'It's my first, yes.'

'I bet the team are making the most of it. Twelve suspects? What did he have for his last supper? Keeping an ear out for banging in the morgue after three days.'

'You're as bad as them.' Thinking, *probably worse*. 'So, what about you?'

'Same old, same old. Torturing prisoners in the secret subterranean cells...'

The flippant remark was a little too close for comfort. Not only the parallel with what had been done to Dominic Orford, but also an unwelcome reminder about the situation with Virgil Balan and what that might lead to.

She leaned towards him, rested her hand on his when she saw his expression.

'I'm kidding. It's not the nineteen seventies. Although sometimes I wish it was.'

The continued joking only served to reinforce what he became aware of every time they met. She knew everything about him—except for the developing situation with Balan—whereas he knew precisely nothing about her.

It hadn't taken long before he'd realised that was how she

liked it, always finding a way to deflect his questions whenever he'd tried to focus the conversation on her.

He was about to try again now, when she headed him off before he'd even started.

'I want to ask a favour. I'm going up to London next weekend to stay with an old friend...'

He raised an eyebrow at her.

'*Female*,' she said, her smile growing wider. 'The thing is, she's allergic to dogs. How do you feel about dog-sitting Jasper?'

'No problem. At your house or mine?'

'Up to you.' She paused, the mischief in her eyes telling him what was coming next. 'If you stay at mine, you'll be able to root through my drawers while I'm not there.'

He matched her, grin for grin.

'I'd rather wait until you're there in person.' Almost saying, in *them*.

'Are you sure your mother won't mind having him in the house?'

'She's staying with my sister for the weekend.'

She narrowed her eyes at him. Trying to decide whether he was teasing because she'd just told him she was away for the weekend herself.

'I'm not sure I believe you.'

'Reschedule your friend and find out.'

'I can't. It's taken forever to arrange. Besides, she's very needy.'

'As well as being allergic to dogs.'

'She's vegan, too.'

'This is the person I'm playing second fiddle to, is it? A needy vegan who's allergic to dogs? Has she got a problem with personal hygiene, as well?'

'Now that you mention it...'

They both took a sip of their drinks, enjoying the gentle flirting. Then she put her hand on his a second time.

'Any other time, I'd say come back to mine tonight, but we're in the middle of an inspection. I shouldn't really have come out tonight at all.'

He nodded like now he understood the score.

'So now it's a bunch of jobsworths with clipboards making sure the prisoners have got big enough TVs in their cells who're pushing me aside?'

'Afraid so. You have no idea how much I'd love you to say that to them.'

He leaned in closer, dropped his voice.

'If I stay at your place tonight, I'd have time to catch the first ferry with you tomorrow morning, say it to them, and still be at work on time.'

'Is your salary sufficient to support us both after I get fired?'

He scrunched his face.

'I knew there'd be a fly in the ointment.'

The evening carried on in the same vein until she made an early night of it, claiming she still had work to do if she even got to bed at all.

Jilted in favour of a bunch of jobsworths, he thought watching her drive away. *Whatever next?*

17

'Ruby is better than ground penetrating radar any day of the week,' PC Matt Holder said proudly, sounding as if he'd fathered his German shepherd himself, as he let her out of the back of his liveried *Avon and Somerset Police Dog Section* Skoda in the lane bordering Kilstock Court.

Listening to his thick West Country accent, DS Dave Garfield wouldn't be surprised if he actually had. Winter nights can be long and lonely in rural Somerset

'GPR doesn't eat as much as a cadaver dog does,' Vicky Cook pointed out. 'Or—'

'Ruby didn't cost anything in the first place,' Holder countered, cutting her off before she became too graphic. 'She was a rescue dog before we got her. Half-dead from malnutrition due to her crack-addict owner not feeding her.' He reached down, gave the dog an encouraging pat on the shoulder. 'Okay, lead on.'

Garfield led the way, following the same route he had previously. There were six of them in all, if you included the dog. Garfield, Cook, Holder, and two uniformed PCs armed with shovels. They all entered the field bordering the grounds of Kilstock Court twenty yards down the lane from where the sender of the email would have parked. As before, they kept off the unploughed verge, climbing the barbed-wire fence at the same spot Garfield had used the last time. Ruby easily leapt right over.

A quarter mile later they were standing at the edge of the trees surrounding the clearing behind the boathouse. Holder let Ruby off the leash, and they all stood back to watch her do her stuff, zig-zagging up and down the clearing, nose glued to the ground, tail wagging furiously.

'You owe me,' Vicky whispered to Garfield as Holder watched his baby at work.

'How did you persuade the boss to give the thumbs up?'

She raised an eyebrow at him.

'Do you really want to know?'

'Probably not,' Garfield admitted.

'GPR wouldn't be any good around here,' Holder said without taking his eyes off Ruby and still singing her praises. 'High electrical conductivity in fine-grained sediments such as clay and silt causes signal loss. There's plenty of that around here. Rocky ground scatters the signal, too.'

'Sounds like you're better off with a dog every time,' Cook said, with a wink at Garfield.

'They're amazing,' Holder went on, unaware of what had passed between the two detectives. 'They can tell the difference between decomposing animal and human remains, and even different types of decomposition. They can smell remains buried up to fifteen feet underground, or thirty metres underwater.'

'How do you actually train them?' Vicky said, Holder's enthusiasm putting a temporary dent in her scepticism and mocking attitude.

Holder laughed, then looked a little uncomfortable answering.

'The dogs associate the odour of a dead body with play. They're trained to look for decomposing remains as if they're playing fetch.'

'I bet they're disappointed when they're not allowed to eat what they find.' She pointed across the clearing at where Ruby was now sitting watching them, her mocking tone back. 'GPR doesn't get tired, either.'

Holder shook his head as he looked where Ruby waited, his excitement palpable.

'She's not tired. That's what she does when she's onto something.' He set off across the clearing, the others following close behind.

'It's hard to tell who's more excited,' Vicky whispered as Holder spent a solid minute congratulating and petting his canine partner.

'It's all yours,' Garfield said to the waiting uniformed officers with an expansive sweep of his arm. 'Give us a shout if you get tired and I'll get Vicky here to take over.'

She gave him a look that told him she hadn't been joking earlier about favours.

'I think you're forgetting who owes who, Sarge.'

The two PCs set to it, putting their backs into it as they dug carefully and methodically.

'What's the success rate?' Garfield asked Holder.

The dog handler rocked his hand.

'Anything between sixty-five and ninety-five per cent in trials. Obviously, it's impossible to say in the field because you don't know if there was a body there in the first place.'

An hour later and Garfield was starting to think that even sixty-five per cent might be on the optimistic side as the piles of earth grew steadily higher. He was in the hole now, taking his turn. It was better than sitting watching, waiting, feeling the excitement drain slowly away with every empty shovel of dirt.

Vicky, who hadn't contributed anything to the growing pile of earth, caught his expression when he paused to wipe the sweat out of his eyes.

'Maybe Ruby's having an off day.'

Yeah, and I'll be the laughing stock of the station, Garfield thought, and went back to digging.

Holder heard the remark, but ignored it, his eyes scanning the expanding hole for the first sight of bone or clothing.

It was another fifteen minutes before he saw it, his arm rigid as he pointed.

'*There!*'

Garfield and the uniformed PC stopped digging, climbed out of what was now officially a shallow grave and rested on their shovels. The other uniformed cop brushed the soil gently away with a blue-gloved hand, then sat back on his heels, the satisfaction of a job well done in his voice.

'Looks like a human skull, if you ask me.'

'There's no avoiding the long arm of the paw,' Holder laughed and patted his panting dog, groans of complaint from Vicky and the sweating PCs filling the air.

If Garfield hadn't been too busy thinking how the woman behind the *never_forgotten2012@gmail.com* email address wasn't such a time-wasting crank after all, he'd have happily brained him with his shovel.

'Looks like you could've held your breath, after all,' Maeve Kelly said, when she'd been put through to Gulliver.

His pulse immediately picked up at how pleased she sounded with herself.

'You spoke to your sister? Erin, wasn't it?'

'You've got a good memory.'

And a notebook, he thought, and didn't spoil the illusion.

'Did she remember any of Dominic Orford's past girlfriends?'

'She had a crush on him, but he wasn't interested in her. So she remembers the names of all the girls who he *was* interested in.'

'She used to stick pins in dolls of them?'

Maeve laughed with him, then ran through a list of names that meant nothing to him. He didn't know if it was random chance or she deliberately left the best to last, finally mentioning the name he was interested in.

'And she remembers Juliet Cross, although she's Juliet Sharp now.'

'Does she have contact details for her?'

He listened patiently while Maeve took him through a convoluted chain of associations involving friends of friends and ex-husbands and brothers-in-law and Facebook friends and the local Women's Institute and the book club until all he wanted to do was scream down the phone at her.

Yes, or bloody no?

Jardine was watching him, the grin on her face growing wider in line with his frustration as he made a circular, rolling motion in the air with his hand.

'So, yes, I've got a phone number and an address for her,' Maeve said finally. 'Have you got a pencil ready?'

If we were talking face-to-face, you'd know whether I've got a pencil or not, he thought. *Although I'd have to pull it out again to be ready to use it.*

'Ready when you are, Ms Kelly.' He scribbled the details down as Maeve recited them, slammed the phone down with barely a word of thanks or goodbye. '*Halle-fucking-lujah!* I thought you liked to talk, but you're almost mute compared to her.'

'You need to learn how to interrupt.'

'Not much chance of that, is there? Not spending all day with you.' He started punching in the number Maeve had given him. 'It better be bloody worth it.'

That remained to be seen, but five minutes later they had an appointment with Juliet Sharp, née Cross.

'Let's hope she doesn't talk as much as Maeve,' Jardine said, a mischievous smile on her lips as they headed out.

'I'm staying in the car if she does. The two of you can battle it out for gob of the year.'

'I READ ABOUT IT IN THE PAPER,' JULIET SHARP SAID, HER BACK TO them as she busied herself making tea. 'It took a minute before I realised it was him. We all called him Tom when I knew him. Is it really true he was crucified?'

'That's not the sort of thing the paper would make up,' Gulliver said, avoiding a direct answer and getting a slack-jawed look from Jardine that Juliet didn't see.

Juliet shuddered, horror mixing with relief that she hadn't stayed with him in her voice.

'It's made me come over all funny to think I might know something that might be connected to him being killed like that. Do you think I might be in danger?'

In danger of taking what you watch on TV too seriously, Jardine thought, and said something different.

'Definitely not. Going back to Dominic, we understand he suffered a nervous breakdown in the middle of training to be a doctor.'

'That's right. The pressure had been building for a while. It's actually how we hooked up again. He was spending most of his free time back home with his parents and we bumped into each other in Bishop's Waltham. We'd been in a relationship before he went off to university.' She smiled the smile of the girl who'd been left behind when her boyfriend threw off his small-town shackles. 'That came to an end when he started meeting new people, but then we picked it up again. Shortly after that, he suffered the breakdown, and his parents sent him to a private clinic in London.'

'Do you know anything about his time in the clinic?'

'Not really. Except it wasn't anything like in *One Flew Over the Cuckoo's Nest*.'

Jardine smiled with her, moved on.

'And afterwards, you went travelling together? Recuperation for him. What about you?'

A scowl passed over Juliet's face. It seemed to Jardine it started at the first mention of going travelling, rather than a reaction to the question about Juliet's own circumstances.

'I was in a dead-end job I hated. It was no loss to give it up.' She dropped her eyes to the table top. 'If I'm honest, I was hoping the relationship with Tom . . . I mean Dominic . . . would stay permanent this time, and I might not have to worry about a career going forward.' She looked directly at Jardine, a woman who had clearly decided she wanted a career for herself, to see if there was any criticism or scorn in her face. She carried on when she saw none. 'This sounds so awful, but I knew that even if he didn't go back to medicine, his parents were loaded. He had plans to work at his father's company after we got back from travelling while he made up his mind about being a doctor. I even thought he could get me a job there if I wanted one, without having to go through all that horrible interview process.' She looked at them both, now. 'You must think I'm so shallow.'

About a thousandth of an inch, Jardine thought, and kept it off her face while Gulliver said the right thing.

'Not at all.'

Juliet smiled gratefully, not caring if it was sincere or not. She then dipped deeper into her personal well of shame.

'That's also how I was able to go travelling. I didn't have any money saved up. I couldn't have afforded to give up work and spend three months on a beach. But Dominic was happy to pay for us both. His parents' answer to his breakdown was to throw money at it. They paid for the best clinic in London. Then told him, take off for as long as you like, we'll pay for it all. Just come back the person you used to be.'

'Can you tell us a bit about the trip itself?' Gulliver said.

The scowl was immediately back on Juliet's face, and Jardine knew she'd been right earlier.

'There's not a lot to tell. The plan was to spend a while touring Europe, then head south. Dom always wanted to go to Marrakesh. After that, head east towards Thailand and Bali, stop off in India on the way. It was pretty flexible. Stay longer in one place if we liked it, move on if we didn't.'

'That doesn't sound like *not a lot to tell* to me,' Gulliver said. 'Didn't it work out like you'd planned?'

'Not for me, it didn't. We started in Scandinavia. Flew to Stockholm, then Copenhagen and from there to Hamburg, ending up in Amsterdam after we'd been travelling for about ten days.'

'Amsterdam's great,' Jardine said, sounding like she wished she was relaxing in one of the city's many brown bars.

'I felt the same,' Juliet said, the sour twist to her lips at odds with the words. 'To begin with. Then we met *her*.' Making it sound like a cross between Myra Hindley and the antichrist.

Gulliver and Jardine shared a look. If they'd found whoever *she* was nailed to a home-made cross, they'd be putting the cuffs on Juliet right about now. As it was, the depth of loathing behind that one small word, *her*, was sufficient to make them come alert.

'Met who?' Jardine said. 'What was the woman's name?'

'Jasmijn. I never found out her last name.'

'It sounds like you didn't want to. I know this is hard—'

'Not any more, it isn't. I got over it a long time ago.'

'What exactly happened?'

Juliet got up and went to the fridge, took a bottle of chilled water out, filled a glass.

You'll need more than water to wash the bitterness out of your mouth, Jardine thought.

'It started out okay,' Juliet went on, eyes out of focus, the flare to her nostrils suggesting she could tell herself she'd put it behind her until the cows came home, but that didn't make it true. 'We met them in a bar. She was with a guy with a big beard whose name I can't remember. Doesn't matter. We never saw him again. With hindsight, I should've noticed the way Dominic and Jasmijn hit it off. There was a chemistry between them that was never there with us. Dominic was really into alternative religions when he was younger, and so was she—at least that's what she claimed. Anyway, we all agreed to meet up the next day. Except it was only her. After that, we couldn't get rid of her. Not that Dominic wanted to. He was completely obsessed with her.'

'I'm guessing you said something to him about it,' Jardine said.

Juliet gave a quick flash of her eye teeth, remembered malice in her eyes.

'You bet I did.' She waved her hand angrily in the air. 'I won't bore you with the details, but I came home the very next day. I reckon he was in her knickers before I'd boarded the plane. As far as I know, he went on the trip we'd planned to do together with her. I never saw or heard from him again, so I can't say for sure.'

'You wouldn't know if he brought her home with him?'

Juliet shook her head, eyes still out of focus.

'Sorry. He was so obsessed with her it wouldn't surprise me if he'd married her.'

'His wife's called Louise,' Gulliver said. 'They didn't meet until after he qualified as a doctor. Do you know anything at all about this woman, Jasmijn?'

Juliet finished the water in her glass as she thought about it, then re-filled it from the tap, even though the bottle was still half-full.

'Not really. She was Dutch. Lived in Amsterdam. She was a few years older than us.' Her mouth twisted into a sour moue to match the bitterness in her words. 'The sort of real woman who can teach a young man like Dominic a thing or two about life. I didn't have a chance once she set her sights on him.'

'Was that how it was?' Jardine said.

'Definitely. That's not me trying to make myself feel better, instead of thinking he was bored with me and looking for someone new. She went after him.' Glaring at Jardine as if she could imagine her doing the same.

'I don't suppose you've got any photographs?' Gulliver said, knowing it was a waste of breath as the words rolled out.

'I would've destroyed them years ago, but I don't think I ever had any. Dominic's probably got millions of them.'

'Not if things ended badly with her, as well.'

Juliet immediately brightened at the prospect.

'That's true. He obviously didn't stay with her.'

Gulliver was aware that he shouldn't be asking what he now did, inviting Juliet to speculate based on a few days spent together fifteen years previously.

'Do you think she was the sort of woman who would bear a grudge if she thought he'd wronged her?'

'Definitely. She was a real bitch. She knew exactly what she wanted, and God help anybody who got in the way or crossed her.' She gave a dismissive, self-aware shrug. 'That might be the bitterness at being rejected in me talking.'

They both shared an unspoken thought as they called it a day and left Juliet to her resentful memories.

Yes, but that doesn't mean you're the only one who's bitter.

18

'You should've brought this to me earlier, Dave,' DI Jay Chopra said.

Yeah, right, Garfield thought. *It would've been a different story if we hadn't found anything.*

'Well done, anyway.' Slapping Garfield on the back as he said it.

Here it comes, Garfield thought. *I'll take it from here...*

'Are you happy taking the lead on this?' Chopra said, instead.

'Absolutely, sir.'

An hour earlier and he wouldn't have been so enthusiastic. Being nominated as the SIO would have been something of a poisoned chalice, had they not already had an early piece of good luck—the victim had been wearing a gold necklace when they went into the ground. Currently, it looked like a piece of scrap metal, but who knows what it might lead to once it was cleaned up.

They were still at the burial site, as were a large number of SOCOs and the pathologist, busy inside the crime scene tent that had been erected over the shallow grave.

The majority of the skeleton—now nothing more than a collection of disarticulated bones after the connective tissue had degraded—had been recovered and bagged, waiting to be transferred to the pathologist's lab. There, it would be reassembled and examined in detail with the assistance of a forensic anthropologist, a botanist, a geologist and any other *ists* who wanted to give their two pennyworth.

Hearing them talking outside, the pathologist, Dr Howard Lowe, took a breather from the cramped, claustrophobic tent to step outside. He carried an evidence bag containing the skull in his hands, as if returning to his seat from the prize table at a Royal College of Pathologists charity raffle.

'You never look happier than when you've got decomposing human remains in your hand, Doc,' Chopra said.

'And you, Jay, never look happier than when I tell you what they tell me.'

Garfield was getting a little lost following who was telling who what, but waited to see what the pathologist was prepared to commit to without the benefit of a full examination in the lab.

'Subject to all the usual caveats,' Lowe started, 'the overall size and shape of the skull as well as the appearance of the brow bone and jaw would suggest a female. It's not conclusive, of course. A woman can have a square jaw and a man can have a small head.'

'What about a child?' Garfield said.

'It's possible, although the skull is pretty much adult size by the age of ten, so size alone won't tell you.' He indicated the squiggly line running the length of the skull. 'As you can see, the sagittal suture is not yet completely fused. That suggests we're looking at someone younger than thirty-five.' He then turned the skull this way and that, showing them every part of it, as if, after winning it in the raffle, he was hoping to sell it to them. 'You'll notice a complete lack of obvious trauma. No fractures or holes. However, the same can't be said for the hyoid bone.'

'It's fractured?' Garfield said, almost expecting Lowe to produce it from his pocket.

'It is. Suggesting the victim was strangled. That may or may not be the cause of death, of course. The victim might have been stabbed as well, for example. From a cursory inspection of the ribs I haven't seen any nicks that might have been caused by a blade, but the victim might have been stabbed in the stomach, for example, which would now be impossible to determine . . .'

'I think we'll work on the basis of strangulation for now,' Chopra said, clearly as keen as Garfield was to stop the pathologist from listing all the things that might have happened that it would now be impossible to prove.

Lowe nodded, *as you wish*, then tapped the skull with his finger.

'As I said, I'm not relying on this as an indicator of sex and age. The pelvis is a far more reliable indicator. Its width suggests we have a young female. I'll check for pitting and parturition scars once it's cleaned up, then I can let you know whether she'd ever given birth.'

Garfield's head was immediately filled with the desk sergeant, Nick Ensign's words.

The call handlers put a young woman through. She wanted to know who was in charge of mispers. I gave her your name.

Have we just dug up your sister? he asked himself. He gave the shallow grave that his perseverance and gut instinct had led them to a last look, then followed behind Jay Chopra as they made their way back towards their cars.

Lowe watched them go, then went past the tent and around to the side of the boathouse. Looking out across the small lake and the trees beyond it to where he knew the house sat hidden from view, a very different thought troubling his mind.

Were all the rumours true, after all?

'I WAS STARTING TO THINK YOU'RE AVOIDING ME,' STUART Beckford said, when Angel finally decided to answer the call.

Well done, Stu. Good to see those detective's skills haven't deserted you.

'Don't be ridiculous.'

In truth, he *had* been avoiding him. He'd needed to allow himself time until he was confident he wouldn't lay into Beckford for putting all the blame on him about giving Virgil Balan the go ahead.

Beckford snorted down the line at him.

'You're confusing me with somebody who's never met you before. Anyway, I wanted to apologise for Cath coming in the other day and giving you a hard time.'

'Don't worry about it. I get the feeling I got off lightly compared to you.'

Beckford gave a nervous, stuttering laugh that made Angel think of a man cowering in a corner under the onslaught of his wife's fury.

'Don't remind me.'

'Have you sorted it out between yourselves?'

Beckford was back to snorting.

'Cath thinks she has. She said if Balan finds Florescu and we go to Romania, she might not be there when I get home. She's taking it as read that we'll beat Florescu to a pulp in a filthy basement cell in some medieval Romanian prison.'

Maybe we will, Angel thought, something coming alive in his gut he didn't want to analyse, lest it look like excited anticipation.

'She's watched too many bloody horror movies, if you ask me,' Beckford complained.

'I hope you didn't tell her that.'

'I'd be speaking in a much higher voice if I had.'

'Do you want me to call Balan off?'

Immediately, he regretted the choice of words. It was too late. Beckford was on it in a flash.

'*See!* You make him sound like an attack dog.'

Yes, one with perfect English and impeccable manners, but who knows what that hides on the inside.

'Is that yes or no?'

'I don't bloody know.'

And I sound like a man who does? Angel thought.

They ended the pointless discussion with an agreement for them both to give it some more thought.

Except Angel knew in his heart that if he went at all, he would go alone.

'YOU LOOK LIKE YOUR DOG JUST DIED,' KINCADE SAID, COMING back into the room after re-filling the coffee machine water tank in the ladies' toilets.

He was very grateful she'd been out of the room when Beckford called. Although if she hadn't been, he wouldn't have needed to lie.

'It's the prospect of having to talk to Orford's parents yet again.'

Kincade rolled her eyes in agreement.

'I know what you mean. I can feel the Chief Constable's name being dropped into the conversation soon. And the word *harassment*. You'll probably hear *grieving parents*, too.'

'Maybe if they told us the whole truth, didn't drip feed it to us when they can't squirm out of it, we wouldn't need to.'

She held up her hands, *whoa.*

'You don't need to convince me. So? Shall we go?'

He got up and shrugged his jacket on, hoping the irritation and bad temper Beckford's call had brought on had subsided by the time they got there.

No, that's not true, he thought, following Kincade out of the room. *I hope it festers all the way there.*

Nigel Orford's face said it for him when he opened the door to them half an hour later.

You again!

His actual words made sure they got the message.

'What is it this time?'

Drip, drip, drip, Angel wanted to say, *here comes the truth little by little*.

'Just a few things we'd like to clarify, Mr Orford.'

'Who is it, Nigel?' came from inside the house, his wife's voice. She appeared at his shoulder. '*Oh!* It's you.'

Don't you mean, you again? Angel thought as Orford stepped aside, ushered them in with as much bad grace as he could muster.

Both Orfords stayed where they were after Nigel Orford closed the front door, clearly hoping that remaining in the hall would ensure a brief discussion.

Hope on, Angel thought, and headed for the conservatory where they'd held the first interview. Kincade gestured to the Orfords, *after you*, and they all trooped through the house to where the afternoon sun warmed the back of the house.

Angel dropped into the nearest rattan armchair, waited for everybody else to seat themselves.

'I can see from your face that you're getting as sick of this as we are, Mr Orford.' He glanced at Helen Orford. 'Although not as sick of it as you, Mrs Orford. So, unless you want to make this a regular feature of your lives, why don't you stop forcing us to squeeze every little bit of information out of you and start volunteering what you know, in the hope of catching the people who murdered your son.'

Neither Orford said anything. Nobody played the stupid card, claiming they didn't know what he was talking about. No bluster from Nigel Orford, no snooty nose in the air—*how dare you, you grubby little policeman*—from Helen. The Chief Constable's name went unspoken.

'We talked to Juliet Cross,' Angel went on. 'She told us she came home from Europe after only ten days because your son became infatuated with a woman they'd met called Jasmijn. She thinks he continued the trip with her.'

'She also thinks Jasmijn had an agenda,' Kincade cut in.

Angel nodded his thanks, went back to the Orfords, both admiring the terracotta-tiled floor with its little diamond-shaped inserts.

'Is that true? Please bear in mind what I said about volunteering information. Do not feel obliged to limit yourselves to monosyllabic *yes* or *no* answers.' He leaned back in his chair, *the floor's all yours*.

Nigel Orford took a deep breath. Angel hoped it signified a decision to tell everything he knew. He wouldn't bet money on it.

'Dominic spent three months travelling in total. He was with Jasmijn for the whole of that time. I assume you're not interested in where they went?'

'Not unless you think it's relevant,' Angel said.

"They didn't go to Jerusalem to visit the site of Christ's crucifixion, if that's what you mean,' Helen snapped.

Angel smiled at her.

'It wasn't, Mrs Orford, but thank you for that, anyway. We can't ever have too much information in a case like this.' He went back to her husband. 'Did Jasmijn return to the UK with your son?'

'She did—'

'But we never met her.' Helen again.

'Why was that?' Addressing Orford. There was no need to address questions to Helen. She'd answer when she felt like it, whoever he asked.

'This is only my personal opinion,' Orford said. 'but I always thought Dominic wanted to introduce her to us, but she wasn't interested.'

Angel thought about the implications, threw out the most obvious one.

'Was she trying to isolate him from his family and other friends?'

'That's what we thought, yes.'

'And he was happy to go along with that?'

'So it would appear.'

'I'm sure she had her ways of manipulating him,' Helen said.

And you'd know about things like that might have felt appropriate to Angel, but he kept it to himself. What he did say wasn't a lot better.

'Why did you lie about her?'

'We didn't lie,' Helen said, almost before the question was out.

Angel gave her a long-suffering look everybody in the room interpreted correctly.

I'm not here to play word games.

He re-phrased the question.

'Why didn't you tell us about her? We're looking for unusual events in your son's life that may be behind his death. He dumped his regular girlfriend—'

'They'd only been together again for a short while.'

'You're splitting hairs, Mrs Orford. He dumped Juliet, took up with a controlling older woman and went on a three-month trip with her—'

'That *you* paid for,' Kincade added pointedly, and got a sour look—*don't think we've forgotten*—from both Orfords.

'That's the sort of situation you must have known we'd be interested in,' Angel said. 'The fact that you didn't mention it makes me wonder if you know something about her, and the time Dominic spent with her, that you don't want to tell us. The implication is that it's something bad.'

'I can assure you we know nothing about her,' Orford said, as Angel and Kincade both fixed them with uncompromising stares. 'We said nothing about her because we knew we'd only end up in this exact situation, telling you we know nothing about her.'

And me not believing you, Angel thought, and said something different that had a small chance of being answered truthfully.

'How did it end?'

He knew he was wrong about the truth as soon as Orford opened his mouth.

'We don't know. One day it was all over and Dominic refused to talk about it. We tried to bring the subject up once or twice but soon gave up.'

'Was he upset about it?' Kincade asked. 'Relieved? Or did it send him back into the darkest days of his breakdown?'

'It didn't do that, thank God,' Helen said, effectively not answering for both of them.

'Do you have any idea what happened to her?'

'None whatsoever,' both Orfords answered together, as if reading from a script.

'This was while he was working for your company before going back to his medical studies, was it?'

'That's right,' Orford said.

'Where was he living?'

Orford hesitated momentarily before answering.

'Here, with us.'

'Wasn't that a bit claustrophobic? He worked with you all day long, and he was living here with you as well.' She glanced around the large conservatory. 'It's a big house, but even so. I couldn't have done that with my parents.'

'That might say something about you or your parents,' Helen said, the enjoyment she took from it written all over her face, 'but we didn't have a problem and nor did Dominic.'

'One last thing,' Angel said, getting to his feet, the Orfords up on theirs almost before him. 'Did Dominic ever have any contact with her after this time?'

'If he did, he never told us,' Orford said.

Clever answer, Angel thought, bringing the interview to a close.

'How much more do you think they're withholding?' Angel said, as they drove down the Orford's drive, the ancient cobblestones rumbling under the car's tyres.

'At least double what they did say.'

'And how much of that was lies?'

The answer didn't come as quickly this time as she ran through the interview in her head.

'I believe they never met Jasmijn. Helen Orford would've made specific catty remarks about her if they had.'

He smiled at the way her mind worked.

'That's an unusual test to apply, but if it works . . .'

'But I think they know how it ended.'

'Badly? And now she's come back and killed him?'

She rocked her hand, stuck out her bottom lip.

'The jury's out on that one. I definitely think they were lying about him living there with them.'

'Me, too. Were they embarrassed because they bought him a

flat or rented a house for him and didn't want to admit to yet another example of spoiling him?'

She shook her head slowly.

'No, there's more to it than that.'

It wouldn't be long before they found out exactly what.

19

They were still kicking it back and forth when Gulliver and Jardine piled into their office shortly after they got back. Kincade glanced at their new coffee machine, wondering if Gulliver had raided it while they were out, he was so wired.

'What's up, Craig?'

'The results are back from trawling Orford's personal and work computer systems.' He handed her a sheet of paper. 'That was sent to his work email address two days before he was killed.'

She glanced at it without comment, passed it to Angel.

'Call this number at eight p.m. tonight,' Angel read aloud, not bothering to read the number itself. 'Is it the same number Orford called two days before his death?'

'It is, sir.'

'What else have you got in your hand, Craig?' Kincade said.

'The email attachment. The reason Orford called the number and didn't delete the email as junk.'

He handed it to her. Angel was out of his seat by now, at the side of her desk where he could also see it.

'That has to be the same house.'

They all knew which house he meant—the property Gulliver had identified on Google maps as Kilstock Court in Somerset where the mobile phone used to call the journalist, George Leather, had been briefly switched on but no call made. They'd assumed to take a photograph.

The picture of the substantial Georgian property surrounded by perfectly-manicured grounds they were all studying looked like the sort of property that would be called Kilstock Court.

'You said the entrance gates were locked and the grounds were completely overgrown?' Angel said to Gulliver.

'That's right, sir. You can't see the house at all because the drive curves away out of sight.'

Angel took the photograph from Kincade. Not that he needed a second or closer look to state the blindingly obvious.

'These grounds aren't overgrown.'

'Either it's a different house,' Kincade said, 'or it's the same house before it fell into disrepair.'

Jardine took the photograph being passed around, confusion creasing her brow.

'If the killers already had this photograph which they knew would make Orford sit up and take notice, why go back down to Somerset and take another one, which they then didn't send?'

There was nothing to be achieved by speculating. Angel had a feeling he'd be visiting Kilstock Court in the near future.

'We'll have a word with the locals. See if they know anything about the place. Whatever's going on, the photograph was sufficient to make Orford agree to meet them and take a shotgun with him. How long did the call he made last?'

'It was short,' Gulliver confirmed. 'I remember thinking it was just long enough to make arrangements to meet.'

'More proof the picture of the house told him everything he needed to know. They didn't have to spell it out for him.'

'The email address it was sent from suggests the same thing. *Never_forgotten2012@gmail.com.* Something happened there in two thousand and twelve that he won't have forgotten.'

'Something he wanted to make sure didn't come to light,' Angel added.

Kincade had tuned them out as the other three talked, her own thoughts going in a different direction.

'Maybe that's where Orford was living,' she said, more to herself than anyone else, then brought Gulliver and Jardine up to speed on what they'd learned from Orford's parents.

'Hell of a commute to get to his old man's offices,' Jardine said. 'It's got to be seventy-five, eighty miles, at least.'

Kincade, who made a thirty-mile commute every day from where she lived with Angel's father just north of Salisbury, didn't pass comment on the viability of the journey. It wasn't out of any desire to keep Gulliver and Jardine in the dark about her living arrangements. The thought that had just crossed her mind eclipsed any worries about her secret getting out.

'If he ever actually worked there.'

'I don't believe it,' Angel said, feeling like he wanted to pull his hair out. That, or throttle Nigel Orford. 'Somebody else can go and talk to the bloody Orfords next time, or I won't be held responsible for my actions.'

'We don't know for sure he didn't work there,' Kincade said, arguing against her own previous comment.

'*I* know,' he said, prodding his gut. 'In here.'

Funny how he didn't hear anyone arguing.

There was one thing they were all agreed on. Jardine brought it up.

'Sending the email to his work email address means they knew where he worked, but didn't have his personal email or phone number. They wouldn't send it to work where somebody else might see it, if they knew his personal email. Maybe they're one of his patients.'

'Not necessarily,' Gulliver said. 'I bet the surgery uses standard format email addresses like we do. If you've got a name, it'll be easy to work out their email address.'

Everybody knew what that implied. They would need to look at every patient at the Oaks Medical Centre, not only Orford's.

'Past and present,' Kincade added, making the task ahead even more daunting.

Don't forget Uncle Tom Cobley, Angel thought facetiously, as the other three got into a competition to see who could add the most potential suspects—cleaners, delivery drivers, medical reps . . .

'ARE YOU GOING TO CALL THE CARROT-CRUNCHERS OR SHALL I DO it?' Kincade said, when Gulliver and Jardine had gone back to their desks.

Angel gave her a disapproving look.

'I think you've just disqualified yourself.'

'Ooh arr,' she replied as he made the call.

He was put through to a DS Dave Garfield, who didn't have much of an accent at all.

'Strange request,' Angel said, 'but is there anything you can tell me about a big old house near Knighton called Kilstock Court?'

There was a slight pause, as if Garfield wasn't sure he'd heard correctly.

'What? Apart from the fact that we dug up the remains of a young woman there yesterday, you mean?'

Both men were silent for a long moment, getting over their mutual surprise and assimilating the implications.

'Ooh arr,' Kincade said in the background.

'You first,' Angel said.

'There's not a lot to tell, so far,' Garfield replied. 'A shallow grave in the grounds. Nothing left but bones. The pathologist gave us his opinion at the scene—'

'He's nothing like ours.'

'—and reckons it's a woman under thirty-five. The hyoid bone was fractured, so we're working on the basis she was strangled. Why were you asking about the house?'

Angel had been surprised by Garfield's revelation. He felt confident he could go one better.

'We've got a crucified man...'

'Seriously?'

'Yep. Nailed through the wrists to a DIY cross.'

A sharp intake of breath came down the line at him.

'Nasty.'

It gets nastier.

'A picture of what we suspected was Kilstock Court, and what I'm now positive about after talking to you, was emailed to him. It was sufficient to lure him to a derelict barn and take a shotgun with him. Clearly, he was overpowered. He was then tortured before he was killed.'

'Because they're sick bastards, or to get information?'

'We think information. They also notified the local paper in case we weren't forthcoming with all the gory details.'

'It's got to be the same person or people.'

As often happens, each of them was taking the new information and fitting it into what they already knew, assuming the other party also knew their side.

'What's got to be the same?' Angel said.

'A young woman called our front desk to ask for my name. She then emailed me map coordinates telling me where the body was buried. I ignored it to begin with. Then she emailed again...'

'And you had to scratch the itch.'

'Yeah. I went and had a look around. It looked as if somebody had been there recently. When she emailed again, I twisted my DI's arm and we got a cadaver dog out there.'

'What was the email address?'

'*Never_forgotten2012@gmail.com*.'

Angel didn't even need to check.

'Same one the killers used to email the photograph to our victim.'

'What was his name?'

'Dominic Orford.'

Angel sensed Garfield shaking his head before the words were out.

'Means nothing to me.'

Again, a brief silence stretched out as they tried to make sense of what was going on. Angel was the first to break it.

'Cell-site data indicates she or they were at the house recently. We thought it was to take the photograph they emailed the victim. Except it must have been an old photograph, because the house was well-maintained. I understand the place has fallen into disrepair.'

'Yeah. The grounds are a jungle, too.'

'Do you know anything about it before it was abandoned? Or how long ago?'

'Nope. I was about to look into it before events took over. Try to find an old-timer who remembers it. I'll be looking into past owners, obviously, and people who might have worked there. A house and grounds like that need a lot of maintenance. There's also the chance it was a secluded, convenient disposal site that's got nothing to do with the house, of course. What about your end? Anything?'

Nothing I can put my finger on, Angel thought, then took Garfield through his misgivings about the whole Orford family.

'The victim had what now feels like an unaccounted-for, missing three-year period in his life about fifteen years ago. He was also in an intense relationship with a woman in her late twenties called Jasmijn. We don't have any other details about her. The victim's parents claim they don't know how the relationship ended. They said he refused to talk about it.' He glanced across at Kincade, now giving his conversation all of her attention, jokes about country bumpkins long forgotten. 'And my DS doesn't believe the victim was living with his parents as they claim.'

'Do you believe in coincidence?'

No, but I believe in things falling into place too easily even less, he thought.

'Anything on the body to identify it? Jewellery? Scraps of clothing?'

'A necklace.'

'That's something.'

'Yeah. Apart from that, it's just bare bones. Even with the necklace, it's going to be a nightmare identifying her.'

In other circumstances, Angel would've said, *rather you than me*. Except they both knew they were in it—whatever *it* was—together.

They ended the call with an agreement to keep each other updated.

'That sounds promising,' Kincade said, before the phone was down.

'It is. Promising and confusing . . .'

He half-expected her to get up and pour a cup of coffee as he explained, but it seemed she'd hit her caffeine quota for the time being. That, or they'd run out of coffee.

'What's confusing?' she said, when he'd run through it all.

'Orford was at Kilstock Court with Jasmijn. Doesn't matter why for now. He strangled her and buried her in a shallow grave...'

Olivia Finch had been passing in the corridor. Theirs was not a large office, their conversations easily audible to anyone passing the open door. She stuck her head in the room.

'What's that about strangled and buried in a shallow grave?'

Angel waved her in, then took her quickly through his conversation with Garfield while she helped herself to a cup of coffee from what used to be her machine.

Kincade then suggested one obvious scenario.

'Somebody close to Jasmijn knew or suspected Orford killed her and buried her in the grounds. They're extensive grounds, so they tortured him to get the exact location, then killed him. They then contacted Garfield anonymously to ensure their loved one was dug up and would get a proper burial.'

Finch sipped thoughtfully at her coffee, then made a couple of valid observations.

'First of all, why wait all this time? Secondly, don't they realise they'll be the obvious suspects when the body is identified?'

'*If*, ma'am,' Kincade said. 'Not *when*. Orford's ex-girlfriend said Jasmijn was Dutch. According to Garfield, there's nothing to identify the remains apart from a necklace which is only any use if we have somebody to ask about it. You need high-quality DNA to perform familial DNA testing. Blood, semen or saliva are best. Bones aren't always good enough. You also need a reference sample from a relative to compare it to. They can sleep easy—'

'After torturing and crucifying a man?'

'—knowing that what they consider to be justice has been done.'

Angel listened to the exchange in silence. Kincade's theory had things going for it. It explained why Orford had been unwilling to discuss Jasmijn's exit from his life with his parents.

If they suspected something was badly wrong, it explained their lies and reluctance to volunteer information. But Finch's point about the time delay was also valid, even if he tended to side with Kincade on the chances of identifying the body.

Finch handed Angel her empty cup to put in his wastepaper bin, her brow furrowed in thought as she prepared to leave. Except it wasn't anything he or Kincade expected.

'Tell you what, Cat? I'll bet you my . . . sorry, *the* coffee machine on it.'

Kincade didn't even bother to look at Angel. As far as she was concerned, it was her machine.

'What do I get if I'm right?'

'I'll buy you the coffee for—'

'A year?'

'A month.'

'Six.'

'Three.'

The two women nodded their acceptance of the wager, a handshake unnecessary.

'She'll bankrupt you if she wins, ma'am, the amount she drinks,' Angel said. 'You shouldn't have agreed to more than a week.'

'We'll see, Padre.' She gave them both a broad smile. 'Enjoy the coffee while you still can.'

20

Kincade's theory was too neat and easy for Angel. Even if it hadn't been, he would never drop other avenues of investigation and pursue only one, however promising. He couldn't deny the Jasmijn angle was intriguing. It had all the hallmarks of a theory he was often accused of favouring—the more unusual, the more he liked it.

Even so, Caitlin Fox's behaviour in walking out of Orford's consulting room as he started to examine her felt as if it had potential, too.

He sent Gulliver and Jardine to talk to her. The Oaks Medical Centre had provided an address for her, but the phone number they had on file was no longer in service, necessitating a visit in person without calling ahead.

Caitlin Fox's door was opened by a man in his early thirties who clearly recognised them for what they were. It was mutual. He looked familiar, even if neither of them could bring his name to mind. The attitude he projected, the expression on his face as if he'd caught a whiff of something on the bottom of his shoe, was also something they recognised, although it had long ago ceased to bother either of them.

'We're looking for Caitlin Fox, Mr . . .' Jardine said, warrant card thrust towards him.

'She's not here.'

Jardine wasn't sure whether he'd deliberately failed to give his name at her prompt, or whether he'd taken her use of *mister* as an alternative to *mate*.

'Fair enough. What's your name, sir?'

'Damien.'

She waited. No more came. Her next question sounded as if she was addressing a small child.

'Do you have a last name, Damien?'

'Burke.'

The reason for his reluctance to volunteer his name was immediately clear—and it wasn't because he was embarrassed by the name Burke. They knew who he was now. They would check on the PNC when they got back for details, but they both knew he had a string of convictions to his name.

Burke saw the recognition on their faces. It put a scowl on his, an edge of aggression into his voice.

'Like I said, she's not here.' Starting to close the door as he said it.

Jardine stopped it dead with her foot.

'Has she moved out?'

'Nah. She's at work.'

Sullen and uncooperative he might have been, but Burke finally caught on that the faster he answered, even volunteered information, the quicker they would leave him alone.

'She works at the Mazda dealership in Eastleigh. You can Google the address.'

Jardine felt the pressure against her foot increase. She dug her heel in.

'Do you have a current phone number?'

'What for?'

She looked at Gulliver. Gulliver nodded sadly, *yes, some people really are that stupid.*

'Because we want to call her, Mr Burke. Avoid another wasted trip. Stop us from having to come back here tonight.'

The number poured out of Burke's mouth so fast, it was like a continuous blur of noise neither of them caught. Jardine made him recite it again more slowly.

'We'll probably need to come back tonight, anyway,' she said, removing her foot from the door. 'See you later.'

Except the door was already shut.

'I'M POSITIVE WE'VE ARRESTED HIM FOR CAR THEFT AND BREAKING and entering,' Gulliver said, back in the car. 'Assault, too.'

'Makes you view things differently,' she admitted, 'finding out she's with someone like him. You start asking yourself if there's a scam going on, and her walking out of the examination was stage one.'

Neither of them needed to state the obvious.

There wouldn't be a stage two. At least not with Dr Dominic Orford.

'He'll be on the phone by now,' Gulliver said, his hand to his ear, thumb and little finger extended in the universal sign for a phone. 'Warning her we're on our way.'

'Definitely. Strange that he didn't ask us what it was about. It suggests he already knows.'

'Or he realised the less questions he asked, the quicker we'd get off his doorstep.'

'Be interesting to see if she's still at work when we get there.'

'Bit of an indicator of guilt if she isn't.'

'Does that mean she's not guilty if she is?'

If only it was that easy, he thought and concentrated on driving.

. . .

They were fifty per cent right in their assessment. Burke had indeed called Caitlin Fox to warn her of their imminent arrival, but Caitlin hadn't taken off as a result.

Pragmatic, Gulliver thought, while they waited for her in reception. She knows we won't give up. Might as well get it over with.

Caitlin was a couple of years younger than Burke. She wore her brown hair short in a pixie cut and was pretty enough to carry it off, even if Jardine thought the eye makeup was a little on the heavy side. Despite that, she could've done a lot better for herself than the petty criminal Damien Burke.

She opted to talk in Gulliver's car, not wanting to use one of the dealership's private offices or even a nearby café.

Jardine got in the back with her while Gulliver twisted in his seat to face her in the nearside back seat.

Her attitude was markedly different to that of her partner. She was relaxed and open, confident that whatever they wanted to ask, she would have a valid and reasonable explanation.

Jardine took the lead, woman to woman. Gulliver didn't think it ever worked with Jardine, but *hey ho*.

'Is this about Doctor Orford?' she asked, before Jardine got her first question out. 'I saw it in the paper. It's just awful.'

'It is about Dr Orford, yes, but not in relation to his death.'

Caitlin relaxed visibly.

'I've been so worried ever since I read about it. I knew you'd hear about what happened when he started to examine me . . . that's what this conversation is about, isn't it?'

'It is,' Jardine confirmed.

Caitlin relaxed further, then glanced quickly at Gulliver as if worried he was about to play bad cop to Jardine's good cop.

'I don't know what came over me,' she said. 'I feel so stupid now. I'll never be able—' Her hand flew to her mouth as she realised what she'd been about to say. 'I know I can't go back to Doctor Orford, but all the other doctors will be saying, here comes that crazy bitch. Make sure you don't touch her. They probably all think I'm planning on suing them.'

Jardine ignored the reference to their own, earlier thoughts, carried on.

'What exactly happened?'

Caitlin shook her head like she wished she knew.

'I don't know. Damien keeps on at me. *Are you sure he didn't grope you?* Obviously, I'm sure. All he did was touch my stomach. We'd even been joking about his hands being cold. Suddenly, I felt this anxiety come over me out of nowhere. I used to suffer from panic attacks, but I haven't had one for years. This was like a mild version. All I could think about was getting out into the fresh air.'

'Had you had a bad experience before? In the days before there was a chaperone in the room.'

'No, never.'

In the front seat, Gulliver cleared his throat.

Caitlin anticipated his question, immediately closed it down.

'If you were about to ask if I'd been abused as a child or anything like that, the answer's *no* to that, as well. Not everybody has, despite what the newspapers and TV like to make out. I don't suppose happy childhood memories sell many papers.'

Gulliver cleared his throat a second time. Not only because it looked as if he'd got Caitlin onto a pet hate and they didn't have all day, but because the question he was about to ask often felt like slapping cooperative witnesses across the face.

I hear what you say. Now prove you're not guilty, anyway.

'Can you tell us where you were last Friday night?'

'At home with Damien. We'd normally go out on a Friday night, but he wasn't feeling well.' She gave Jardine a knowing smile—*men are big babies, every last one of them.* 'I know it's not much of an alibi.'

'It is what it is,' Jardine said, taking hold of the door handle to signal the end of the interview. 'One last thing. The press are very persistent. They'll try to do exactly what we're doing, digging into Doctor Orford's past life. They might find you, like we did. I'd recommend you don't speak to them, even if they offer you money.'

Caitlin nodded dutifully. They noticed how she didn't agree out loud.

Que sera, sera, Jardine thought, as Caitlin headed away across the car park, then glanced at Gulliver, also watching Caitlin.

'Roll your tongue up, Craig. Somebody might trip on it.'

He ignored the remark, although his response suggested she wasn't so far off the mark.

'What on earth does she see in someone like Damien Burke?'

'Some women like a bit of rough.' She caught the start of a grin on his lips. '*No*, that doesn't include me.'

'So, what did you think of her story?'

She looked across the car park again to where Caitlin was standing in front of the dealership's glass and steel mesh facade watching them. She saw or sensed Jardine look her way, immediately went inside.

'Not sure. Something must have provoked the reaction when Orford touched her.'

'You think she's lying about being abused? She was very quick to mention her happy childhood memories.'

'Could be.' She fell silent briefly as Gulliver pulled away, half-expecting to see Caitlin at an upstairs window looking down on them. 'Even if she was, what's it got to do with Dominic Orford?'

21

DAVE GARFIELD HAD BEEN KICKING IT BACK AND FORTH IN HIS mind ever since the remains had been discovered. Was the person behind the *never_forgotten2012@gmail.com* email address the person responsible for killing and burying her, or a witness?

If they were the killer, they would follow their own agenda whatever he did. It would make no difference if he replied to the email or not. Worst case scenario, the killer would taunt him.

If they were a witness, they needed a helping kick up the backside to make them come forward.

The time delay was confusing.

He would have a better idea of how long the body had been in the ground after the post mortem and all the various experts had weighed in with their opinions, but they were looking at a number of years—and the date 2012 in the email address was too big a clue to ignore.

Why would the killer suddenly send an email after all that time?

It made more sense that it was a witness.

There were plenty of valid reasons for not coming forward

earlier, from being worried about being implicated to being scared of reprisals from the killer.

All they needed was a helping hand. Garfield started tapping out an appropriate response.

A young woman's remains were disinterred yesterday in the grounds of Kilstock Court.

He re-read the sentence, thought about changing *disinterred* to *dug up*, then left it as it was and got to the point.

I need you to identify yourself so we can arrange for you to come into the station to explain how you knew the body was there.

He glanced at DI Jay Chopra's closed door. Decided he didn't want to have to explain the ins and outs of a duck's arse for half an hour just for Chopra to tell him to leave it with him. Nor did he want to wait for the mighty Google to perhaps give them the details they had for the owner of the email address. He already knew the number of the burner phone it would be linked to. The young woman had used it to call the front desk, after all. Being told it was owned by Ms M. Mouse of 1 High Street, East Bumfuck wouldn't move the investigation along much, either.

He hit *send*.

'They've found the body,' she said, bounding into the room as if she was six years old.

He crumpled his empty beer can in his fist, then muted the sound on the TV as he came off the sofa, her excitement infecting him.

'How do you know?'

She held her phone out towards him like it was a winning lottery ticket.

'Garfield replied to my email.'

To *our* email, he corrected mentally, taking the phone from her. His smile grew wider as he read the message, then an incredulous bark of laughter.

'Yeah, right. Identify yourself! Like we're going to waltz in there with our arms out to be cuffed.' Extending his arms, wrists pressed together as he said it. 'We should email him back. Say we've done enough of his job for him already.'

She hesitated, knowing what she was about to say would cause an argument, spoil the moment.

'We're going to have to do the rest of it for him anyway.' They'd had the argument so many times before, she didn't need to spell it out. She did so, nonetheless. 'Tell them who she is.'

He dropped back onto the sofa, grabbed the TV remote. Turned the sound back on.

She stood in front of the TV, blocking his view. Less risky than snatching the remote out of his hand.

'Please don't ignore me.'

'Why not? I'm sick of talking about it.'

She came towards him, lowered herself to her knees in front of him, elbows resting on his knees. He tried to look around her at the TV, but she shifted her body from side to side to continue blocking his view. She took the remote gently from his hand when he gave up, switched the TV off altogether.

'I know we've been over it, but now it's real. They've actually dug her up.'

The calm reasonableness of her tone, the warmth of her body against his, did the trick, as she'd hoped, the tension in his shoulders and jaw relaxing. That didn't mean he was ready to roll over just yet.

'Give them a bit of time to identify her themselves.'

The reasonableness was instantly gone from her voice, now quarrelsome.

'How much time? A day? A week? A month?'

'I don't know. But more than twelve hours, for Christ's sake.'

It annoyed the hell out of her that he wouldn't listen to what she'd told him over and over, as if she'd made it up. She'd spent so many hours on the internet researching, she felt like she could head up a pathology department, if not run a whole murder investigation herself.

'They might never identify her.'

'All the forensic crap you see on the TV is bollocks, is it? DNA and all the rest of it.'

'*See!* You don't even know what the rest of it'—making quotes in the air—'actually is, but you're convinced it'll help them identify her.'

'Pardon me for not being a bloody expert.'

She resisted the urge to push herself off his knees, let him go back to the football on the TV and send Garfield a reply with Rosie's name anyway. Except, they needed to stick together.

'There's no point in giving them time to try to identify her, and then we have to tell them anyway when they can't. How do we know if they ever do it themselves? They're not going to email us and give us an update.'

They held each other's gaze for a long moment. She could see he knew she was right. It was only his male pride preventing him from admitting it.

'Let me up,' he said. 'I need to take a leak.'

She smiled to herself, didn't let it show. She'd won. But he couldn't simply give in. He was creating a break, a diversion. Then he could come back as if he'd been giving it serious thought while he peed the blue toilet cleaner off the bowl, trying to get all of it before he ran out of piss.

She used his knees to push herself to her feet, let him get up and leave the room. Telling herself not to look too smug when he came back and agreed.

'I've been thinking it through,' he said, when he came back a couple of minutes later, drying his hands on his jeans. 'I think it's best if we tell them, after all . . .'

DAVE GARFIELD KNOCKED ON JAY CHOPRA'S DOOR AND WENT IN without waiting to be invited.

'Rosie Laing. Born twenty-second of February, nineteen ninety-seven.'

Understandably, Chopra didn't know what Garfield was talking about. His face made that very clear. Garfield put him out of his misery.

'That's the victim's name and date of birth.'

With the bones still in packing cases waiting to be reassembled into a human skeleton in the pathology lab, Chopra knew Garfield's revelation wasn't based on scientific evidence or solid police work. There was only one other option.

'They emailed you the name?'

'Yep.' Forgetting to mention he'd emailed them first.

'Just the name and date of birth?'

Garfield gave him an incredulous look—*some people are never satisfied.*

'I'll get back to them, shall I? Ask for more details.'

'The way this is going, they'd probably supply them. They didn't give the date she was killed?'

'I'd have said if they had, sir. But the email address suggests some time in two thousand and twelve.'

Chopra nodded a grudging acknowledgement, then asked the impossible question that was hanging in the air.

'I wonder why they told us?'

The question had been front and centre in Garfield's mind ever since the email arrived. He threw out an obvious reason that felt too straightforward to him.

'Because they wanted her identified and laid to rest properly.

They're also sensible enough not to believe everything they see on the TV about identification and plucking clues out of thin air.'

Chopra leaned back in his chair, hands clasped behind his head, the yellowing discolouration on the armpits of his white shirt clearly visible.

'Is that really her name? Or are they playing with us?'

Garfield had wondered the same thing. He felt like a giant puppet master was jerking his strings. Except his gut told him there was a lot of feeling behind the emails, despite their brevity. These people wanted Rosie Laing dug up and her death acknowledged.

'With the name and date of birth, it should be easy enough to find her. I'll make a start.'

'Don't forget to notify the people in Southampton.'

'Will do.'

Except his phone rang the moment he got back to his desk and it went right out of his mind.

22

Seventy miles away in Southampton Central police station, Gulliver caught Jardine grinning at him after he'd just ended a call.

'What?'

'Your cake delivery is here.'

Sounds like your medication delivery is late, he thought, no idea what she was talking about.

'Not with you.'

'Jack Bevan called while you were on the phone. Dorothy Bancroft is in reception asking to see you.'

The name took a moment to register, then Jardine's remark fell into place. Ms Bancroft was the witness who'd encountered a rude man while walking her dog, a man they were hoping might be one of Orford's killers checking out the derelict barn— the same witness who'd plied Gulliver with fruit cake when they interviewed her.

He jumped up, pulled on his jacket.

'Better not keep her waiting.'

He knew Jardine was only winding him up, but he couldn't help the pang of disappointment when he saw Dorothy in reception, not a carrier bag or Tupperware container in sight. There weren't even any cake-shaped bulges in her coat pockets. Her dog, Lola, was with her on a bright-yellow retractable dog leash of the sort Gulliver believed were designed specifically to trip unwary pedestrians.

He held up his first two fingers towards Bevan—*two teas*—then led Dorothy to an empty interview room, where Lola took an immediate interest in the interview table legs.

'I felt so bad not being able to remember the registration number of the car I saw,' she started, looking as if it was all she could do to not wring her hands. 'I've always prided myself on being observant and having a good memory, then the one time it matters, I can't remember a thing.'

'Your presence here today suggests something's come back to you.'

'It has, yes. After I got over being annoyed at how rude the man was.'

The door opened without a knock preceding it, and Bevan carried two plastic cups of anaemic-looking tea in. Dorothy, who'd served tea from a bone-china teapot, looked horrified when Bevan placed one in front of her.

Wouldn't be so bad if you'd brought cake with you, Gulliver thought, not touching his own cup.

'I was in Bishop's Waltham yesterday doing some shopping. I was waiting at a zebra crossing. I always wait for somebody to stop. I don't step out onto it like some people do, as if it's their God-given right. A car was approaching and it looked as if it was slowing down. I stepped onto the crossing and the next thing I knew, it accelerated again.'

'Are you suggesting it deliberately drove at you?'

Gulliver watched the effect of too much TV going to work in Dorothy's mind, memories of crime dramas where vital witnesses were mowed down in the street playing in her mind.

She took a sip of tea without thinking as she considered her answer, the spasm that twisted her mouth suggesting she wouldn't take another.

'I don't think so. They were probably on the phone which is why they slowed, and then they accelerated again when they finished the call. Anyway, I had to jump backwards, and the car went past and beeped its horn at me. It was so inconsiderate, it made me think of the car in the lay-by that parked so close to me. I got a vivid mental image of the number plate—'

'On the car that nearly hit you, or the one in the lay-by?'

'The one in the lay-by, of course. I could see the one that nearly hit me. I'm not blind. The thing is, I can't remember the complete registration.' She glared at the cup of undrinkable tea as if it was responsible for her memory loss.

'What was the part you did remember?'

'HK67. Is that helpful?'

'Definitely. With the car model and colour and a partial registration, we can search the PNC—'

'The what?' Sounding as if it was a new food additive she hadn't heard of.

'The Police National Computer. Unless it's a silver Ford Focus in London or another big city, there's never going to be more than one or two matches.'

Dorothy soaked up the praise as if the murderer was as good as behind bars already.

Shame you didn't bring some cake as well to really make my day, he thought, showing her out.

Upstairs, Kincade had just finished a call as the afternoon wound down towards the weekend, snatches of which Angel had overheard without meaning to earwig.

'That sounded very complicated.'

She gave him a look that suggested members of the public wouldn't be happy to hear the remark coming from a man responsible for running complex investigations that impacted directly on their safety.

'Not really. What are you doing tomorrow?'

'Dog-sitting.'

She narrowed her eyes at him, as if suspecting he'd made something up on the spot to get out of whatever she was about to suggest.

'Really? Who for?'

Vanessa Corrigan, but I'm not telling you that.

'A friend.'

'I'd worked that out for myself. Anybody I know?'

'Nope.'

But you'd love to.

Momentarily, he thought she was going to push him. Point out that the question, *anybody I know?* is actually a softer way of saying, *who is it?*

'What's the dog like with children?'

The question surprised him, but he soon recovered.

'The owner assures me he only eats one a day.'

She gave a satisfied nod, *that's settled.*

'That's okay. I've got two daughters. They're coming to stay for the weekend—'

'At my father's house?'

'Where else? It's where I live. The bunk beds he bought specially have never been slept in, and he keeps threatening to sell them if they don't get used soon. Anyway, you're invited. You can bring Rover, too.'

'*Jasper.* He's a border collie. What are the arrangements? I assume Elliot isn't putting them on the train on their own.'

He got the look again.

'It's lucky Jasper's owner didn't hear that. You don't sound as if you can be trusted with a dog, let alone children. Anyway, I'm catching the seven-fifteen train from Salisbury. It only takes an hour and a half. Elliot's meeting me at Waterloo with the girls at nine o'clock.'

'Really?'

'I know. I can't get used to it. Elliot's started behaving like a human being ever since I—'

'Told him he'd won?'

She'd recently confided in him that she'd reluctantly given up on any hope of having her daughters come to live with her. The list of factors in her estranged husband's favour was too long, almost as extensive as the list against her.

'Don't remind me.'

'You should've pushed him to drive them down to Salisbury.'

She shook her head as if she'd considered it, but decided against it.

'No. He'd want to see where they're staying.'

'You're not ashamed of my father, are you?'

The look she gave him made it clear that of the two remaining males in the Angel family, his father would be the last one she was ashamed of.

'*No*. It's just that having got Elliot to be more amenable, I don't want your dad spoiling it all by punching him in the face after all the dreadful things I've said about him.'

He nodded, *fair point*.

She clapped her hands together, a gesture her girls would recognise.

'That's settled then. Come over about twelve.'

'And if I wanted to have a peaceful chat with my own father before the bedlam begins?'

'You know, I'm glad we've had this chat. It's reminded me to get my mind right before I spend a day with you, your father, two excited children and a dog you probably can't control.'

'How about we invite Grace . . .'

She pointed a finger at him, even though she knew he wasn't serious.

'I think your old man would punch *you* in the face if you do.'

He didn't bother asking if she'd be standing right behind him, waiting to take her turn.

'STAYING LATE?' KINCADE SAID AN HOUR LATER, AS SHE PULLED ON her coat.

Only until you've gone. I'm not risking you watching me from the window.

'Not much longer. I thought I'd give DS Garfield in Bridgwater a call, see if there's anything new.'

She gave him a knowing—or what she thought was knowing—smile.

'Anything to avoid going to the Jolly Sailor on the way home, after you saw your mother there with another man, eh?'

He shrugged, *you got me.*

If only you knew.

'Did you ask her about it?' she said, making her way slowly towards the door.

'Uh-uh. What would I say?'

'No idea. I've never caught my mother on a date with another man in my favourite pub. Were you going to mention it to your dad tomorrow?'

He made a big fuss of looking at his watch.

'Hadn't you better get going? Friday night traffic and all that.'

The smile on her face broke out into a full-scale grin.

'I think tomorrow's going to be interesting.'

'In the Chinese curse sense of the word, you mean? May you live in interesting times.'

'We'll see.'

He reached for the phone in an attempt to move her on. She took the hint and skipped out of the room, *see you tomorrow* floating back over her shoulder.

His mobile pinged before he had a chance to make the call to DS Garfield. He checked the screen, thinking he'd have to assign a distinctive ring tone to her when he saw the name —Vanessa.

I'm here. I caught an earlier train.

Here was across the road in Southampton Central railway station. The original plan was for him to wait for her in what was fast becoming his new local, the Pig in the Wall, less than a ten-minute walk away.

He breathed a retrospective sigh of relief that Kincade had already left and wouldn't be watching him walk down the street with Vanessa and her dog to the Pig. It wasn't that he was deliberately keeping his budding relationship with her a secret. But with so many things in his past to keep the team amused at his expense—his lost years as a priest, in particular—he wanted to keep a part of him private. Her job as Deputy Governor of HMP Isle of Wight provided too many opportunities for puerile comments about being chained up in a dungeon by a dominatrix in stilettos wielding a whip.

Five minutes later, he met her coming out of the station, Jasper straining at the leash to greet him.

'I hope he gets on as well with your cat as he does with you,' Vanessa said, as Jasper jumped excitedly up at him.

'Not a problem. My mother's staying at my sister's for the weekend. Leonard will spend the whole time asleep on her bed.'

She linked arms with him as they walked down Western Esplanade. It put him in mind of Isabel Durand—as did their destination, the Pig. No doubt he'd get a few curious glances from the staff there.

Vanessa waited with Jasper at a table outside while he

went in to get the drinks, his hopes of not being remembered immediately dashed when the barman smiled at him.

'Same as usual? Campari and soda and a Margarita, heavy on the salt?'

'We've only got time for a quick one,' he said, ordering a beer and a small glass of Sauvignon Blanc.

Vanessa was texting on her phone when he carried the drinks outside. She finished it and pocketed the phone, raised her glass in a toast.

'Here's to Jasper not eating your cat.'

He clinked glasses.

'You haven't met Leonard.'

'One day perhaps.' A wistful note in her voice.

If it was an unsubtle reminder that most glaciers moved faster than the relationship was proceeding, he soon put a stop to it.

'Unless you want to meet my mother as well . . .'

'Why not? I've already met your father.'

As a result of fate up to its tricks, she'd worked at HMP Whitemoor in the Cambridgeshire fens at the same time as his father spent eleven years there at Her Majesty's pleasure for killing a man.

'If you weren't going to London for the weekend, you could've met him again,' he said, then told her what he had lined up for the following day.

She patted her pocket where her phone sat, the mischief running high.

'Maybe I could text Amanda, try to reschedule. It sounds like it'd be more fun coming with you.'

He pulled out his own phone and took a quick photograph of her, the glass of wine held to her lips.

'For when my father asks who Jasper belongs to.'

She considered him carefully, not sure whether he was being serious or not.

'Okay by me. Aren't you worried your sergeant will see it?'

He didn't reply, momentarily distracted by a young woman who'd come out and sat at a nearby table. She looked vaguely familiar. From the expression on her face, she thought the same thing. She'd probably seen him with Durand. They exchanged a fleeting polite smile, no more than a twitch of the lips, then both looked away.

Vanessa downed the last of her wine, got to her feet.

'Might as well go to the loo while I'm here. The ones on the train are bound to be out of order.'

He spent a minute giving Jasper a good rub behind the ears while she was away. The young woman wasn't paying him any attention. If she'd been looking at him, he might have started a conversation. Except *do I know you* sounded like a cheesy chat-up line. She'd think he was an old letch making moves on a woman half his age while the woman his own age was in the loo.

His thoughts segued easily into imagining what the young woman whose remains had been dug up had been like in life. He didn't have a daughter, but he got the feeling that if he did, what he saw in his job on a daily basis would make him overly-protective of her.

Vanessa came back out a minute later, her reapplied lipstick making her smile all the more vibrant.

'It's lovely in there.'

'I know.'

'I really do wish I could reschedule.'

'The food's excellent, too.'

'I told you Amanda's a bloody vegan, didn't I? Wears a hazmat suit just to walk past a butcher's shop.'

'The steaks are particularly good.'

Her grin was wide enough to eat him whole.

'You're not making this any easier.'

He pointed at where her phone sat in her pocket.

'Send her a text. Tell her something's come up.'

'What? Like a juicy steak? That'd end the friendship forever. Anyway, don't tease. You know I can't.'

He shook his head, *I don't know any such thing.*

She looked around at the elegant building behind them, indecision on her face and something else in her voice that entered the world not long after the planet cooled and had been men's downfall ever since.

'It's a hotel, too.'

'I know. Did you check if they've got any availability when you went to the loo?'

She raised an eyebrow at him.

'You made that sound as if you don't believe I went to the loo at all.'

'That's just your guilty conscience.'

Angel noticed the young woman watching them. It would've been hard not to. He wouldn't have been surprised if she'd yelled at them.

Just book a bloody room!

He downed the last of his beer, inclined his head towards the station.

'C'mon, I'll walk you to the station. I don't want an enraged vegan after me brandishing a sharpened carrot.'

23

Unlike Angel and Kincade, Gulliver and Jardine were still hard at work.

As Gulliver explained to Dorothy Bancroft, searching the PNC for a blue Alfa Romeo with the partial registration HK67 had resulted in only one hit—for Mr Graeme Laing of Brookvale Road, Southampton. It was an encouraging result. The address was less than two miles as the crow flies from where they now sat. The letter *N* in PNC stands for National for a good reason, and a search could equally have thrown up a match in Aberdeen.

So, while Kincade was doing battle with the traffic on the A36 to Salisbury and Angel was taking custody of Jasper the border collie, they were making the short drive to Brookvale Road.

There was no answer when they knocked on the door, nor was there the sound of a TV or music playing too loudly to mask their knock. Gulliver tried the house to the right, Jardine to the left.

He had more success than she did. A middle-aged man wearing baggy grey tracksuit bottoms and a matching grey T-shirt opened the door immediately, as if he'd been waiting behind it for a delivery of more shapeless grey clothes.

'We're looking for Graeme Laing,' Gulliver said, warrant card held in front of him.

The grey-clad neighbour checked his watch.

'He'll be walking the dog at this time.' He smiled, displaying teeth that thankfully weren't a matching grey. 'Although he doesn't do much walking these days.' He pointed due west where the warm orange glow of the setting sun backlit the houses opposite. 'We used to go together before my old dog went to the big kennel in the sky. We always used to sit for a few minutes on a bench overlooking the Ornamental Lake on the common while the dogs chased the ducks. These days, he spends more time sitting than walking. That's where you'll find him.'

The neighbour seemed sufficiently au fait with Laing's habits for Gulliver to feel comfortable asking his next question.

'Any idea how long he'll be?'

The grey neighbour consulted his watch again.

'A while yet. Generally, he's out for a couple of hours. I'd get over there quick, if I was you.' He tipped his hand to his mouth a couple of times as if taking an imaginary drink. 'Always takes his hip flask with him, too. I reckon he'd forget the dog—it's an old black Labrador—before he left the house without his hip flask.'

Gulliver and Jardine reconvened at the car a minute later. Jardine drew in a deep breath of the fresh, early-evening air.

'I don't fancy waiting in the car until his hip flask runs out.'

Gulliver couldn't disagree. Besides, it was a pleasant evening, perfect for a walk on the common. Jardine opened Google maps on her phone and they made their way towards the lake, following the most direct route, the same route they guessed Laing would follow if his aim was to minimise walking time and maximise quality bench and hip-flask time.

'That must be him there,' Jardine said breathlessly, after a ten-minute route march trying to keep up with Gulliver. She was pointing towards a middle-aged man sitting on a bench overlooking the lake, a black dog asleep at his feet. 'I know we need to catch him before he drinks too much, but it would help if we've still got some breath left to talk to him.'

That's a first, Gulliver thought and kept to himself. *Lisa Jardine unable to talk.*

The man turned towards them when he heard them talking as they approached, the dog also coming awake and yawning.

'Mr Laing?' Gulliver said.

'That's right.'

'Your neighbour told us where to find you,' Gulliver explained, anticipating the question Laing was about to ask. 'We'd like a quick word.'

'What? Here?'

'Wherever suits, sir.'

Laing pulled his collar up, shivered.

'Let's do it at home. I'm feeling a bit chilly today.'

Jardine smiled like she knew how it was, a different thought in her mind.

We'll soon warm your ears up for you.

Laing pushed himself to his feet like it was all he could do to achieve it, disturbing the dog as he did so.

'You go on ahead if you want. Harvey doesn't walk very fast these days.'

I know what he feels like, Jardine thought, as they all set off together.

It took them a lot longer to get back, Laing's remark about his dog not an exaggeration. It suited Jardine down to the ground, even if Gulliver looked as if he was taking two steps forward, one step back.

Laing parked them in the front sitting room while he went

upstairs to the bathroom, an all-pervading smell of breath mints coming back down with him a couple of minutes later—as if they hadn't already smelled the booze on his breath every step of the way home.

They shared a look as he entered the room. Apart from his embarrassment at being caught drinking on a park bench like a wino, he didn't appear concerned by their visit. He didn't have the air of a man who might have been seen crossing a field towards a derelict barn where he planned to crucify a man.

'We'd like to ask you what you were doing on Sunday the twenty-second of September at about seven p.m., walking across the fields near Warren Wood Farm,' Jardine said. 'That's about a mile south west of Bishop's Waltham.'

'That's easy. I wasn't.'

'We have a witness who saw your car parked in a lay-by on the B3035, close to a stile leading into the fields.'

'Your witness is mistaken.'

'Do you own a blue Alfa Romeo, registration . . .' She pulled out a printout of the car details taken from the PNC, read out the registration.

'That's my car,' Laing confirmed. 'If your witness saw it parked in a lay-by near Bishop's Waltham, it must have driven itself there, because I didn't drive it there. How reliable is your witness?'

'As reliable as any other witness,' Gulliver said, not answering the question, and no mention of any doubts about the accuracy of Dorothy Bancroft's memory.

Laing sensed the evasion, took advantage of it.

'Did they give you the full registration?'

'Not the full registration, no. But the system—'

'I don't care what your system can do or what your witness thinks they saw. I wasn't there.'

'Have you ever been there?'

Laing didn't even need to think about it.

'Not to my knowledge. Why would I drive there to walk my dog when I've got the common on my doorstep?'

To recce a derelict barn as a suitable place to crucify a man felt as if it would be jumping the gun.

'Where were you?' Jardine asked, instead.

'Same place you found me tonight, I should think. I go there most nights unless it's pissing down with rain.'

'Can anyone confirm that?'

'My dog.'

Jardine gave him a tight smile that didn't get close to her eyes.

'Anyone who is capable of giving a statement to corroborate your alibi?'

'Alibi for what?'

'Please answer the question, Mr Laing.'

This time, Laing took a moment to think about it. The mention of alibis, with everything people associate them with, had changed things for him. His facetious answer about his dog backing him up demonstrated how confident he'd felt earlier. Some of that confidence had now slipped away.

'I talked briefly to a bloke fishing the other day. It's the first time I've talked to him, but I've seen him there loads of times. He probably recognises me, too.' He coughed out a bitter laugh. 'The saddo who sits on the bench secretly drinking.'

He saw what went through both their minds.

I'm glad my liberty doesn't depend on an alibi that flimsy.

'What about the evening of Friday the twenty-seventh of September?' Gulliver said.

Laing gave him a look as if he expected Gulliver to have a good understanding of his routines by now.

'The same. Sitting on the bench.'

'What about later in the evening?'

'Falling asleep in front of the TV, I should think. Waking up cold and stiff at two in the morning. And before you ask, no, there's nobody who can corroborate that.'

'Do you own a tweed field coat? The sort of coat people wear for shooting.'

Laing studied him as if he suspected Gulliver had peeked in the utility room while he was upstairs swallowing breath mints.

'I do, yes. I can't remember the last time I wore it.'

'Do you shoot, Mr Laing?' The memory of Dominic Orford's missing shotgun prompting the somewhat tangential question.

'Not any more, I don't.'

It felt like an unnecessarily forceful way of putting it to Gulliver. He didn't let that distract him, getting back on track.

'Can we see the coat, please?'

'What's all this about?'

Most of the confidence was now gone from his voice, the question about the coat unsettling him. It was obvious they weren't about to answer his question. He had no choice but to get up and leave the room, returning a minute later carrying a heavy herringbone tweed field coat with two large cartridge pockets on the front and a contrasting collar.

'There must be millions of people with a coat like this,' Laing said defensively, handing it to Gulliver like it was an exhibit in a courtroom. 'Anybody who shoots probably has one exactly like it.'

My father's got two, Gulliver thought, *one of them identical to this*.

He kept the thought to himself as he took the coat, inspected the lower half of the front of it. Immediately below the right-hand cartridge pocket he saw a mark that might have been the remnants of a muddy paw print, although the age and general condition of the coat added to the herringbone pattern made it difficult to say for sure with the naked eye.

'If that's mud you've seen, what do you expect on a field coat?' Laing said, pointing at where Gulliver was turning the fabric back and forth in the light. 'A field coat owned by somebody with a dog. Do either of you have a dog?' Looking from one to the other of them.

Gulliver handed the coat back, neither of them answering the question.

'What happens now?' Laing said, some of his earlier confidence back after seeing his remarks about the ubiquity of field coats register with them. The alcohol he'd drunk, now more noticeable after the breath mints had worn off, played a part, too. 'Are you arresting me?'

This time, he was looking for an answer.

'We're not, Mr Laing,' Gulliver said, 'but it's likely we'll want to speak to you again in the future.'

'You know where to find me if you do,' Laing said, the bitter note in his voice aimed at him alone.

ALTHOUGH THE LIGHT HAD GONE BY THE TIME THEY FINISHED WITH Laing, it was still a pleasant evening. With The Cowherds pub less than half a mile from Laing's house, it would be rude not to pop in for a quick one to discuss what they thought of Graeme Laing and his vehement denials.

Jardine nabbed one of the picnic tables in front of the pub while Gulliver went inside to get the drinks, memories of a recent case in which the pub had played a major role difficult to ignore. He was sure the barmaid who served him remembered the last time he was there, asking questions other than *what flavour crisps have you got?*

'I think you've got worms,' Jardine said, when Gulliver deposited three bags of crisps on the table along with the drinks.

'I couldn't decide what flavour to get.'

'Lucky they didn't have ten different flavours.'

He shook his head as he ripped open the first packet and spread it on the table.

'No. I wouldn't ever buy prawn cocktail.'

She nodded like it was good to know, his obsession with food prompting her next remark.

'You think maybe Dorothy Bancroft was mistaken? And you were too busy thinking about her fruit cake to notice.' She held up her hand. 'Feel free to finish eating before you answer.'

He did so, washed the bits left between his teeth down with a swig of beer.

'It's a hell of a coincidence if she is. She gives us a partial registration that's wrong by one digit, say, and it still comes back with a blue Alfa Romeo that's registered to a man who lives half a mile over there.' Pointing in a north-easterly direction.

Jardine couldn't argue with the statistical improbability, but she still wasn't convinced.

'But he was so confident he wasn't there. That felt genuine to me. A guilty man who's worried he's about to be caught doesn't joke about his dog being his alibi.'

'He wasn't so confident when we mentioned the coat.'

She scrunched her face, struggling to put what she felt into long enough words for her partner.

'That almost makes his initial confidence more genuine. He really does believe what he's saying, and then he thinks, shit, I could get wrongly accused because I own a coat like a million other people do.'

'My dad's got two of them. One of them herringbone, like Laing's.'

She grinned at him.

'Has he got an alibi?'

'Yeah. Counting his money, like normal.'

They sat in a companionable silence for a while, on the face of it just another couple like those at the other tables around them enjoying the evening, the feeling of the working week winding down, the weekend stretching out ahead of them.

Gulliver picked up the open crisp packet, folded it into a funnel and tipped the last few broken bits into his mouth. Then ripped open the second packet.

'Worms,' Jardine said. 'Hungry ones, too.'

'Help yourself.'

'What? Salt, fat, chemicals? I don't think so.'

'I was forgetting. Your body's a temple.' He almost got carried away, said something about it being a big one, room for plenty of worshippers. He caught himself, went back to safer ground. 'What did you think about the way he answered when I asked him if he shoots?'

She took a thoughtful sip of beer, almost reached for a crisp without thinking.

'A bit sharp, perhaps. Like we were talking about a murder where the victim had been blown away with a shotgun, and then you asked him about shooting. Why'd you ask him, anyway?'

'It just sort of popped into my head. My subconscious trying to make connections to Orford taking a shotgun with him, and it's now missing.'

They kicked it back and forth for a while longer, not getting anywhere.

'Why does Laing drink?' Gulliver said, thinking out loud when they'd exhausted the subject.

'Why do you eat junk food?'

'Cake's not junk food . . .'

Needless to say, no more work was discussed that evening.

24

DS Dave Garfield couldn't believe how difficult it was trying to identify who had lived in Kilstock Court—not only at the time when the body was most likely buried, but at any time.

It had been easy enough to establish that the property was owned by a rich American called Earl Hooper Jr., who liked the idea of owning an English country estate in the county his ancestors had left behind for the promise of the New World three hundred years previously.

Having bought it, the view was that he'd never actually set foot in it. It had been rented out to a succession of tenants over the years through a property letting agency in London called Rise Lettings. The agency had gone bust in 2015.

Of course, they had, Garfield thought.

Nor did anybody know what happened to the company's records when they went belly-up. It was coming up for ten years ago, after all, and the Inland Revenue only require records to be kept for six years. In practice, they get shredded a lot earlier than that, most people gambling that the tax man will never come knocking.

The agency had provided a full service for their no-doubt

exorbitant fee taking advantage of an absentee landlord three thousand miles away. As part of that service, they dealt with all of the utilities—gas, water and electric—the cost of those utilities rolled into the rent.

The tenants would have been responsible for paying their own Council Tax, but Garfield reckoned he'd be nothing more than a collection of bones in the ground himself by the time the local council got around to doing anything about his request. Never underestimate the ability of a government employee to do precisely jack shit all day long.

It was now Friday night at the end of what had been a very frustrating day. The time had come to take the bull by the horns, go directly to where the real information would be found—the Rose and Crown, located in the village of Klive, two miles as the crow flies from Kilstock Court.

Garfield thought about taking DC Vicky Cook with him, then dismissed the idea. Her feminine charms would work wonders on the old boys who might have worked as gardeners or odd-job-men at the property, but she would want to bat on afterwards and Garfield didn't feel he had it in him after the week he'd had.

At the Rose and Crown, he bought a pint of Tangle Foot Golden Ale and a bag of pork scratchings, then identified himself to the landlord.

'You think I can't recognise a copper when I see one?' the publican said. 'Even if Kilstock Court hadn't been crawling with police and forensics and God knows what else.'

It was a fair point.

'Any of your locals ever work there?'

A smile broke out on the publican's face as he pointed to a man in his sixties sitting alone at a table beside the unlit fire.

'See Joe Skinner over there, crying into his beer?'

Garfield could obviously see the man, but he didn't know what the reference to crying in his beer was about.

'Uh-huh.'

'He used to be the head gardener there. Have you seen the state the place is in now?' He waited for Garfield to confirm that he had. 'It breaks old Joe's heart every time he drives past. I tell him, don't drive past, but he doesn't take any notice.' He shrugged, unable to comprehend people who refused to take his advice, then went to serve another customer.

If he hadn't moved away, Garfield would've asked for a pint of whatever Skinner was drinking to help loosen his tongue. As it was, he drifted across with his own beer and his pork scratchings, then introduced himself.

He got a similar reaction as he had from the publican.

'I was wondering when somebody would get around to talking to me. It's about the bones dug up in Kilstock Court, isn't it?' He looked pointedly at Garfield's full, untouched pint, then at his own glass with an inch of beer in the bottom.

'What are you drinking?' Garfield said.

'I'm not fussy when somebody else is buying.'

Garfield took the hint, put his pint in front of Skinner. Went back to the bar and bought two more. Something told him he'd caught Skinner on a thirsty night.

He was proved right when he got back to the table. What had been his beer until a minute ago was now half-gone. It didn't look as if there were many pork scratchings left in the packet, either.

Garfield took the seat opposite Skinner, sipped his beer and waited.

'I worked at Kilstock from the late nineties until two thousand and ten,' Skinner started. 'I don't remember the names of any of the tenants and it won't do any good checking my bank account.' He raised a thick finger that looked as if it had spent most of its life buried in dirt. 'That's not because they paid cash. I always paid my taxes—'

'The agency paid your wages?'

'That's right. I reckon they took half of what should've come to me, too.'

Lucky they did, Garfield thought, as Skinner drained the second half of what had been his beer. *Or you'd have drunk yourself to death before now.*

'Anyway, doesn't matter who the early tenants were,' Skinner said, 'I reckon you should be looking at the last lot.'

'Why's that?'

'It was a cult.' Then, when Garfield's surprise stopped him from immediately answering, 'You know, like Charles Manson.'

A similarly-aged man to Skinner standing with a couple of friends on the other side of the fireplace had been paying more attention to their conversation than that of his friends. He heard the word *cult* and nudged one of the men with him.

'Old Joe's on about cults again.'

'Give it a rest, Joe,' the friend called out.

'I'm telling you, it was a bloody cult,' Skinner replied, his voice similarly raised.

'I suppose the bones that were dug up was a human sacrifice at one of their black masses, was it?' the first man jeered.

Garfield got to his feet, showed his warrant card to the three men.

'I'd appreciate it if you didn't interrupt again.'

The man who'd referred to black masses hooked his thumb at the door, spoke to his friends as if Garfield wasn't there.

'I'm going outside for a fag.'

The other two followed behind him, a parting comment coming from one of them.

Waste of taxpayers' money.

'Sorry about that,' Skinner said, when Garfield took his seat again.

'It's not your fault. Tell me why you think it was a cult.'

'The name for one thing. The church of something. I can't remember exactly what. There must have been nearly twenty of them living there at one point.' He leaned in, lowered his voice. 'A lot of them were young women.'

'Do you know the names of the people in charge?'

Skinner took a long swallow of beer, made a show of trying to remember.

'It was a man and a woman. Both mid-twenties to thirty, but I can't remember their names. She was foreign. Dutch, I think. Everybody had to call him *master* or something stupid like that, so I never heard his real name spoken. Probably got kicked out for taking his name in vain.'

'What did they believe in?'

Skinner twisted around to look through the window where the three men who'd mocked him were all smoking outside.

'It wasn't human sacrifices or anything like that prick said. I never went into the house, so I don't know what might have gone on inside. It's not like they asked me to build them an altar in the garden.'

Garfield instinctively knew he'd got most of the information he was likely to get when Skinner first said the word *cult*. Despite that, he pressed on.

'What did they do all day? Work in the grounds turning the place into a self-sufficient community?'

'No, nothing like that.' Jabbing his chest to indicate who did all the hard work around the place.

'Big property to look after on your own.'

Skinner immediately backtracked, his tone defensive.

'They helped out some of the time, but nobody knew their arse from their elbow. I had to supervise them.'

'Did they work locally? They must've needed money.'

Again, Skinner glanced out of the window to where the three men were still smoking, then leaned in and dropped his voice as if it were open.

'They asked me to look into how much it would cost to repair the big old Victorian greenhouses. I asked them what for. The next thing I know, I'm out on my ear.' Hooking his thumb at the door as he said it. 'They told the agency they didn't like my attitude. Got some foreigner in to replace me. That's when the place started to fall apart. A few months later, I heard a rumour they were selling drugs in Bridgwater and Taunton. Glastonbury, too, when the festival was on.'

He gave a satisfied nod that his suspicions about the greenhouses had been proved right.

Now, it was Garfield who looked at the three men outside who'd finished smoking but weren't making a move to come back in. Probably due to his presence. They wouldn't be able to make fun of Skinner after he'd asked them to stop. But he couldn't help wondering if they had a point.

'Did you have much interaction with the cult members?'

'Not really. I was too busy.'

'Did anything unusual or suspicious happen you're aware of?'

'It was all unusual if you ask me.'

'I mean like one of the girls suddenly not being around anymore?'

'I've been asking myself the same thing ever since the bones were dug up. I can't think of anything. The disciples or whatever they called themselves came and went on a regular basis.'

'Do you know how it ended?'

Skinner shook his head, *no idea*.

'I drove past one day and the gates were padlocked. It still breaks my heart to see it how it is today. My own blood and sweat is in that ground, not only that young woman.'

Garfield bought him another pint on his way out. If any of the three men had still been outside, he would've stopped to question them on why they were so dismissive of Skinner's story.

But they weren't.

Still, it was a good evening's work. The way forward felt closer, despite the complete lack of detail or names in Skinner's memories and the need to filter what he had said.

He'd worked with less.

25

Angel got to his father's house at a little before 11:30 A.M., Jasper sitting upright on the passenger seat beside him with his nose poking out of the window. The front door was open, although Carl was nowhere in sight.

It wasn't forgetfulness—either due to Huntington's or everyday old age. It was more a sensible precaution, given that his father was expecting two small visitors who would go through it if it wasn't already open.

He went inside and called out.

'I'm up here,' drifted down from upstairs.

Angel fixed Jasper's leash to the boot scraper beside the front door, took the stairs up two at a time. He found Carl putting fresh sheets on the bunk beds in the third bedroom.

'You're early,' Carl said, without stopping what he was doing.

'Nice to see you, too, Dad,' Angel said to his father's hunched-over back. 'Why don't I get Grace to come up and do that for you?'

Carl paused tucking in a sheet long enough to wag a finger at him.

'Gotta try harder than that, Max. Cat told me you already

used that line on her yesterday. Besides, hasn't Grace got your mother staying for the weekend?'

Yeah, the one weekend Vanessa's away, Angel thought, and shortened it.

'Yeah.'

'How is she?

Having a whale of a time, meeting new people...

He almost asked, *do you care*, then softened it.

'Are you interested?'

Carl finished smoothing every last crease out of the bedcovers, angled his head to check from a different perspective, then finally turned to face him.

'If she's come all the way from Belfast hoping to watch me die, it would serve her right if she went first.'

Angel knew full well his old man was being deliberately provocative to disguise any residual feelings he had. He didn't rise to the bait, said something equally inflammatory.

'Are the two of you planning to meet at all?'

Carl grinned at him now.

'There's a worrying amount of desperation in your voice, Max. Got a vested interest, have you? You're stuck with her until we do, eh?'

Angel was starting to ask himself why he hadn't simply done as Kincade told him and turned up at midday.

'Are you planning on meeting or not?'

'She hasn't phoned me to suggest it.'

'You've only got a one-way telephone, have you?'

Carl nodded to himself as if something that had been confusing him for a long while had suddenly fallen into place.

'I can see where Cat gets some of her cheek from. She spends too much time with you.'

Angel knew better than to try to defend himself as they made their way downstairs.

'Who left that dog there?' Carl said, when they got down, making it sound like somebody had left an unwashed cup in the sink.

'I did. I'm dog-sitting. I thought Cat mentioned it.'

'Not to me she didn't.'

This time, Angel couldn't stop himself from wondering if his father's memory was on the way out—for whatever reason.

Carl went over to Jasper, scratched him behind the ears.

'Who does he belong to?'

'A friend.'

'I didn't know you had any friends with a dog.'

Maybe not, but you know this one, Angel thought, tempted to get out his phone, show his old man the picture of his ex-gaoler.

'Cat's girls are going to love him,' Carl said, moving on and saving Angel from having to explain further. 'What's his name?'

'Jasper.'

Carl took a moment to think about the name, as if he was deciding whether it was appropriate.

'If I had a dog, I'd call it Max.'

'That's my name.'

'So? Who said a man can't have a son and a dog with the same name?'

'Might cause a problem when you take them both to the park.'

'Only if you've got a son stupid enough to chase a tennis ball and bring it back in his mouth.'

There wasn't a lot Angel could say to that.

Not that Carl gave him a chance, another brisk rub on Jasper's head before he headed for the kitchen.

'Must get on.'

'Need a hand?' Smiling to himself as he said it. It'd be a cold day in hell before his father accepted help from anyone with anything.

'No thanks. You'll have to do more than enough of that when the Huntington's really kicks in.'

Angel couldn't stop himself from laughing at the way his father not only refused to take his daughter's concerns seriously, but openly mocked them.

'You wouldn't say that if Grace was here.'

The Huntington's remark had been thrown over Carl's shoulder as he headed for the kitchen. Now, he stopped to fix Angel with a stare that told him how wrong he was.

'Wouldn't I? Maybe we should invite her next time.'

'Mum too?'

'The more the merrier.'

'I think I'm busy.'

Carl looked as if he was going to say more—a pithy but untrue remark about Angel avoiding the big issues, perhaps— but decided against it, turning back towards the kitchen.

Angel untied Jasper, then sat on the old bench underneath the front-room window to relax for a minute before the onslaught began. Jasper got settled at his feet as if thinking the same thing.

'Sensible dog,' Angel said to himself as much as Jasper. 'You're going to need all the energy you've got.'

He was proved right ten minutes later when Kincade's car turned up. Isla and Daisy exploded out of the back seats before it had even come to a complete standstill and made straight for Jasper who'd sat up at the sound of the car approaching.

Kincade climbed out of the front, her smile saying it all as they petted him.

Welcome to my world.

The affection pecking order had changed once again.

She had been eclipsed by Angel, the strange man with a mouth organ who used to be a priest, his parish located on one of the farthest planets in the solar system in their young minds.

He, in turn, had been ousted by a dog.

He was relieved his father was out of sight inside the house, or else the girls might have had a difficult decision. Either that, or Carl Angel a disappointing first meeting.

Hearing all the commotion, Carl now appeared, giving Jasper a much-needed break before he was loved to death.

'And this is Carl,' Kincade said.

Carl had been adamant he wanted the girls to address him by his first name. Angel was simply *Angel* to them, so that was already taken. The alternative was *The General*, Carl having been unofficially promoted from Warrant Officer Class One to General by Isla when Kincade first told her daughters about Angel's father's military background.

The girls said a quick *hello* and went back to Jasper.

'Nobody with only two legs and no tail can compete,' Kincade said apologetically.

Despite the truth in her words, Daisy, the youngest, grew bored with stroking Jasper and turned her attentions on Angel.

'Did you bring your mouth organ?'

He patted his pocket where the instrument lived, worked a sorry note into his voice.

'I did, but I'm afraid Jasper doesn't like it. It makes him sad. He'd probably run away and you'd never see him again.'

'Especially the way he plays it,' Kincade said under her breath, marvelling at his ability to think on his feet.

Daisy nodded solemnly, although it wasn't clear whether it was her mother's contribution that convinced her the mouth organ should stay firmly in Angel's pocket.

'Grab your bags out of the car, girls,' Kincade said. 'I'll show you your room.'

'Has it got a view of the sea?' Daisy asked, demonstrating a six-year-old's grasp of geography, but understandable, nonetheless. Before moving in with Angel's father, Kincade had lived in a penthouse apartment in the up-market Ocean Village Marina owned by one of her estranged husband's friends.

'Depends how good your eyesight is,' Angel said, then pulled a serious face as if explaining a complex mathematical problem. 'I've heard lots of fizzy drinks can help improve the eyesight.'

Both Kincade and Carl glared at him, their joint thought easy to read.

Says the man who's not staying the night and doesn't have to get them settled down.

Except Carl was up to the challenge, thinking of ways to wear them out.

'We'll get your bags later, girls. How about we all go for a walk with Jasper down by the river?'

Kincade pointed a finger at Angel as the girls fought over Jasper's leash, eyes narrowed and words unnecessary.

You say anything about a prize for the first one to fall in and you're dead.

If Angel thought he'd had the last laugh, he'd seriously underestimated Kincade's deviousness, as Isla demonstrated once they were all heading towards the river.

'Who does Jasper belong to?'

Angel didn't need to look at Kincade to see the satisfied smile on her face.

'A friend.'

'What's his name?'

Now, he gave Kincade a smug look—*you didn't prime her very well, did you?*

'It's a secret.'

'I like secrets,' Daisy joined in.

'Everybody does,' Angel agreed. 'The thing is, they're secret.'

I've got all the time in the world, Kincade thought. *They'll wear you down in the end.*

26

'Get the girls settled down okay on Saturday night?' Angel asked, when Kincade walked in on Monday morning looking exhausted.

'Eventually. No thanks to you. I'm surprised Daisy didn't try to climb onto the roof after drinking a two-litre bottle of Coke, hoping to see the sea. Luckily your dad bored them to sleep. His war stories might be exciting stuff, but he needs to cut down on the detail for a six and eight-year-old audience. *We killed all the bad guys* is more than sufficient for them. How about you? Jasper recovered okay from his ordeal?'

He knew what she was doing bringing the dog into the conversation. Despite what she'd thought, her girls had not worn him down with their persistence. They didn't think Jasper's rightful owner would agree to transferring ownership to them, so they weren't actually that interested.

'He's fine,' he said, then moved swiftly on. 'I bet the girls are driving Elliot insane about getting one.'

She grinned at him, the pleasure she got at imagining her estranged husband being badgered night and day outweighing her disappointment at not knowing who Jasper's owner was.

'Yeah. Great, isn't it?'

Talk of the dog brought back the concerns he'd had at his father's house before they went out of his mind when Kincade turned up with her girls.

'Did you tell my dad I was bringing Jasper with me?'

'Of course. Not everybody likes dogs.'

'He claimed you hadn't mentioned it.'

She knew exactly what his concern was. At times, she felt as if she was a spy in Carl Angel's house, watching for symptoms of Huntington's disease to report back to his children.

'I told him on Friday night.'

'And less than twenty-four hours later, he said you didn't. Was it after he'd been to the pub for his three pints?'

'Uh-huh.'

They both knew he was clutching at straws, as her next words proved.

'It wasn't as if I told him and he might not have heard properly. He said it would be great. Take the pressure off him trying to think of ways to keep the girls amused.' She smiled softly. 'He even said he might get one himself if the girls were going to stay regularly.'

'A Carl Angel-style hint.'

'Exactly.'

They held each other's gaze for a long moment. Then he asked the question she was praying he wouldn't.

'You would tell me if you saw any definite symptoms, wouldn't you?'

She took a long time answering.

'I don't know.'

At least you're honest, he thought. He knew as well as she did his father would do everything in his power to hide any symptoms, should there be any, from his children. She would find herself in an impossible position. Torn between their understandable desire to be kept informed about their father's health and betraying his trust.

'I hope I never have to find out.' She still had her coat on and her bag slung over her shoulder. She deposited them on her chair and went straight to the coffee machine. 'You want one?'

He jumped at the opportunity to put an end to the awkward conversation.

'Might as well, before we have to give the machine back to Finch.'

'You think I'm wrong?'

He didn't know what he thought.

Her theory was that Dominic Orford hadn't worked at his father's company at all. Instead, he'd been at Kilstock Court with Jasmijn, the woman he met while travelling. There, he'd killed her and buried her in a shallow grave, which had recently been dug up. Somebody close to Jasmijn knew or suspected he'd killed her, but didn't know where exactly he'd buried her in the extensive grounds. They had then tortured Orford to get that information before killing him.

'Not sure. We need to speak to Orford's father again. See if he can provide proof of Orford working for him.'

Just saying the words reminded him of how sick he was of having to prise every little piece of information out of Nigel and Helen Orford. Having been to their house twice and them having come into the station once, it was their turn to come to him—if he wanted to view it in dinner party terms.

'You can call him to ask him to come in, seeing as you're the one risking our coffee machine on it.'

My coffee machine, she corrected mentally, dialling Orford's mobile.

'His phone's switched off.'

They shared a look. *Why are we not surprised?*

'He's avoiding us,' Angel said. 'I'm going to call his office.'

'I can do that.'

'No. You drink your coffee. You look as if you need the caffeine more than an argument.'

Nothing like having your mind made up in advance, she thought, but happy to do as he said.

'I bet Orford's told the receptionist to say he's in a meeting,' he said, as he dialled.

'Don't tell them who you are.'

'I wasn't planning to.'

As it turned out, the situation was even worse. Angel felt as if the phone might crack in his grip as the receptionist responded to his request to be put through.

'I'm afraid Mr Orford is unavailable. He's taken compassionate leave for the foreseeable future. He's recently suffered a personal tragedy. Is there anybody else who can help?'

The immediate spike of irritation that went through him was short-lived when the significance of the opportunity that had been presented to him hit home. He was now free to interview Orford's employees without Orford himself breathing down his neck and making them feel uncomfortable.

'Is there a general manager? Somebody who's been with the company a long time?'

'Stan Kowalski is your best bet. He's been here twenty years at least. Who shall I say is calling?'

'Max Angel.' Glancing at Kincade as he said it, getting a thumbs up for dropping the *Detective Inspector*.

'Can I ask what it's about, Mr Angel?'

'It's a private matter.'

There was a brief pause while she made the obvious connection between Orford's compassionate leave and his use of *private matter*. If she made the next, easy leap and realised he was a police officer, she chose to say nothing about it, asking him to hold, instead.

He changed gear as soon as Kowalski came on the line.

'This is Detective Inspector Max Angel, Mr Kowalski. We need to come in to talk to you as a matter of urgency. We can be there in half an hour...'

Thirty seconds later—long enough to tell the confused Kowalski, *no, he couldn't ask what it was about*—and they were pulling on their coats, Kincade throwing the last of her much-needed coffee down her throat.

They were shown into a modern conference-cum-boardroom on the top floor with a view over the car park. Looking down on it while they waited for Kowalski to join them, Nigel Orford's conspicuously-empty private parking space nearest to the front door seemed to be laughing at them.

We'll see who has the last laugh, Angel thought, as he came away from the window when Kowalski entered the room.

Stan Kowalski was a thickset man in his early sixties, his steel-grey hair cropped close to his head. If he'd worked for Nigel Orford for twenty years, he'd been in the country for at least that length of time, possibly a lot longer. If he'd had an accent, it was now long gone. He wore a blue suit with a white shirt and a striped tie. Nigel Orford went up in Angel's estimation if he was behind his staff dressing smartly in the current era of casual and often downright scruffy attire in the workplace. It might have been Kowalski's own sense of pride in his appearance, of course.

They shook hands and made the introductions, then all took a seat at the big, pale-wood table.

'I understand you've been with the company a long time, Mr Kowalski,' Angel started.

'Twenty-two years.' Sounding like it was two hundred and twenty-two. 'Where does the time go, eh?'

I can tell you where I wasted ten years of mine, Angel thought, and was about to get to the point when Kowalski carried on.

'Liz on reception said it was a private matter relating to Mr Orford. I don't see how I can help. Mr Orford is a good employer, but we don't socialise or anything like that.'

'It's actually his son, Dominic, that we're here about.'

'*Ah*.' There was an awkward silence as if somebody had told a dirty joke on the church steps, before Kowalski found his voice. 'I read about that. It was terrible. Is it true what the newspaper said?'

'I'm afraid so. But Dominic Orford's death isn't why we're here today.'

Kowalski relaxed visibly, his brief worry that he was about to be asked to account for his movements fading away.

'We're interested in the period when Dominic worked here. The three years from two thousand and nine to two thousand and twelve.'

He was very careful to not say where their information came from. Attributing it to Nigel Orford, Kowalski's boss, would have a negative effect on Kowalski's willingness to disagree with anything his employer had told them.

Angel needn't have worried.

Kowalski coughed out a knowing laugh, his voice filled with the acceptance that some things will never change, that people will always put the interests of themselves and their family above all else.

'I don't know if you got your information from the Inland Revenue, but even if Dominic was officially on the payroll, he never set foot in the place.'

Angel caught Kincade's eye, saw what went through her mind.

The coffee machine is halfway safe.

'We're talking about after Dominic had his breakdown, aren't we?' Kowalski carried on.

'We are.'

The amused contempt Kowalski displayed a moment ago disappeared at the mention of Dominic's breakdown. Perhaps due to feelings of sympathy in a man who might have been worked like a dog himself, but had managed to come through it unscathed.

'Everybody knew about the breakdown. Mr Orford paid a fortune to have him treated in a private clinic up in London. Then Dominic went travelling around the world—'

'That's right.'

'—and he was supposed to join the company when he got back. We were all thinking, bloody marvellous, the spoilt little rich boy is going to come back and start bossing us around, and we'll just have to suck it up. Except it never happened. Every time we asked when he was due to start, we got fobbed off. *Soon. Next week.* In the end, we forgot about it and stopped asking. I've never thought about it until you just mentioned it.'

'Do you know what he was doing when he was supposedly working here?' Kincade said.

A sudden wariness came over Kowalski, uncomfortable at being asked to venture into the realms of speculation. They expected a quick negative response followed by an even quicker question about whether they were done.

Kowalski surprised them.

'You should talk to my son Keith about that. He knew Dominic back then. The whole situation with Dominic supposedly joining the company really pissed me off at the time. I asked Mr Orford if he could find a position for Keith, and he said no, there weren't any available. Then suddenly he invents one for his own son.' He held up a large, square hand to stop them from stating the obvious, then stated it himself. 'I realise it's his company. He can do what he likes. But it still pissed me off. Anyway, you're not interested in that.'

You got that right, Kincade thought, and said something more constructive.

'If I could take Keith's details, please.'

'No need.' He pointed at the floor. 'He's downstairs. Mr Orford didn't give him a job at the time, but ten years later he did.' He smiled the smile of a proud parent, then blew his own trumpet. 'I like to think that after I'd worked here for another ten years, Mr Orford decided he'd employ any Kowalski who wanted to work here.'

ANGEL AND KINCADE STOOD SIDE-BY-SIDE AT THE FLOOR-TO-ceiling window looking out over the car park while Kowalski went to fetch his son.

Who's having the last laugh now? Angel thought, looking down on Nigel Orford's empty space. *Let's see if it gets better still.*

From the length of time he was away, Stan Kowalski's son must have either been in a meeting or on a long phone call. That, or, more likely, Stan was taking him through the conversation he'd had with them.

After a perfunctory knock on the door, Keith Kowalski entered the room alone, then closed the door behind him. Angel gave his father a mental *attaboy*. Not only did Stan Kowalski dress smartly in a suit and tie, he recognised when his presence was no longer required.

If they hadn't been paying close attention, they might have thought Stan himself had come back into the room. Keith was a carbon copy of his father, to the extent that Stan would never have harboured suspicions about his wife being unfaithful.

'Dad tells me you want to talk about Dominic Orford,' Keith

started, addressing Kincade more than Angel after they all sat down at the conference table.

Looks like you've got an admirer there, Angel thought, reading Keith's body language. He leaned back in his chair, happy to let her take the lead.

'That's right. The period when he was supposedly working here. Your dad thought you'd know where he actually was.'

It was obvious Keith was concerned about how much his father might have built him up, billing him as the last person they would need to talk to before they slapped the cuffs on Dominic Orford's killer.

'I don't know anything for sure. But I can tell you the rumours that were going around at the time...'

'Before we get into that, can you tell us how you knew him, how well you knew him?'

Keith smiled, swept his hand around the spacious room on the top floor of the whole building owned by Dominic Orford's father in preparation to answering.

'I certainly didn't go to the same school as he did. Dom was at some fancy boarding school. I went to the local comprehensive. But there was a group of us used to hang out together during the school holidays. I didn't know him that well myself, but I knew the same people he did, especially some of the girls. This was all before he went to university to train to be a doctor, of course. I didn't keep in touch, but I kept in touch with people who did.'

'We appreciate what you're going to say is based on hearsay,' Kincade said, to stop Keith from spending another five minutes distancing himself from whatever he was about to tell them.

Keith nodded, then glanced up and down the completely clear table.

'Didn't Dad offer you anything to drink?'

'We're fine,' Kincade said, not wanting to waste more time. 'Tell us what you heard.'

'The rumour was that he was down in the back of beyond in Somerset. You probably don't think that's very interesting—'

Kincade shared a look with Angel—*we think it's more than interesting*,

'—but it's what he was doing there. Apparently, he joined a cult.'

The word *cult* had the effect Keith had clearly been hoping for. A momentary stunned silence filled the room before Kincade spoke again.

'Would this have been in a big old house called Kilstock Court?'

'I don't know what it was called, but it was in a country estate, yeah. He'd had a breakdown—'

'We know about that.'

'—and went travelling and met some woman. They both joined the cult when they got back.' His brow creased as if unhappy with something. 'Actually, some of the rumours say they started it themselves. They'd been to India and got into all that hippy shit. Although living in a country mansion doesn't exactly fit with turning your back on the material world and all that peace and love crap.'

Kincade caught Angel's eye, saw that he was thinking the same as her. It would be a very small step into conjecture and gossip based on nothing more than pre-conceived ideas and too much TV.

'Do you know anything about the woman he started the cult with?' Angel said.

'Only that he met her travelling.'

They wrapped it up after that. The time Keith had spent stressing that what he knew was second-hand hadn't been wasted.

Angel kept hold of Keith's hand a little longer than strictly necessary when they shook hands on the way out.

'We won't mention what you've told us about Dominic to Nigel Orford, but feel free to do so yourself, if you want to.'

Keith didn't need to put his thoughts into words as Angel released his hand.

Do I look stupid?

'I'M GETTING THE FEELING OUR COFFEE MACHINE IS SAFE,' KINCADE said in the lift on the way down.

'It's more encouraging than if Kilstock Court had been used as a residential management training school,' Angel admitted. 'It also explains Orford's parents' reluctance to tell us the truth.'

'Yes, but do they know how it all ended?'

'Do you mean how it actually ended? Or how you think it ended?'

'Same thing.'

I hope you're right, he thought. *I don't want to go back to the brown sludge that comes out when you press the "coffee" button on the drinks machine by the lifts.*

27

'A cult?' DI Jay Chopra said, sounding as if Garfield had told him Kilstock Court had been used as a staging post for an alien expeditionary force. 'Are you having a laugh?'

'That's what the ex-head gardener reckons. The church of something or the other. Lots of young women cavorting and taking drugs.'

Chopra gave him an incredulous look.

'*Cavorting?* That's a fancy word for a gardener.'

'He didn't actually use that word.'

'No? It's a fancy word for you, too, Dave.' He shook his head at the strange ways of the world. 'Shame we can't have California's weather if we have to have their cults. I suppose it fits with them having a crucified man in Southampton.'

Shit, Garfield thought. He'd completely forgotten to update them with the name of the young woman whose bones had been dug up—and how they'd come by that information.

'I'll give them a call now.' Already dialling Angel's number as he left Chopra's office, making sure the door was firmly closed behind him.

'I was about to call you,' Angel said. 'You'll never believe what Kilstock Court was used for—'

'A cult.'

There was a brief lull after Garfield stole Angel's thunder, then Angel carried on.

'Our information is a bit sketchy. Rumours and gossip. How about you?'

'I spoke to the head gardener who used to work at Kilstock. He claims they called themselves the church of something or the other. He was a bit vague, couldn't remember names. He claims he didn't see anything suspicious, or notice that one of the young women wasn't around anymore, but he was only there until two thousand and ten.'

'Any luck identifying the tenants yourself?'

Garfield took a minute to update Angel on what he'd been doing, in particular the lack of success he'd had on account of everything being handled by the property letting agency who had subsequently gone bust.

'What about council tax records?' Angel said.

'I'm waiting for them to get back to me.'

Angel gave a knowing laugh.

'It's a race to see who gets nowhere first.'

'Not quite nowhere. We know the identity of the woman whose bones we dug up.' He held up a hand to stop Angel interrupting, a pointless instinctive reaction given that Angel couldn't see him. 'Or at least the same person who told us about the body in the first place has given us a name.'

'Really?'

'Uh-huh. And a date of birth.'

'They were right about the body being there, so who knows? What's the name?'

'Rosie Laing.'

Angel was quiet for so long Garfield thought the line had been cut.

'It sounds to me as if the name means something to you.'

'You could say that,' Angel replied eventually, then told him why.

'What's up?' Kincade said, when Angel ended the call.

He pointed at the coffee machine, the taste of brown sludge already in his mouth.

'Unplug it and take it back to Finch.'

'What for?'

'The woman whose bones were dug up was called Rosie Laing, not Jasmijn. The same people who emailed Garfield to tell him the body was buried there sent him the name.'

She glanced at the coffee machine, her words hopeful if not the voice behind them.

'They might be wrong.'

'They were right about the body being there.'

They spent five minutes speculating on why the sender of the emails had done so, arriving at the same tentative conclusion Garfield had—they wanted her identified and laid properly to rest, and had a good enough grip on reality to know how difficult an identification might be after so many years, despite what they saw on TV.

The brief discussion temporarily eclipsed the more significant development. It couldn't be coincidence that the man Gulliver and Jardine had interviewed about the car parked in the lay-by close to the derelict barn where Orford was killed and who denied ever being there was called Graeme Laing.

It was a given that they would interview Laing again at some point, this time under caution. It was just a question of whether they accumulated sufficient evidence to arrest him and charged him with Orford's murder.

'Let's have a word with Finch,' he said, knowing they were a long way from being in that situation. 'Might as well bring the machine with you.'

He waited while she unplugged it, looking as if she was packing her daughters' suitcases in preparation for her husband and his gold-digging bunny boiler, Hannah, to emigrate to Australia with them.

Once it was unplugged, she marched ahead of him to make sure she got to Finch's office first.

'I thought it was unfair to keep it, ma'am, seeing as it was only a broken fuse,' she said, carrying it in.

Finch looked at her and Angel following behind over her glasses.

'Really?' Sounding as if Kincade had said the Tooth Fairy had told her to return it. 'So? What part of your theory was wrong?'

Angel replied for her while Kincade put the machine back on top of Finch's filing cabinet.

'It wasn't Jasmijn buried behind the boathouse.'

'I'm not grubbing around behind there plugging it in again,' Kincade muttered, as Angel took Finch through the latest developments.

Finch got up from her desk as she listened, opened the bottom drawer of the filing cabinet and pulled out an extension lead. She plugged one end into a more accessible wall socket and the coffee machine into the other.

'That'll make it easier to unplug when we win it back again,' Kincade said, again under her breath.

'Anyone like to say something on the matter?' Angel asked, after he'd finished explaining about Rosie Laing.

Finch took her seat again, steepled her fingers and threw it back in Angel's court.

'What do you think, Padre?'

'Definitely easier to unplug it next time, ma'am.'

He got the look he deserved.

He was not to be an arse his whole life.

'I don't think we can charge Graeme Laing yet,' he said, wiping the smile off his face. 'We need confirmation of the identification first, not just the emailed word of an anonymous sender. We'll start by checking to see if a Rosie Laing, born in February ninety-seven, has ever been reported as missing. We also need to check to see if Laing had a daughter called Rosie. And we need to get to the bottom of what's going on with his car. Jardine is pretty convinced Laing was telling the truth when he denied being there.'

Finch rocked her head from side to side, unconvinced.

'If you've had twelve years to plan your revenge, you probably make sure you're good at lying before you make your move.'

'True. But we also don't know for sure the body was buried during the time the cult was in residence.'

'The date included in the email address suggests it was in two thousand and twelve.'

'Okay, but we're back to believing the anonymous email sender. I admit it's all pointing one way, but we don't have a single piece of hard evidence to suggest Orford ever set foot in Kilstock Court, started a cult and buried Rosie Laing in a shallow grave there.'

Finch couldn't disagree. Instead, she made shooing motions at them.

'Don't just stand there. Go and find some.' A pause, long enough to let the satisfaction creep into her voice. 'And thanks for fixing *my* coffee machine.'

. . .

ANGEL FELT HIS BLOOD RUN COLD WHEN HE GOT BACK INTO HIS office with Kincade. He'd left his mobile on his desk when he went to update Finch. He'd missed a call while he was away, the two initials jumping off the screen at him.

VB

Virgil Balan.

At the time, he'd felt stupid when he used Balan's initials instead of his full name against his number. Not so stupid now. Kincade knew the score, but it was still better to be safe than sorry. Risk Superintendent Horwood wandering in and wanting to know why an Inspector in the Poliția Română was calling Angel on his private phone.

He checked it. Balan had left a voicemail. His heart was thumping, a feeling of nameless dread settling in his stomach as he called it. The message was short, to the point and not informative at all.

It's Virgil Balan, Padre. Call me immediately.

Angel's pulse quickened again, a single thought in his mind. Balan had found Bogdan Florescu. He wanted an answer from Angel. Do we go this official route? Or do you want me to hide him away while you and Stuart Beckford book your flights and polish your brass knuckles?

Kincade couldn't fail to see the effect the voicemail had on him. But living with his father, and after the conversation they'd had first thing that morning about Huntington's symptoms, she jumped to the wrong conclusion.

'It's not your dad, is it?'

He shook his head, her voice breaking the grip of his escalating panic.

'It's Balan.'

'He's found Florescu?'

'I don't know. He left a message to call him.'

As Finch had, she made shooing motions with her hands towards the door.

'Off you go to the men's toilets, like you normally do.'

He was already on the way. Except he needed fresh air, not the claustrophobic atmosphere of the ground-floor toilets. He took the stairs down, too wired to wait for the lifts. Blew through the front lobby without a word to Jack Bevan on the front desk and out into the open, his phone clamped in his sweaty hand.

He hit the missed call like he was trying to crack the screen, clamped the phone to his ear.

Voicemail.

An irrational surge of anger ripped through him. Balan was deliberately not answering to prolong his anxiety. He didn't leave a message. This was no time to be playing telephone tag. Instead, he kept the phone in his hand, counting to sixty before he tried again.

The phone rang in his hand at fifty-four, the initials *VB* on the screen.

He took a deep breath, kept his voice level as if they were about to arrange dinner together.

'Sorry I missed your call, Virgil.'

Like they had all the time in the world for pleasantries.

'Likewise, Padre.'

Nothing.

Forcing him to ask.

Reminding him who was in control.

'Have you found Florescu, Virgil?' Knowing that if he'd said, *found him*, Balan would have replied, *found who?*

'Not yet, no.'

Relief hissed out of Angel like air from a punctured balloon. *No decision to make today!* He didn't want to think about what that implied about him.

'It's a delicate matter, Padre. Stuart Beckford contacted me directly.'

The surprise stole the words out of Angel's mouth as Balan continued.

'I wanted to ask if that was something you'd agreed between yourselves? Whether you'd asked Stuart to liaise with me, given he has time on his hands.'

Angel wanted to know how Balan did it. How he managed to catch him off balance every single time they talked. It made him feel like a child dealing with an adult.

He felt the knowing smile in Balan's voice long before he heard the words.

'Your silence tells me it's news to you, Padre. Your friend has gone behind your back.'

Angel knew Balan had deliberately chosen to state it bluntly, provocatively. Phrase it in terms of how it impacted on him, Angel, the implication of betrayal. A harder note entered Balan's voice now, one Angel guessed was more at home there compared to the easy conversational tone that characterised their discussions.

'If I am to continue, I need to be confident I'm dealing with two people singing from the same hymn sheet. That's the correct expression, isn't it, Padre?'

'It is, Virgil.'

'There is no place for a loose cannon.'

And that's enough demonstrating your knowledge of English idioms, Angel thought.

'I totally agree, Virgil. What exactly did Stuart say?'

'Simply that he wanted to introduce himself. He'd heard you talk about me so much, he wanted to put a voice to the name, if not a face.'

All he has to do is close his eyes and think of the devil.

'However,' Balan went on, 'I believe that was merely an

excuse. I can give you my own opinion of why he really called, although I must warn you that you won't like it.'

Angel worked a confident note into his voice, no easy task.

'What sort of a man would I be if I said *no* after that?'

Balan left the slightest of pauses. Just long enough to emphasise his unspoken reply.

I can give you my take on that, too, if you're up for it.

'This is only my opinion, of course,' Balan said, the caveat merely highlighting the validity of everything that came out of his mouth. 'I believe he wanted to ask me to contact him in the first instance, should I find Florescu. Except he lost his nerve. What concerns me is what that implies.'

Angel would've bet everything he owned on Balan leaving the sentence hanging, not stating the implications that concerned him. He duly played his part.

'What implications, Virgil?'

'That he is worried you are not sufficiently committed to our joint endeavour. Are you committed, Padre?'

So many things Angel wanted to say.

Committed to what, exactly?

Is your offer official or unofficial?

Stop playing fucking games with me.

'I'm as committed as I've ever been.'

'An interesting answer, Padre.'

'I'm totally committed, Virgil.'

'I'm glad to hear it. I was worried you might have discussed it with Vanessa Corrigan, and she'd advised you to back off. She didn't want you as her guest at HMP Isle of Wight.'

Angel felt as if he'd been punched in the gut, his mouth flapping uselessly like a landed fish on the riverbank. His mind was spinning, and not only from being blindsided yet again. Was the crack about being Vanessa's guest that rarest of creatures, a mistake by Balan? An inadvertent admission that what he was offering might lead Angel into committing an act that might land him in prison?

Balan said nothing, enjoying the effect his words had caused.

'How do you know about her?' Angel croaked.

'I make it my business to know everything about the people I deal with, particularly when the matter is out of the ordinary.'

'Out of the ordinary in what way?'

Praying that Balan compounded his admission—*because it's unofficial.*

It wasn't to be.

'Because it's not only a police matter, it's personal, too. I need to know who I'm dealing with. Surely you are the same, Padre?'

Yes, Angel thought, *but I don't have the resources to spy on a police officer in Romania.*

Balan chuckled, the sound Angel knew so well that hid so much, made him wonder if Balan chuckled as his men attached electrodes to a prisoner's genitals.

'I'm guessing you haven't told anybody about your relationship with her? In particular, not your sergeant.'

'I'm waiting for the right moment. So? Any news on Florescu at all?'

Balan chuckled again at Angel's very obvious attempt to move the conversation away from his personal life.

'Not so far, no.'

How is it you can spy on me in the UK, but you can't find a man in your own country?

It was as if Balan read his mind.

'My country is very rural and mountainous in places, Padre.' He laughed again. 'Don't forget, what was Transylvania now lies within Romania.'

Yes, and we both know who that makes you.

. . .

Angel had walked as he talked without paying much attention. By the time they ended the call with an agreement that Balan would continue to liaise with Angel, he was halfway down West Quay Road, on the way to The Pig in the Wall. He was sorely tempted to keep going, pop in for a beer and a sit down to try to collect his thoughts.

And there were plenty of them to organise, all clamouring to be heard.

He felt a pang of professional shame to learn he'd been followed and hadn't been aware of it.

He was concerned to know that Vanessa had also been followed—it wasn't as if she wore a name badge with *Deputy Governor, HMP Isle of Wight* on it as she walked down the street. She didn't need his shit in her life, especially given that he hadn't even mentioned the situation to her yet. Would it end their fledgling relationship before it got off the ground?

More than any of that, what did the fact that Balan had kept him under surveillance imply? He wouldn't have done so if all he was offering was official assistance.

An uncomfortable conversation with Stuart Beckford awaited him. Would it also be the end of what remained of their friendship, even before they were faced with any difficult decisions? In a way, he couldn't blame Beckford. Sitting at home all day long without the demands of a busy job to take his mind off Balan's offer. Angel wasn't sure how he'd cope, himself.

One thing he knew for sure. If he could turn back time, he would've told Balan he wasn't interested the first time he called with his toxic offer. With hindsight, *let sleeping dogs lie* sounded like good advice.

For now, he turned back towards the station. A team briefing was scheduled for 6 p.m., and he didn't want to breathe beer or Margarita fumes over everybody.

Kincade looked up as he entered their office.

He gave a small, multi-purpose shake of his head before she opened her mouth.

Balan hasn't found Florescu.

I don't want to talk about it.

Fifteen minutes later and he was almost feeling sorry for Beckford. He had a mountain of paperwork to get through and occupy him, but he still couldn't get the conversation with Balan out of his mind. He suspected if he was the one on long-term sick leave with time on his hands, he'd have booked a flight to Bucharest long ago.

28

'Everything okay?' Kincade said three hours later as they headed towards the incident room to take the team briefing.

'Define okay.'

She pulled her head down into her shoulders, turtle-style, thinking, *that's the last time I show any concern.*

'As bad as that, eh?'

'Worse. I'll tell you about it later.'

It was standing room only in the incident room, detectives and uniformed officers and civilian staff assembled for the latest in what was turning into a very unusual investigation. As far as Angel knew, nobody in the room had experience of dealing with cults, beyond keeping the peace when Hare Krishna followers strayed too close to town-centre pubs filled with rowdy Southampton F.C. supporters—and even that never involved anything more serious than returning a stolen tambourine.

Angel took the room through the various pieces of evidence pointing at, but not proving, Dominic Orford had been involved with a cult based out of Kilstock Court, finishing with the latest update.

'DS Garfield from Bridgwater called me this afternoon. The

ex-head gardener from Kilstock got in touch with him again, told him he'd been wrong about the name. It wasn't the church of whatever, but Heaven's something or the other.'

'Heaven's Gate?' Gulliver called out facetiously from the back.

'I think you'll find they all committed suicide in nineteen ninety-seven, Craig.'

Gulliver's hand immediately shot up.

'Permission to go to California to see if any of them survived, sir?'

Angel gave a firm nod.

'Permission granted, Craig. In your own time and at your own expense.' He caught Finch's eye. She was sitting at the side of the room, the cup in her hand and the smile on her face suggesting she was making the most of having her coffee machine back.

She nodded back at him.

'Seconded.'

'Don't forget to send us a postcard, Craig,' Angel said, moving on. 'Okay. Heaven's something. It's a tenuous connection to Orford being crucified, although the fact that he was nailed to it still says punishment to me rather than symbolism. We'll be getting in touch with organisations that help survivors of cults and their families, see if we can get any more information. We'd very much like to find out more about Jasmijn, the woman Orford met whilst travelling. We're also hoping a friend of Orford's from the relevant period will supply us with the name of a young woman Orford tried to recruit. Depending on how much detail we get, we'll consider making an appeal for information, both here and down in Somerset.'

A uniformed PC at the front raised her hand.

'Down the hall on the left,' her partner beside her said, and got a small ripple of laughter.

'Go ahead,' Angel said.

'Are we taking it that the same people who emailed the details of the body also killed Dominic Orford?'

'We are. The same email address was used to send him the image of Kilstock Court that made him arrange to meet them.' He looked around for Jardine, almost hidden behind Gulliver.

'Did you find him on the electoral roll down in Somerset, Lisa?'

'No. He was registered at his parents' address for the whole three-year period. If he was down in Somerset during that time, his parents actively colluded in hiding that fact. That's not the same as knowing what he was up to, of course.'

'True.' Thinking, *but unlikely*. 'We need a look at Nigel Orford's bank accounts to see if they were paying the rent.' He looked at Finch again.

This time, she rocked her hand.

'I don't think we've got enough to apply for that at the moment, Padre.'

He knew she was right, handed over to Kincade.

'Rosie Laing,' she started, then indicated a photograph of a dark-haired teenager pinned to the incident board. 'Aged fifteen. A search of the missing persons' database shows she was reported as missing on the eighteenth of August, two thousand and twelve by her parents, Graeme and Vera Laing—'

'The same Graeme Laing whose car was seen in the lay-by near to where Orford was killed,' Gulliver interrupted.

'That's correct.'

'But who denies ever being there,' Jardine added.

Gulliver came right back at her.

'The PNC doesn't lie.'

'No, but old women's memories do . . .'

Kincade held up a hand to put an end to the private discussion-soon-to-be-argument.

'Without doubt, Graeme Laing is a person of interest in the murder of Dominic Orford, but there are still unanswered questions. Did he know Rosie was buried there all this time and he's been waiting twelve years to take his revenge rather than see his own daughter laid to rest? It's unlikely, but you never know. We'll be speaking to Vera Laing first regarding Rosie's disappearance. She's updated us with her contact details every time she's moved, so she's clearly not giving up on Rosie or her remains being found. Bridgwater have sent us images of the pendant discovered with the bones dug up at Kilstock Court. We'll be asking Vera if it belonged to Rosie.'

'We're not going anywhere near Graeme Laing until we've got a positive ID,' Angel said, leaving nobody in any doubt. 'We can't risk spooking him.' He extended his hand towards Kincade, the interruption over.

'We need to pick Rosie's life apart. When and why did she join the cult? Was she running away from problems at home? The original file has details of a boyfriend, Christopher Jordan, and a best friend, Lindsey Howe. We need to speak to both of them and anyone else who knew her at the time. You all know the drill. Let's get to it.'

'Is it later yet?' Kincade asked, walking beside Angel back towards their office.

'No, it's always now.'

'Pedant.'

'If you mean, do I want to talk about Balan's call, the answer's *no*—'

'That's fine.'

'—but I'm prepared to, nonetheless.'

She threw him a sideways glance.

'What is this? Pedants' half hour?'

He followed her into their office, closed the door behind them—something neither of them ever did.

'Shall I sweep the office for bugs, or will you?' she said.

He pointed a finger at her, but he was struggling not to smile.

'Any more of that and there'll be nothing for anyone to overhear.'

'Shame we haven't still got the coffee machine. The noise of that would've been useful cover.'

'We all know whose fault that is.'

She shrugged, *that's the way it goes.*

The light-hearted exchange was exactly what he needed, even though he'd decided to confide in her before they went into the briefing.

Despite her outward confidence, she felt herself being compared to her predecessor, the much-loved and sorely-missed DS Stuart Beckford, at every turn—and by both her superiors and those reporting to her. Angel hadn't helped ease her concerns when he recently went behind her back and asked Beckford to approach a confidential informant on his behalf.

She needed to hear that Beckford wasn't perfect every once in a while. That it would take a lot more than him saying he wanted his old job back before he got it.

'Stu contacted Balan directly...'

She leaned back in her chair as he explained, hands clasped behind her head, although still looking at him and not the ceiling. When he finished, she dropped her hands into her lap and rocked forward, looking like she was the one whose life kept on getting more complicated.

'What are you going to do?'

'I don't know. We can all pretend it didn't happen. I continue to liaise with Balan.'

She was thoughtful a long moment. He wouldn't have been

surprised if she'd accused him of sticking his head in the sand. Except he was wrong.

'Maybe Balan's playing a game? Beckford didn't call him, and he's trying to cause trouble, make the two of you fall out?'

It was the day for tired, but true, clichés. After *let sleeping dogs lie* earlier, he was struck by the wisdom behind *a problem shared is a problem halved*. The very obvious possibility she'd suggested hadn't even crossed his mind, too busy concentrating on the potential problem dealing with Beckford.

'It's possible.'

'Then it's best if you don't say anything for now.'

He nodded, *sounds good to me*.

'Just one thing...'

She threw her eyes, knowing the serious discussion was over.

'What?'

'How can somebody who provides such a useful insight into my personal life get it so wrong about the woman buried at Kilstock Court, to the point that we lose our coffee machine?'

She shrugged apologetically—*you win some, you lose some* —rather than answer.

It had been the right decision to confide in her, talk it through. That didn't stop him from feeling guilty that he hadn't said a word about the bigger bombshell Balan dropped regarding Vanessa.

He hoped Balan never gave Kincade tips on surveillance.

29

Angel was relieved they'd got the discussion about Balan's call out of the way before they set off to interview Vera Laing. It meant he didn't have to suffer the oppressive weight of Kincade's curiosity, allowing him to concentrate on the task ahead. As for her, she was more energised. As if any bad press regarding Stuart Beckford was the verbal equivalent of blood doping, boosting her self-confidence and enthusiasm rather than her red blood cells.

'You want to take it?' he said, pulling to the kerb outside Vera Laing's house.

She was usually happy to let him take the lead. Claiming he was so good at it, that his past life as a priest somehow softened the blow that a loved one had died a violent death.

Except, in this case, that fact had yet to be proven. In a cruel twist of fate, what they wanted the most from the interview—for Vera Laing to confirm the necklace had belonged to her daughter—was the worst outcome for Vera herself. Life, in this instance, truly was a zero-sum game.

'If you like,' she said, then, with a smile on her lips, 'Not much of a reward for providing such a useful insight into what Balan might be up to, is it?'

'On the other hand—'

She nodded, *I know*.

'The perfect punishment for the person who gambled and lost our coffee machine.'

'Exactly.'

Things got off to a bad start as soon as Vera Laing opened the door, Kincade in front, Angel at her shoulder.

'No, thank you,' Vera said none too politely, already closing the door.

Kincade stopped it with her foot.

'We're police officers, Mrs Laing, not Jehovah's Witnesses.'

Vera opened the door fully again, looking as if she'd like to close it on them, too.

'You better come in.'

She led them into a cosy sitting room that doubled as a shrine to her lost daughter. There were photographs of her everywhere, on the walls, on every flat surface. Angel recognised the original of the one from the missing persons file that was now pinned to the incident board.

They couldn't help noticing, and Vera couldn't miss them noticing.

'Is it about Rosie?'

'We think it might be, Mrs Laing,' Kincade said. 'A young woman's remains were recently disinterred. She was wearing a necklace we're hoping you can identify.' She produced two close-up shots showing both sides of the necklace taken from the email DS Garfield had sent, handed them one-by-one to Vera looking hungrily at them.

They never knew how the next-of-kin would react. The number of reminders of her missing daughter in this one room alone suggested Vera would be one of those who crumple at the knees and have to be caught before they injure themselves.

That might have been the case had it been twelve weeks since Rosie Laing went missing, but not today after those weeks had become months and then years, the period of absence almost as long as the time spent together.

'It looks like hers,' Vera said, no catch in her voice or hand held to her throat. 'I'd need to see the original to be absolutely sure, but she had one exactly like it.'

She went over to a sideboard sagging under the weight of framed photographs, scanned them quickly with the practised eye of the person who dusted each of them individually every week. Then selected one in a plain, silver frame that showed her daughter wearing an open-necked white blouse.

'That looks like it there to me.'

Kincade took the photo frame. Vera continued to point as if there might be some misunderstanding about where on her body her daughter would've worn a necklace.

'Me, too.'

Angel took his turn studying the photograph, made it three out of three.

Vera took the photograph back, breathed on the glass a couple of times and gave it a quick rub with her sleeve, then set it down on the sideboard again.

They then got their first introduction into how deeply Vera Laing had thought about Rosie's disappearance over the past decade and more.

'How did you know to come to me? I never gave a DNA sample and I know my ex-husband didn't, either. If we're talking about bones after all this time . . .' She raised an eyebrow at Kincade, got a small nod back. 'I thought you needed better DNA for familial testing than bones are likely to provide.'

'The science is constantly evolving,' Angel said, admiration in his tone, 'but you've obviously done your homework,'

'And you obviously don't have a missing daughter.'

'I have two,' Kincade said, to save Angel from having to respond. 'Daughters that is. Thankfully not missing. I know I'd be the same.'

Vera ignored the attempt to introduce a human element, repeated her question.

'How did you know to come to me?'

Kincade wished they'd found a passport or some other ID, knowing where the truth would lead.

'We received an anonymous tip-off.'

Vera's face darkened, anger in her voice more than surprise.

'Somebody knew all this time and never said anything.'

'It looks like it.'

Angel had drifted into the background after Vera's rebuke, scanning the photographs on the sideboard. Nothing jumped out at him. He picked one up at random, only to have it whisked out of his fingers by Vera. She held it close to her body, the first outward display of emotion, as she asked the obvious question.

'Do you think it's the person who killed her? Their conscience has finally made itself heard after all these years?'

'We think it's unlikely,' Kincade said, and was about to add some unnecessary blather about pursuing a number of possible avenues of investigation, when Vera interrupted.

'Where was she found?'

'A country house called Kilstock Court in Somerset.'

'What was she doing there?'

It was an automatic, obvious, but stupid question people always asked. It never occurred to them that their missing loved-one remained missing precisely because they were in a place nobody expected them to be. In most cases, they didn't have an answer. Kincade almost wished that were true now.

'We believe she joined a cult,' she said. Vera started to ask further, obvious questions, but Kincade talked over her. 'At present, we don't know very much about it. We don't even have a definite name. Heaven's something. Does that ring a bell with you, Mrs Laing?'

'Why should it?'

'It's possible you might have heard Rosie mention it.'

'Well, she didn't. Don't you think I'd remember something like that?'

Kincade bit her tongue, didn't point out that sometimes memories need a bit of prompting, coaxing out into the open.

Despite her quick denial, Vera was even quicker to jump to a conclusion based on her new-found knowledge, as well as popular misconceptions about the arcane rituals surrounding cults.

'Is this anything to do with that man who was crucified that I read about in the paper?'

'There might be a connection,' Kincade admitted, then added a white lie. 'We don't know what it is.'

Vera gave a solid nod. It suggested she'd upgraded the possible connection to an indisputable fact and written off the remainder of what Kincade had said as lies.

This one's sharp, Angel thought to himself, as Kincade struggled to regain control of the interview. He winced silently to himself at the way she chose to do it, Vera's attitude so far telling him how she would react.

'Do you have any idea why she might have run away?'

Vera narrowed her eyes at her, the thoughts passing back behind her eyes easy to read.

I know what people like you think, with your nasty suspicious minds.

'You're talking about family problems, aren't you? Abuse.' She shook her head, leveraging the power of a personal admission. 'I don't have a lot of good to say about my ex-husband, but I can tell you this for a fact. He never laid a finger on our daughter. Not hitting her or anything . . . else.' The wrinkle in her nose making it very clear what she was talking about.

'That's not the only factor,' Kincade said, her voice level despite being accused of having a dirty mind. 'There might be problems at school. Bullying. Drug or alcohol abuse. Cults often recruit from the vulnerable. People with a lot of things going for them in their lives are less susceptible to the bullshit peddled by a bunch of charlatans.'

Angel didn't miss the heartfelt venom behind her words, the way they touched on her own troubled past. She'd wrecked her marriage and derailed her career when an undercover operation to infiltrate The Order of Nine Angles—a militant Satanic terrorist network and magnet for crazy sick freaks—went disastrously wrong. The cult Dominic Orford had started wasn't in the same league, but it meant she had zero tolerance for delusional self-styled prophets of good or evil.

Vera shook her head throughout the brief diatribe, as if refusing to listen more than dismissing each individual factor.

'She was well-liked at school. And she didn't have a problem with drugs or alcohol.' She carried on before Kincade said, *that you know of*. 'I'm not a naive idiot, Sergeant. I know when I went away with Graeme, she'd have her friends round, drinking all our booze. And she smoked a bit of weed. But it wasn't a *problem*.' Making quotes in the air to go with the dismissive contempt she filled the word with.

'Could a friend have led her astray? A girlfriend? She had a boyfriend at the time, didn't she?'

Some of Vera's dismissive attitude slipped away. She became thoughtful, the framed photograph clutched tighter to her body.

'Yes, she had a boyfriend. Christopher something. He was a

nice boy. I think he was more interested than she was. She didn't have any weird girlfriends that I can think of. Her best friend, Lindsey, moved to Bristol.'

Halfway to Somerset, Angel thought, catching Kincade's eye. A big city. A good place to prospect for new recruits.

'Did you talk to Christopher or Lindsey about Rosie's disappearance?' Kincade asked.

'Of course I bloody did. So did your lot at the time. I think they suspected him at one point. Typical bloody psychology for idiots. He was obsessed with her, she wasn't interested in him and dumped him, he killed her. Case solved. Except anyone with eyes in their head could see he was devastated.'

'What about the friend who moved to Bristol?' Angel said, Vera's sarcastic criticism like water off a duck's back.

Vera nodded to herself as the memories trickled down.

'At first, I suspected that's where she'd gone. It made sense. I spoke to Lindsey on the phone. She claimed she didn't know anything about it. At the time, I thought she was lying.' She scrunched her face, re-living the acrimonious exchange. 'Later, I realised it was probably me imagining things. Thinking she sounded evasive when she was just confused, that sort of thing. I was a bit intense back then.'

A bit? Kincade thought, and kept the incredulous look off her face.

'What did you think happened?'

Vera shook her head, eyes out of focus, lost in a place only she could see.

'We didn't know what to think. We tried not to think the worst, but you can't help yourself. Your mind is your own worst enemy.' Tapping her temple with her middle finger as she said it. 'No wonder Graeme started drinking heavily. And, *no*, it wasn't because of his guilt because he'd abused her. I get the feeling I can repeat myself until I'm blue in the face and you still won't believe me. It's a sick world we live in.'

And we are merely a reflection of it, Angel thought, then started them down the road that might lead to arresting Vera's ex-husband for the murder of Dominic Orford.

'I'm assuming Rosie's disappearance is what caused your marriage to fail.'

Vera waved her hand as if to say, *what's the point of raking over it now?*

'It was everything. Rosie's disappearance. Graeme's drinking. My father died at about the same time. Graeme wasn't supportive at all...'

'About what?'

'My father's death. It was like, I've just lost a daughter, don't bother me with your father. As if I hadn't lost a daughter as well as my father. Anyway, we were doing okay for a while. Daring to hope we were the one couple in a million who survive the loss of a child.' She shrugged, a defeated gesture that fate had put them in their place, exacted a price for their naive arrogance. 'But then the arguments started. Petty bickering at first, before it got more bitter and all we were doing was trying to hurt each other. Graeme was old fashioned. Very strict. I used to accuse him of pushing her away. Have you told him yet?'

'Not yet, no. The fact that you updated your contact details so regularly tells us how desperate you are to learn the truth. We thought it was only fair to tell you first.' Telling himself it was only a white lie. She would feel better about herself. Nothing to do with not wanting to spook her ex-husband.

Except it backfired. Panic gripped Vera, a desperate plea in her eyes, in her voice.

'Do I have to tell him?'

'Not unless you want to.'

'You do it. Please.'

He smiled, *of course. We understand*. But her reaction didn't sit well with him. Something needed poking.

'It sounds like you try to avoid any contact with your ex-husband.'

'I do. We haven't spoken for years.'

The sentence felt incomplete to Angel. He felt a *but* hovering in the background, sensed the internal dialogue in Vera.

'I get the impression you want to say more, Mrs Laing. I shouldn't have to remind you this is a murder enquiry.'

She hesitated, torn between what she knew she should do and the last remnants of loyalty to a husband she'd split from a long time ago but who would always be the father of her lost daughter.

'He called me last week. Somebody hand delivered a note to his house. It said they knew what happened to Rosie and gave a number to call. He reckoned it was a scam to get money. He wanted to warn me they might contact me after he told them to piss off. Like I'm the sort of idiot who'd fall for anything.'

I think he was right, Angel thought. *All they needed to do was mention the name Rosie and you'd be hooked.*

Vera escorted them to the front door, her face showing signs of more inner turmoil, another battle with her conscience.

'What is it, Mrs Laing?' Angel said, as she hesitated with her hand on the door latch.

She shook her head at him when she saw the hope in his eyes that a further revelation was on the way.

'I can't let you tell Graeme about Rosie. It's not fair. I'll do it.'

He nodded his approval at the right decision. It would be harder now, but she wouldn't live the rest of her life giving herself a harder time for not being stronger. He didn't patronise her by putting it into words.

. . .

'WHAT DO YOU THINK?' ANGEL SAID, WHEN THEY WERE BACK IN the car. 'Graeme Laing really did ignore the note, or it's a different burner phone?'

It was too much of a coincidence to think it wasn't the same people who'd contacted Dominic Orford and DS Garfield. Except they'd reviewed the call logs for the number Orford had called and it hadn't contained a received call from a number subsequently identified as Laing's.

'Hard to say without having met Laing myself.'

'We need to see that note. It looks like the people behind it and the other emails and calls were trying to get Laing to do their dirty work for them. The question is—'

'Did Laing play ball or not? Did they have to do it themselves?'

He put the key in the ignition but didn't start the car, the conclusion he'd arrived at prompting more questions to come crowding into his mind, speaking them aloud as they came to him.

'How did they know about Rosie's death in the first place? About Graeme Laing? They must realise if they pointed him at Orford and he killed him, he'd be the obvious suspect. What have they got against him to the extent they're prepared to sacrifice him?'

He glanced at Vera Laing's house, the memory of her words in his mind.

He never laid a finger on our daughter. Not hitting her or anything... else.

Kincade was thinking along the same lines.

'It must be somebody who knew her at Kilstock Court. Somebody she confided in. Told them why she'd run away.'

The echo of Vera's words seemed to fill the car.

He never laid a finger on our daughter. Not hitting her or anything... else.

They were both staring at Vera's house now. As if by doing so long enough the answers would come to them.

'Is she lying?' Kincade said, putting their shared thought into words.

To us or herself? Angel thought, finally starting the car and pulling away.

'Home or work?' he said, once they were on the move, the decision to interview Graeme Laing a given, the only question being where to find him at four-thirty on a weekday afternoon.

'Try work first.' Already entering the address Laing had given Gulliver and Jardine into Google maps as she said it.

Ten minutes later, they pulled into the staff car park in the University of Southampton's Highfield Campus where Laing worked as a Senior Business Analyst.

'Maybe he cycles to work to clear his head after all the booze he drinks sitting on the park bench every night.' Kincade said when they failed to see Laing's car in the car park.

'Or maybe his ex-wife called him, warned him we were on our way?'

'I doubt it. You saw the way she almost fainted when she thought she might have to tell him about Rosie's death.'

He couldn't disagree. But there's a world of difference between having to tell your ex-husband face-to-face that the one good thing to come out of their failed marriage was now as dead as it was, and a quick phone call to warn him the police were on their way to speak to him.

The receptionist on the front desk soon proved him right.

'Graeme's left for the day.' She glanced at the clock on the wall. 'He's normally here a lot later, of course, but something urgent came up. He didn't say what.'

Us, Angel thought sourly, as they came away again. *We have that effect on people.*

'What do you reckon now?' he said, as they navigated through the traffic towards Brookvale Road.

'She definitely warned him.' Then, a second later, 'He's not going to be at home either, is he? Or on the park bench with his hip flask.'

He let his silence answer for him, not wanting to put into words what his gut was telling him was true.

Ten minutes later, they were proved right when there was no answer to their repeated knocks. Nor did they have any joy knocking on the doors on either side.

He called Gulliver, asked him for directions to where they'd found Laing on the common, then walked there themselves, knowing they were wasting their time.

'There's more chance of seeing a hippo in the lake than Laing sitting on a bench by it,' he said, as they followed Gulliver's directions.

'Wrong pond?' she said, when they arrived at the empty bench.

'You're clutching at straws.' Dropping onto the bench as he said it, feeling as if he wouldn't say no to a nip of whisky from a hip flask himself.

She sat down beside him, her own thoughts booze-related but along different lines.

'Why does he sit here and drink every night?'

'Because he lost his daughter twelve years ago, then his marriage fell apart? People drink for a lot less. And today, his ex-wife called him to confirm what he's spent all this time trying not to think about, dulling his pain with whisky.'

It sounded good and it made sense, but it didn't stop Vera Laing's words from echoing in their minds.

He never laid a finger on our daughter. Not hitting her or anything ... else.

30

'*Jesus!* We're as bad as the bloody Americans,' Jardine said.

Gulliver took his eyes off the road to glance at her, see if it might give him an idea of what she was talking about. She had her phone in her hand, eyes glued to the small screen.

'In what way?' he said, when she continued to read rather than elaborate. 'Obesity? Political correctness and woke bollocks?'

She gave an exasperated head shake at her partner's inability to read her mind.

'Cults, what do you think? Earth calling Craig. Where are we going?'

They were on their way to meet with Andrew Foster, the founder of the Cult Victim Support Trust, a charity that provided advice and assistance to former cult members and their families. That didn't mean Gulliver was wrong to question what she'd been talking about. If he had to choose one word to describe what came out of her mouth, it would be *random*.

'I can't believe we're as bad as them.'

She waved her phone at him as if the little screen never lied.

'This article says there are more than five hundred cults

operating in the UK. That means on a per capita basis we're as bad as America.'

'Really?'

'According to this. At least our nutters can't buy automatic weapons.'

'Do I take it that *nutters* is a technical cult term?'

'If it isn't, it should be.'

She pocketed the phone, gave him her full attention.

'No,' he said, before she could ask.

'You don't know what I was going to say.'

He gave her a long-suffering look.

'How long have we been partners?'

'Too bloody long.'

'Amen to that. Which means I know how your mind works. If *works* is the right word. You were going to ask if I'd ever thought about joining a cult.'

She rolled her eyes at his continued ignorance.

'People don't wake up and think to themselves, *it's about time I joined a cult*. You get recruited.'

'Okay. *No*, I've never been recruited.'

'The article said a lot of it goes on at university, that's all. Despite what people think, the average cult member comes from a well-off family background, and is well educated with above average intelligence. I almost expected to see a picture of your face.'

'Really? Are there any cults that have a compulsory oath of silence?'

'Don't be a twat, Craig.'

'I might start one if there isn't. I'll call it—'

'*The Jardine Cult*. And sign me up as founder member.' She held her hand over her mouth, yawned unrealistically. '*Sooo* boring.'

'Female only membership, of course . . .'

'Boring.'

'Geordie accents preferred.'

She looked out of the side window rather than respond in her own Geordie accent, a smile on her lips she'd die to stop him from seeing.

As ever, it passed the time.

'You sure this is the right address?' Jardine said, when Gulliver pulled up outside a very ordinary-looking residential property. 'You'd think they could afford a sign.'

'What? So that all the nutters, as you call them, can find him? They might not have automatic weapons, but that's not much consolation when you've been brained with a baseball bat by some zealot chanting, *death to all unbelievers.*'

'True. If you're the Big Orifice or whatever you call yourself, and you've got dozens of semi-naked acolytes waiting to be anointed with your special holy water, you'd be pissed off if some do-gooder tries to spoil it for you.'

He might have objected to the term *do-gooder*, had all his mental prowess not been busy trying to get his head around Jardine's lurid example.

Special holy water?

The front door opened as they approached, suggesting the fiftyish man who opened it had been watching from a window. He proved their remarks about potential reprisals right by asking to see their warrant cards before they'd had a chance to get them out.

'Can't be too careful,' he said, standing aside to let them in. 'There was a similar support group to mine in America called the Cult Awareness Network that were forced into bankruptcy by the Church of Scientology.'

Gulliver almost expected Jardine to hook her thumb at him.

And you think he looks like John Travolta or Tom Cruise?

Foster led them down the hall and through the kitchen into an office housed in a purpose-built extension on the back of the house. Although it was a big step up from a computer on a wobbly Ikea desk in the spare bedroom, it still lacked meeting facilities. Foster sat behind his desk, Jardine took the single visitor's chair in front of it, and Gulliver leaned against the wall.

'We use the front room if I'm talking to parents or an ex-cult member,' Foster said, apologetically. 'It's more relaxed and comfortable, but I thought you'd be interested in what's on here.' Patting his computer suspended underneath the desk as he said it.

He then took a minute to tell them a little about himself. How, as well as providing advice and information, he was also a cult deprogrammer, or exit counsellor, working with individuals to help them recover from the damaging effects of cults and other extremist groups.

'I have personal experience of exactly how dangerous these organisations can be,' he added, sadness tempered by stoic acceptance in his tone. 'My youngest son, Daniel, was recruited into a cult and indoctrinated. He ended up taking his own life as a result. That's what started me on my vocation.'

'I'm sorry to hear that,' Gulliver said, with a reproachful glance at Jardine sitting staring straight ahead, eyes fixed on Foster like he was the most interesting man she'd ever met.

Want to reconsider your use of the term do-gooder now?

'It was a long time ago,' Foster replied, as if that ever made anything any easier. 'So? What can I help you with?'

'We haven't got much to go on,' Jardine admitted. 'Not even a complete name. Heaven's something . . .'

'Not *gate*, I hope,' Foster said, and everybody smiled.

'That's what we're hoping you can tell us. They operated from two thousand and nine to two thousand and twelve, based in a country house called Kilstock Court near Knighton in Somerset. We think one of the founders was a Dutch woman called Jasmijn.'

Foster had started typing as Jardine talked, continuing to do so after she finished.

'What are you searching on?' she asked.

'My own database compiled over the last twenty years . . . here it is. Heaven's Testament. All the other details match what you told me. But no names, I'm afraid.'

'Does it say why it shut down?'

'No, sorry. I do have some images, if you're interested.'

He angled the monitor so that they could all see it, Jardine leaning to the side.

'That's definitely the same house,' Gulliver said, recognising Kilstock Court as it was in the photograph that had been sent to Dominic Orford. The next three images were also of the house. The fourth wasn't.

'You're in luck,' Foster said, enlarging it and immediately reducing it again when all enlarging achieved was to make it more blurred.

Not sure about that, Jardine thought, as they studied what might have been a generic photograph taken in the 1970s, not at some point between 2009 and 2012.

It showed a young man with long hair tied back in a ponytail and a huge, bushy beard that no doubt provided safe refuge for all manner of small creatures. He was dressed in faded jeans and a white linen shirt unbuttoned halfway to the navel, his feet bare. His wife or parents might have been able to say whether it was a younger Dominic Orford, but they could not, even though he wasn't wearing sunglasses or obscuring his face in any way.

The woman beside him—presumably Jasmijn—looked almost identical, apart from the beard and her shirt being more modestly buttoned. From the back, they would have been almost identical, his shoulders a little broader, her hips and backside a little fuller.

They were standing holding hands on a well-kept lawn, mature trees in the distance behind them under a cloudless blue sky.

Just buried Rosie Laing in those trees, have you? Jardine thought.

'Recognise them?' Foster said, his tone suggesting he expected a negative reply.

'Afraid not,' Gulliver confirmed. 'Are there any more?'

There were. Foster opened the next one.

'That's more like it,' Gulliver said, as they all looked at what was clearly a photograph of the back of the previous image. On it, somebody had written in neat script:

Jasmijn and Tom, Kilstock Court 2012

'*More* like it, but not quite there,' Jardine corrected, then added for Foster's benefit, 'Tom is the name our victim went by.'

Foster shook his head at himself, irritation in his voice.

'I must have been tired or having a bad day. I would normally enter any names or details handwritten on a document into the system. I'll do it now.'

They waited while he entered the names, then Jardine asked an obvious question.

'Where did the photograph come from?'

'Impossible to say. If I'd known at the time, I would have made a note of it. Unfortunately, I don't know whether the fact that I didn't do so is also down to my own incompetence or because I never knew.'

Jardine wanted to tell him not to be so hard on himself, but she knew he'd dismiss the attempt to excuse his human failings, perhaps draw a parallel with their own job where the smallest detail can make the difference between success and failure.

'How do you normally acquire photographs and other documents?'

'A lot of them come from ex-members who come to me for help. Unfortunately, they're often poor quality. The leaders do everything in their power to preserve what they would call their privacy. *Secrecy* is a more appropriate word. Other times, parents have employed investigators. If crimes are committed, there might be newspaper reports. I subscribe to Google alerts for relevant keywords. I also swap information with other people doing the same work as me.'

'Is there anyone you can think of who might have more information?'

Foster smiled, nodded.

'I'll make a few calls, see what I can do. But don't get your hopes up. This was a small, short-lived set-up. Some people might argue it wasn't a cult at all.'

'What's the definition?'

Foster took hold of his little finger, started to recite the key factors from memory.

'The use of psychological coercion to recruit, indoctrinate and retain members. The leader is self-appointed, dogmatic, messianic, and accountable to no-one, but they do have charisma. And they believe the end justifies the means. I'm guessing your presence here today is proof of that particular pudding.'

'I'm afraid so. The remains of a young woman were found in the grounds of the property.'

Foster didn't immediately go to his keyboard, but they knew he'd be tapping away by the time they were back in the car.

Gulliver was ready to call it a day, but Jardine's interest was piqued.

'You mentioned psychological coercion. What exactly does that involve?'

Foster raised a finger, *let me show you*, then went back to his computer, opened up a document showing a long list of coercive techniques.

Jardine and Gulliver ran their eyes down the first half dozen or so lines, almost feeling themselves losing the power of independent thought as they did so:

Hypnosis
Rejection of old values
Confusing doctrine
Uncompromising rules
Verbal abuse
Sleep deprivation
Chanting
Confession

'The victim is broken down physically and mentally,' Foster explained as they read. 'They become highly vulnerable to the suggestions and wishes of the group and, in particular, its leader. The process only takes three or four days. It causes a sudden, drastic personality change. The victim is left unable to reason, to make choices or critically evaluate the world around them. They're dependent on the cult and the leader to interpret reality and the reason for their own existence.' He smiled without humour at the sceptical expressions on their faces. 'I know what you're thinking. *It would never happen to me.* I hope you never have to find out whether you'd be strong enough to resist it.'

'How does anyone ever break away from it?' Jardine said.

The sadness and loss that had filled Foster's voice when he mentioned his son was immediately back, what he now said akin to self-accusation.

'Generally, it requires intervention from outside. Your family rescue you, for example. A small cult in its early days like Heaven's Testament might not be as adept at psychological coercion, making it easier for members to escape. But one thing's for sure. Nobody comes out of it unscathed.'

We've got more than enough proof of that, Jardine thought, now happy to wrap things up.

Foster emailed them the photograph of Jasmijn and the bearded man they were hoping was Dominic Orford while they waited, then confirmed his intention to make further enquiries on their behalf as he showed them out, immediately closing the front door behind them.

'Looking for tips about psychological coercion, were you?' Gulliver said, when they were back in the car.

'I don't need psychological coercion with you, Craig. All I need is a packet of chocolate digestives, and I can get you to do whatever I want.'

'Really? Interesting what he said about cult leaders. Self-appointed. Dogmatic. Messianic. Not accountable. Remind you of anyone?'

'You forgot charismatic.'

'I left it out deliberately.'

'Besides, I'm not self-appointed. And I have to answer to the boss.'

'What about the other two?'

But she wasn't listening anymore, staring out the window at the ordinary-looking house that contained the evidence of so much pain, so many ruined lives. The bitter self-recrimination that filled her voice made him think he'd never fully understand her, no matter how long he was partnered with her.

'I feel like a real bitch for suggesting he's an interfering do-gooder.'

JARDINE'S BOUT OF SELF-LOATHING HAD WORN OFF BY THE TIME they got back to the station and piled into Angel and Kincade's office to update them.

'Heaven's Testament,' she announced, making it sound like

the sort of mantra cult members would've used when greeting one another. 'Although after listening to Andrew Foster, I think Heaven's Twats would be more appropriate.'

'We've got a photograph,' Gulliver said, before Angel or Kincade commented on Jardine's unorthodox suggestion.

He placed the image he'd printed out from the email Andrew Foster sent on Angel's desk, then laid the one of Dominic Orford taken from the incident board beside it.

'What do you think?' Angel said, comparing them.

'We can't decide,' Jardine answered for both her and Gulliver.

Kincade came out from behind her desk to take a look. She picked up both photographs, held them up side-by-side.

'It's him. Let's get Finch in here asap. We'll have a bet with her, see if we can win our coffee machine back.'

'You're that confident it's him, are you?' Angel said, taking the photographs back from her.

She rocked her hand.

'I think so. Everything was pointing towards him, anyway. If the photograph showed him as bald and only five-foot tall, we'd have a problem, but it doesn't.'

Interesting way of looking at it, Angel thought, studying the photograph again, but concentrating on the woman this time.

'I wonder what happened to her?'

'A hand-written annotation on the back confirmed it's Jasmijn,' Jardine said. 'Orford was still using his middle name at that point. Foster didn't have any more details, I'm afraid.'

'I'll give DS Garfield in Bridgwater a call tomorrow, see if he's got anything more,' Angel said, checking his watch. 'Let's call it a day.'

'We're going for a quick beer,' Jardine said, 'if you're interested.'

Kincade grabbed her jacket off the back of her chair.

'Sounds good.' Looking at Angel as she said it.

'I'll pass.'

He caught her eye, fully expecting her to come out with her usual line.

I don't believe it! A prior arrangement with Doctor Death, again!

Except she didn't. And he knew why not. It was linked to her suspicions about who owned the dog he'd brought to his father's house. That didn't mean she had nothing to say on the matter.

'I hope you're not going to the Jolly Sailor on your own.'

'Not tonight, no.'

He saw the smile she almost managed to keep off her face, knew what she was thinking.

Don't want to catch your mother with her new boyfriend again, eh?

He made shooing gestures towards the door.

'Off you go.'

'We'll talk about you, sir,' Jardine said with an insubordinate grin.

'No,' Gulliver corrected. 'We were going to discuss cult leaders. How they're self-appointed, dogmatic, messianic, and accountable to no-one . . .'

'Don't know why you're all looking at me,' Angel said, then shooed them away some more.

'He's accountable to the man upstairs,' drifted back to him after they'd all filed out—and he knew they didn't mean Superintendent Horwood.

He pulled out his phone as soon as they were gone. Thinking about Kincade wanting to know who Jasper belonged to made him think of the visit to his father's house on the weekend. The thought he read in her mind about the Jolly Sailor brought his mother to mind. Combined, they prompted him to call his sister.

'I'm honoured,' Grace said by way of greeting. 'To what do I owe this pleasure?'

'I was wondering how your weekend with Mum went.'

'Really? Hoping she's decided she wants to stay with me instead of you, by any chance?'

He laughed with her, thinking, *if only*.

'You were at Dad's, weren't you?' Grace continued. 'With your sergeant—'

'Her name's Cat.'

'—and her daughters?'

'Uh-huh.'

'She's really getting her feet under the table, isn't she?'

He ignored her attempt to start an argument, said the last thing she wanted to hear.

'I can't remember when I've seen Dad have such a good time.'

'That's because you hardly ever see him, Max.'

Again, he refused to be drawn into an argument, got to the point.

'I was wondering if Mum said anything about meeting up with him.'

Grace hesitated momentarily. Nobody else would've noticed, but he knew his sister. He'd touched on something she wasn't comfortable talking about. His earlier mind-reading exchange with Kincade about catching his mother in the Jolly Sailor with another man was instantly in his mind.

'What? She hasn't told you she wants a divorce, has she?'

'Don't be stupid.'

If nothing else, Grace's dismissive response told him their mother hadn't even mentioned it to her. There was the very real possibility it was all in his mind, after all.

'You really don't know, do you?' Grace said.

'Know what?'

'*Jesus Max*, how can you be so blind? No wonder you spend your whole time prosecuting innocent people. You'd certainly never be able to catch the real criminals with your head up your arse.'

He knew what she was doing. Grace was a criminal defence lawyer. She believed her brother and his goose-stepping colleagues were agents of the devil. But her barbed remark hadn't simply been the same old criticism of him she always rolled out, that he was an enthusiastic guardian of a fascist regime hell-bent on persecuting innocent citizens on the basis of colour and creed. She was so uncomfortable with the way the conversation had progressed, she was actively trying to start an argument. Anything to change the subject.

'Blind about what?' he said, feeling a small worm of apprehension come alive in his gut.

'What was it Dad said?'

'*She's come over to watch me die,*' Angel quoted.

Grace snorted, her voice almost despairing.

'Ignoring the provocative language—it's where you get it from, by the way—do you really think she'd come over for the first time in all these years when it might be too late? Why would she do that? So they can tell each other, *we shouldn't have waited all this time?* It's over between them, Max. If you want my opinion, she still hasn't forgiven him for Cormac, and I don't think she ever will.'

'Then why is she here? Living in my house?'

A long silence stretched out. He pictured his sister with her eyes closed, or staring up at the ceiling.

'I wish I was there with you, Max. Then I could draw you a picture.'

Her prevarication was annoying him, exacerbated by the growing unease he felt.

'Just tell me, Sis. I've had a long day. I'm not up to this.'

He heard breath being sucked in on the other end of the line, then it exploded out of her.

'She's scared you're going to do the same as Cormac, you fucking idiot.'

The longest silence enveloped them. New life forms developed, flourished and died out again before he finally found his voice amongst the jarring emotions running riot inside him.

'That's ridiculous.'

'Is it?' Her voice softer now, a million miles from the habitual bickering that characterised their relationship.

'Don't tell me you think the same thing?'

He knew she was serious now. At any other time, she'd have come back at him—*sometimes I wish you would.*

'It's crossed my mind.'

'Did—'

'*No*, it wasn't me who put the idea in her mind. But we all think—'

'All? Does that include Dad, too?'

'—we all think Claire's death hit you harder than you want to acknowledge. You still feel guilty about it. You live alone—'

'I've got Leonard.'

'You have a stressful job—'

'Stressful? I thought I plucked innocent citizens off the street at random and opened my little black book of trumped-up charges...'

He trailed off, feeling the pursed lips on the other end, knowing she was right.

'So, yes, we're worried.'

'I'm surprised you haven't mentioned Huntington's. *Oh!* I forgot. I'm clear. Booked a blood test yet, Sis?'

'Don't change the subject. And try not to be unnecessarily spiteful.'

Don't blindside me like that, he thought, the surprise and disappointment in himself for needing to have it spelled out to him by his little sister continuing to sour his words.

'She's on suicide watch, is she?'

'If that's how you want to phrase it, yes.'

'Any timescale involved? *If he hasn't topped himself by Christmas, I'll go home*?'

A weary sigh came down the line, Grace's voice equally so following behind it.

'Try to see it from her point of view, Max. She's your mother, for Christ's sake. She's already lost one son. If you had children, you'd understand.'

'Well, I don't.'

'Then maybe you shouldn't have wasted the best ten years of your life as a priest. Besides, isn't that supposed to have given you an understanding about people and their weaknesses?'

There wasn't anything he could say to defend himself. Like everyone, he went on the attack, instead.

'You didn't answer my question. Is Dad involved in this . . . this . . .'

'Words fail you, Max? Conspiracy? Is that the word you were looking for?'

'I was thinking *meddling*.'

'Yeah, well, maybe if somebody had *meddled* in Cormac's life a bit more, he wouldn't have put his rifle in his mouth and blown the top of his head off.'

He didn't know whether she was accusing him alone, or including herself in the list of people who'd failed their younger brother. Nor did he get a chance to ask her, the phone already dead in his ear.

31

'You look as if your dog just died,' Kincade said, breezing into their office the next morning. 'You didn't go to the Jolly Sailor after all and have too many beers with your mum and her new friend, did you?'

She looked at him more closely when he didn't reply, a look of horror on her face as she remembered their discussion from the previous day.

'You challenged Stuart Beckford about calling Balan?'

He shook his head, already feeling too weary for so early in the day, but determined he wasn't going to burden her with his discussion with Grace the previous evening.

'No. You told me not to.'

She pulled a face.

'And of course you do everything I tell you to.'

'If I know what's good for me, yeah.'

A mischievous grin crept over her face, her eyes bright.

'In that case, go and get our coffee machine back from Finch's office.' Her arm rigid, pointing at the door as if sending her girls to their rooms.

'I thought you were going to win it back betting on the man in the photograph.'

'I asked her, but she refused the bet. So? Shall we go and get a definitive answer?'

Although Dominic Orford's parents were arguably better qualified to say whether the bearded man in the photograph was their son than his wife was, the Orfords had made themselves unavailable. Even if they were contactable, Angel wouldn't have approached them in the first instance.

'After all the other lies and half-truths they've told, they'd deny it was him even if he had his name tattooed on his forehead,' he said.

Kincade studied the photograph once more as he drove them to Louise Orford's house in Bitterne Park, her voice more confident than ever.

'I'm sure it's him.' She waved the photo at Angel. 'There's something else I'd like to bet on—'

'That photo is going to turn Louise Orford's world on its head.'

'And some. She's going to end up wondering if she ever knew him at all.'

Louise looked at their hands when she answered the door to them, as if she thought they were there to return her dead husband's shotgun to her, her words confirming it.

'You haven't found the shotgun?'

'Not yet,' Angel replied, thinking, *I hope the first we see of it won't be when we go to arrest your husband's murderer.* 'We have something we want to show you.'

Louise let them in, then led them into the same large sitting room as on their previous visit. Kincade pulled out the photograph, kept hold of it for a minute while she gave Louise a very edited explanation.

'This is a photograph of a man we think might be Dominic. It was taken in two thousand and twelve—'

'That's four years before I met him.'

People recognise their partner as a baby or small child, Kincade thought, and phrased it differently.

'We'd like you to take a look anyway.'

Louise took the photograph, an immediate bark of surprised amusement popping out.

'*My God!* What on earth possessed him to grow that beard?'

'You're confirming that the man in the photograph is Dominic.'

'Definitely. Even with that awful beard.' She ran her fingers over her own chin and cheeks, her voice filled with fond reminiscence. 'Dom used to get through a razor blade every couple of days, his beard growth was so strong. But I never imagined he could grow something like that.' Her mouth twisted in disgust. 'It must smell, however much you wash it. And be full of bits of food.'

They listened and smiled politely as Louise marvelled at how her husband used to look. It saddened Angel that in the next minutes that surprise and amusement would become a thing of the past, the monstrous beard paling into insignificance compared to the other things they would tell her about the man she believed she knew better than anyone in the world.

Louise then began the process of bringing what remained of her world crashing down around her ears.

'Who's the woman?'

'Somebody he met when travelling after his breakdown,' Angel said. 'Her name is Jasmijn.'

Louise studied the photograph more closely now, then gave her opinion.

'I don't like the look of her.'

You've got good instincts, Angel thought.

'I'm sorry to tell you it looks as if Dominic never worked at his father's company after he got back from travelling.'

Louise wasn't as surprised as they'd expected her to be, nodding to herself as she continued to scrutinise the photograph.

'He was always a bit vague about what he did there. I used to suspect he spent his whole time wining and dining clients, never did any real work.' She waved the photograph at them. 'He was with her, was he?' Filling the word, *her* with contempt.

Angel confirmed it with a nod and a private thought.

You might well make her sound like a she-devil.

'Doing what?' Louise demanded. 'They look like a pair of hippies. Where was this taken?'

'A country house called Kilstock Court in Somerset,' Angel said, taking the easy question first. 'It looks like they set up a . . .' He cleared his throat. 'An organisation called Heaven's Testament.'

Finally, Louise dragged her eyes away from the photograph to look at him, the expression on her face like she'd spotted two people frolicking naked in the background.

'That sounds like a cult.'

'We think it probably was.'

They'd remained standing so far, the photograph consuming all of Louise's attention, distracting her from offering them somewhere to sit. Now, she dropped onto the sofa behind her, the photograph still in her hand but almost forgotten.

It only took a moment for her mind to process the implications.

'Is his death something to do with this cult?'

'We think so,' Angel confirmed, lowering himself into an armchair facing Louise. 'A young woman's remains were recently disinterred in the property's grounds.'

The photograph fluttered to the floor as Louise's hand flew to her mouth.

'Surely you're not suggesting Dom killed her? And that's why he was killed?'

'We don't know, but we have to consider that as a very real possibility.'

Louise slumped listlessly on the sofa, her mouth hanging open. Kincade took a step towards the door.

'How about a cup of tea? Or something stronger?'

Louise gestured at a drinks cabinet against the side wall.

'Whisky, please. Don't worry about ice or water.' She turned back to Angel while Kincade hopped to it, retrieved the photograph from where she'd dropped it on the floor, waved it at him again. 'Is this the woman you dug up?'

'No.'

'Have you identified her?'

Angel nodded.

'We believe her name was Rosie Laing.'

'Doesn't mean anything to me.' Mild surprise in her voice, as if she'd have expected her husband to tell her the names of young women he'd murdered while heading up a cult.

Kincade came back with a generous slug of whisky in a chunky, cut-glass tumbler. Louise took it from her, sipped gratefully.

'Do his parents know about this? Has everybody been deceiving me all these years?'

'Obviously Nigel Orford would know whether Dominic worked at the company,' Angel said. 'That doesn't mean they knew what he was doing, even if they knew he was living in Somerset.'

'With *her*,' Louise spat, looking as if she wanted to tear the photograph into pieces. 'I bet she was behind it.'

That fits with what his girlfriend at the time told us, he thought, and kept to himself, even though it was what Louise desperately wanted to hear.

Anything for it not to have been her Dominic's fault.

Louise didn't stir from the sofa as they let themselves out. Kincade was tempted to put the whisky bottle on the side table, save her from having to get up at all.

As for Angel, he couldn't think of a time when he'd destroyed a person's memory of a murdered loved one more comprehensively, left them with a new set of memories about the person they thought they knew.

The sound of the front-door latch clicking shut was like a thunderclap in his ears as they left her to her misery. He doubted Louise even noticed, at this very moment losing herself in Johnnie Walker's warm embrace.

'WHAT WORD DO YOU SUGGEST, MA'AM?' ANGEL SAID.

Olivia Finch looked as if she knew a few she'd like to call him, but none that would resolve their current problem. Instead, she repeated herself.

'I don't care, but you can't say *cult*. If you use that word in a media appeal you'll have the phone lines jammed solid with every nutter from here to California.'

Louise Orford's confirmation that it was her husband in the photograph with Jasmijn at Kilstock Court in 2012, added to Andrew Foster supplying the cult's full name had been sufficient to convince Angel the time had come to issue a media appeal, as well as post a request for witnesses on the websites of both the Hampshire Constabulary and the Avon and Somerset Police.

The wording was proving to be troublesome.

Finch threw it back into Angel's court.

'You ought to be able to think of something. All those sermons you had to write must have helped your vocabulary.'

'I don't think we can refer to Kilstock Court as paradise or the promised land, ma'am.'

The remark diverted Finch's concentration from the current problem, prompting a different question.

'Is that really what you used to talk about in your sermons, Padre? It sounds a bit happy-clappy to me.'

Angel grinned at her.

'If I hadn't given it all up, I'd suggest you need to come to the next service to find out.'

The tongue-in-cheek response put a knowing scowl on Finch's face.

'That's what you lot are all about, isn't it? The promise of something that can't ever be delivered. Or at least not while you're alive and able to tell other people.'

'It's called faith, ma'am. But we're straying from the point. How about sect?'

'That's even worse.'

'Organisation?'

She scrunched her face, still not happy, but the best so far of a bad bunch.

'Community?'

'Everyone will know what you mean.'

'There's not much point in the appeal if they don't.'

She pointed the arm of her reading glasses at him in acknowledgement.

'True. Let's go with community.'

'And should we describe Kilstock Court as a community centre? Or do you think that will make people think of bingo and bring-and-buy sales?'

'Just go and write it, Padre. And stop being an arse.'

'How about movement?'

She gave him a pained look. The only movement she was interested in was her right foot moving swiftly in the direction of his backside if he wasn't out of her office in the next three seconds.

'Thank God I got my coffee machine back,' followed him down the corridor. 'I don't think I could deal with you without it.'

THE INTERVIEW WITH LOUISE ORFORD AND THE NEED TO PUT together a media appeal had pushed Angel's planned call to DS Garfield down the list. He'd just sent the final draft of the appeal off for approval when Garfield got in first.

'We've got a name. Jasmijn de Vries.'

'Definitely sounds Dutch to me.'

'Me, too. She was the only person registered for council tax during the relevant period.'

'Not Dominic Orford?'

'Afraid not.'

'It's not actually a problem . . .'

He took Garfield through the interview with Andrew Foster from the Cult Victim Support Trust, gave him the cult's full name, Heaven's Testament, and told him about the photograph Foster had supplied of a bearded man called Tom standing with Jasmijn—a man Orford's widow subsequently confirmed was her husband during the period he was known by his middle name.

'I'm not surprised Jasmijn was the only person registered,' Garfield said. 'It sounds as if Orford was determined to keep under the radar. Almost as if he knew it was going to end badly.'

What cult doesn't? Angel thought, and didn't waste his breath saying.

'When was the council tax account closed?'

'Two thousand and twelve.'

It was confirmation of what they'd suspected. Whether or

not other cult members had known about the death of Rosie Laing, Dominic Orford and Jasmijn de Vries had decided it was a good time to shut the operation down.

'Who closed the account?'

'Not Jasmijn de Vries.'

It was an unusual way to answer. Garfield explained.

'The woman I spoke to told me they were notified over the phone. Normally they require written notice, but all they got was a quick call from a man who refused to identify himself.'

'Dominic Orford?'

'Probably.'

'Why didn't she do it?'

The answer was forming in his mind as the words rolled out. Garfield's knowing laugh told him he'd asked himself the same question.

'It felt off to me, too. I did a bit of digging. It helps that it's an unusual name, at least it is in Somerset. Given we'd already got one dead young woman in the grounds, I started with the coroner's office in Taunton...'

'She's dead?'

'Yep. Unsolved hit and run in October, two thousand and twelve.'

'What was the coroner's verdict?'

Garfield tut-tutted, disapproval in his voice.

'You shouldn't have to ask.'

'Open.'

'Correct.'

Garfield had been right. Angel shouldn't have needed to ask. Despite that, he decided to waste some breath.

'Any witnesses?'

'Nope. It happened on one of the small country lanes close to the property. Who knows why she was out walking the lanes as darkness was falling, but she was. This was after the cult had shut down and the members had dispersed, so there was nobody to ask. As you'd expect, they'd either never kept details of the cult members or Jasmijn and Orford had been busy destroying them before leaving the property themselves.'

'Any suspicion of foul play?'

'The car drove over her while she was lying in the road after being hit. Your guess is as good as mine.'

Angel knew how difficult it would've been to determine exactly what had happened. It was possible the victim had been knocked down directly in front of the car and the driver panicked and kept on going. Equally, the driver might have backed up, then driven over the body a second time to make sure. Hence the coroner's open verdict.

'Was the car found?'

'Burned out in a field. It had been stolen.'

Again, it wasn't conclusive. A car thief or joyrider wouldn't admit to causing a fatal accident, the same as a killer who stole the vehicle for that specific purpose wouldn't.

None of that changed what Angel's gut was telling him. She'd been deliberately knocked down and driven over to make sure she was good and dead.

The question was whether the same killer had nailed Jasmijn's partner to a cross twelve years later.

32

'We've got up-to-date details for Rosie's boyfriend at the time of her disappearance, as well as the best friend who moved to Bristol,' Kincade said, dropping the original missing person file on Angel's desk.

'Where are they now?'

'The friend, Lindsey Howe, is still in Bristol. She's now Lindsey Pritchard. The boyfriend, Christopher Jordan, lives in Winchester.'

'You choose.'

'Let's take the boyfriend. Send Gulliver and Jardine to Bristol.'

'Not getting fed up with all the commuting back and forth to my dad's house, are you?'

She shook her head.

'Never.'

He couldn't help smiling as his sister's words came back to him.

She's really getting her feet under the table, isn't she?

'What are you smiling at?' she said, narrowing her eyes at him.

'Nothing. Just happy that you're getting settled.'

'Unlike your sister.'

Not for the first time, he wondered if she'd bugged his phone.

Half an hour later and they were on the road headed for Winchester and an appointment with Christopher Jordan in the Basepoint Business Centre leaving Gulliver and Jardine to prepare for the hundred-mile-plus hack to Bristol.

Rank had to have some privileges, after all.

As often happened when delving into the past, Angel experienced a slight temporary disconnect when they first met Jordan. Until that point, he'd been *the boyfriend*, aged sixteen. Not exactly still in short trousers, but not at all the six-foot-two man in his late twenties who pumped their hands energetically, then ushered them into one of the business centre's ground-floor meeting rooms.

'Is this about Rosie Laing?' Jordan asked, almost before their backsides hit their chairs.

'It is,' Angel confirmed. 'The grapevine's obviously working efficiently.'

'Yeah. You know how it is.' He glanced at Kincade as if she were living proof of how all women spend their whole lives gossiping. 'And it was the only other time I've been interviewed by the police, of course.'

In Jordan's case, the suffix *of course* felt appropriate. Dressed in an expensive suit over a crisp, open-necked white shirt and with highly-polished leather shoes on the ends of his long legs, he didn't look like the sort of man who'd had regular run-ins with the police.

'Let's start by going back to that interview back in two thousand and twelve,' Angel said.

As expected, some of the *oomph* went out of Jordan. The fact that Rosie's remains had been found was proof he could have been more helpful at the time.

'Okay.'

'You told the interviewing officers you had no idea where Rosie had gone. Do you still stand by that?'

Jordan checked his shoes, cleared his throat.

'I thought she'd gone to Bristol to see her friend, Lindsey.'

'Lindsey Howe?'

'That's right.' He linked his two middle fingers together like links in a chain. 'They were like that until Lindsey's dad got a job in Bristol and they moved away.'

'Why didn't you say that at the time?'

Jordan shook his head as he tried to get back inside the mind of the sixteen-year-old boy he'd been at the time, his hormones running amok.

'Because I wasn't worried about her safety.'

He forced himself to meet their eyes. Offering them the chance to give him their most disapproving looks, get it out of the way.

'You'll have to explain in more detail,' Angel said. 'Give us some background on the relationship.'

'The first thing you need to know is that it was on the way out. We were drifting apart. I know that doesn't excuse anything. The other thing is that I was a typical sixteen-year-old boy.'

They both nodded knowingly.

That explains a lot.

'I was going through a rough patch with my parents. They were always on my case, and I was pushing back as hard as I could. So there's me being a rebellious pain in the arse. I was hardly going to snitch on Rosie at the same time, side with her parents and the police, even if the relationship was over. It wasn't like we hated each other. We just drifted apart. I might have been a teenage twat, but I wasn't going to be a two-faced teenage twat. My friends would've treated me like a leper.'

'And you didn't think there was anything to worry about,' Angel said, throwing Jordan a lifeline.

'Exactly.'

'What about when the days stretched into weeks? Didn't you start to worry then?'

Jordan laughed nervously. No humour, merely another acknowledgement of what he used to be.

'I'd met somebody else by then. I forgot all about Rosie. We weren't at the same school, so it's not like I saw this empty chair in class every day. Besides, I'd heard Rosie's mum had called Lindsey. She would've told you about her. There was nothing more I could add.'

It was a fair point, and one that gave Jordan's conscience an easy get-out. But, so far, all Jordan had done was explain why he'd done nothing at the time. It was all about him. He hadn't provided any insight into Rosie's life.

'Tell us about the relationship,' Angel said. 'Before it was on the way out.'

'It's the fact that it was ending that's important. I'd always been more interested than Rosie was. You start making excuses why. She's a nice girl who's been brought up to believe you don't open your legs for every boy who says he loves you.' Glancing at Kincade as if she epitomised the opposite, getting a stony-faced glare back. 'Then I started thinking, is it me? I'm too skinny, I've got bad breath or too many zits—'

'We get the picture,' Kincade cut in before Jordan went into unnecessary detail.

'Then I started thinking, maybe it's not me, personally, it's all men. She bats for the other side.'

Angel held his tongue. Didn't volunteer another reason why

a young girl might not be interested in the opposite sex, Vera Laing's words in his mind.

He never laid a finger on our daughter. Not hitting her or anything... else.

'That's what I think happened,' Jordan went on. 'Rosie had a crush on Lindsey. That's why she ran away to Bristol, why I didn't think she was in danger. And I didn't want her hating me because I told her parents and they dragged her back home again.' He blew the air from his cheeks, ran his hand through his hair—hair that Kincade guessed got a lot of attention in front of the mirror each morning and every time he went to the gents' toilets. 'I also didn't want to say I thought she was gay because everyone would've laughed at me. Accused me of making it up because my pride wouldn't let me admit she just didn't like me.'

It wasn't necessary to say it again, but they all heard it.

I was sixteen, for Christ's sake.

Angel leaned back in his chair and crossed his arms over his chest, let Kincade take over and get the same questions they'd asked Vera Laing out of the way. Was there any trouble at school? Bullying? Drug or alcohol abuse? Any other problems in her life they should know about?

Jordan gave a negative response to them all, as Rosie's mother had. If it hadn't been for Vera's words still in Angel's mind, he'd have wrapped it up then and there. But they *were* in his mind, and he couldn't escape the feeling that Vera's denials had been too vehement. As if she was trying to convince herself as much as them.

'What you said makes sense. It paints a picture of Rosie choosing to go to Bristol to be with her friend. Is it possible she was actually running away from home and something that might have been happening there?'

Jordan's response was much as Vera Laing's had been, a contemptuous sneer twisting his mouth.

It always comes back to this with you people.

'You mean abuse?'

'Physical or sexual, yes.'

'Just because she had a crush on Lindsey, doesn't mean she wasn't being abused,' Kincade added. 'That abuse might also put her off men.'

Jordan breathed in and out deeply, as if calming himself. That, or preparing himself to say what he'd always known was going to come out.

'If there was anything like that going on, she never said a word to me about it.'

Angel cocked his head at him.

'That's a revealing answer, Mr Jordan. Why didn't you simply say that she never said anything to you? It suggests to me you might have suspected something was wrong.'

'She had bruises on her upper arms one time. I asked her about them and she made up some excuse. She got annoyed when I kept on at her about it, so I dropped it.' He gave them a tight, defiant smile. 'I wasn't in the business of pissing off the girl who was already starting to give me the cold shoulder.'

Angel felt fate's hand at work as Jordan made his excuses about why he'd said nothing. The Jimmy Saville sexual abuse scandal broke in late 2012, a few months after Rosie Laing had run away. If it had come to light a year or six months earlier, Jordan might have aired his suspicions in the knowledge that he was a lot more likely to be believed.

'Did you know Rosie's father?'

Jordan shrugged.

'I'd met him. And her mother. But I didn't know them or spend much time with them. If you're asking if I think he was capable of abusing her, I have no idea.'

He fell silent, and both Angel and Kincade knew it was the time to say nothing. Sadly, there was no sudden *aha* moment, the memory of an unexplained incident shaken loose by their questions. The opposite, in fact.

'If you forced me to say one way or the other, I'd say *no*. They had a good relationship in a normal, healthy way. I know that's not what you want to hear. And I'm not just saying it to excuse me for being blind to what was going on under my nose.'

'ABUSER OR NOT?' ANGEL SAID, AS THEY WALKED BACK TO THE Colebrook Steer car park. 'That's two witnesses who say not.'

'Does it even matter? Ignoring the fact that an unpunished abuser might be sitting on a park bench every night.'

She had a point.

It didn't actually make any difference one way or the other to the murder of Dominic Orford. If Graeme Laing killed him after receiving a tip-off that Orford had murdered his daughter, it didn't make a lot of difference if Laing was assuaging the guilt he felt for abusing her and driving her away, or he was simply a bereft father taking vengeance on the man who took away his raison d'être.

'I care,' he said. 'I'd rather put away an abuser for murder than a grieving father. I'm not sure how that'll sit with me if that's all he turns out to be.'

They walked on in silence for a minute or two, the memory of Christopher Jordan describing his behaviour as a sixteen-year-old prompting what he said next.

'I know it's a long way off yet, but I bet you wish your girls could jump from fourteen to eighteen, skip the problem years.'

She gave him a look—*shows how much you know*.

'Fourteen? It starts a lot earlier than that.'

'At least that's something I don't have to look forward to. There are some advantages to not having kids.'

· · ·

Mercedes Cortés stood on Central Station Bridge, the railway station behind her, the tracks below. Southampton Central Police Station was directly ahead, its upper stories visible above the trees that lined Mountbatten Way.

Back in 2011 when it first opened, it would've been a shining example of modern architecture. Now, the dirty grey-brown staining that dripped from the roof discolouring the pale grey concrete made it look tired. A permanent reminder to the thousands of motorists who drove past it every day that architects might win awards for designing efficient buildings with impressive green credentials, but they didn't know jack shit about the British weather.

Mercedes was convinced she felt her subconscious trying to turn her legs around, a brisk, fifty-yard walk back to the station and then a short train ride out to her grandparents' house. Back to the safety and comfort of the familiar, not a step into the unknown.

The same questions kept on running through her mind with the same regular predictability of the trains on the tracks below.

What was she hoping to achieve after all this time?

Would she be believed?

Or, looking at it from the other side, *what was she so afraid of?*

But try answering that when your heart's going like a triphammer and your stomach's churning with a nameless fear, turning back the clock until you're a child again, frightened of the monsters that live underneath the bed.

She took a deep breath, told herself to get a grip, concentrate on what she did know.

Except her mother had told her so little about that brief, magical period in her life that came to such an abrupt, unforeseen end. Valentina Cortés wasn't one for mawkish sentimentality, but Mercedes had heard her describe it as a taste of heaven.

She knew if she stood too long, some busybody would phone the police, say a young woman was loitering on the bridge, looking as if she was about to throw herself under a train.

A mischievous smile curled Mercedes' lips at the thought of it.

That'd get her some attention.

She started walking...

33

Sergeant Jack Bevan on the front desk waved Angel over when he walked in with Kincade.

'You've got a visitor, Padre. It's not anybody you'd expect.'

Bevan's face was uncharacteristically deadpan, no sign of the smile that usually accompanied the good-natured banter they indulged in. Angel's heart sank, his worst fears all jostling to be heard.

'Not Catherine Beckford again?'

He relaxed when Bevan shook his head, irrational hope replacing the panic.

'It can't be a response to the media appeal already, surely? I know the crazies are quick off the mark, but even so.'

Now, Bevan let the smile come.

'Not that either, Padre.' He pointed at the ceiling, his habitual irreverent smirk on his face. 'Somebody up there is definitely on your side. It's Graeme Laing. I've put him in confessional number one.'

The name took a moment to register, despite them having discussed him so recently.

'Laing? He walked in off the street?'

'Uh-huh. Said he'd heard you were looking for him.'

Angel shared a look with Kincade. Then held up his hand, fingers splayed.

'Give us five minutes. And Jack...'

Bevan nodded, *yes, I know*.

'Don't let him go anywhere.'

They took the stairs rather than wait for the lifts, one of which was out of order for scheduled maintenance.

'Talk me through it,' he said, as they ran up side-by-side.

'No. You talk me through it. *Sir*. I haven't got the first idea. Maybe he took himself off somewhere last night to give himself a bit of breathing space, think up a plausible story.'

'If he killed Dominic Orford ten days ago, he's had plenty of time to get his story straight. I can't believe he'd wait until his ex-wife calls him to tell him we're on our way. If he was that stupid, he'd have left something incriminating at...'

The words dried up as a thought went off in his mind. Kincade mistook his sudden silence for breathlessness.

'You need to do more exercise. Especially now your mother's fattening you up.'

They burst through the doors from the stairwell before he had a chance to reply, narrowly avoided a collision with a uniform carrying four cups of brown sludge from the drinks machine, then down the corridor to their office almost getting jammed in the doorway trying to go through it at the same time.

A minute later and they were back out again, file in hand, moving at a more sedate pace. If Graeme Laing had gone to the effort of coming in—perhaps to give himself up—the least they could do was have the breath to caution him without wheezing their way through it.

They stood in front of the interview-room door for a long moment holding each other's gaze. Kincade voiced their shared thought.

'There's something not right about this.'

'Definitely.'

'I certainly wouldn't want to bet our coffee machine on what's going on.'

He extended his hand towards the door.

'Let's go find out what it is.'

Is he taking the piss? Angel thought, when they entered the room and saw Laing seated at the interview table. He was wearing the same tweed field coat the witness Dorothy Bancroft had described, the one Gulliver and Jardine had asked him about.

Laing stood up as they entered.

'I heard you were looking for me, Inspector.'

'I need to stop you there, Mr Laing. This interview will be recorded, both audio and video.' He crossed the room, started the recording, then went back to Laing. 'I also need to caution you, sir.' He cleared his throat. 'You do not have to say anything. But it may harm your defence if you do not mention when questioned something which you later rely on in Court. Anything you do say may be given in evidence. Do you understand?'

'I do.'

'And lastly, I need to offer you the opportunity to have a solicitor present. We can provide a duty solicitor, or you can use your own.'

'Do I need one?'

'That's not for me to say, sir. But we always recommend it.'

Laing didn't give it a moment's thought.

'It's not necessary.'

'Are you sure?'

'Definitely.'

Angel indicated the seat Laing had been seated at, took the one opposite beside Kincade, then introduced everybody for the recording.

'As I said,' Laing began, 'I heard you were looking for me.'

'We were looking for you yesterday, sir. We got the impression you might be avoiding us.'

Laing shook his head, *that's your problem.*

'It's still a free country. Just about.'

'Can you tell me where you went, and why?'

'I checked into a hotel in Swanage. I would've thought the reason was obvious. My ex-wife had just told me the remains of our daughter who's been missing for twelve years had been dug up. I needed time by myself to come to terms with that news. I suppose you could say I was avoiding the whole human race.'

'Your wife seems to have already come to terms with it.'

'Bully for her. She was always better than me at controlling her emotions.' He smiled, a wistful nod to better times between them. 'She used to accuse me of being an emotional cripple. You could probably arrest her for using that word these days, couldn't you?'

Strange and stranger, Angel thought. Laing wasn't a stupid man. It wasn't possible he didn't realise the seriousness of his predicament after Gulliver and Jardine already interviewed him and accused him of being at a murder site. And yet he still found time to make a snide remark about political correctness.

Angel had a nasty feeling it was going to get stranger still.

'Why did you choose Swanage?'

'It's where Vera and I used to go after Rosie first disappeared. There are happy family memories associated with it that I'm prepared to take you through if you feel it's necessary—although I probably won't be able to remember Rosie's favourite ice-cream flavour.'

'You seem extremely relaxed for a man in your position, Mr

Laing. I realise people react differently to stressful situations, but we don't tend to see much humour or experience suspects mocking us.'

Laing smiled as if Angel had paid him a compliment.

'Not so much relaxed, Inspector, as confident you'll get to the bottom of this misunderstanding. I'm aware of all the old clichés about detectives who like a nice, easy result to keep the statistics looking good, reassuring a nervous public and helping their own promotion prospects at the same time. Are you one of those tired old clichés, Inspector?'

'No, Mr Laing, I'm not.' He raised his hand as Laing's head swivelled towards Kincade. 'Nor is DS Kincade, if that's what you were about to ask.'

'I don't see what I've got to worry about, then.'

'As I'm sure you appreciate, we'll be getting onto that very soon. Before we do, I'd be interested to hear what you were thinking about last night. Obviously, I realise you were remembering Rosie and your lives before tragedy struck—'

'And that's exactly what it was, Inspector.'

'—but you must have thought about other things that prompted you to come here voluntarily. I'd be interested to hear your thought process.'

Laing studied him for a long moment, then asked for a cup of tea and a biscuit, if they had one. For once, Angel got the impression he was genuinely thirsty and a bit peckish. He wasn't buying himself time or avoiding an awkward question. Angel was only surprised Laing hadn't specified what sort of biscuit he wanted. He suspended the interview, left the room with Kincade.

She immediately checked her watch.

'Have I got time to nip upstairs, have a bet with Finch that Laing is innocent?'

'He's certainly acting like it. I feel like we should ring the

Chief Constable, ask him if Laing was at a dinner party at his house on the night of the murder before Laing tells us.'

'You get the teas, I'm going upstairs.'

They were back outside the interview room door five minutes later, three teas and a couple of small packets of biscuits on a tray in his hand, a big shit-eating grin on her face.

'Finch took the bet.'

'Don't you think that's a bit unfair, given she hasn't seen Laing's confidence?'

'I briefed her, told her how confident he is.'

'It's not the same.'

'I know. That's why we'll have our coffee machine back in no time.'

'What does Finch get if we're wrong?'

'You don't want to know.' Opening the interview room door as she said it.

He carried the refreshments in, handed them out and re-started the recording, then extended his hand towards Laing, currently struggling to open the plastic wrapper on one of the packets of biscuits.

'You're right, Inspector,' Laing said, finally getting the packet open and removing one of the biscuits. 'I did a lot of thinking. As I said, I checked into a hotel, but should you check, the staff will confirm the bed hadn't been slept in. I sat on a bench overlooking the sea all night.' He took hold of the collar of his field coat, tugged it. 'Hence the coat. It's the warmest thing I own and I knew I wouldn't be able to sleep at all last night.'

He held Angel's gaze and Angel knew Laing had guessed what he'd thought, that he was being provocative by wearing it.

'What conclusions did you arrive at, Mr Laing?'

'I thought about the interview with your colleagues. The fact that my car was allegedly seen parked close to a murder scene and somebody wearing a coat identical to this one'—

tugging the collar again—'was seen crossing the fields. It was very clear they didn't believe me when I told them that it wasn't me, that there must have been some misunderstanding. And I thought about the fact that I don't have a verifiable alibi for that occasion, or another date they asked me about but didn't tell me why. I made the connection afterwards, of course. It was the date that man was crucified, if the newspaper can be believed.'

'It can, on this occasion, Mr Laing.'

'The exception that proves the rule, eh? So, it was obvious you suspected me of that murder. The fact that I hadn't been arrested suggested you needed more. A motive. Then Vera called me and told me Rosie's remains had been found in the grounds of a property being used by a cult called Heaven's something or the other.' He raised a questioning eyebrow at them.

'Heaven's Testament,' Angel obliged.

'And there's your motive. My daughter murdered by a cult with a religious-sounding name. A man crucified in revenge.' He held his arms outstretched across the table, wrists together. 'Get the cuffs on the father asap. Page one of murder enquiries for idiots.'

'You can drop your hands now, Mr Laing,' Kincade said. 'We're not in America. We're not going to cuff you in here.'

Laing looked at his hands as if surprised he was still holding them out. He dropped them, picked up his tea and took a sip.

'There's a step missing, isn't there, Mr Laing?' Angel said, as Laing followed the tea with half a biscuit.

'There is, Inspector. How was I supposed to know that the crucified man had been a member of this cult, the leader even, and he'd murdered Rosie? Even if I did, how did I find him?'

'Have you got it with you?'

Laing nodded, smiling as if it was only a game, each of them trying to out-guess the other. He dug in the inside pocket of his coat, came out with a crumpled piece of paper.

'I threw it away as soon as it arrived. But the recycling hadn't been collected, so I dug it out again.'

He placed it on the table in front of them, turned it so they could read it.

'*I have information about Rosie,*' Angel read aloud, not bothering to read out the phone number following it. He opened the file they'd brought with them, found the call log for the burner phone used to call Dominic Orford. The numbers weren't the same. Meaning Laing could have called it without them knowing.

'Did you call the number?' Kincade asked point blank.

'I told you, I threw the note away immediately. I thought it was a scam. A cynical, heartless attempt to get money out of me by somebody who'd been trawling through old missing persons reports.' He angled his head to look at the note, as if he didn't already know it by heart. 'It's quite clever, isn't it? No details. Not too obvious. Enough to get my attention, get my own mind doing the work for them.'

'You weren't tempted to call it?'

'No. If this person genuinely has information, they've held onto it for a very long time. It suggests they have an agenda. I didn't want any part of that.'

'Even if it meant missing the chance of finding out what happened to Rosie? That must have been a difficult decision.'

'Not really. My initial gut reaction was that it was a scam, they had no information.' His brow furrowed and Kincade saw a light go on back behind his eyes. 'The fact that you're labouring the point suggests I was wrong. Did they have information?'

'There's evidence to suggest they did.'

'Evidence you're not going to share with me?'

'I'm afraid not.'

Laing looked back and forth between them, then addressed the space between them.

'All I can do is to repeat that I did not call the number. Nobody gave me the details of what happened to Rosie. And I did not go out and crucify the man they said was responsible. It should be obvious whoever sent the note did it themselves after I ignored them.'

They didn't have to say out loud what was in their minds.

If you ignored them.

'Let me put something to you, Mr Laing,' Angel said, after the accusatory silence grew awkward. 'You're clearly an intelligent man. You've thought about this, worked out what we're most likely thinking, realised it all points to you being the murderer. What does an intelligent man do next? Go on the run and as good as confirm our suspicions? Or does he walk in here and put himself at our mercy, believing we don't have sufficient evidence to charge him, let alone convict him? A grieving father who's recently had his worst fears confirmed, the small flame of hope he's kept alive all these years extinguished. We feel sorry for him. He's such a reasonable man, a man who's lost so much. How could a man like that possibly have nailed another man to a home-made cross? And even if he did, who can blame him?'

Laing had finished his tea and the biscuits while he listened. Now, he crumpled the plastic wrapper and stuffed it into the cup, pushed the whole lot to one side. It felt almost symbolic, clearing all the clutter away ready for an admission.

'You're half right. I came here today because I realise not doing so makes me look guilty. For all I know, you might have armed men on standby, ready to break down my front door at six o'clock tomorrow morning and drag me out of bed. But I am not cynically manipulating you in the way you're suggesting. Give me some credit, for Christ's sake. I know that even if the pair of you were sobbing your hearts out with sympathy for me, you'd still arrest me for the murder if you could. I'm sure you're not happy about the way your job eats away at your humanity, but I'm sure it does.'

'You're right, it does. We don't feel good about ourselves when we charge and convict a man who's done what we know in our hearts is what we and everybody else would do if we could ignore the law and avoid the consequences. But you know what makes it easier to swallow?'

'I'm sure you're about to tell me.'

Angel nodded, *you got that right.*

'When the person who ends it is also responsible for starting it.'

'I'm not sure I like what I think you're implying, Inspector. You're going to have to spell it out for me.'

Angel took a deep breath, knowing things were about to go rapidly downhill.

'This whole sad sequence of events started when Rosie ran away from home. What, or who, made her run away in the first place?'

Laing went very still, jaw clenched and eyes hard, an endless expanse of blackness behind them.

'If we were two men in the street, I'd punch your fucking lights out for insinuating what you just did.'

Angel returned Laing's uncompromising stare, feeling the rush of adrenaline inside him as if it might well happen anyway, right here in interview room number one.

'I wouldn't blame you for trying.'

'Do you have a daughter, Inspector?' Laing squeezed out, through teeth gritted hard enough to crack enamel.

'I don't, Mr Laing. But please don't presume to give me a lecture on how that makes me incapable of knowing how insulting the suggestion of abuse is. But, like it or not, I have to ask. And I have to watch you as you answer so that I can decide if I believe you or not. Did you abuse your daughter, Mr Laing? To the point where she ran away from home?'

Kincade felt the table vibrating, not sure if it was coming from Laing, Angel or herself, barely daring to breathe, almost wishing they were in America after all, with Laing securely chained.

Laing dropped his head, then raised his eyes to look at Angel from under his eyebrows, nostrils flared and breath hot like a fighting bull preparing to charge.

'No, I did not. And I hope that when this mess is finally resolved, you'll be man enough to apologise for asking.'

'Count on it, Mr Laing. My next question is the obvious follow-on from any suggestion of abuse being unfounded. Do you know why she ran away?'

Laing suddenly grew weary, the support his anger had provided leaching away.

'I know you said you don't have a daughter, but even you should be able to understand that a fifteen-year-old girl does not confide in her father, however good their relationship. The young are a law unto themselves, and only a foolish man tries to understand them. You'd have more luck asking my ex-wife, but I'm sure you already did.'

'You're right, we did. Unfortunately, she couldn't help us, either. But she went to great pains to stress that you never touched Rosie in any way.'

Something passed behind Laing's eyes, as if he was surprised his ex-wife had supported him. Then it was gone, a satisfied half-smile on his face.

'There you go, then.'

Angel saw what went through Laing's mind, the words he chose not to say.

All that unpleasantness of a minute ago for nothing.

But Laing wasn't the only one able to keep his thoughts to himself, Angel's unspoken response difficult to deny.

The worst abusers are the ones who hide it the best.

FINCH CAME OUT OF THE VIDEO SUITE AND MET ANGEL AND Kincade in the corridor after Laing had been taken to a holding cell pending a decision on whether to charge him with Dominic Orford's murder.

'Thought I'd come and watch my coffee machine walking out the door, myself.'

'*Our* coffee machine, ma'am,' Kincade corrected.

'You seemed pretty hung up on the question of abuse, Padre,' Finch said. 'I'm not sure I can see it myself.'

'How much of the interview did you watch?'

Finch grinned at him.

'If you're asking whether I saw him threaten to punch your lights out, yes, I saw that. He's a bloody good actor if that was put on.'

Kincade immediately jumped on the anti-Angel bandwagon.

'I don't see it either, having listened to him.'

'Nor me,' Angel said flatly.

Both women stared at him as if they'd misheard.

'We're listening, Padre,' Finch said, sounding like they could listen until the cows came home but it still wouldn't make a blind bit of difference.

'I'm not convinced, but it looks like the killers are. They sent the note hoping Laing would call, they'd give him Orford's details, and he'd go out and kill him. They didn't care if he got caught. But if Laing's telling the truth and he ignored the note, it means they killed Orford themselves. Then they set out to frame him for it.'

'Whatever's going on with his car being seen in the lay-by suggests that's a possibility,' Finch admitted.

'If so, they'd have to be pretty callous to set up an innocent man. The dead girl's own father.'

'They were prepared to nail Orford to a cross.'

'That's brutal, and sadistic, but not callous. Orford killed Rosie. They want him to suffer. Why would they also want Laing to suffer? It must be because they think he's guilty of something. If they believe he was abusing Rosie, one obvious possibility is because that's what Rosie told them.'

'Which doesn't fit with the impression all three of us have got after interviewing Laing,' Finch said, a note of despair entering her voice. 'So? What's next?'

He raised his right hand to his shoulder, threw it outwards as if casting a fishing rod, then mimicking reeling a fish in with his left hand.

'I think it's a nice evening for a spot of fishing in Laing's favourite lake on the common.'

34

A LITTLE OVER A HUNDRED MILES AWAY, GULLIVER AND JARDINE didn't feel as if they'd drawn the short straw after all. Lindsey Howe, now Pritchard, owned a small, independent flower shop in Bristol's trendy Wapping Wharf, situated on the city's historic floating harbour.

Making their way past the eclectic mix of bars, restaurants, and food and lifestyle shops on the way to The Wharf Flower Yard, they wished they could stay longer.

Jardine breathed in deeply as they entered, sucked the fresh aroma of cut flowers and foliage deep into her lungs.

'Better than being in a stuffy interview room.'

'The lilies are a bit overpowering for me,' Gulliver said. 'Mind you don't get the pollen on your clothes. It stains.'

'We do have flowers in the North East, Craig.'

'I know. Cannabis, poppies...'

Lindsey came out from a storeroom at the back of the shop, putting an end to the conversation before it deteriorated too far.

Jardine introduced them, then looked admiringly around the shop with its weathered wood shelving and galvanised metal flower buckets and vases.

'Nice shop.'

'Thank you.'

Behind Jardine, Gulliver sneezed.

'The whole area has got a really good vibe,' Jardine added.

'Yeah. They only allow independent shops and restaurants.'

Gulliver sneezed again.

Jardine turned to him.

'I hope you're not going to do that all the way through, Craig.'

Gulliver was too busy sneezing again to answer.

'We can talk outside, if you like,' Lindsey said.

'No. I like the freshness in here. Have you got a peg for my colleague's nose?'

'I think I've stopped now,' Gulliver said.

Jardine gave him a look—*make sure you have*—then went back to Lindsey.

'We'd like to ask you about Rosie Laing.'

'Do you mind if I work as we talk?' Picking up a pair of blue-handled secateurs as she said it.

'Go ahead.'

Lindsey took a bunch of white lisianthus from a conical galvanised bucket, started to trim excess foliage from the stems.

'I need to start with some bad news,' Jardine said, while Gulliver pinched his nose between his finger and thumb. 'Rosie's dead.'

Lindsey stopped snipping.

'How?'

'I'm afraid I can't go into the details. We want to talk about when she ran away from home back in two thousand and twelve. We've been told she came here to Bristol to see you.'

Lindsey resumed snipping, more to avoid Jardine's eyes than fulfil an urgent order.

'We're not interested in the fact that you lied to her mother when she called you,' Jardine added.

Thinking, *your own conscience will punish you sufficiently for that in the days and weeks ahead.*

'What do you want to know?'

'Let's start from the beginning. Why did she run away?'

A faint pink flush that went very well with the white of the lisianthus crept up Lindsey's neck.

'She had a crush on me. We'd been best friends for a long time. I'm not gay, but Rosie was starting to suspect she was. She had a boyfriend—'

'Our colleagues have talked to him.'

'—but she wasn't interested. My dad got a new job and we moved here, and I suppose it came at the wrong time for her. She was really confused, didn't know what she wanted. I think she came to me to find out if she really was attracted to me, or it was just that the idea of it was growing in her mind because I was out of reach.'

'So she left home specifically to come here? It wasn't that she was leaving anyway, and this was a good place to come?'

Lindsey laid the white lisianthus down, selected a vibrant purple bunch and started to trim them. It seemed to Jardine she went at them a lot more violently—and it wasn't because the foliage is tougher on purple varieties.

'If there were problems at home, she didn't say anything about them to me.'

Jardine experienced a brief, very unprofessional thought as she watched Lindsey snip away.

Would the answer be any different if she snatched the secateurs out of Lindsey's hand, put her little finger between the blades?

'I told you Rosie was dead. I didn't say this is a murder enquiry.'

Lindsey stopped snipping.

'It doesn't change my answer. I'd assumed that, anyway. The police don't interview people if someone dies young of cancer.'

Off to the side, Gulliver blew his nose noisily. It was almost like a pre-arranged signal to change tack. Both women glanced at him, then Jardine resumed.

'What happened when she got here? Did she tell you how she felt?'

Lindsey nodded, the pink glow on her neck intensifying, although not as dark as the purple lisianthus. Taken altogether, it would have made a very nice, colour-coordinated display.

'She talked around it, but eventually it all came out. I had to tell her I didn't feel the same. I'd just met a new boyfriend and things were going really well. It didn't last, but it was enough to make the situation very clear at the time.'

'How did Rosie take it?'

Lindsey shrugged, *it is what it is*.

'She was fine. I think in her heart she knew it was one-sided. That's why she came here. She had to find out one way or the other before it drove her crazy.'

'Then what happened?'

Lindsey hesitated. Jardine could almost see her mind working, the implications of what she hadn't yet said reflected in her face.

'Where was she killed?'

'In Somerset.'

'Was it at a big old country house?' Her face compacted. 'Something court or manor?'

'I think you better tell us what you know, Lindsey.'

Lindsey dropped the flowers she'd been holding onto the bench, laid the secateurs beside them amid a pile of trimmed foliage. Then sat on an industrial-looking stool with a round, wooden seat and a spiral thread for adjusting the height.

'We were in the city centre, and there were a couple of

people handing out leaflets. A man and a woman. They had a sandwich board with a name on it. *Heaven* something.' She looked at Jardine, a question in her eyes, then continued when she got no acknowledgement. 'I was taking the piss. Saying what kind of an idiot falls for all that crap. Suddenly I notice Rosie's mesmerised by it. She wandered over to them and I followed behind. The woman made a bee-line for her and it's like, *Bang!* There's this immediate attraction between them. You could feel it coming off them. They're in their own little world. The next thing I know, Rosie went off with the woman. I say woman, but she wasn't much older than us. Maybe a couple of years? The guy stayed there, handing out shit. Rosie said she'd call me later. I was relieved. She'd only arrived the day before and had to sleep in the garden shed. My parents would've phoned her parents if they'd known she was there. I was already worrying about what I was going to do with her, and she was so happy to go with the woman, it was like fate. I'd told her I wasn't interested in a relationship with her and then, out of the blue, she meets someone who's almost got her tongue hanging out.' She dropped her eyes, took a breath before carrying on as if bracing herself for Jardine's disapproval. 'You have to remember, I was only a kid, too, whatever I thought at the time. I was thinking about me. Thinking how if my parents found out about Rosie, I'd be grounded, then I wouldn't be able to see my new boyfriend. You know how it is.'

Jardine did indeed, but that was a story for another time and place.

'Did she call you later?'

'Yeah. I'd never heard her so excited. Told me about the big house in the middle of all this land, and how the people were really nice and she was going to stay for a day or two to see how things panned out.'

Long enough to be halfway to brainwashed, Jardine thought, Andrew Foster's words in her mind.

'But she stayed longer?'

Thinking, *twelve years if you include the time in the ground.*

'Yeah. She called me again after a few days. Said everything was still great, and she was going to stay a bit longer. It was a cult, wasn't it?'

'We think so. Heaven's Testament.'

'That was it!'

'Did she say anything about the woman who'd recruited her?'

Lindsey laughed out loud at the memory.

'I couldn't shut her up about her. She told me they were already a couple. She was really apologetic, like I'd be pissed off.'

'What about her name?'

Some of Lindsey's enthusiasm for her friend's wonderful new life slipped at the memory of an aspect that wasn't so wonderful.

'She never told me. I got the impression they weren't allowed to talk to outsiders about who was there and what went on.'

'Is there anything at all you can tell us about her? Where she came from, how long she'd been there, herself?'

Lindsey made a show of trying to remember, head down, angled towards the tiled floor, then up at the ceiling where silver ventilation ducts and electrical cables and all the other things that used to be hidden behind suspended ceilings were on show.

'No, sorry.'

'I don't suppose she sent you any photographs of the two of them?'

'She promised she would, but she never did. Like I said, they probably weren't allowed to.'

The charade of trying to remember might not have

produced anything useful, but Jardine's continued questioning caused a spurious connection in Lindsey's mind.

'Do you think she killed her?'

No, we think she probably killed the man who did.

'It's possible, but it's not our main focus. Did you get the impression she was in charge?'

'Definitely not. The leaders were older. Mid-to-late twenties. They got all the members to go out recruiting for them.'

'So, what happened? Rosie just stopped calling?'

'Yeah. I tried calling her but it always went to voicemail. But I wasn't worried for her safety. I thought she wanted to stop all contact with her past life in case her parents came looking for her and tried to take her back.'

To safety, Jardine finished in her mind.

THEY TOOK THEIR TIME MAKING THEIR WAY BACK TO THE CAR, stopping for a burger and chips on the way, then eating it in a converted shipping container overlooking the River Avon.

'Looks like we've got a prime suspect for our killer,' Jardine said, through a mouthful of burger. 'All we need is something to help identify her.'

Gulliver, who'd been sent to private school at great expense by his parents, finished his mouthful before answering.

'What about the accomplice? She didn't nail him to a cross on her own.'

Jardine, who'd attended the local sink school, pointed a soggy chip at him.

'Something else. If she was gay, who does she get to help her? It can't be her new man.'

'Unless she's changed sides again.'

'Or putting it on until he's outlived his usefulness.'

His burger, which had been on its way to his mouth, stalled halfway.

'Only a woman could think like that.'

'Lucky we do, if it turns out that's what's going on.'

He was thoughtful a moment, chewing in a slow, bovine way as he mulled it over.

'It would make sense if he was also at Kilstock Court.'

'Yeah, but he can't have been in a relationship with Rosie as well.'

'Why not?'

She pulled her head back to look at him, mischief in her eyes.

'You surprise me, Craig. A threesome? I didn't think public schoolboys knew about things like that.'

He ignored the jibe, pointed at the chips she'd left on her plate.

'Do you want those?'

'They're a pound each.'

'Yeah? What a coincidence. It's a pound a mile to drive you back to Southampton. I think it was a hundred and four miles, but I'm willing to round it down to a hundred.'

She looked around, soaking up the atmosphere.

'I'm not sure I want to go back.' Smacking the back of his hand with her fork when he snaffled a chip.

'*Ow!* I'll start a collection for your leaving present as soon as we get back.'

'You'll miss me when I'm gone.'

'We'll see.'

'Just think, you might get partnered with someone who wants to eat all of their meal themselves.' Whacking the back of his hand again, harder this time.

'*Ow!*'

'Big baby. Next time I'll do it with the prongs.'

'They're called *tines*.'

'Not where I come from, they're not.' The fork poised in anticipation of his next foray.

'I'm going to make a complaint about police brutality.'

'That's boring. How about sexual harassment?'

'Is any imminent?'

'It's a long drive back . . .'

Sometimes, he just didn't know what to make of what came out of her mouth.

35

'Any luck?' Angel said.

The fisherman—the third one Angel and Kincade had approached—took his eyes off the red tip of his float two rod-lengths out, his thoughts easy to read.

I'd have more luck if every idiot didn't stop to talk and scare them all away.

At least I haven't got a dog that jumps in, Angel replied in the conversation in his mind.

'I've had a couple of nice rudd.'

'Do you come here a lot?'

The fisherman looked past Angel to where Kincade was watching the red-tipped float intensely. Again, his thoughts were easy to read.

If she'd asked that I'd think she was chatting me up.

'Now and again.'

'How about in the last couple of weeks?'

'I think you just had a bite,' Kincade said.

The fisherman's head snapped towards the water.

'Maybe not,' Kincade admitted. 'It might be my eyes.'

Angel repeated his question.

'Why are you asking?' the angler said.

Angel pulled out his warrant card. The angler nodded, then picked up a bait catapult, opened the lid of his bait box and dropped a dozen fat, wriggling maggots into the catapult's pouch. He held the catapult upside down, pulled back gently and let go, a rain of maggots peppering the water around his float a second later.

'Good shot,' Kincade said.

'It's easy when there's no wind.'

'Have you noticed a man sitting on that bench drinking from a hip flask?' Angel said, pointing at the bench and promising himself he'd push Kincade in the lake if she distracted the fisherman again.

'Why? What's he done?'

Maybe crucified a man.

'Nothing that we're aware of. Have you seen him? He sits there most days in the early evening.'

'Bit of a saddo, is he?'

He certainly doesn't come to watch the excitement of all the fish being caught, Angel so desperately wanted to say.

'Have you seen him, sir?'

'Nah. I hardly ever come here.'

Angel made a lightning-fast mental calculation involving the length of the man's fishing rod and whether he'd need to remove the reel first before sticking it where it would be going very shortly.

'Definitely a bite that time,' Kincade said.

The fisherman grabbed his rod and struck without looking, almost hitting Angel in the face with the rod that would soon be doing a disappearing trick.

'*Bollocks*. Missed it.'

He reeled his tackle in, inspected the single maggot that had been sucked dry on the hook.

'You need a fresh one,' Kincade said.

The angler grinned at her.

'Want to do it for me?' Fully expecting her to squeal in disgust.

'Why not?' She caught the float swinging in the air in front of her, slid her hand down to the hook. Selected a lively, fat maggot and pinched it at the pointy end—the head—which made the rear end bulge, then nicked it lightly with the hook.

The angler nodded approvingly.

'You've got the job, luv.' Then to Angel, 'Mind yourself.' Casting before Angel had a chance to get out of the way.

Angel gave Kincade a questioning look—*finished now?*—then started to move away.

'You should talk to my mate Rob,' the fisherman said. 'He comes here all the time.' He glanced around the lake. 'I'm surprised he's not here today.'

'Have you got a number for him?' Kincade said.

The fisherman beamed at her—*for you, luv, anything*. He pulled out his phone, scrolled through his contacts.

'What's your number? I'll send it to you.'

Kincade returned his smile—*in your dreams*.

She pulled out her phone anyway, opened the camera and took a photograph of the angler's phone screen as he held it towards her.

'Full marks for trying.'

He shrugged, *always worth a go*.

'I've never been out with a policewoman.'

'I'm a detective. I don't have a truncheon.'

'Yeah, but you've got handcuffs.'

'Time to go,' Angel said, steering Kincade by the elbow. Then, when they were out of earshot, 'I actually think he fancies you because you were able to bait the hook.'

'What's wrong with that? Better than a man who's only

interested because he thinks you'll be good at cooking and ironing his shirts.'

'Let's call Rob,' Angel said, identifying a road he did not want to go down.

'Engaged,' she said a minute later.

They both looked at the fisherman. He was looking directly back at them, his phone clamped to his ear.

'At least your call isn't going to be unexpected,' Angel said.

They continued watching the fisherman as he talked and laughed with his friend. Kincade re-dialled as soon as he pocketed his phone. This time, it was answered immediately.

'I'm actually on my way now,' Rob said. 'I got held up at work. I'm about five minutes away...'

'Might as well sit on Laing's bench while we wait,' Angel said. 'Unless you want to help your new friend instead.'

Kincade glanced at where the fisherman was still watching them, his float and fishing forgotten.

'Yeah, why not?'

Angel watched her as she went back to the fisherman, unable to hear what they were saying. She nodded and he gave her the bait catapult, then she grabbed a handful of maggots, loaded the pouch. Tried a similar upside-down method of firing, cursing loudly when the shower of maggots fell short. She immediately refilled the pouch, tried again. This time, she overshot. The fisherman took the catapult back from her before she emptied his bait box.

Angel drifted over to the bench. He hadn't been sitting down for more than a minute when a man laden with fishing tackle walked up.

'Are you the cop?'

'One of them. DI Max Angel. My colleague's busy with your friend.' Pointing at Kincade, now crouching down on bended knees. 'You must be Rob.'

'Yeah. You were asking about the bloke who always sits here? Sipping out of a hip flask the whole time and trying to hide it?'

'That's right. You've seen him?'

'Yeah. Pretty much every time I'm here.' He hefted his rod bag off his shoulder, leaned it against the back of the bench. 'I spoke to him for the first time the other day.'

'What day was this?'

Rob thought about it, then got out his phone, checked his diary.

'Last Wednesday.'

Angel cursed under his breath. It was ten days after the day the witness Dorothy Bancroft encountered a man on his way to the derelict barn where Dominic Orford had been killed.

'What about the twenty-second of September?'

'What day was it?'

'A Sunday.'

'Yeah, I was probably here. Over there.' He scowled, pointing at the swim where his friend was fishing. 'Andy wouldn't have got that swim if I hadn't been held up.'

'I wouldn't worry. He hasn't exactly emptied the lake. Do you take photographs of the fish you catch?'

'If they're worth photographing, yeah. Want me to check for the twenty-second?'

'Please.'

Angel waited while Rob scrolled through his image gallery, hoping he was a better angler than his friend.

'Here you go. A nice little tench.'

He showed Angel a photograph of him squatting with the fish held in both hands towards the camera, a wide grin on his face.

'I wouldn't normally take a picture of something that size, but I'd had a bet with a mate that I could catch a tench here. There's not many of them in here.'

The explanation went in one ear and out the other as Angel studied the photograph. It had been taken facing towards the lake, Rob holding his catch with his back to the water.

'Have you got any taken facing the other way?'

'Depends who I asked to take it. Other fishermen don't mind going down to the water's edge, but dog walkers take them from the path.' He swiped across as he talked, Angel not daring to breathe. 'That's better.'

Angel almost snatched the phone out of Rob's hand.

The image showed the same subjects, man and fish, but taken from the water's edge facing away from the lake. The bench he was currently sitting on was clearly visible in the background—as was a man's leg sticking out, the rest of his body and his head hidden behind Rob smiling at the camera. He swiped across again. The next photograph was a close-up of the fish. The third one was another distance shot, but taken from a different angle. The bench was still visible, as was the whole of the man sitting on it.

Graeme Laing.

He was looking directly at the camera watching the fish being photographed, no doubt the highlight of his evening aside from the contents of his hip flask.

Angel tapped the *info* icon at the bottom of the screen and the date and time appeared—Sunday, 22 September 2024; 18:56—as well as a map showing the location.

As he'd claimed, Laing had not been in the vicinity of Dominic Orford's murder scene on 22nd September, supposedly carrying out a reconnaissance of the derelict barn where Orford was murdered five days later.

He'd been sitting where Angel was sitting now.

Kincade's interest in fishing had clearly waned, wandering back towards them. She picked up on the excitement coming off

Angel when she got to within ten yards of the bench. He handed her the phone, her response predictable.

'*Yes!* We've got our coffee machine back.'

'Send all the images to me, please,' Angel said to the confused fisherman, then recited his number as Rob did it there and then.

'Not quite back yet,' Angel said, after Rob had left to discuss the evening's unusual goings-on with Andy. 'But it does look as if somebody is trying to set him up. And why would you do that if you hadn't killed Dominic Orford yourself?'

Kincade sat on the bench beside him while Angel reviewed the photographs Rob had sent him.

'We should ask them how long he sits here,' she said, immediately getting to her feet again.

He stayed where he was as she went down to join Rob and Andy on the bank. A three-way conversation followed, then she was back again.

'They reckon he's generally here for a couple of hours unless it starts pissing down with rain. And he's regular as clockwork. I'd say there's time for somebody who knows his routines to break into his house, borrow the car to drive to the lay-by on the B3035—'

'While wearing his field coat.'

'And have a quick tramp across the fields—'

'Making sure you park inconsiderately and are rude to anyone you encounter so they can't fail to remember you.'

'Exactly.' She was thoughtful a moment. 'That requires a specific skill set.'

'Only to break into the house. Assuming Laing leaves his car key lying around, doesn't keep it on the same ring as his door key. I don't.'

'Nor me. Maybe I will, going forward.' She checked her watch. 'I suppose we better get back and let Laing go.'

. . .

AN HOUR LATER, GULLIVER AND JARDINE WERE COMING IN AS Graeme Laing was leaving the station on a tide of justified self-righteousness, his head held high as he sailed through the reception area.

Jardine stopped dead, head swivelling around to watch him go, her voice incredulous.

'Is he taking the piss, or *what*? Did you see the coat he's wearing? It's the same field coat we asked him about.' She resumed walking as the door banged shut behind Laing. 'I wonder what's happened to make them let him go?'

Gulliver barely heard her, certainly didn't attempt to second-guess his superiors. After a hundred-plus-mile drive back from Bristol with his head full of the implications of what Lindsey Howe had told them, the sight of Laing in his field coat had brought to mind a quick exchange he'd had with him, an off the cuff question that suddenly didn't feel so random.

Do you shoot, Mr Laing?

Not any more, I don't.

At the time, he'd been struck by how forceful Laing's response was. As if he had a very good reason for giving up shooting.

Now, that feeling was ten times stronger.

36

HALF AN HOUR LATER, EVERYBODY ASSEMBLED FOR A DEBRIEF IN Olivia Finch's office.

Kincade went directly to the coffee machine sitting on top of one of the DCI's filing cabinets and patted it lovingly.

'Soon be back where you belong.'

'Who wants to start?' Finch said, ignoring her.

'Lisa wants to request a transfer to Bristol, ma'am,' Gulliver said. 'She's going to open a flower shop.'

'Sounds good to me,' Finch said, looking at Jardine. 'I think I might join you. So?'

'Lindsey Pritchard, née Howe, provided us with a very solid lead...'

'Someone else with a motive for crucifying Dominic Orford,' Finch said, after Jardine finished taking them through Lindsey's account of her friend Rosie's relationship with another young woman resident at Kilstock House. 'Equally as strong as her father's. You want to update us all on that, Padre?'

Angel started by extending his hand towards Kincade.

'Cat is now officially a fisherman's friend.'

Finch gave him a quizzical look.

'I thought fisherman's friends were lozenges for sore throats and congestion.'

Angel glanced at Kincade giving him a look of death, her mind easy to read.

Anyone who suggests sucking me is dead.

Angel handed his phone to Finch for her to view the images the angler, Rob, had sent him, then explained how it had been Kincade's willingness to bait the fisherman's hook that contributed to him putting them in touch with Rob.

'Really?' Finch said to Kincade. 'Don't all the maggot's innards ooze out when you impale them on the hook?'

'Only if you squeeze too tightly.'

'People put them under their tongue back home to keep them warm in cold weather,' Jardine said. 'At least my dad always did.'

Finch shuddered as if she had a particularly wriggly specimen under her tongue at the moment.

'It's a wonder your parents still managed to have two children.'

'I think the word you're looking for is *shame*,' Gulliver said, very quietly indeed.

Finch passed Angel's phone around, Gulliver and Jardine taking their turn to study the proof of Laing's alibi.

'Karma,' Jardine announced without warning. 'One suspect has to be released, and bingo, another one appears.'

'Laing isn't completely off the hook,' Finch pointed out with a fond look at her coffee machine. 'It wasn't him Dorothy Bancroft saw checking out the barn, but he could still have killed Orford, or been involved in his death.'

'Clutching at straws, ma'am,' Kincade muttered under her breath.

'He came in voluntarily,' Angel pointed out. 'It does look as if the killer is trying to frame him.'

'Can I interrupt a minute,' Gulliver said, 'before we get onto that. Going back to Laing himself. When we asked him about the coat, I also asked him if he shoots. He said, *not anymore, I don't*. As if he had a very good reason for stopping. I didn't get the chance to ask him about it, but it struck me as too forceful.'

Everybody mentally nodded their agreement. You don't question your gut instincts.

'More than because it was making him go deaf in his right ear,' Angel said.

'An accident, perhaps?' Finch suggested.

Something was scratching away at the back of Angel's mind he couldn't put his finger on. He had a picture of Vera Laing's face in his mind, the memory of her voice complaining in his ears. Then it came to him.

'Laing's ex-wife said part of the reason they split up was his attitude when her father died. He wasn't very supportive.'

'Perhaps her father had an accident with a shotgun,' Finch said. 'And Laing's attitude was, you play with guns, accidents happen.'

'But then he gave up shooting himself?' Gulliver said.

Jardine had the perfect answer to that.

'Better to learn from somebody else's mistake.'

They could have speculated all day long. Finch cut it short, throwing it back into Gulliver's court.

'Find out how he died, Craig. Take a deeper look if you think it's necessary.' She looked around the room, her gaze settling on Angel. 'So? Where were we? Somebody's setting Laing up. You were about to tell me who, Padre.'

'I was, ma'am.'

She extended her hand towards him, *go on then*.

'The people who really killed him.'

'Thank you for that, Padre. I don't know where we'd be without you.'

Another long, pointless discussion about abuse then followed. Everybody agreed that the chain of events made sense.

Rosie was abused and ran away from home.

She met another young woman at Kilstock Court and fell in love with her.

She was murdered by Dominic Orford for whatever reason.

Twelve years later, her lover killed Orford in revenge and tried to frame Graeme Laing for it, believing he was the abuser who'd set the tragic chain of events in motion.

Trouble was, everybody also agreed they didn't think Laing had abused his daughter.

'What if Vera Laing's father was the abuser?' Kincade said, and gave everybody something to think about.

Finch pointed directly at Gulliver.

'Get onto his death asap, Craig.'

'Want to bet the coffee machine on it, ma'am?' Kincade asked.

'But if you win, that means you've won it twice over.'

'Exactly. You'd have to do the same to get it back.'

'You know, I think I'm just going to order a new one from Amazon.' Scrolling and clicking as she said it. 'There's one here for thirty quid.'

'Yes, but where's the fun in that?'

'I THOUGHT I'D FIND YOU HERE,' LORRAINE WATTS SAID, TRAILING her fingers across Graeme Laing's shoulders as she walked behind the bench, then sat down beside him on the opposite side to where Harvey the black Labrador raised his head, sniffed, then settled back down.

Laing wasn't surprised to see her, even though it had been more than ten years since they'd last met, a tearful, acrimonious exchange that even now could set the bitterness surging inside him. He didn't object when she sat pressed close to him, thighs and arms touching, then laid her hand on his leg. He looked at it, thought about putting his on top of it, then didn't bother.

'I heard they found Rosie's remains,' Lorraine said, the tremor in her voice telling him she was as afraid of where the conversation might lead as he was, torn between that fear and the desire to comfort him. 'I'm so sorry, Graeme.'

So you should be! was instantly in his mind, mercifully not on his tongue. Because he was as guilty as her, if not more so.

He stared directly ahead, not seeing the lake, not knowing if he was glad she'd come or not, whether he wanted to be left alone or needed the comfort of another human being close by. Praying she didn't give his thigh a reassuring squeeze, tell him not to blame himself. He might slap her if she did.

'It gets worse,' he said, to head off the possibility, stick with the nightmare of the present, anything but the endless recriminations of the past.

'I wouldn't have thought that was possible.'

'Nor me. The police almost charged me with murdering the man they think killed her.'

'They couldn't blame you if you did.' Jumping at the chance to talk about anything but them, their relationship, their obsession with one another, and the tragedy it had brought about. 'What happened?'

'Did you read about the man who was crucified . . .?'

He took her through it all as it had been explained to him, his anger growing steadily as he talked.

'The cop in charge as good as accused me of abusing her, implying that's why she ran away in the first place.'

'Oh my God.' Now, she did squeeze his thigh, her voice filled with a mix of horror and incredulous disbelief. 'How can they be so wrong? Did you tell them the truth?'

He shook his head slowly from side to side, breathing deeply through his nose, trying to control the anger inside him.

'No.' He turned to look at her for the first time, felt the same animal attraction he had all those years ago, a force of nature that was always going to triumph over any man's pathetic attempts to resist it, and to hell with the consequences. 'How could I do that to Vera? After everything else.'

She dropped her eyes, not wanting to look at the hunger she saw in his.

'It'll all come out, anyway.'

He looked away again, knowing she was right.

'Why didn't they charge you,' she said, 'if you didn't tell them?'

He smiled, something he hadn't thought he was capable of anymore. Patted the bench.

'I'm in the background in a photograph one of the fishermen took. I'll have to buy him a beer next time I see him.'

'Will there be a next time?'

He heard what she really meant.

Are you going to sit on this bench every day for the rest of your life?

'I don't know.' Feeling so very weary now.

She snuggled up closer to him, squeezed his thigh again. It wasn't a gesture of comfort this time.

'It's not good for you to sit here brooding like this. You shouldn't be alone.'

'I've got Harvey.'

She glanced at the dog which hadn't stirred at hearing its name.

'Fat lot of use he is.'

'Don't worry. I'm not going to top myself.'

'I know that.'

'I'd have done it years ago if I was.'

'Come back to my place tonight. It can't remind you about it all any more than events already have. You can bring your dog with you.'

He twisted on the bench to face her, thought about taking her hands in his, something inside him preventing him.

'We're the reason Rosie's dead.'

'*We're not!*' They'd had this argument a thousand times before, back when everything was falling apart. Then, it had always ended with bitter accusation. Now, the passage of time had mellowed him, allowed him to accept her denial rather than scream in her face that they were both going to hell for their selfishness and lust.

She stood up, grabbed his hand and pulled gently.

'C'mon. Don't make me beg.'

He allowed himself to be pulled to his feet, wishing he could find comfort in her reassurances. Except he couldn't. The guilt would always be there. But he'd suffered more than a decade of the pain. It was about time he re-acquainted himself with the pleasure that had led to it.

Eighty miles away as the Angel of Infidelity flies, Vera Laing parked on the grassy verge a hundred yards down from the rusting gates of Kilstock Court. She knew she should have set off earlier because it would soon be dark. But was that a problem? Rosie had been in the cold darkness of a shallow grave for a dozen years. Maybe it was fitting that her mother should feel the creeping cold in her own bones, the paralysing fear in her own heart as the creatures of the night came to observe the intruder in their midst.

She'd studied Google maps and knew exactly where to go, even though there was no evidence that the place had recently been a crime scene, no tattered remnants of crime-scene tape caught on the barbed wire she now clambered over.

She followed the path around the perimeter of the field, then scrambled over the fence separating the field from the small wood in Kilstock Court's grounds. She made her way through the trees, startling at every unexpected sound, telling herself that the really dangerous creatures on this earth, the ones that set out to hurt and kill for nothing more than their own pleasure, all walk on two legs.

A strangled sob escaped through gritted teeth as she stood on the edge of the small clearing, the derelict boathouse on the far side.

Because it's all well and good telling yourself to be strong when you're in the driver's seat setting off from outside your house, but it's a very different story in the quiet of the evening, a pair of bats darting and flitting through the still air the only other living creatures stopping you from thinking you're already dead yourself.

She forced her legs into reluctant action, marched across the clearing to where a mound of fresh earth marked where Rosie's remains had been dug up. Dropping to her knees on the damp soft ground, her whole body was wracked with uncontrollable sobs, heaving in shuddering breaths, a keening wail filled with pain and loss shattering the silence, tears and snot streaming down her face.

And when she was spent and left feeling empty and hollow but somehow better for it, cleansed and more able to think about a life beyond the nightmare of the past twelve years, she went to stand a while on the bank of the small ornamental lake. She inspected the boathouse deck, decided it didn't look up to taking her weight. If she went through its rotting boards, she wasn't sure she'd have the strength to pull herself back out again.

Then she dug in her bag, came out with a cheap prepaid phone she'd heard called a burner on the crime dramas she watched on TV. It had served its purpose well, but now its usefulness was over. Drawing back her arm, she hurled it far out into the middle of the pond. It landed on a thick pad of water lily leaves and she thought she might have to wade out through the mud and silt to get to it. But as she watched, the lily leaves dipped and tilted under its weight, the phone sliding silently into the water like a dead mariner buried at sea.

She stood for a while longer as the last of the daylight leached out of the cloudless sky, feeling no fear now as darkness enveloped her. She almost understood why Graeme spent every evening sitting on a bench overlooking a lake similar to this one. The still water added another dimension to the peacefulness, should you be in the enviable position of being able to feel at peace with the world and yourself.

That understanding did nothing to reduce the bitterness she felt, now that the pond in front of her had brought him to mind.

May you rot in hell, you cheating bastard.

37

Isabel Durand stuck her head around the door to Angel and Kincade's office as Angel was thinking about calling it a day. Kincade had left twenty minutes earlier, saving him from having to suffer rolled eyes now and a ribbing in the morning—*not dinner with Doctor Death again!*

'Still here, Padre?'

'No rest for the wicked, Isabel.'

'Very true.' She made a show of looking around the Kincade-free office, her brow compacting. 'So how is it that Sergeant Kincade has gone already? She should be here twenty-four-seven on that basis.'

Angel wagged a finger at her.

'You're as bad as she is. So? Is this business or pleasure?'

'Both.'

He'd asked her to liaise on his behalf with Howard Lowe, the Somerset pathologist performing Rosie Laing's post mortem. He'd also sent her a copy of Rosie's dental records from the missing person file, obtained at the time she went missing. With NHS dental practices only required to retain patient records for eleven years, it made sense to obtain them in advance when remains might not be found until decades later. In turn, Durand had forwarded the records to Dr Lowe who had passed them on to the forensic odontologist for a detailed comparison with the disinterred body's teeth.

'Is it Rosie Laing?'

'Definitely. The forensic odontologist is one-hundred-per-cent convinced, despite the two upper front teeth being missing from the recovered skull. There are sufficient other matches.' She smiled as an ironic fact struck her. 'Funny how a forensic odontologist is always hoping people don't look after their teeth. If everybody had a full set of perfect teeth, it would make it a lot more difficult to get a match.'

He touched his own teeth.

'What about the missing front teeth?'

'That's consistent with the meagre findings resulting from the post mortem. The hyoid bone was fractured. As you're aware, that is most commonly associated with manual strangulation as opposed to ligature strangulation. There are no other obvious signs of injury on the bones. No nicks from a blade or fractures resulting from blunt force trauma, apart from what might be a faint zygomatic fracture.' Touching her left cheekbone as she said it. 'Given the missing front teeth, one possible scenario is that this was a frenzied physical attack using the fists which knocked out or loosened the front teeth and potentially fractured the cheekbone. After battering her, the attacker then manually strangled her.'

'Sounds like somebody in a rage.'

'It does.'

'I wonder what she did to annoy him so badly?'

'That's for you to determine, Padre.'

One obvious possibility was already in Angel's mind after listening to Gulliver and Jardine describe the homosexual relationship that developed between Rosie and the young woman who recruited her. Dominic Orford in his role of leader tried to exercise his *droit de seigneur* with Rosie and was turned down. He then showed her what happened to anyone who dared to say *no* to him.

'Is that the end of the business?'

'It is, Padre. I've given you a positive identification and as good a cause of death as you're likely to get from a collection of bare bones after all this time.' She smiled again, very uncharacteristic mischief behind it. 'I can't do your whole job for you.'

'You're in a very good mood for somebody who's spent the whole day elbow-deep in dead bodies.'

'You're right, I am. It's the reason why I'm buying you dinner.'

Angel had a good idea what lay behind the offer. He didn't say anything, didn't steal her thunder, happy to let her tell him in her own time—a time which he knew would not come to pass until they were both enjoying a pre-dinner drink.

'The Pig in the Wall?'

'Where else?'

Twenty minutes later and they both had a Campari and soda in their hands, Angel deciding against his usual Margarita. There would be wine with dinner as well. He raised his glass in preparation for a toast.

'What's the occasion?'

'You've probably guessed already. Oliver has decided he doesn't want to become an Army surgeon, after all. I don't know what you said to him to put him off, but it worked.'

He leaned forward and clinked glasses with her.

'That's great news. But I'm sure it was nothing to do with anything I said to him.'

'You're probably right. I feel stupid for asking you to get involved in the first place.'

'Don't,' he said, her son's words in his head, spoken in this very room with undisguised venom behind them.

You're part of the reason my parents got divorced.

She never shuts up about you. Padre this, Padre bloody that.

She rested her hand on his, a gesture that would never be innocent again.

'Dinner is the least I can do in return.'

He dipped his head, *offer accepted*.

'Has he decided what he does want to do, instead? Médecins Sans Frontières are always looking to recruit young doctors.'

She pulled her hand away, narrowed her eyes at him.

'Offers of dinner can always be withdrawn, Padre.'

'So it's back to square one? Anything so long as it isn't a forensic pathologist?'

She sipped her drink, didn't bother confirming it.

'Sometimes I envy you not having children, Padre. You'll never have to experience what being a disappointment to them feels like. Anyway, enough about me. What about you?'

Movement caught Angel's eye on the far side of the room. A young woman who looked vaguely familiar stuck her head in as if looking for somebody, then immediately went away again. But it was enough for him to remember her. He'd seen her when he met Vanessa to take charge of Jasper.

'Somebody you know, Padre?' Durand said, twisting in her chair to look. 'I hope it's not Sergeant Kincade.'

He shook his head—*it's nobody*. He wasn't about to tell her the truth.

Durand had moved on anyway, repeating her question about what was new in his life.

And seeing as they had all evening, he told her—or worked his way towards it.

'Grace told me my mother isn't over here to see my father...'

'Of course she isn't.' Looking at him as if he'd told her the world wasn't flat after all. 'She's worried about you.'

He shouldn't have been surprised by her reaction. She was a mother herself, after all—even if he was twice Oliver's age.

'Did you really not realise?' she carried on, curiosity in her voice as if she'd seen an organ twitch in a corpse she was cutting open.

'It never crossed my mind.'

She grinned at him.

'Much as it pains me to agree with Sergeant Kincade, I know what she would have to say on the matter.'

She didn't even have to spell it out. The words were bouncing off the walls.

Head up your arse.

'If people would stop murdering one another for two minutes, I might have a chance of taking a step back,' he said, in response to the unspoken accusation.

'There's none so blind as those who refuse to see.' She then proceeded to run through all of the factors Grace had thrown at him on the phone the previous day, adding her own take on the most serious issue.

'This situation you've got involved in with the Romanian detective—'

'Virgil Balan.'

'—suggests you haven't got over Claire's death as much as you like to pretend.'

'Really? Am I pretending to myself, or to everybody else?'

'The fact that you're being argumentative and provocative proves you know I'm right.'

They both took a sip of their drinks, an unspoken agreement to back down from what had somehow escalated to where it might easily become an argument. He was trying to think of something light-hearted to say to break the tension, when she beat him to it.

'You being on your own must worry your mother. I'm sure if you were to start a new relationship, she'd feel comfortable enough to go back home again. So long as she thought the new woman was kind and loving and understanding...'

'Am I supposed to join in volunteering admirable qualities?'

'It wouldn't hurt, Padre...'

38

Gulliver didn't think the team had been as convinced about his gut instinct as he'd have liked. But they'd all sat up when Kincade suggested Laing's father-in-law might have been abusing Rosie, Finch in particular.

Call it pride or stubbornness, but Gulliver knew he was onto something. Rather than come at it from the point of view of the father-in-law's death—difficult, since they didn't even have a name and he was reluctant to go back to Graeme or Vera Laing if he could avoid it—he decided to approach it from the firearm side.

Two minutes later, after searching the PNC for the data transferred from the National Firearms Licensing Management System, and he knew he was right.

Graeme Laing's shotgun licence renewal had been refused on 29 September 2012, approximately six weeks after his daughter was reported missing. The reason given was a fatal accident-cum-suicide involving Laing's AYA Nº2 shotgun. The victim's name was Duncan Hamilton.

Gulliver pulled up the details of Laing's original application for a licence, Angel's words about Laing not being supportive when his wife's father died in his mind.

The referee's name was Duncan Hamilton. His relationship to Laing was described as father-in-law.

Gulliver spent a minute thinking about the situation from Vera Laing's point of view. Her father had been instrumental in her husband obtaining a shotgun licence. He had then used her husband's gun to commit suicide. And Laing hadn't been supportive. No wonder Vera was pissed off at him. But was Laing's lack of sympathy a reaction to his own guilt over not keeping the shotgun secure enough, or was it something else? Thinking *good riddance* because his father-in-law had been abusing his daughter?

Gulliver went back to his computer, found the details of the investigation into Hamilton's death. He didn't want to wade through it himself, made a note of the SIO's name, Gareth Awbrey, instead. Then went to find somebody in the firearms licensing team, hoping to flesh out the reasons behind refusing Laing's licence renewal.

He knew it was likely to be a painful process. Cops who choose to spend their careers processing applications, assessing suitability and ensuring licence holders maintain adequate security and safety in their homes are likely to be on the pedantic side of the spectrum, getting an unnatural amount of satisfaction from each box they tick.

Sergeant Arthur West was a case in point. His movements were painfully slow as he brought up the details on his screen, as if he'd hit the wrong key one time and inadvertently licensed a serial killer to own a fully-automatic assault rifle.

'I remember this one,' West said. 'I refused the renewal myself.'

Why am I not surprised? Gulliver thought, and kept quiet as West droned on.

'A fatal accident or suicide using a licence holder's gun doesn't necessarily mean the licence will be revoked, of course. I wasn't concerned about contributory negligence. The gun cabinet was locked, even though everybody knew where the key was kept.' He tapped his temple with his middle finger. 'I had bigger concerns over his mental state. His daughter had gone missing only six weeks beforehand, and it hit him hard. He was drinking heavily, and not social drinking, either. I couldn't blame him for it, but I decided it was best if an easy answer to his grief wasn't conveniently to hand. Especially after his father-in-law had recently done the same thing.'

'Are you suggesting that's why the father-in-law killed himself?'

West held up a large hand that had rattled many a gun cabinet's door to test its secureness during a home visit.

'I don't get involved in that side of things.'

Thank God for small mercies, Gulliver thought and thanked West for his help before making good his escape.

His attempts to avoid having to read the file on Duncan Hamilton's death were thwarted when he was told Gareth Awbrey, now a DI twelve years later, was halfway through a Caribbean cruise. Awbrey wouldn't be pleased to receive a call from a junior officer with a few questions about a twelve-year-old case when that junior officer had full access to the file himself.

He went back to his computer and got stuck in, the first surprise on page one. Not only had Hamilton used Laing's shotgun, he'd killed himself in Laing's house, the same house Laing still lived in.

Gulliver immediately pulled up the transcript of Awbrey's interview with Laing, skimming the preliminaries to get to the meat of it.

Awbrey: Tell us exactly what happened, Mr Laing.

Laing: I'd been out with my wife that evening for a meal. It was our anniversary and we decided we shouldn't put our whole lives on hold because of Rosie's disappearance.

Awbrey: Try to take your mind off it for a short while.

Laing: Exactly. Anyway, the respite was short-lived. As soon as we got back to the house, I went to check my email, see if there was any news. The computer was in my study. It's not really a study, of course—'

Awbrey: I understand, sir.

Gulliver heard the unspoken part—*just get on with it.*

Laing: I thought it was unusual when I saw the door was closed, but I didn't think anything of it. I tried to open it but it wouldn't budge.

Awbrey: Is it lockable?

Laing: No. Anyway, my wife came downstairs at that point and said her father wasn't in bed.

Awbrey: If I could stop you there, Mr Laing. Was your father-in-law staying with you?

Laing: He lived with us.

Gulliver smiled to himself as he pictured the look on Laing's face, surprised that Awbrey didn't know all the things he hadn't yet mentioned.

Laing: My wife's mother had died a few years before that. Her father's health was deteriorating and it was decided he would sell his house and move in with us. We put the money in the bank in case he got so bad that he needed to go into a care home.

Awbrey: How long had he been living with you?

Laing: Three years.

Awbrey: Longer than you expected?

Laing: Yes.

Gulliver smiled again at the terseness of Laing's answer, pictured the face that went with it. He knew what Awbrey had been thinking—*it's lucky for you that you've got a good alibi or we'd be taking a long, hard look at you.*

Awbrey: Right. I know the score now. So, he wasn't in bed . . .

Laing: No. And he'd never go out without telling us. We started to get worried. My wife saw me standing in front of the closed study door and started screaming, telling me to kick the door down. That's what I did. My father-in-law had wedged a chair under the handle but a good kick dislodged it. That's when we saw him.

Awbrey: What exactly did you see?

Laing: He was slumped in the swivel chair behind the desk, his head hanging down backwards behind him.

Awbrey: Thank you for the demonstration, Mr Laing. You can sit up straight again now.

Laing: There was blood all over the wall behind him. My shotgun was lying on the floor. There was a glass on the desk and a half-empty bottle of vodka. It was horrible. The blood was going *drip, drip, drip* onto the floor behind him. It's polished oak. Not real oak, of course. It's stained pine . . .

Awbrey: I get the picture, sir. What happened next?

Laing: My wife tried to push past me into the room, but I stopped her. She was hysterical, screaming and crying and fighting against me. Our daughter was missing and now this. I held her until she stopped struggling, then took her into the kitchen and made a cup of tea. Then I called you.

Awbrey: Going back to the scene . . . I know it's difficult, but are you sure there wasn't a suicide note?

Laing: Definitely. I can see the scene perfectly if I close my eyes. The vodka. Grey Goose. The good stuff. Bottle half-empty, the cap on. One of our best cut-glass tumblers. The rest of the desk was clear apart from my keyboard and mouse and a pen tidy. I don't like clutter.

He's going to say, tidy desk, tidy mind any minute, Gulliver groaned to himself, cringing on Awbrey's behalf.

Awbrey: Had your father-in-law received any bad news regarding his health recently? Or a family decision that it was time for him to go into a care home?

Laing: Nothing like that.

Awbrey: Was he upset about anything else? The disappearance of his granddaughter, perhaps?

Laing: Not that I know of. He was very fond of Rosie, but he was old-school. Stiff upper lip. He was too pragmatic to kill himself over something like that. She might have turned up the next day.

Awbrey: You say he was fond of her. What was Rosie's attitude towards him?

Laing: Typical teenager. Barely knew he existed except when she wanted a new pair of shoes or the latest computer game. Then she could twist him around her little finger.

Awbrey: Did he spoil her?

Laing: No more than any other grandparent.

Gulliver felt Awbrey aching to ask—*did you have any concerns about their relationship?* But it was the first interview when things were still very raw.

He skimmed ahead, saw nothing more of interest, cursing Awbrey for being unavailable. His thoughts would have been invaluable, his assessment of the non-verbal aspects of the interview as enlightening as the words themselves.

As it was, Gulliver went back to the file. The autopsy report was as he would expect, using a lot of medical jargon to say what everybody could see with their own eyes—Duncan Hamilton had blown the back of his head off. It was before Isabel Durand's tenure began, making a discussion with the forensic pathologist impractical, but the autopsy findings were sufficient to suggest he'd put the shotgun barrel into his mouth, breaking two of his front teeth when he pulled the trigger. Doing so was perfectly feasible, his arms sufficiently long to reach the trigger, given the twenty-eight-inch barrel length of Laing's shotgun. Traces of blood, saliva and tooth enamel found on the gun's barrels supported the hypothesis. All of those facts, coupled with the door wedged shut from the inside, were sufficient for the coroner to record a verdict of suicide.

Yes, but did you abuse your granddaughter before you bid the world farewell? Gulliver thought, closing the file.

39

'Don't you think you should've come into my office?' Finch said, entering Angel and Kincade's after he'd called her. 'I am the ranking officer, after all.'

'We were all in here already, ma'am.' Indicating Kincade, Gulliver and Jardine as if there was a chance she might not have noticed them all crowded into the broom-cupboard-sized room.

'You could have brought our coffee machine with you,' Kincade said.

'You think you've won it twice over, do you?' Finch replied, then addressed Gulliver. 'So? Did Laing's father-in-law abuse Rosie?'

'Impossible to say, ma'am. But he did blow his brains out with Laing's shotgun shortly after she disappeared.'

He took them through what he'd learned, pointing out that they might have a better idea when DI Awbrey returned from his Caribbean cruise.

'No need to wait for him,' Kincade said. 'Something made her run away. I reckon it was the father-in-law abusing her. Especially if he'd been living in the house since she was twelve.'

'I agree,' Angel said, 'but why did Orford's killers try to set Laing up for it?'

'It was too late for them to get to his father-in-law,' Jardine pointed out, stating the obvious. 'Maybe Laing knew about it and didn't do anything about it. That makes him partly responsible for her running away. He needs to be punished, too.'

Angel didn't buy it.

'If that's the case, everybody needs to be punished. Why not blame the mother? Surely she would've seen the signs. Or teachers at school? Or the boyfriend? He admitted he saw bruises on her arms, backed down when she got annoyed.'

'Should we prepare ourselves for a lot of overtime, sir?'

It was a typical, tongue-in-cheek Jardine remark. But it gave everybody pause for thought. It had been ten days since Orford's murder. There was nothing to say the killers were finished with punishing wrongdoers.

'Best catch them first,' Finch said pointedly, heading for the door.

Angel's phone rang before he had a chance to reply. It was Jack Bevan on the front desk.

'I think we might have had another one, Padre.'

Angel knew exactly what he was talking about. Nobody would've described the media appeal as a roaring success, but there had been some response, even if all of it had been from time wasters.

Then Angel's brain retrospectively caught up with his ears.

'What do you mean *had*? Or is that just your peculiar Welsh way of speaking English?'

'*Had,* as in past tense, Padre. She's gone again.'

'I'll be down in a minute.'

'What's up?' Kincade said when he put the phone down.

'Jack Bevan's just lost another potential witness from Kilstock Court.'

'Given the response so far, that doesn't sound like much of a loss to me.'

'I'm going to have a word with him, anyway.' Already on his way towards the door.

'What for?'

The question stopped him in his tracks.

'I'm not sure. Everything is shifting so fast, I don't want to let anything slip through the cracks. If Gulliver hadn't picked up on Laing's tone of voice when he said he didn't shoot anymore, we wouldn't even have looked at the father-in-law.'

She shrugged, her voice dismissive.

'It's not going to happen twice.'

'We'll see.'

He took the stairs down, walking slowly, thinking through what he'd said to Kincade, the comparison he'd made to Gulliver. Gulliver had the benefit of meeting and talking to Laing allowing him to make a judgement. He hadn't even seen the young woman Bevan called about, let alone talked to her.

So why the uneasy churning in his gut?

'It's not my fault, Padre,' Bevan said, as soon as Angel came through the door from the stairwell. 'Not unless you want me to start arresting everyone who walks in and asks for you.'

'What exactly happened?'

'She walked in—'

'How old?'

'Early twenties.'

Already Angel was on the verge of going back upstairs again. The young woman would've only been ten or eleven at the time Heaven's Testament were in residence at Kilstock Court. It was possible the members might have included a family with a ten-year-old child, but it felt unlikely.

'She walked in and asked to speak to you,' Bevan went on. 'I asked her if it was related to the media appeal and she said yes. Although she was a bit distracted. I got the impression she'd have said yes if I'd asked if she wanted you to hear her confession.'

'I was hoping that's exactly what it would've been.'

'You know what I mean. Anyway—'

'How did she seem?'

'Like I said, distracted. But also nervous as hell.'

'It's understandable, especially if she'd come to admit she'd witnessed a murder twelve years ago and she's said nothing about it in all that time.'

'She might have been abroad. She had a slight Australian twang. Maybe it's the first time she's come back and she happened to see the media appeal.'

It was on a par with Gulliver picking up on Laing's tone of voice. As Kincade had said, things like that don't happen twice in as many days.

'What made her leave again? You didn't smile at her, did you? All those sheep back in Wales could tell a story about how scary that is.'

'I asked her name, that's all.'

'Did she tell you?'

'Uh-uh. That's when she walked out again.'

'Without a word of explanation?'

Bevan shook his head in frustration.

'Something like, *I can't do this.* She had her back to me by then and the door half open, so I might have misheard. And unless you wanted me to chase her down the street, there was nothing I could do.'

There was nothing more Angel could do, either—except hope she came back. Already, he felt his hopes starting to run away with him. The crazies don't walk out again. The time wasters don't walk out again. People who know something that scares them who're struggling with their conscience are the ones who get cold feet.

'Send me the CCTV footage, will you, Jack. I get the feeling you might have let the wrong one get away this time.'

KINCADE WAS STANDING IN FRONT OF ANGEL'S DESK WHEN HE GOT back upstairs, his phone clamped to her ear.

'Thank you, Doctor. Hope to speak to you very soon.'

His immediate thought was that she'd answered his phone to Durand calling with an update. Except she would never end a conversation with the pathologist saying she hoped to speak to her soon.

'Who was that?'

'Doctor Howard Lowe. The pathologist who performed Rosie Laing's post mortem.'

They did a little shuffling dance around each other as he went behind his desk and she moved out of the way and back to her own.

'He's taken a second look and found something he missed the first time?'

'No, nothing like that. He was discussing it with his wife, Bernadette. She's also a doctor. Works in Musgrove Park Hospital in Taunton. It reminded her of an incident that happened about twelve years ago. A young man who'd overdosed on cocaine was brought in. Dumped at the front door by a young woman who immediately drove away again. An ambulance crew saw it happen, but they were too busy to take the car's registration or give a description of the woman. Lowe's wife said he'd have died if he hadn't been brought in. He refused to say who'd driven him to the hospital or give any details about what or where it happened. But he had a tattoo on his forearm. A cross, plus the words—'

'Heaven's Testament?'

'Got it in one. She also remembers his hands. They were blistered and rubbed raw.'

'Like somebody unaccustomed to physical work who'd just dug a shallow grave, perhaps?'

'My thoughts exactly. I don't need to tell you the rest of it . . .'

With her parting words on the phone—*hope to speak to you very soon*—in his mind, she didn't, but he said it, anyway.

'She can't remember the young man's name.'

'Nope. But she's going to try to find the details in the hospital's records.'

'As a doctor, I presume she recommended we don't hold our breath.'

She smiled with him, but couldn't disagree.

'You think it's the accomplice who helped nail Orford to the cross?' she said, after they'd both sat thinking the implications through.

'It makes sense. To do that to Orford, he must have either hated Orford himself or owed the young woman who did. Saving your life is about as big a debt as you can get.'

'He might have had a grudge against Orford as well. If he overdosed at Kilstock Court—'

'To take his mind off being forced to dig a shallow grave.'

'—Orford and Jasmijn would have been against taking him to hospital, risking the attention that might have focussed on them. The young woman probably took him behind their backs. That explains why she dumped him and immediately drove off again.'

'But why did he keep silent?' Angel said. 'Protecting them, in effect.'

'Because he was worried he'd be blamed for killing Rosie himself. I'm assuming nobody actually saw Orford kill her. This guy's the one who overdosed and looks like he's just dug a shallow grave. Orford and Jasmijn would stick together, say he killed Rosie while he was off his head on cocaine. He'd be playing into their hands.'

The phone call and its implications had eclipsed Angel's trip down to the front desk to speak to Jack Bevan. The prospect of a potential cult member coming forward paled into insignificance compared to the possibility of learning the identity of one of Orford's killers.

Kincade asked, anyway.

'What about the young woman asking for you at the front desk?'

Angel couldn't help the laugh that slipped out, fuelled by his own perverseness and self-awareness.

'I'm more interested because she walked out,' he said, then explained his thought process.

'Typical bloody you. Anything of interest not based on the attraction of her unavailability?'

'She's a bit young according to Jack. Early twenties, making her ten or eleven at the time.'

'Rosie Laing was only fifteen.'

'True. But a lot of growing up happens in those three years, as you'll find out soon enough.'

'Not for a few years yet, please God.'

'Anyway, Jack's going to email me the CCTV footage. We can make our own minds up about her age.'

'It won't make any difference how old she is if she doesn't come back.' She studied him for a long moment, a sly smile creeping across her face. 'If she does, let's hope she's not as perverse as you are, wanting to tell us all the things she *didn't* see going on.' She shook her head, the smile getting wider as it became more insubordinate. 'Can you imagine it? Two people in the world just like you.'

40

Doctor Howard Lowe's wife, Bernadette, wasn't the only person to have their memories jogged by the recent events at Kilstock Court, even if Father Dermot Curran didn't have such a direct connection to the case as Lowe's wife did through him.

Father Curran had been the parish priest at St Mary's in East Quantoxhead, a little over two miles from Kilstock Court. The rumours that had been circulating about the existence of a pseudo-religious cult in the middle of his parish, tempting his flock away from the path of true righteousness with the promise of wild orgies and satanic rites had been a constant worry to him at the time, but it was one particular incident that had weighed heavily on his conscience for the past decade and more.

It had taken the discovery of a young woman's remains in the grounds of Kilstock Court to make him finally come forward, hoping that what he was about to describe to DS Dave Garfield was as a result of that young woman's death and not a precursor to it.

Garfield had driven from Bridgwater after Father Curran made the call. They were now seated on a weathered bench against the church's ancient stone wall, overlooking the original graveyard, long since full. There was a fresh breeze off the sea half a mile away, but the sun was shining and the bench protected from the worst of the wind by the projecting porch.

Father Curran's housekeeper, Mrs Rossi, was busy making tea in the presbytery. It was on account of her sharp ears that Curran decided to admit his failings to DS Garfield on the old bench in the sun. Mrs Rossi was an integral part of the local gossip machine, and Father Curran didn't want his shortcomings getting back to the bishop.

'I'm afraid I can't give you an exact date when this happened,' Curran started.

'It's not a problem Father. We're unable to say exactly when the victim was killed. Even if you'd made a note of the date, we wouldn't be able to say whether it was before or after she was killed.'

Father Curran was sure Garfield had all the best intentions in mind, trying to excuse his own lack of detail. Unfortunately, it had the opposite effect, leaving open the possibility that he might have been able to prevent the tragedy.

'We didn't used to lock the church back in those days, and I wish we didn't have to now. Anyway, I came across a young woman sitting in one of the pews one evening. She was crying and from the look of her eyes, she'd been doing so for a long time. She looked utterly wretched. It looked to me as if she'd been beaten up. Her lip was swollen'—touching his own bottom lip—'and her cheek was bruised. I'm sure recent events are affecting my recollections, but I remember thinking she'd come from Kilstock Court.' He gazed out across the ancient crooked gravestones in front of them in the direction of the cult's property, looking as if he wished he had a crucifix in his hand to ward off its evil. 'I was worried about the rumours I'd heard, and I suppose I was attributing every bad thing that happened to the damn place.'

'Subsequent events suggest your gut instinct was right, Father.'

Don't bloody rub it in, Curran thought, then carried on.

'She wouldn't tell me what had happened, of course, no matter what I said. I tried to get her to agree to go to the police, but she refused point blank.'

Mrs Rossi came bustling down the path at that point, carrying a tray containing a teapot and a couple of mugs, as well as a plate of assorted biscuits.

'You do know the tea's going to be stone cold in no time at all, don't you, Father?' She touched the side of the teapot. 'It's going cold already in this wind. You should come inside.'

'It'll be fine, Mrs Rossi,' Father Curran said. 'Besides, you're always telling me I slurp when I drink it too hot.'

Mrs Rossi gave Garfield a dirty look.

'I don't suppose this officer is going to arrest you for slurping, Father, although you never know these days.'

'Dunking your biscuit, perhaps,' Garfield said, with a good-natured smile, 'but not slurping. Half of my colleagues would be in their own cells if we did that.'

'Don't blame me if your chest infection comes back, Father,' Mrs Rossi warned, reluctantly leaving them alone.

'She means well,' Curran said, 'even if she is a bit too keen to gossip.'

'You were saying, Father...'

'The young woman wouldn't tell me anything, and I suppose I was getting frustrated with her. I wanted to shake her, ask her, *how can I help you if you won't talk to me?* I didn't, of course. But I did ask her what she was doing in my church. She said she needed somewhere quiet to think. Not pray for answers or anything like that. She told me she had a very difficult decision to make.'

'Did she tell you what it was?'

Curran shook his head, sipping absentmindedly at his tea, which was cold as Mrs Rossi had predicted. Personally, Garfield suspected she'd added cold water after it had brewed in an attempt to force them inside for a fresh, hot one.

'No. But ever since I heard about the bones being dug up I've been worrying that she was thinking about blowing the whistle on something going on there, and they found out and killed her for it.' He looked directly at Garfield, as if the roles were reversed and he was looking to Garfield for absolution. 'I could've prevented her death if I'd gone straight to the police myself.'

'Only if she was the young woman who was killed, Father. We now know her name was Rosie Laing. Do you know the name of the woman in your church?'

'I do,' the priest said, and told him.

Garfield forced the excitement rising up inside him back down, took a step back.

'How can you be so sure, Father? You said she wouldn't tell you anything.'

Curran looked back towards the presbytery to make sure Mrs Rossi wasn't watching them, then tipped his tea out onto the ground at the side of the bench.

'I told her she was welcome to stay as long as she liked. She was shivering by then, wrapping her arms around herself to try to keep warm.' He reached out to touch the church's stone wall. 'It costs a fortune to heat this place. Anyway, I suggested we go inside the presbytery so she could get warm, have a cup of tea and a bite to eat if she wanted it. I was surprised when she jumped at the offer. Mrs Rossi had gone home by that time, so I made her a sandwich and a cup of tea. By the time she'd finished eating, it was getting dark. I said she could stay the night if she wanted. On the sofa, or in the spare bedroom if she wasn't too scared of all the dreadful things she'd read about Catholic priests.'

'She chose the sofa?'

'She did.' He smiled at the memory. 'I was very grateful. It meant I didn't have to re-make the bed in the morning to avoid an interrogation from Mrs Rossi.'

'And she was gone in the morning?'

'She was. No note of thanks or anything. But I couldn't sleep that night. It's hardly surprising. I had a distraught runaway from a cult in my house. I came downstairs in the middle of the night to check on her. To be honest, I expected her to have snuck out as soon as I went to bed. But she was still there, crashed out on the sofa. She looked even younger, more vulnerable.'

He dropped his head, and Garfield finished the story for him.

'You sneaked in and looked in her purse?'

Curran nodded, eyes still on the ground as if he'd admitted to putting his hand inside her bra.

'She was only seventeen, but she had a provisional driving licence. That's where I saw her name. It's stayed in my mind ever since, expecting to read about something dreadful that happened to her after she left my house.'

'At least you don't have to worry about that now, Father.'

Garfield saw from Curran's face that his words gave the priest no comfort. The young woman he'd helped hadn't spent the last twelve years in a shallow grave a few short miles from his church, but he understood his fellow men well enough to know the evil that put a different young woman there was still at large in the world.

'YOU'RE VERY QUIET OVER THERE,' KINCADE SAID. 'IF YOUR EYES weren't open, I'd think you'd dozed off.'

Open they might have been, but they weren't seeing anything in the room, nor in the present, his thoughts elsewhere. Thinking about how different life might have been, how fate hides the things from us we need to know the most.

Kincade's voice brought him back to the here and now.

'Just thinking,' he said, a stock answer that always hides a multitude of sins.

'Has Jack sent that CCTV footage yet?'

'Just received it,' he lied, having watched it all the way through twice already.

Kincade was out of her chair before he could offer to forward it to her, standing at his shoulder a moment later.

Angel hit *play* for the third time and watched it with her.

'What do you think?' she said as it finished, beating him to it.

I saw her in the Pig in the Wall the other night and the time before that when I was there with Vanessa, remained firmly unspoken.

'What do you mean? Do I think she looks like a nutter or a time waster?'

'*No*. About her age.'

'I'd say Jack's right. Early twenties. Maybe mid-twenties.'

'Which would make her roughly the same age as Rosie Laing was back in two thousand and twelve. Maybe Orford and Jasmijn liked to recruit them young. Play it again.'

Angel did so, knowing exactly when Kincade would tell him to pause it. The young woman was looking almost directly at the camera behind Bevan when she did so.

'Stop it there.' Assuming Kincade position #1 as she said it. 'I wonder what made her change her mind?'

Angel mirrored Kincade's pose, left arm across his body, right elbow resting on it, forefinger pushed into his top lip. It would've looked comical had somebody walked in, the pair of them looking as if they were practising dance moves.

Then his phone rang.

They both glanced at the screen as the innocent-looking

instrument that was capable of making or breaking their day or week or the whole case vibrated on the desk.

Dave Garfield.

Without knowing how, Angel knew everything was about to fall into place. He snatched up the phone, hit the green button.

Garfield didn't bother with *hello.*

'I've got a name for the young woman who might have been in a relationship with Rosie Laing,' he said, then took him through the story Father Curran had told.

Angel immediately put the phone on speakerphone, aware of Kincade's eyes on him as they listened, as if picturing him in Curran's role. He looked up to meet her eyes when Garfield gave them the name, a shared thought in their minds.

We missed it.

Angel ended the call with a promise to keep Garfield updated, Kincade already headed for the door. She waved excitedly at Gulliver and Jardine as they went past, the two DCs dropping everything and following as they picked up on the urgency in their boss' stride.

'This looks ominous,' Finch said, as everybody piled into her office.

'Caitlin Fox,' Angel said. 'The woman who walked out of Orford's surgery while he was examining her. She was Rosie Laing's lover.'

'You already interviewed her, didn't you?'

There was no accusation intended in her words, but Gulliver looked as if she'd stood up and called him an incompetent idiot when he interrupted.

'We did, ma'am.'

'We also spoke to the man currently staying with her,' Jardine added. 'Damien Burke.'

Finch shrugged—*it happens*—then went back to Angel.

He extended his hand towards Kincade, *over to you.*

Kincade took them quickly through the conversation with the Somerset pathologist, Howard Lowe, and how his wife hadn't been able to remember the name of the young man who'd overdosed.

'We'll give her Burke's name. I'm confident she'll have no problem finding him in the hospital records.'

'It must have been Caitlin Fox who dumped him at the hospital,' Finch said, stating the obvious.

'Too much of a coincidence otherwise,' Kincade agreed. 'She only had a provisional driving licence. She wouldn't have been insured. That's another reason she didn't want to hang around at the hospital and answer awkward questions. She must have borrowed Orford or Jasmijn's car without them knowing.'

'And Damien Burke ends up owing Caitlin for his life.'

'Until Caitlin calls in the debt,' Angel finished, then summed up his thinking.

They'd seen a photograph of Dominic Orford as he'd been at the time, almost unrecognisable with his big bushy beard and long hair. They knew he'd gone by his middle name, Tom, the other cult members ignorant of his first name or surname. It meant that when fate stuck its oar in and arranged a doctor's appointment for Caitlin Fox with Dr Dominic Orford, she didn't recognise his name. Nor did she recognise his clean-shaven face as he sat at his desk asking questions and typing at his computer while she sat on a chair off to the side glancing around the room. But when he was leaning over her and placed his fingers on her flesh, something went off inside her, a deep subconscious connection was made, and all she could think of was getting out of the room as fast as was humanly possible.

Whether she'd stayed in contact with Damien Burke as a result of their shared trauma at Kilstock Court, or she went searching specifically for him after the unexpected encounter with Orford, was unclear.

What was clear was that Burke, like most people recruited into a cult, had his entire life course altered for the worse. People suffer financial, psychological, social, and health consequences, amongst other things. In Burke's case, it led to a life of petty crime, providing him with the perfect skill set to break into Graeme Laing's house and steal his car in order to impersonate him as he supposedly reconnoitred the murder site.

'It all makes sense, Padre,' Finch said, when Angel had finished, 'except why did they torture Orford with a blowtorch? If Burke was forced to dig the grave, he'd have known where Rosie Laing was buried.'

'Unless his subconscious had blanked the memory. Or he'd continued to fry his brain with hallucinogenic drugs or a million other reasons.'

'Or they wanted to make doubly sure and enjoy themselves at the same time,' Jardine said. 'We already know they're sadistic bastards.'

'We'll ask them when we interview them,' Angel said, cutting short the pointless supposition. 'Crack of sparrow fart tomorrow morning, everybody.'

A shared thrill of trepidation tinged with excitement went through everybody at Angel's reference to a dawn raid on Caitlin and Burke's property. And with the shotgun Orford took with him when he went to meet his killers still unaccounted for, the men with the helmets and Heckler & Koch HK416 carbines would be going in first.

41

At 4:45 a.m. as the deep navy blue of the night sky gave way to the pinkish-orange glow of a new day, two Armed Response Vehicles, each with four officers from the Tactical Firearms Unit squeezed inside, stopped in the middle of the road twenty yards down from Caitlin Fox and Damien Burke's house, Angel's Audi immediately behind it, Gulliver's A-class Mercedes bringing up the rear. Two unmarked vans coming from the opposite direction blocked the road a similar distance away on the other side of the house.

The eight TFU officers dressed in full ballistic gear piled out of their vehicles and formed up at the rear of the lead vehicle to make final preparations—body cameras activated, radios live, Heckler & Koch HK416s loaded and safety catches on.

Angel, Kincade and Finch joined them, Gulliver and Jardine following behind, everybody getting themselves comfortable in their ballistic vests. The adrenaline that had started flowing on the journey to Waltham Chase heightened every sense as the moment that had kept them all from enjoying a good night's sleep approached. Uniformed officers from the unmarked vans assembled by their vehicles. A ginger-haired officer built like a brick shithouse hefted the heavy steel battering ram like it was made from expanded polystyrene.

A sergeant called Meyer from the Tactical Firearms Unit, dressed all in black with his balaclava tucked under his chin and goggles pushed up over his helmet, finished the final briefing with his men and turned to Finch.

'Waiting for your say so, ma'am.'

She nodded once, an understated gesture that could potentially end lives—those of the house's occupants or her own men.

'Go.'

The officers from the TFU moved silently down the pavement like a giant black arachnid, the deadly HK416s that comprised its lethal sting raised to its eight shoulders, eight pairs of goggle-encased eyes scanning the street and the target ahead as they converged on the house with a single-minded purpose. Uniformed officers crept silently forward from the other direction, the big, red-headed man with the battering ram in the lead.

Not for the first time, Angel was acutely aware of Kincade beside him. The feeling of something inside her eager to be let off the leash and God help anything or anyone who got in its way, her eyes bright and filled with something he didn't ever see when she was behind her desk. And under her breath, a whispered mantra fuelled by her impatience.

'C'mon, c'mon, c'mon.'

At 5:04 a.m. all hell broke loose as night reluctantly relinquished its grip on the quiet street and a new day started in a way few residents were likely to forget.

The ginger-haired brick shithouse swung the battering ram, a single driving blow with his full weight and his reputation behind it, door frame splintering with a sharp crack, bursting the lock out of the frame, the door flying open and crashing against the wall, the mass of armed officers flowing through the open doorway like a toxic black cloud filling the space, their shouts fuelled by adrenaline and honed by training and procedure bouncing off the walls.

Police! Armed police!

Bodies flooded into the narrow hallway like an uncontrolled stampede, except everybody knew exactly what they were doing and where they were going. Up the stairs or down the hallway, weapons trained on doorways, and into the front room and the kitchen and the back room, carbines sweeping the empty rooms, voices shouting above the sound of boots pounding up the stairs.

Clear!

Kitchen clear!

Living room clear!

And then from upstairs a different shout, the voice more urgent, the voice of a man with a gun trained on another human being, a person he will shoot dead without hesitation if lives are threatened, his warnings unheeded.

Police! Armed police! Do not move!

More bodies thundered up the stairs as Angel and Kincade sprinted into the house, the ground floor completely clear, everybody's attention concentrated on the rooms upstairs.

A second shout rang out as Angel and Kincade followed behind, a different voice, a different room.

Police! Armed police! Stay where you are!

At the top of the stairs Angel went one way, Kincade the other. In the front bedroom Caitlin Fox sat bolt upright in her bed, naked from the waist up. Arms crossed in front of her to cover her breasts and her hands gripping her shoulders, eyes wide with fear. Two armed officers already in the room, leaning forward with their weight on the front foot, carbines raised, the red dots from their laser sights trained on the intersection of Caitlin's crossed wrists.

Angel stepped into the room, looked behind the door but didn't see a dressing gown hanging on the back of it. Caitlin was shaking with fear or cold, he couldn't tell and didn't care which, but he didn't want to be hauled over the coals for violating her human rights. A messy pile of clothes had been thrown on a chair at the bottom of the bed.

'Get out of bed,' he said, sorting through the clothes. 'Slowly. Keep your hands in sight at all times.'

'I haven't got anything on.'

'We're not here for a cheap thrill, Caitlin. The quicker you get out of bed, the quicker you can put these clothes on.'

'Fucking pervert.' She glared at the two armed officers. 'You two, as well. I can hear you panting behind your balaclavas.'

Angel threw her bra to her.

'Put that on first.'

She caught it one-handed, gave everyone a quick eyeful as she put it on, the laser sights' red dots still trained on her chest as she reached around behind her to fasten it.

'Give me my panties.'

'After you get out of bed. I've got no idea what you might have hidden under the covers.'

He saw her trying to think up a smart-arse remark, some insult about how no sensible woman would let him, a policeman, into her bed so that he might find out. In the end, she mouthed *pervert* at him again, swung her legs out from under the covers and put her feet on the floor, the sheets still covering her belly and upper thighs. Angel relented and threw the panties to her. She bent at the waist to put her feet through the leg holes, pulled them on and stood up in one fluid motion, as if she was accustomed to dawn raids led by pervy old policemen looking to start their day with a lecherous smile.

Angel checked the pockets of her jeans before passing them across, then did the same with her hooded sweat top. She gave them all a sour smile once she'd got dressed that was easy to interpret.

Show's over boys.

Angel asked her to turn around, then cuffed her and cautioned her.

'Caitlin Fox, I am arresting you on suspicion of murdering Dominic Orford...'

A commotion broke out in the back bedroom as Angel was finishing the caution. He left Caitlin in the charge of the TFU officers and went to see what was happening, an indignant shout coming from the bedroom as he was crossing the landing towards it.

'You can't fucking pin that on me.'

He found Kincade in the middle of cautioning Damien Burke, his hands cuffed behind his back and dressed in black jeans and a white T-shirt. The tattoo with the words *Heaven's Testament* was clearly visible on his bare forearm.

'I didn't kill anyone,' Burke yelled over his shoulder as he was led away and guided safely down the stairs.

'Any trouble?' Angel asked, once Burke's protestations had faded out of earshot.

'Not until I charged him with Orford's murder.' She tapped her breastbone. 'Not many people resist arrest when they've got two red dots doing a little dance on their chest.'

'No sign of Orford's missing shotgun?'

She hunkered down and peered under the bed.

'It's not under there. Probably hidden in the loft. How about you? Any trouble with Caitlin?'

'Apart from being accused of being a pervert, no. She was naked in bed.'

Kincade grinned at him, an insubordinate remark on its way.

'Lucky you had all those years as a priest practising how to resist temptation, eh?'

He ignored the attempt to bait him, Damien Burke's urgent denials in his mind.

'Burke's not a happy bunny. We'll start with him.'

They made their way downstairs, where the SOCOs had arrived ready to take the house apart. Outside, people were standing in their open doorways in dressing gowns or hastily-thrown-on clothes, some of them filming the comings and goings in the now-busy street, others simply watching or drinking tea as they chatted to equally nosy neighbours over the garden fence, their excited faces illuminated by the blue flashing lights.

Angel removed his ballistic vest, handed it to Kincade who'd already taken hers off, then headed towards the lead ARV where the TFU sergeant, Meyer, was giving Finch a quick debrief on what had been a very successful morning's work.

That wasn't to say the rest of the day would go as smoothly to plan. A development that would turn their thinking on its head was only a few short hours away.

42

By nine o'clock that morning, Angel was feeling a lot happier about the upcoming interview with Damien Burke.

After returning from the dawn raid, he'd gone with Kincade to an early-morning café in the railway station concourse for an egg and bacon sandwich and a cup of tea, then called the Somerset pathologist, Dr Howard Lowe, to give him Burke's name and date of birth. Lowe passed the details to his wife, who'd gone to work early to check the hospital records. Bernadette Lowe called Angel back herself an hour and a half later to confirm that Damien Burke, born on 9th July 1994, was indeed the young man admitted to Musgrove Park Hospital on 20 September 2012 suffering from a cocaine overdose after being dropped at the front door by an unidentified young woman.

Burke's silver Volkswagen Golf had been caught exceeding the speed limit by a camera on the B2177 as it entered Bishop's Waltham at 8:35 p.m. on Friday, 27th September. From there, it was only a mile and a half to the lay-by on the B3035 adjacent to the public footpath that passed within fifty yards of the derelict barn where Orford was crucified.

Similarly, in Somerset, Burke's car had been recorded by an

ANPR camera on the A39, three and a half miles from Kilstock Court, on the day DS Dave Garfield received an anonymous email supplying the details of where Rosie Laing's remains would later be found.

The news from the SOCOs pulling apart the house in Waltham Chase where Burke and Caitlin had been arrested wasn't so encouraging. The fact that they didn't find Dominic Orford's shotgun was particularly worrying.

Angel had an uneasy premonition they hadn't heard the last of it.

He would also have to wait for any trace evidence the SOCOs might find. Orford's blood on clothing found in the house or in Burke's car would be a welcome bonus, given the current lack of any physical evidence linking Burke or Caitlin to the murder.

What he was hoping for was a confession from Burke, implicating both himself and Caitlin. She had remained silent while Burke continued to protest his innocence—although two minutes in Burke's company was sufficient to convince Angel he was the sort of whinger who always looked to blame other people, the establishment and all of its nefarious agencies, or life itself. Aliens weren't out of the question.

Burke sensibly accepted the offer of free legal representation. He was deep in conversation with the duty solicitor, Nadeem Akbar, when Angel and Kincade entered confessional number one to begin the interview at 09:45. Angel hoped Akbar was busy persuading Burke that the best option was to make a clean breast of it, rather than counselling him to recite *no comment* endlessly like a guilty parrot.

He introduced everybody for the recording, then cautioned Burke a second time, also for the recording. Akbar immediately interrupted before he asked his first question.

'My client would like to make a voluntary statement

regarding the events that occurred on Sunday, twenty-second of September.'

Angel looked at Burke who nodded.

'I stole Graeme Laing's car and drove it to a lay-by near where Orford was killed...'

Angel immediately stopped him.

'Why did you steal it?'

'To frame him for Orford's murder.'

'And why did you want to do that?'

'Caitlin said he abused Rosie. That's why she ran away from home.'

The way he said it made it clear that what Caitlin said was gospel as far as he was concerned.

Angel was well aware she would have fed Burke edited details to persuade him to help her. They'd be getting back to the question of abuse, but not with Burke whose knowledge of it was third hand.

'Having decided to frame Laing, you learned his routines...'

Burke hesitated, then glanced at Akbar. The solicitor gave a small headshake.

'That's right,' Burke said. 'You only have to watch the sorry sad fucker for a few days to know he sits on the same bench on the common at the same time every day getting pissed from his hip flask. Bloke needs to get a life.'

And how would framing him for murder help with that? Angel thought, and said something more constructive.

'So you waited until he went out... then what?'

'Caitlin followed him and phoned me when he was on the bench. I let myself into the house—'

'Hang on. What do you mean *let*? You didn't break in?'

'Nah. I had a key.'

Akbar cleared his throat.

'We'll get back to that later, if that's okay, Inspector?'

It wasn't okay at all as far as Angel was concerned. But there was an agenda behind Burke volunteering information. For now, he went with the flow.

'What next?'

'I found his car keys and a coat and hat, then drove to the lay-by. Caitlin had seen the old barn and decided it was . . .' He tailed off, dropped his eyes before continuing. 'Where it was going to happen. We were hoping somebody would see me checking it out . . .'

They listened in silence as Burke recounted the same story the dog walker Dorothy Bancroft had told, then confirmed their own suspicions.

'I used a crowbar to break the lock. And I had a hammer and some nails. There were a lot of planks of wood lying around.' He closed his eyes, falling silent as he re-lived the moment. This time, he didn't continue.

'You made a cross out of a couple of the planks of wood?' Kincade prompted.

'Yeah.'

'Why a cross?'

Burke looked at her as if it would be better if Angel didn't let her do any of the talking. He pushed up the sleeve of the top he'd been given after being booked, thrust his forearm towards her, the tattoo with the words *Heaven's Testament* facing her.

'Because of that fucking place and all the religious bollocks they came out with.'

'You liked it well enough at the time to get a tattoo.'

Burke's mouth turned down, at himself as much as the logic behind her comment.

'Yeah, well, I was young.'

And stupid, Kincade finished in her mind. *Now, you're older and stupid.*

'Whose idea was the cross?'

'Caitlin's. She was more screwed up about the place than me. Because of Rosie.' He glanced down at his hands, an involuntary subconscious gesture that spoke volumes, as if he could still see the dirt on them from digging her grave.

'What did you do after making the cross?' Angel said.

Burke looked at him as if he'd been wrong earlier, or maybe they were all idiots.

'Got the fuck outta there, what do you think? Laing wasn't going to sit on the bench all night. I had to get the car back.'

'Did anything else happen on that evening we need to know about?'

'Nah. We went to the pub for a couple of beers, then went home.'

'Are the two of you a couple?'

Burke looked at him as if he'd been right about them all being idiots.

'Are you joking? She's a dyke.' He glanced at Kincade as if she might be one too. 'Sorry. She's a lesbian. Like Rosie. They were a couple while we were all at Kilshit Court.'

'Kilstock Court?'

'Yeah. I call it Kilshit.'

Yes, you probably do, Angel thought and moved on.

'Is there anything else you'd like to tell us?'

Burke glanced at Akbar, got a definite nod back.

'Yeah. I drove her down to Somerset so she could go and see where Rosie was buried.'

Angel bit his tongue, knowing Kincade was doing the same, not wanting to ask Burke about digging the grave until later.

'I also got involved in sending the messages to the cop down there. Garfield. I didn't want to give him all the information so quickly, but Caitlin couldn't wait. She wanted Rosie dug up and buried properly. With a funeral and all that, even if there was nothing left except bones. Closure. That's what Caitlin called it.'

Closure with added revenge, Angel thought, then worked towards confirming what they already suspected.

'Why were you prepared to do all this for Caitlin? As you've made very clear, you're not in a relationship with her.'

'She saved my life—'

'She drove you to the hospital after you overdosed?'

The interruption took Burke by surprise—maybe they weren't all idiots, after all.

'You know about that?'

'We do. We're guessing Orford and Jasmijn didn't want to get involved.'

Burke's face twisted, an ugly mix of disgust and loathing, his voice filled with the same.

'Bastards would've let me die. Then Rosie wouldn't have been the only one buried there and forgotten.'

'Except who would've dug your grave?' Kincade said, as if it was an innocent question.

The surprise of a moment ago was as nothing compared to the look on Burke's face now, realising that perhaps he was the stupid one, after all.

'They forced you to dig Rosie's grave, didn't they?' Kincade carried on. 'That's why you went and got off your face. Except you went too far. Didn't the first hit stop the images in your mind, Damien? So you tried another, and another, until suddenly there wasn't anything at all except blackness.'

Burke's face confirmed it for them, his sullen silence, too. Angel pushed him harder back into the worst night of his life.

'What happened to Rosie?'

Burke shook his head, and the confusion behind his next words had the ring of truth about it.

'All I know is Jasmijn told me there'd been a terrible accident and Rosie was dead. She said if the police got involved, the whole place would be shut down.' He thrust his forearm towards them again, the tattoo on show. 'Like you said, I was really into it. They brainwash you until it's the only thing in your whole life that matters.' He smiled suddenly, except there was no pleasure in it, only bitterness. 'And I fancied the pants off Jasmijn. I would've done anything she asked me. She said I was the only person she could trust.'

'Things changed when you started digging, didn't they?' Angel said quietly.

Burke looked down at his hands again, horrified at what they'd done.

'Suddenly it was real. I'm digging the hole with a shitty old shovel that's rubbing the skin off my hands and the pain's keeping my mind sharp. And I'm thinking, they're going to put Rosie in this hole and forget about her like she never existed. By the time I'd finished, I was ready to slit my wrists and lie down beside her. Jasmijn gave me some coke, told me to go and get wasted.'

His expression made it clear he was remembering what he'd been told in hospital when he was out of danger—the same hard facts Bernadette Lowe had explained to Angel when he spoke to her earlier.

'She'd spiked it, hadn't she? The doctors reckoned fentanyl. It wasn't an accidental overdose. You were the only one who knew where the body was buried, and she wanted to make sure you kept that knowledge a secret permanently. All the bullshit she fed you about being the only one she could trust, but in the end, she didn't trust you enough to let you live.'

Burke's scowl was easy to interpret.

Don't remind me.

Angel let him reflect on it a moment, then moved on.

'What happened to Heaven's Testament?'

'It all fell apart. Suddenly Rosie wasn't around anymore. I never went back myself after I got out of the hospital. I think somebody must've overheard me when I was off my head and ranting. Rumours spread, people got scared and left. Orford and Jasmijn weren't interested in trying to keep it together. I never saw Caitlin again until she got in touch a couple of months ago.'

It was clear any knowledge Burke might have of subsequent events—Jasmijn's death in particular—would have been gained from Caitlin, suitably edited. Angel decided it was pointless asking him about it.

'Let's go back to how you happened to have a key to Graeme Laing's house.'

Burke immediately turned towards Akbar, *over to you.*

The solicitor cleared his throat. Interlaced his fingers, hands resting on the table in front of him. The confident pose of a man who has something to offer that they would be well-advised to listen to.

'My client has information regarding the involvement of a third party who is crucial to your understanding of this murder enquiry. He is prepared to share that information with you on the understanding that his cooperation will be taken into account, both when deciding what offences to charge him with and the sentences recommended.'

'We're always amenable to doing a deal,' Angel confirmed, skipping the excess verbal garbage.

'Go ahead, Damien,' Akbar said, then sat back in his chair to enjoy watching his client take the wind out of their sails.

'Rosie's mum, Vera, gave us a key. She didn't know if he'd changed the locks, but we were welcome to it. And she told us about his habits. We didn't need to watch him every night for a week. She told us he'd been doing it for twelve years.'

Angel used every ounce of self-control to keep his face impassive, his tongue under control, not blurt out, *the bitch fooled us every inch of the way.*

Worse, he had a worrying premonition Vera hadn't been the only one to trick them.

After arresting Caitlin, he'd exercised his power to delay her right to make a phone call, offering instead to notify someone of her arrest on her behalf. She'd given him the number for her mother, Bree.

At the time, he'd thought her mother's voice sounded familiar. He'd dismissed the idea, blamed it on tiredness and the after-effects of the dawn raid. Now, he wasn't so sure.

'How was she even involved?'

'Caitlin contacted her after she recognised Orford at the doctor's surgery. She knew Laing had abused Rosie and thought his ex-wife would be happy to help frame him if she told her about the abuse. If she didn't already know, of course.'

'And Vera was happy to help?'

Burke coughed out a bitter laugh that summed up how easily and how badly love can change to hatred between two people who've been so close.

'Happy? She bit Caitlin's fucking hand off.'

'Was this before or after Caitlin contacted you?' Kincade cut in.

'Before.'

'Then the two women needed some muscle, is that it?' Looking at Burke's scrawny tattooed forearm as she said it.

Burke gave her a tight smile back.

'*No*. They needed a man to impersonate Laing.'

Angel felt the weight of all their misconceptions in the contempt in Burke's voice. And he had a feeling they were about to find out Burke's claims of innocence were true.

'Tell us what happened on the night Dominic Orford was killed. Your car was caught on camera in the vicinity at approximately eight-thirty p.m. I don't believe that's a coincidence.'

'It's not. I drove them there, then went with them to the barn. I'd left the cross leaning up against the wall. We put a camping lantern on the ground behind it so it was lit up. All the rest of the barn was in shadow except for where the moon was shining through a hole in the roof. It was creepy as hell. Caitlin stood in front of the cross when we heard Orford's car. We'd left one of the barn doors open so he'd see her standing there like she was some high priestess. Vera was in the shadows behind the closed door. I hid behind a pile of all the old shit farmers leave lying around on the other side. We were hoping he'd only be expecting two of us. He came creeping up, and it was like, *what the fuck*, when he sees Caitlin with the cross lit up behind her. He stepped inside, but he was wary as hell. Vera scraped her foot on the floor like she was trying to sneak up on him. He spun around—'

'Risky, when Orford's got a shotgun and must have been suspicious,' Kincade said.

'You didn't see the look on her face when we were planning it. She didn't know what fear was. Anyway, Orford swung around to face her. I stepped out from behind him and brained him with a cricket bat. The flat face, not the edge.'

Like it matters to a man who's about to be crucified, Kincade thought.

'He was out cold, flat on his face. We put the cross on the floor and laid him on it, then fixed his wrists to it with cable ties. Tied his feet to it with rope. That's when I left and went to wait in the car. I owe Caitlin my life, but I'd already helped those two crazy bitches as much as I was prepared to. I didn't want to be involved in actually killing him.'

'You're still an accessory, a secondary party,' Kincade said, 'if we even believe you.'

Akbar cleared his throat again.

'If I could refer you to our earlier discussion about cooperation, Sergeant?'

Kincade nodded her reluctant agreement, told Burke to carry on.

'I went back to the car to wait for them. The plan was I'd call Caitlin if anybody turned up.'

'He was a lookout,' Akbar said, as if nobody had worked it out for themselves.

'Can you prove you weren't an active participant?' Angel said.

He expected a sorry headshake, a mumbled *no* under Burke's breath. Instead, he got a derisive snort.

'Vera called me a *fucking pussy*. I'm sure she'll be happy to tell you that herself. She won't want anybody taking credit for avenging her daughter who didn't earn it.'

I'm glad I'm not relying on that as a defence, Angel thought, moving on.

'Do you know who actually did what to him?'

Burke shuddered at the memory of what Caitlin had no doubt taken him through in excruciating detail.

'I didn't want to know.'

'Why didn't you simply tell Caitlin where you dug Rosie's grave?'

'You sound just like Caitlin. I couldn't remember. She kept on and on at me like I was deliberately not telling her. I looked it up on the internet. It's called dis-something amnesia.'

'Dissociative.'

'That's it. Stress causes it. Nearly dying from an overdose didn't help. Your mind protects you from bad shit so you don't turn into a basket case.' He laughed nervously, a spontaneous reaction as something else he'd been protected from crossed his mind. 'Lucky I couldn't remember. If Vera knew I'd dug the grave, she'd have crucified me, too. She would've used the blowtorch on Orford even if she'd found a map in his pocket with a red cross marking the spot. She's one crazy, evil bitch.'

'One last thing. Where is Dominic Orford's shotgun?'

Except Angel knew the answer long before Burke opened his mouth.

'Vera's got it.'

43

'It wasn't Caitlin's mother I rang,' Angel said, as they rushed from the interview room, anger at his own stupidity distorting his voice. 'It was Vera. I thought I recognised the voice. And I should've recognised the number.'

Kincade bit her tongue. There was no point telling him not to be so hard on himself, that they spoke to scores of people day-in, day-out, hundreds of numbers and names and God knows what other details crossing their desks. When somebody's determined to beat themselves up, let them get on with it.

He had his phone out, already dialling Graeme Laing's number. Vera had been happy to set him up to go to prison for a murder he didn't commit. Who knows what she might do now she knew the plan had failed and her accomplices were both in custody? With a shotgun to hand, Angel wasn't taking any chances.

'Voicemail,' he spat, as he waited impatiently for the message telling him to leave a message to end and actually give him a chance to do so. 'It's DI Max Angel, Mr Laing. You need to go somewhere safe. *Right now*. Not home, not work, not anywhere your ex-wife might find you. If she calls you, ignore the call. Call me as soon as you pick up this message.'

'You can't do more than that,' Kincade said, as he ended the call.

What they both heard: *it's probably already too late.*

DCI Finch had been watching the interview from the video suite. She almost collided with them in the corridor as Angel walked and simultaneously left the message, Kincade beside him like they were joined at the hip.

'You weren't to know, Padre,' Finch said, her rank saving her from being told that when he wanted anybody's opinion, he'd bloody well ask for it.

'We'll send cars to his workplace and home,' he said as they moved down the corridor as one. 'To the bench on the common, as well.'

'And the hotel in Swanage he went to when he found out about Rosie being dug up,' Kincade added. 'And to Vera's house.'

'What?' Finch said, as Angel came to a halt mid-stride.

'The derelict barn where Orford was killed. That's where they'll be.'

'You're assuming Vera's already got to him.'

Angel waved his phone in her face, an angry, insubordinate gesture.

'His phone went to voicemail.'

'So? Maybe he's in an important meeting.'

His face said he had no time for *maybe*.

'I'm going to check the lay-by.'

'*We're* going to check it,' Kincade corrected, as Angel gave his orders to Finch.

'We need armed response on standby, ma'am. And the police helicopter.'

Finch watched them disappearing down the corridor, the

voice of the person responsible for budgeting chasing after them.

'You better be right, Padre.'

He was already out of earshot, but she heard him just the same.

Believe me, I am.

KINCADE ANSWERED A CALL ON ANGEL'S PHONE AS THEY WENT under the M27 at Hedge End, four miles from the lay-by.

'Both cars are there,' she confirmed after ending the short call patched through from the driver of the patrol car dispatched to the scene. She called Finch immediately without changing phones.

'Yes or no, Padre?'

'It's DS Kincade, ma'am—'

'Jesus, Cat, don't be so bloody formal. So?'

'Laing and his wife are both at the lay-by.'

'Leave it with me. And Cat . . .'

'Ma'am?'

'Don't let him do anything stupid.'

'I heard,' Angel said, before Kincade had a chance to relay the warning.

'Heard what, sir?'

He grinned at her, and she got an inkling that maybe he'd done more than look after the soldiers' spiritual welfare as an Army padre in Iraq and Afghanistan.

'You're right, Sergeant. The phone signal's appalling around here.'

Finch rang back two minutes later as he pulled into the lay-by, almost shunting the liveried patrol car. He let Kincade answer it again.

'Half an hour before armed response get there,' Finch said before Kincade got a word out.

'Can't wait,' Angel said, taking the phone from Kincade and hitting the red button at the same time.

Thirty seconds later and they were over the stile and striding out along the footpath towards the barn in the distance.

'Laing's got no idea what she's like, has he?' Kincade said, climbing the five-bar gate between the footpath and the farmer's land.

'Not if he agreed to meet Vera here, he hasn't.'

They fell silent as they covered the last fifty yards to the barn. They needn't have bothered. Vera stepped out of the barn, Dominic Orford's missing Beretta 686 Silver Pigeon shotgun in her hands, looking very at ease with it. She swung the barrel towards the barn's interior.

'In here.'

They stopped dead.

'Put down the gun and ask your ex-husband to come outside, Mrs Laing,' Angel said. 'I'm hoping he's in a state to be able to do so.'

'He is.' A short pause. 'For now.'

'A Tactical Firearms Unit is only five minutes away. It'll be better for everybody if we resolve this before they get here.'

Vera shook her head.

'We'd hear the sirens by now if they were that close.' She glanced up at the sky. 'And the police helicopter. I'm going inside now. I'm going to shut the door. It's up to you what side of it you're on.'

With that, she stepped back inside out of sight, pulling the door shut behind her, then leaving it partially open when Angel called out.

'We're coming.'

Vera was twenty feet away by the time they slipped through

the gap, the shotgun pointed directly at them. Laing was sitting cross-legged on the ground in the middle of the barn, staring at the blood-stained dirt in front of him. Vera gestured at the door with the gun when they were both inside.

'Close it properly.'

Angel glanced up at the roof while Kincade did as Vera instructed. The hole was still covered, as he'd instructed the SOCOs to do. The helicopter crew wouldn't be able to see a thing.

'Please put the gun down, Mrs Laing,' he repeated, when the door was closed. 'This doesn't have to get any worse than it already is.'

'It can't get any worse as far as I'm concerned.'

Don't bet on it, he thought, said something different.

'Why are we here? Why have you got Mr Laing at gunpoint? I remember your exact words. *He never laid a finger on our daughter. Not hitting her or anything . . . else.*'

Vera walked to where her ex-husband was sitting, stood behind him, the shotgun barrels six inches off the back of his neck.

'Graeme wants to answer that one.' She gave his neck a vicious jab. 'Don't you, Graeme?'

Laing hissed in pain and tensed.

For a brief moment Angel thought he was going to do something really stupid, take a backhand swipe at the gun.

Vera thought so, too. She took a couple of steps backwards.

Laing relaxed. Or gave in—it looked the same to the untrained eye. And sounded it. Like a man resigned to whatever shit fate sent his way today, whether it was his last day on the planet or not.

'I was having an affair. She became ill—'

'Stupid bitch found a lump in her breast,' Vera interrupted, as if worried he wouldn't put enough venom into the story. 'Thought she had cancer, poor thing. Graeme was so worried about her, he couldn't see what was going on under his nose in his own house.'

'Your father abusing Rosie, you mean?' Angel said.

'*Yes!* My own father. I'd never been able to stand up to him. Not over the smallest thing, let alone accuse him of abusing his own granddaughter. I begged Graeme to say something.' She darted forward, hit Laing across the side of the head with the shotgun barrel, knocked him sideways. 'But he was so obsessed with his poor sick whore, he ignored me. It wasn't until Rosie ran away that he finally took some notice. By then it was too late.'

Laing righted himself, twisted his head towards her.

'You think I haven't tortured myself every day for the past twelve years? It's not all about you, Vera.'

Angel and Kincade held their breath. You don't criticise the person holding the shotgun. Suggest your pain is as great as theirs. Not unless you want them to prove you right with a different kind of pain.

Vera swallowed hard. Took a deep breath, calmed herself.

And Angel was reminded of how much truth lies behind tired old clichés.

The calm before the storm.

Vera sensed it in him, gripped the gun tighter as she pointed it at the back of Laing's head.

'If he hadn't been so blinded by sex, our daughter would still be alive today.'

Don't argue, Angel prayed. *Admit it.*

You're pissing into the wind, fate answered, as Laing did his best to bring his death closer.

'And if you hadn't insisted on bringing your filthy pervert of a father into our home, she would never have run away.'

Shut the fuck up, Angel screamed silently, but Laing kept on going.

'I might have been blind. But at least I wasn't too weak-willed to confront my own bloody father.'

Jesus Christ! Angel cursed to himself. *Why don't you just ask her to prove that weak is the last thing she is right now?*

Everybody looked up suddenly, an instinctive reaction as the pulsating *whop whop whop* of an approaching helicopter's rotor wash grew louder.

Angel strained his ears, knew they were all doing the same, but still no sound of approaching sirens.

In the brief silence before anybody spoke again the final piece of the puzzle fell into place, prompted by the Laings' bitter back and forth about who should've done something about Vera's father.

'You threatened to go to the police about him, didn't you?' Angel said to Laing.

'After it was too bloody late,' Vera screamed.

Laing didn't need to answer, but nodded all the same.

They all knew what had happened next.

Vera's father had been facing the prospect of spending the rest of his life in a secure unit in prison, surrounded by perverts and sex offenders and living in constant fear of the other, so-called *normal*, prisoners getting to him. And despite the fact that their daughter was missing and Graeme Laing was screwing another woman, Vera and Graeme went out for a meal to celebrate their wedding anniversary—leaving her father alone in the house with Laing's shotgun. The abuser had duly played his part, blown the back of his head off as they endured a meal and a bottle of wine together.

And now, one party to that vicarious killing had a different shotgun in her hands. She too was looking at spending the rest of her sad, empty life in prison.

Angel didn't suppose she cared one jot if the Tactical Firearms Unit turned up and stormed the barn, shoot first and ask questions later.

It was now his job to talk her down before she did something to make it a reality.

He caught Kincade's eye.

'Wait outside.'

The insubordinate answer came back as fast as he knew it would.

'No.'

He could've gone the official route, called her *Sergeant* and told her again.

She'd have replied, *no, sir*.

Instead, he pulled out a folded sheet of paper from his pocket, handed it to her. She unfolded it, surprise her first reaction, then a dawning realisation about how wrong people can be about one another, about themselves, about life itself.

'Trust me,' he said.

She held his gaze until it felt as if time itself had ground to a halt.

Then she passed the CCTV image he'd printed out back to him and left him to it. He was walking directly towards Vera, the photograph in his extended hand and Vera hissing at him not to come any closer, as Kincade slipped out and closed the door behind her. She leaned her back against it, asking herself what part of Finch's instruction to not let him do anything stupid she hadn't understood.

Five minutes later as the approaching sirens could finally be heard, she felt the door pushed against her back. She moved away, then Angel came out carrying Orford's shotgun broken over his forearm. Vera was immediately behind him, Laing bringing up the rear.

'*Amor vincit omnia*,' he said, as she cuffed a sobbing Vera Laing.

THE INTERVIEW WITH VERA WAS SHORT, STRAIGHTFORWARD, AND left a sour taste in Angel and Kincade's mouths. She showed no remorse whatsoever for what she'd done. She confirmed Damien Burke's account, corroborating his claim that he'd left the barn after helping secure Dominic Orford to the cross with cable ties and clothesline. She and Caitlin had then nailed Orford's wrists to the cross. As far as she was concerned, it was punishment, pure and simple. Orford had picked the wrong mother's daughter to welcome into his band of delusional followers. She admitted to using the blowtorch on Orford's feet with as much emotion as if describing how to caramelise the sugar topping on crème brûlée. She told them Caitlin had pushed her aside and delivered the fatal knife wound when Orford's screams became unbearable. Vera's only regret appeared to be that she hadn't videoed the whole grisly episode on her phone.

'What was that you said about love conquers all?' Kincade asked, after Vera had been charged and taken back to the custody cells.

'I'll tell you later.'

44

As Angel had hoped, there wasn't a lot left to wrap up with Caitlin Fox. Damien Burke and Vera Laing had both implicated her, Vera explicitly stating that Caitlin had delivered the fatal stab wound.

Like Vera, Caitlin declined the offer of legal representation. Unlike Vera, it had nothing to do with not wanting to be gagged by a solicitor duty-bound to protect his client from herself. It was acceptance. The game was up.

Angel let Kincade take the lead, a consolation prize for excluding her from talking Vera down in the barn. She took the same approach as he had with Vera, running through the account Damien Burke had given, stopping at the point where Burke left the derelict barn.

'Is that a fair representation of what happened, Ms Fox?'

Caitlin didn't immediately reply. It wasn't a question of disagreement. The betrayal they saw in her eyes made that clear. Her one act of kindness—saving Damien Burke's life by taking him to hospital after he overdosed—had been repaid by him implicating her in order to save his own skin.

'Is that a fair representation?' Kincade repeated.

'Yes,' Caitlin spat, the venom behind it suggesting fairness didn't come into it as far as she was concerned.

'Tell us what happened after Damien Burke left the barn.'

Caitlin wrapped her arms around herself as if a cold wind had chilled her. Suddenly she didn't look like an arrogant young woman who'd nailed a man to a cross and stabbed him to death for the crimes she judged him guilty of. She looked like a frightened girl overwhelmed by the enormity of what she'd done.

She gave her account in a monotone as if reading from a prepared script. It matched what Vera had told them in every detail. All that remained was to ask why.

'What made you push Vera aside and stab Orford to death?' Kincade asked.

The colour drained from Caitlin's face at the memory of what she'd set in motion when she first contacted Vera Laing.

'She was possessed. She would've carried on all night. The smell of burnt flesh was making me feel sick. I couldn't stand him screaming.' Clamping her hands over her ears as if she could hear it now. 'It was driving me crazy.'

Angel experienced a minor epiphany in that moment. The viciousness of the way in which Orford had been killed had been troubling him. Vera he could understand. But Caitlin had been in a brief relationship with Rosie twelve years previously when she was still a teenager herself. There had to be more to it.

And now he knew what it was. His old friend. Guilt. Caitlin blamed herself for what happened to Rosie, and Orford's screams brought it all back with a vengeance.

He sensed she was on a knife edge. Torn between wanting to unburden herself and trying to push the memories back into the dark places inside her for another twelve years.

'Let's take a short break. Then you can tell us the circumstances of Rosie's death.'

Caitlin jumped at the offer. Said she was gasping for a cup of tea and was there any chance of something to eat?

'Bacon sandwich?' Angel suggested.

'Remind me to nail a man to a cross next time I'm hungry,' Kincade whispered, as they left the interview room together.

He nipped across the road to the café on the station concourse, ordered his second bacon sandwich of the day and three cups of tea.

'No egg this time?' the woman behind the counter said, remembering him.

'Yeah, why not?'

Ten minutes later and he was back in the corridor outside the interview room, wishing he'd had a bet with Jack Bevan about what Kincade would say.

'Only one sandwich?'

'I don't think she could eat two.'

Kincade gave him a dirty look—*you know what I meant*—then followed him into the interview room. The speed with which Caitlin devoured the egg and bacon sandwich proved how wrong he'd been, but he wasn't going back for another one.

Caitlin now looked like a frightened girl overwhelmed by the enormity of what she'd done who'd eaten an egg and bacon sandwich too quickly. Hopefully the fat and calories would see her through to the end.

'Rosie was really confused and mixed up. She'd had a boyfriend and that didn't work out. Then she thought she fancied her best friend who rejected her. Then she met me. And I was *very* interested in her. But she was still a kid, not sure about her sexuality.'

And she'd been abused by her grandfather, Kincade thought, but decided against bringing it up. She didn't want the added distraction of Caitlin learning she'd got it completely wrong.

'It didn't make for the smoothest relationship,' she said,

instead. 'All those teenage hormones and a massive change in her life.'

Caitlin smiled, and for a brief moment they could almost have forgotten what she'd done to Dominic Orford.

'Yeah. She was difficult to manage. I'm not saying I was perfect. It was up and down like any relationship, except living in that place seemed to make things worse. Then one day we had a massive argument. I can't even remember what it was about now. Something stupid that gets blown out of proportion when nobody's prepared to back down.'

'Business as usual,' Kincade said, and got another tentative smile back.

'The thing is, Orford and Jasmijn were a couple, but Orford had a roving eye. And he was a good-looking guy, if you like that hippy look. Anyway, he saw his latest recruit, Rosie, was down in the dumps and tried to comfort her. One thing led to another and he seduced her. After the argument with me, Rosie was more than willing. Trying to hurt me, I suppose.'

'She got pregnant,' Kincade said, a statement more than a question.

'Yeah. She confided in me. But I was only seventeen myself and she'd been fucking Orford's brains out to try to piss me off, so I gave her the cold shoulder.'

'Which is when she told Orford she was pregnant,' Kincade said, as if they were reading a script together. 'She had nobody else to turn to.'

Caitlin hadn't once shown any remorse about what she'd done to Dominic Orford. Now, she dropped her eyes, started to toy with the greasy paper bag the sandwich had been in, folding it in half and then half again.

'Orford went apeshit. Told her she had to have an abortion. Made it very clear he wasn't interested in her anymore. Rosie was beside herself. She told me she'd die before she had an abortion.' Caitlin swallowed hard at the premonition in her words, sniffed, swiped angrily at her nose with the back of her hand. 'She was crying her heart out. Saying how I didn't want her and Orford didn't want her and the baby was all she had.'

Angel risked an interruption as Caitlin fell briefly silent.

'Did you tell Vera all this?'

Caitlin nodded unhappily, swiped at her nose again.

They shared a look. They didn't want to imagine what Vera must have felt when she was told her dead daughter had been pregnant and even when she was rejected by everybody else, she still didn't consider the possibility of going home to her parents.

The worst was yet to come. They would end up understanding what Caitlin had done, if not condoning it, when she bared her soul to them.

The first crack appeared in her voice when she took a self-loathing step down that road.

'I must have been some special kind of bitch. I gave her the cold shoulder again. Told her she got herself into the mess, she could get herself out again. Have the baby, have an abortion, I don't care. Nothing to do with me. She went back to Orford, told him she wasn't going to terminate the pregnancy. I don't know for sure what happened because I never saw her again. You probably know better than me from the post mortem?' A rising inflection in her voice, a plea for details she didn't want but couldn't stop herself from asking for.

Kincade glanced at Angel, got a small nod back.

'He beat her up, then strangled her.'

Caitlin gave a strangled sob in response.

'That's one way to end an unwanted pregnancy.'

She closed her eyes as the full weight of her guilt crushed her, the flippant remark a random reaction to the conflicting emotions running riot inside her. They gave her time. If they pushed her too hard, she'd disappear back inside herself.

'I bumped into Damien a couple of hours later. He was flushed and sweating like a pig, all his muscles twitching like he had St. Vitus' Dance. He was babbling about a shallow grave and how he was going to hell. And his hands were rubbed raw. I figured out what had happened. I knew Orford and Jasmijn wouldn't take him to the hospital. I snuck into Orford's room and stole his car keys, then drove Damien there myself. But Orford caught me when I was putting the keys back. He stank of booze. I had to tell him about taking Damien to hospital, but I didn't say anything about a grave. He started hitting me, calling me an interfering bitch. He was so drunk I managed to get away from him, ended up at a church a couple of miles away trying to decide what to do. The priest let me stay the night.'

'You decided to bide your time,' Kincade said.

'Yeah. I went back. Forced myself to apologise to Orford for taking Damien to hospital, when all I wanted to do was kill him.' She smiled briefly, a quick twitch of her mouth at her own cleverness. 'I told him I hadn't been thinking straight. I'd had a big argument with Rosie and she'd run away, telling me she was going home to her parents. So he was feeling good about himself, thinking I didn't know anything. He even apologised for hitting me. Things sort of got back to normal for a while.'

'While you waited for your moment. You didn't have to wait long, did you?'

A light entered Caitlin's eyes, not looking like a frightened girl anymore. As if she was re-living the jolt in her car seat as she drove over Jasmijn lying in the road dying.

'Orford worshipped Jasmijn. I know he seduced Rosie, but he was a man, couldn't help himself. It meant nothing to him. Not seducing her or getting her pregnant or killing her.'

'So you took away the one thing he *did* care about.'

Caitlin let her silence answer for her. She was no fool. She couldn't avoid the consequences coming her way for murdering

Dominic Orford, but she wasn't going to hand them anything on a plate.

'Did you run down and kill Jasmijn while she was walking in the country lanes?' Kincade wasted her breath asking.

Caitlin didn't answer, volunteering instead her justification for the crime she couldn't evade.

'For twelve years I've hated myself. I could've persuaded Rosie to have an abortion if I'd listened to her and comforted her, instead of acting like the selfish immature bitch I was. Then she'd still be alive today. I deserve to burn in hell.'

Ordinarily, Angel would've agreed with her. Except, today, he didn't have the heart to be judgemental. The trepidation that had started twenty-four hours previously, now approaching fever pitch, made one thing very clear. He was in no position to criticise anybody for the things they'd done in their youth without a thought spared for the consequences.

45

'Walk with me,' Angel said.

Kincade dropped everything. The paperwork could wait. The cup of coffee she'd been contemplating for the past half hour could wait. Breathing could wait, if necessary.

He didn't say anything in the lift on the way down, his focus elsewhere.

She didn't ask.

'Good result, Padre,' Jack Bevan said, as they passed the front desk.

Angel barely heard him, an automatic response—*thanks, Jack*—on his lips.

Leaving the station, they turned right onto Southern Road, heading towards West Quay Road. She knew where he was headed, knew she wouldn't be going all the way with him. Some roads are made to be walked alone.

It was as if the frantic, unremitting traffic all around them, the noise and the fumes and the sense of life itself chasing its own tail, faded into the background as side-by-side they walked. In their minds, back in the derelict barn. The sound of a circling police helicopter overhead, unseen rodents foraging in the darkest corners. Graeme Laing sitting cross-legged on the ground, a trickle of blood leaking from his ear. Vera standing defiantly behind him, the shotgun pointed at Laing, at them, at anyone stupid enough to try to take it from her.

'Trust me,' Angel had said to Kincade.

She'd held his gaze until it felt as if time itself had ground to a halt.

Then she'd passed the CCTV image he'd printed out back to him, left him to it.

Angel was already walking towards Vera as Kincade closed the door behind her, leading the way with the photograph as if it were a peace offering.

Vera took a step backwards, hissed at him.

'Don't come any closer.'

He kept on coming. Voice soft and measured despite the racing of his heart, the adrenaline coursing through his veins.

'How much joy did Rosie give you, Vera?'

She cocked her head at him, wary at the strange turn the conversation had taken.

'*What?*'

'How much?'

'More than you can ever know.' Her voice filled with contempt for the man who could never understand. She took a step backwards. 'I told you not to come any closer.'

He took another step towards her as if she hadn't spoken, level with Laing on the floor now.

'Would you deprive another person of that joy?'

'What the fuck are you on about?'

'*Would you?*'

'Of course, I wouldn't. What do you think I am? Orford deserved everything he got. But I'm not a heartless monster.'

That's what I'm hoping, he thought, taking another step closer.

'What would you say to a man who'd never known he had a daughter, who suddenly learned he had one?'

She raised the shotgun, pointed it directly at him. Even in the dim light of the barn he saw her finger inside the trigger guard.

'I don't know what you're trying to do. Now back off. I won't warn you again.'

'Answer the question, Vera.'

Something about his insistence registered with her, the aggressive comeback dying on her lips, her curiosity aroused. It seemed to him the weight of her loss bore down more heavily on her as she answered.

'I'd tell him to do everything in his power to make up for his lost years.'

'And what if he was killed before he ever got the chance to meet her?'

Her previous vitriol came flooding back, the memory of what she'd done to Dominic Orford in her eyes, in the satisfaction in her voice.

'I'd say the bastard who killed him deserves what Orford got.'

'Me too.'

He took a final step towards her, bent slowly, his movements smooth and measured, placed the photograph carefully on the ground as if it were a priceless relic. Then took half a dozen unthreatening paces backwards.

'Look at it.'

Vera looked everywhere else. Eyes darting around the dark corners of the barn as if she expected somebody to jump her if she fell for his stupid trick.

'Push it closer to her, please, Mr Laing,' Angel said.

Still on his arse on the floor, Laing reached out, flicked it towards Vera as if it were a live grenade. She darted forwards like a starving animal that can't resist the bait any longer, snatched it up. Clamped it with her left hand against the gun's chequered fore-end, looking down the length of the gun from it to Angel beyond.

'Take a good look,' Angel said, as Vera stared uncomprehendingly at the picture of the young woman caught on CCTV talking to Jack Bevan at the station front desk.

He gave her time, the same creeping realisation dawning in her eyes as in Kincade's five minutes earlier.

'Now look at me.' He took a step towards her, then another. Heart thumping as he stared into the blackness of the gun barrels pointed at him. 'I'm going to take the shotgun, Vera. You have to decide whether you're going to shoot me as I try to do it.'

Her gaze flicked back and forth between the photograph and his face as he approached, her mouth moving soundlessly as she struggled to find the words she wanted, the point behind his seemingly random questions now clear to her.

'This is your daughter?'

'I'm not sure. I'm hoping to find out very soon.' He tried a nervous smile, feeling as if he'd pulled on a death mask. 'If you don't shoot me first.'

The shotgun was shaking in her hands now. He reached slowly for it, an other-worldly calm settling on him. At peace with himself. Prepared to accept the consequences of his stupidly reckless actions based on nothing more than an ache inside him.

Then his hand was on the cold metal of the barrels, gently pushing them downwards and to the side.

Vera sagged as he took the gun from her unresisting hands, all the anger and pain going out of her with it, an empty shell all that was left behind. He broke the gun, ejected the cartridges, then led Vera and her ex-husband to where Kincade waited outside.

'Amor vincit bloody omnia,' Kincade said as he finished his story, the sight of the big blue Ikea store on their left welcoming her back to the here and now. 'Love conquers all.'

'Yep.'

'Now I know why Finch told me not to let you do anything stupid.'

'I haven't done anything quite like that before.'

She gave him a dubious look—*I'm not sure I believe that*.

They walked on in silence for another couple of hundred yards until they were a quarter mile from the roundabout at the bottom where he would turn left up Western Esplanade towards the Pig in the Wall and whatever awaited him there.

Stopping before going their separate ways, she made him think of a human dam wall, the weight of her questions building strength behind her. One day soon, the first cracks would appear and he'd be swept away in the flood of her curiosity. Mercifully, it wasn't today.

'Let me see the photograph again,' she said, instead.

He fished it out, handed it to her. She studied it a long while, didn't need to look at his face to make a comparison.

'Not going to give me your verdict?' he said, when she passed it back.

'Nope. Good luck.'

With that, she was gone.

They say a man's life passes before his eyes in the moment of his death. Angel's passed before his ten times over in that final, endless quarter mile, mercilessly berating himself for every misstep and poor decision that had brought him here, his mind filled with a relentless litany of *if onlys* and *what ifs*.

'I believe this young woman is staying here,' he told the reception clerk at the Pig in the Wall, handing him the image from the CCTV footage.

'Miss Cortés,' the clerk confirmed. If he noticed the

sergeant's epaulette on Jack Bevan's crisp white shirt in the bottom corner, he didn't let it show. 'I'll try her room for you, sir. Who shall I say—'

'Max Angel. I'll be in the bar.'

He took the same seat as he had the last time when he was with Isabel Durand, a picture of Valentina Cortés as he'd last seen her in his mind. A tearful farewell before he left for the seminary, her Catholic upbringing doing nothing to help her come to terms with his decision to become a priest.

He heard a hesitant footstep as he sat with eyes closed reliving the hardest thing he'd ever done. He was on his feet in a heartbeat as Mercedes Cortés came towards him, her mother's smile on her face.

'Hello, Dad . . .'

ALSO BY THE AUTHOR

The Angel & Kincade Murder Mysteries

THE REVENANT

After ex-drug dealer Roy Lynch is found hanged in his garage, a supposed routine suicide soon becomes more insidious. As the body count rises, DI Max Angel and DS Catalina Kincade are forced to look to the past, cutting through thirty years of deceit and betrayal and lies to reveal the family secrets buried below. The tragedy they unearth makes it horrifically clear that in a world filled with hatred and pain, nothing comes close to what families do to one another.

OLD EVIL

When private investigator Charlie Slater is found shot dead in his car on historic Lepe beach, DI Max Angel and his team find themselves torn between the present and the past. Did Slater's own chequered past lead to his death at the hands of the family he wronged? Or was it the forgotten secrets from a lifetime ago he unearthed, old evil spawned in Lager Sylt on Alderney, the only Nazi concentration camp ever to sit on British soil?

FORSAKEN

When DI Max Angel and DS Catalina Kincade are called to a hijacked lorry, what they find inside makes them think its destination was a slaughterhouse, not a warehouse. The discovery of a woman's hairs on a blanket makes it clear that cheap Romanian refrigerators weren't the only goods the murdered driver was transporting. After the human cargo is set free by the killers, Angel and Kincade find themselves caught up in a race to locate the girl before the people traffickers catch her and condemn her to a life of sexual slavery.

JUSTICE LIES BLEEDING

When Angel and Kincade are called to Southampton Old Cemetery, not all of the dead bodies they encounter are ancient relics buried six feet underground. In the untamed wilderness of the cemetery's darkest corner a woman sits propped against one of the old gravestones, her hands bound together as if in prayer. As Angel and his team piece together the final days of her life and it becomes apparent she went voluntarily to her death, two questions vex the team - who did she arrange to meet in a graveyard at night and why?

THE UNQUIET DEAD

When a man is found dead in the New Forest, cold-bloodedly shot in the back as he crawled away from his killer, DI Max Angel and DS Catalina Kincade soon learn the victim was more than the out-of-work truck driver and part-time drug smuggler he appeared to be. He's been sticking his nose into the business of a man whose ruthlessness is matched only by his greed and moral corruption, trying to get to the bottom of the tragic accident that left his life in ruins and a muck-raking journalist dead.

LAMB TO THE SLAUGHTER

When a respected doctor is found murdered in a derelict barn, nailed to a cross and tortured, it's clear to Detective Inspector

Max Angel and his team that it's not just a brutal, sadistic killing, it's a message sent by a killer consumed by rage and hatred. But is the crucifixion nothing more than the bloodthirsty work of a random, religious maniac? Or are the victim's own crimes responsible for his cruel death?

The Evan Buckley Thrillers

BAD TO THE BONES

When Evan Buckley's latest client ends up swinging on a rope, he's ready to call it a day. But he's an awkward cuss with a soft spot for a sad story and he takes on one last job—a child and husband who disappeared ten years ago. It's a long-dead investigation that everybody wants to stay that way, but he vows to uncover the truth—and in the process, kick into touch the demons who come to torment him every night.

KENTUCKY VICE

Maverick private investigator Evan Buckley is no stranger to self-induced mayhem—but even he's mystified by the jam college buddy Jesse Springer has got himself into. When Jesse shows up with a wad of explicit photographs that arrived in the mail, Evan finds himself caught up in the most bizarre case of blackmail he's ever encountered—Jesse swears blind he can't remember a thing about it.

SINS OF THE FATHER

Fifty years ago, Frank Hanna made a mistake. He's never forgiven himself. Nor has anybody else for that matter. Now the time has come to atone for his sins, and he hires maverick PI

Evan Buckley to peel back fifty years of lies and deceit to uncover the tragic story hidden underneath. Trouble is, not everybody likes a happy ending and some very nasty people are out to make sure he doesn't succeed.

NO REST FOR THE WICKED

When an armed gang on the run from a botched robbery that left a man dead invade an exclusive luxury hotel buried in the mountains of upstate New York, maverick P.I. Evan Buckley has got his work cut out. He just won a trip for two and was hoping for a well-earned rest. But when the gang takes Evan's partner Gina hostage along with the other guests and their spirited seven-year-old daughter, he can forget any kind of rest.

RESURRECTION BLUES

After Levi Stone shows private-eye Evan Buckley a picture of his wife Lauren in the arms of another man, Evan quickly finds himself caught up in Lauren's shadowy past. The things he unearths force Levi to face the bitter truth—that he never knew his wife at all—or any of the dark secrets that surround her mother's death and the disappearance of her father, and soon Evan's caught in the middle of a lethal vendetta.

HUNTING DIXIE

Haunted by the unsolved disappearance of his wife Sarah, PI Evan Buckley loses himself in other people's problems. But when Sarah's scheming and treacherous friend Carly shows up promising new information, the past and present collide violently for Evan. He knows he can't trust her, but he hasn't got a choice when she confesses what she's done, leaving Sarah prey to a vicious gang with Old Testament ideas about crime and punishment.

THE ROAD TO DELIVERANCE

Evan Buckley's wife Sarah went to work one day and didn't come home. He's been looking for her ever since. As he digs deeper into the unsolved death of a man killed by the side of the road, the last known person to see Sarah alive, he's forced to re-trace the footsteps of her torturous journey, unearthing a dark secret from her past that drove her desperate attempts to make amends for the guilt she can never leave behind.

SACRIFICE

When PI Evan Buckley's mentor asks him to check up on an old friend, neither of them are prepared for the litany of death and destruction that he unearths down in the Florida Keys. Meanwhile Kate Guillory battles with her own demons in her search for salvation and sanity. As their paths converge, each of them must make an impossible choice that stretches conscience and tests courage, and in the end demands sacrifice—what would you give to get what you want?

ROUGH JUSTICE

After a woman last seen alive twenty years ago turns up dead, PI Evan Buckley heads off to a small town on the Maine coast where he unearths a series of brutal unsolved murders. The more he digs, lifting the lid on old grievances and buried injustices that have festered for half a lifetime, the more the evidence points to a far worse crime, leaving him facing an impossible dilemma – disclose the terrible secrets he's uncovered or assume the role of hanging judge and dispense a rough justice of his own.

TOUCHING DARKNESS

When PI Evan Buckley stops for a young girl huddled at the side of the road on a deserted stretch of highway, it's clear she's running away from someone or something—however vehemently she denies it. At times angry and hostile, at others scared and vulnerable, he's almost relieved when she runs out on him in the middle of the night. Except he has a nasty premonition that he hasn't heard the last of her. Nor does it take long before he's proved horribly right, the consequences dire for himself and Detective Kate Guillory.

A LONG TIME COMING

Five years ago, PI Evan Buckley's wife Sarah committed suicide in a mental asylum. Or so they told him. Now there's a different woman in her grave and he's got a stolen psychiatric report in his hand and a tormented scream running through his head. Someone is lying to him. With his own sanity at stake, he joins forces with a disgraced ex-CIA agent on a journey to confront the past that leads him to the jungles of Central America and the aftermath of a forgotten war, where memories are long and grievances still raw.

LEGACY OF LIES

Twenty years ago, Detective Kate Guillory's father committed suicide. Nobody has ever told her why. Now a man is stalking her. When PI Evan Buckley takes on the case, his search takes him to the coal mining mountains of West Virginia and the hostile aftermath of a malignant cult abandoned decades earlier. As he digs deeper into the unsolved crimes committed there and discovers the stalker's bitter grudge against Kate, one thing becomes horrifyingly clear – what started back then isn't over yet.

DIG TWO GRAVES

Boston heiress Arabella Carlson has been in hiding for thirty years. Now she's trying to make it back home. But after PI Evan Buckley saves her from being stabbed to death, she disappears again. Hired by her dying father to find her and bring her home safe before the killers hunting her get lucky, he finds there's more than money at stake as he opens up old wounds, peeling back a lifetime of lies and deceit. Someone's about to learn a painful lesson the hard way: Before you embark on a journey of revenge, dig two graves.

ATONEMENT

When PI Evan Buckley delves into an unsolved bank robbery from forty years ago that everyone wants to forget, he soon learns it's anything but what it seems to be. From the otherworldly beauty of Caddo Lake and the East Texas swamps to the bright lights and cheap thrills of Rehoboth Beach, he follows the trail of a nameless killer. Always one step behind, he discovers that there are no limits to the horrific crimes men's greed drives them to commit, not constrained by law or human decency.

THE JUDAS GATE

When a young boy's remains are found in a shallow grave on land belonging to PI Evan Buckley's avowed enemy, the monster

Carl Hendricks, the police are desperate for Evan's help in solving a case that's been dead in the water for the past thirteen years. Hendricks is dying, and Evan is the only person he'll share his deathbed confession with. Except Evan knows Hendricks of old. Did he really kill the boy? And if so, why does he want to confess to Evan?

OLD SCORES

When upcoming country music star Taylor Harris hires a private investigator to catch her cheating husband, she gets a lot more than she bargained for. He's found a secret in her past that even she's not aware of - a curse on her life, a blood feud hanging over her for thirty years. But when he disappears, it's down to PI Evan Buckley to pick up the pieces. Was the threat real? And if so, did it disappear along with the crooked investigator? Or did it just get worse?

ONCE BITTEN

When PI Evan Buckley's mentor, Elwood Crow, asks a simple favor of him – to review a twenty-year-old autopsy report – there's only one thing Evan can be sure of: simple is the one thing it won't be. As he heads off to Cape Ann on the Massachusetts coast Evan soon finds himself on the trail of a female serial killer, and the more he digs, the more two questions align themselves. Why has the connection not been made before? And is Crow's interest in finding the truth or in saving his own skin?

NEVER GO BACK

When the heir to a billion-dollar business empire goes missing in the medieval city of Cambridge in England, PI Evan Buckley heads across the Atlantic on what promises to be a routine assignment. But as Evan tracks Barrett Bradlee from the narrow cobbled streets of the city to the windswept watery expanses of the East Anglian fens, it soon becomes clear that the secretive family who hired him to find the missing heir haven't told him the whole truth.

SEE NO EVIL

When Ava Hart's boyfriend, Daryl Pierce, is shot to death in his home on the same night he witnessed a man being abducted, the police are quick to write it off as a case of wrong place, wrong time. Ava disagrees. She's convinced they killed him. And she's hired PI Evan Buckley to unearth the truth. Trouble is, as Evan discovers all too soon, Ava wouldn't recognize the truth if it jumped up and bit her on the ass.

DO UNTO OTHERS

Five years ago, a light aircraft owned by Mexican drug baron and people trafficker Esteban Aguilar went down in the middle of the Louisiana swamps. The pilot and another man were found dead inside, both shot to death. The prisoner who'd been handcuffed in the back was nowhere to be found. And now it's down to PI Evan Buckley to find crime boss Stan Fraser's son Arlo who's gone missing trying to get to the bottom of what the hell happened.

Printed in Dunstable, United Kingdom